Love's Misadventure

Book One of *The Mason Siblings Series*

By Cheri Champagne

pandamoon
publishing

www.pandamoonpublishing.com

Jacket design and illustrations © Pandamoon Publishing

Art Direction by Matthew Kramer at Pandamoon Publishing
Illustrations by Fletcher Kinnear at Pandamoon Publishing
Editing by Zara Kramer, Anya Kagan, Rachel Schoenbauer, and Jessica Reino at Pandamoon Publishing

Pandamoon Publishing and the portrayal of a panda and a moon are registered trademarks of Pandamoon Publishing.

Library of Congress Cataloging-in-Publication Data is on file at the Library of Congress, Washington, DC

Edition: 1

ISBN-13: 978-0997135107
ISBN-10: 0997135107

Dedication

For every hopeless romantic book lover with dreams of adventure.

Gerry,

Enjoy! Best wishes!

-Cheri Champagne

Acknowledgements

I have so many people to be thankful for. My parents for being unconditionally supportive, my husband for pushing me to do what I love, and my children for being content to play while mommy gets some writing in.

I want to thank everyone that helped me through the early stages of my writing career; who offered support, encouragement, and aid whenever and however they could. You have no idea what that means to me.

Lastly, I want to thank the Pandamoon team. You have become a second family to me, that I am so proud to be a part of. You have impacted me in so many wonderful ways. From the bottom of my heart, thank you!

Love's Misadventure

Prologue

Something's gone terribly wrong.

Lane Mason, seventh Earl of Devon, tugged against the ropes binding his wrists in a futile effort to free himself. The room was dark and silent, and Lane hadn't the foggiest idea where he was.

The space stunk of rot, stale cigar smoke, and an unidentifiable acrid odour that stung his nose. But beneath it all, he smelled the faintest amount of lemons.

"Anna?" His whisper echoed like a gunshot in the quiet room. "Annabel, are you here?"

"Lane, oh, Lane, thank goodness you're here!" Her sweet whisper sounded somewhere to his right. "Where are we? Who were those men?"

Lane narrowed his eyes in an attempt to see her through the pitch dark.

"I don't know, Anna, but I'm going to figure a way out of this."

Somewhere in their adventure today something had gone horribly awry. This was not at all what he'd planned.

Chapter 1

"My Lord, Miss Bradley, your luncheon is prepared."

Miss Annabel Bradley's stomach growled in anticipation. She hastily covered her stomach with one hand, a light blush staining her cheeks.

"Thank you, Geoffrey." Lane accepted the basket and blanket from his butler, then turned to face Anna. "Shall we?"

Anna rose from her seat on the thinly cushioned settee and smiled at her closest friend. "I would be delighted."

Lane led Annabel out the wide French doors to the garden, the fresh scent of roses, foxgloves, and sweet violets washing over her in one grand wave. Lane employed the finest gardener in all of England, much to the envy of his neighbours and the very great joy of Anna. She had always loved this garden.

Anna allowed Lane to guide her as they strolled slowly down the path, her face tipped upward toward the sun. She closed her eyes and let her skin soak up the warmth. A gentle breeze blew, picking up the edges of her skirts and loose tendrils of her hair.

A bird chirped somewhere in the distance and Annabel's lips curved upward in one corner. *What are the birds saying?* she wondered.

"Lost again, Anna?" Lane's deep voice penetrated her reverie.

"As always, Lane," she said with a laugh. "Why do you persist on ruining my moments?"

He slid his arm beneath from her touch and placed his hand over his heart, staggering backward in mock affront. "*I?* I *ruin* a moment?" He notched his chin high and pushed out his chest like a proud calling bird. "I daresay I am the maker of moments."

Anna laughed and playfully rapped him on the arm.

"Where do you suppose we shall settle for our alfresco luncheon?" Lane asked as they resumed their stroll through the garden. His chocolate-brown eyes crinkled with mirth.

She grinned up at him. "I haven't the faintest notion, your lordship." But she did. She always did.

It was *their* spot.

They passed several immaculately arranged flowerbeds, both fragrant and colourful, Anna's hand curved familiarly around his elbow. The sound of water trickling over smooth pebbles reached her ears on the breeze, then the copse of cherry blossom trees came into view. At this time of year their petals showered from the branches to look like pink snow in the spring. Soon the blossoms would be replaced by deep red leaves, which were almost as pleasing to the eye and equally as ideal to picnic beneath.

Anna reached one arm out to touch a low-hanging branch with the tips of her fingers, causing pink petals to drift along the air before floating to the ground.

As they reached their spot in companionable silence, Anna released Lane's arm. He placed the basket beside the tree's trunk before spreading out the blanket.

He turned to grace her with a self-satisfied smile and Anna's heart foolishly skipped a beat.

He helped her to her seat on the blanket, where she arranged her lavender skirts to cover her stocking-clad ankles. Lane sat across from her and began to remove items from the basket.

He was an exceptionally handsome man, with his light-blonde hair, brown eyes, square jaw, full lips, and a figure fit from physical sports. At the age of eight and twenty he was a wealthy Earl, a caring landlord, the most sought-after gentleman of the season, and her best friend and confidant. Anna considered herself very fortunate to have Lane as a friend.

They grew up on neighbouring estates, their families spending a great amount of time in each other's company and bringing their children together.

Part of Anna had always thought—nay, *hoped*—that she and Lane would begin a family of their own one day. But so many years had passed since she had come of age, without a hint of romantic interest from Lane, that she had given up hope on becoming anything more than his very good friend.

Any intimate interference at this stage could be detrimental to their amity. She must satisfy herself with that fact, despite how he made her feel inside. She would never force her attentions on any man, her friend most especially.

Perhaps that was one of her troubles, her failure at flirting. If she had flirted with Lane, would he have offered a proposal? She sighed. Most probably not. It must be her, then, as lowering as that thought was.

Early in her debut season, Anna had received many callers hoping to begin a courtship with her, but she had always offered a polite refusal, secretly hoping that Lane would come to his senses and see her for the woman she had become.

She was not a raving beauty by any means, with her dull, dark-blonde hair, ample hips, and too-large bosom, but she was rather fond of her blue eyes. Small and thin women were among the most desirable, and fuller figures were out of fashion, as her modiste was wont to remind her. Though she had never considered herself unattractive, her voluptuous body and her age of five and twenty put her firmly on the shelf.

It was all but inevitable that her youth and eligibility would come to its quick conclusion, leaving her a mob-capped spinster. Perhaps if she practiced flirting, some man would begin a courtship of her, despite her advanced age.

She looked across the blanket at Lane as he arranged slices of meat upon two plates. *He will never make me an offer of marriage*, she told herself. *Find a willing man, accept a proposal, and live a life of contentment with the children he can give you.*

"Are you feeling well, Anna?" Lane paused with his arm hanging in mid-air, a plate with roasted lamb on it resting in his fingers.

"Quite well, thank you," she replied quickly. Perhaps too quickly.

His left eyebrow rose in suspicion.

She waved a hand through the air before accepting the plate from Lane. "Merely a troubling thought," she said through a smile, "but I assure you it was just in passing. I am quite well now."

Lane watched Anna for another moment before deciding to allow her falsehood to pass. He knew something bothered her, but he would not press the matter. Once she felt comfortable sharing it with him, he would be there to listen.

"Tell me, Anna, what new novel have you lost yourself in of late?"

Her anxious expression altered immediately into one of joy. "I found a splendid new novel at Hatchard's Bookshop that just came in. It is authored by a man named Mr. Mystery." Her eyes lit with excitement, and Lane's chest constricted at the sight. "Some say it is a silly name, but I happen to think it quite clever. The author is very talented; he knows just the right way to keep the reader enthralled."

"The story itself is fascinating. It's about a young woman who finds herself lost in a forest but comes across some very disreputable scoundrels who kidnap her for ransom. Then the blackguards learn that her parents are deceased and left her penniless, so instead, they attempt to sell her to a pirate captain as a female slave! Meanwhile, her closest friend's brother, who has been missing for years, appears from nowhere and turns out to be the very same pirate captain!"

Lane listened to her continue on about her newest book acquisition, his heart pounding in his chest. There was something about the passion in her expression—her eyes bright with enthusiasm and her body language at ease with her wild gesturing.

It had him...*feeling*.

His gaze lowered to her lips—her full, luscious, tempting lips. *Blazes*. He couldn't count how many times he had fantasized about those lips on his, her hands on his bare chest, her body moving beneath his... His breeches began to tighten, and he internally scolded himself. *Neither the time nor the place, Lane.*

If only he hadn't that *problem*...

"...just happened to be the same place that he had gone missing!" Anna finished breathlessly.

Lane grinned, a bead of sweat forming on his upper lip. "That sounds like quite the grand adventure," he improvised. "I would be pleased if you would allow me to borrow the book from you once you have finished reading it."

"Oh yes, you must read it! I am so anxious to finish it myself, I could hardly tear myself away." She paused, smiling. "Of course, you are worth the distraction."

His heart pounded like the smithy's hammer on an anvil. How she could not hear it, he would never know. That teasing smile of hers always put his heart to beating erratically.

He schooled his expression into a mild smile. "Why thank you, my dear. Now let us eat; I'm afraid our food has gone cold."

"Goodness! I had forgotten all about it."

They both turned their attention to their meal, eating in comfortable silence. The cherry blossom tree provided shelter from the unseasonably warm April sun while the breeze blew its petals around them. The stream, rustling leaves, and nearby birds provided a pleasing ambient noise.

Lane finished first and sipped at his Madeira while Anna licked berry juice off of her fingers. Lane grit his teeth before finishing his drink in one large gulp.

"That was delicious. Thank you for inviting me, Lane."

"You are quite welcome. I shall have to pass the compliment on to Cook." He began returning the dishes to the basket.

"I should be very happy if you did so." She smiled at him, and his stomach knotted. What was the matter with him? "Would you care to take a stroll about the garden?"

"Indeed I would, as long as you promise to let me trounce you in a game of chess when we return home." He wiggled his eyebrows.

Annabel laughed, shaking her head. "Ah, now that I cannot do. I can promise to play the game with you, but I shall *not* allow you to win. You will have to achieve that on your own…if you can."

"A challenge! I accept." He stood and held his hand out to her.

The touch of her skin sent his blood thundering through his veins, raging through him. *Blazes.*

When she was balanced on her feet, he quickly let go of her hand and offered his elbow, instead. The material separating them allowed a trifling comfort that he would not scandalize his friend and embarrass himself.

You cannot have her, he reminded himself. *You cannot have* any *woman. Not until you've fixed yourself.* Anna was his friend, besides. He would not dare to risk their friendship for the sake of a small amount of lustful feelings.

They left their basket and blanket to stroll through the garden. They spoke of literature, the new works of their favourite authors, the flowers and sights that surrounded them, life, and the agreeably warm weather. All the while, Lane was aware of her…the way she moved, the way she smiled, the way she gestured with her hands while she spoke.

He had known her since they were children; they played together, learned together, and yet he still adored the way she looked at the world and went about living and loving life. He had gained and lost countless friends from Cambridge and Oxford, the majority of the friendships ending in a slow separation due to boredom or change of interests. Yet his friendship with Anna had never waned.

They reached the portico of his large town house and entered into the empty family parlour.

"What a lovely day," Anna breathed as she removed her bonnet to place it on the side table near the door.

"It is." He went to the hallway to summon Geoffrey.

"My lord? I trust your luncheon was satisfactory," Geoffrey said from the door.

"Indeed. Please send our compliments to Cook."

"As you wish, my lord. Shall I arrange refreshments? Some tea, perhaps?"

"Please do. And if you would be so good as to have someone fetch the basket and blanket; we left them among the cherry blossoms."

The butler bowed. "Right away, my lord." Geoffrey hesitated slightly, catching Lane's attention.

"Is there something amiss?"

The butler cleared his throat. "I should inform you, your lordship, that there is a new addition to the family."

Lane refrained from rolling his eyes. "What has Emaline brought home this time?" His younger sister was forever bringing home sick, injured, or lost animals.

"It is a small tabby that she has named Whiskers."

"Thank you for informing me, Geoffrey."

"Not at all, my lord." He bowed and quietly exited.

As soon as Geoffrey closed the door, Lane gestured for Anna to precede him to the chess table. "If you dare." He winked.

She sent a sly glance and a smile at him as she took her seat at the table.

He sat across from her, and they played in earnest. A maid came with their tea tray, which sat on a side table, cooling and untouched. They each took time with their turns to ensure the best possible move, both focused, both dedicated to the challenge of the game.

As the final moves of the game came into view, Lane realized that he was going to lose. He looked up at Anna across the table to see a smug smile on her beautiful face.

"What do I win?" Her blue eyes twinkled with humour.

"I was not aware that we had agreed to wager anything."

"We hadn't, but I would still like to win something."

"Isn't being the victor prize enough?" His lips pulled upward in a grin.

"No," she stated baldly. "I would like proof that I am the victor. Prestige isn't enough when I have no one to tell other than you."

One loud bark of a laugh escaped him as his mind worked. "Tell me, what do you feel about a surprise gift?"

She outwardly feigned consideration, but Lane could tell from the glint in her eye that she was both intrigued and excited by the prospect.

"What sort of surprise gift?"

"It would not be a surprise if I told you what it was. Besides, I have yet to think of what it will be."

She nodded once. "I accept. Shall we shake hands?" She reached her right hand out across the table.

Lane's gaze locked with hers as he clasped her hand. "Congratulations."

Chapter 2

It happened again. It blasted well happened again!

"Hell and blazes," Lane muttered. Head resting in his hands, he sat on the edge of one of the beds in Madame Bordeau's flash house, and cursed his inability to take care of his needs.

"'Appens te lots 'a gents, love," the perfumed whore named Harriet said from behind him on the bed.

The room was adorned in deep red and darkened wood furnishings. The stench of stale perfume, sex, liquor, and smoke permeated the air. It was nauseating.

Lane grabbed his breeches off the rumpled counterpane and stepped into them. "I apologize for wasting your evening, Harriet. I will pay you for your time nonetheless."

"T'was a pleasure, love. Though not *too* much of a pleasure, if'n ye get my meaning." She winked at him.

He hid a grimace.

His chest tightened, and he filled with self-loathing. "Bloody hell."

He tucked his shirt into his breeches, pulled his waistcoat and coat on, and began tying his cravat in a simple knot. He tossed his soiled condom in the hearth. *Why the devil does this always happen?* Something must be physically wrong with him. This wasn't normal, and it certainly wasn't healthy. Perhaps he should consult a doctor. Surely men were supposed to be able to have sexual relations without so much trouble.

He was able to get himself going well enough; it was keeping himself going that was the difficulty. He was damned tired of paying women extra money to keep their mouths shut about his problem. He'd visited every flash house in London and its outskirts at least once. He'd travelled to Scotland and tried several there as well, yet his problem continued.

He was still a virgin, for Christ's sake.

Not that he hadn't any experience. He had done plenty of other very interesting and entertaining acts, but he had never once been able to complete the act of lovemaking. He left every establishment feeling unclean, and in dire need of a stiff drink to rid his senses of the taste and smell of his own failure and heavily perfumed whores.

With a groan, he reached into his breast pocket and handed the lightskirt a small purse with her pay, in addition to the extra amount he offered to keep the story to herself.

Running a frustrated hand through his hair, he bid her good night and left.

Lane met his coach around the street corner, climbed in, and rapped on the roof with his fist to signal his coachman to take him home. He sat back against the squabs with a self-deprecating sigh.

"Bloody rotten hell!" He ran a hand over his face and pinched the bridge of his nose in the vain hope that he could stop the headache forming behind his eyes. He was certain that no other man at the age of eight and twenty had never had sex. In fact, he was certain that many men lost their virginity before their twentieth birthday.

How was he ever to take a wife if he could not perform his husbandly duties? How could he ever recite his vows before God and his family if he knew he could never produce an heir?

Shame burned through him, weighing heavily on his heart. At this rate, he would never be the man a wife would need him to be. He would never be a father.

He groaned and shook himself from his miserable reverie. His thoughts were too damned depressing.

He forced himself to change the course of his musings. He'd had another lovely time with Annabel. Her triumphant grin at winning their chess game flashed through his mind. He made a mental note to think of something special to award her with as a prize.

His lips split in a toothy grin. She always brightened his mood, no matter how ill his humour. Having Anna for a best friend was the greatest thing in his life; she knew him better than anyone, though she did not know about his…*problem*. He, likewise, knew her better than anyone. He knew that she adored books, chocolate, teacakes, and cherry blossom trees. She was an adequate artist and a terrible pianist.

Lane's grin turned into a smile as the coach rolled to a stop in front of his town house. He loved how she felt free enough to laugh at herself. He stepped down from the carriage. In fact, he loved her sense of humour; her alluring, crooked smile; their long talks; the way she always smelled like lemons and soap; and her expressive way of talking. He loved…*her*.

He halted mid-step, his foot poised in the air over the front steps of his town house. His heart began a rapid, staccato beat in his chest, and his eyes grew wide.

Good God. He loved her!

"My lord?" Geoffrey stood waiting with the door open.

"Not now, Geoffrey," Lane mumbled absently.

8

"Very good, my lord."

How long had he loved her?

"Oh, Lane." A fourteen-year-old Annabel opened her arms to him.

He rushed to her and held her close, tears welling in his eyes.

"I am so sorry, Lane," she whispered into his collar.

Her shoulders shook, and he knew she was doing her best to be brave for him. He would be the man of the house now. With three sobbing younger sisters and a mother to take care of, his work would be great indeed.

But he had Annabel. He hugged her tighter and let her soft warmth seep into him. He had Annabel.

Lane staggered slightly at the bottom step. Eleven years. How could he have been so blind? For *eleven damned years*! What a fool he was!

He started up the stairs and marched past the butler. He needed a drink.

"I won't be going out again tonight, Geoffrey; you are free to retire." He paused. "Oh, but please have a bath sent up to my chambers."

"Thank you, your lordship. Right away."

Lane stormed into his study and went straight for the brandy in his Tantalus. With shaking hands, he poured himself four fingers of his best French brandy and took a large gulp, relishing the burn as it went down.

Love.

He left his empty glass on the Tantalus and retrieved a cigar from the box atop his desk. In a daze, he lit it on a sconce and returned to his seat before the fire.

Blazes.

What was he going to do? Annabel. Sweet, lovely Anna. He thought about her luscious lips. Did she taste as sweet as she smelled? He wanted to run his lips down her neck and dip his tongue in the crevice between her breasts. Her perfect, full, rounded... He shifted in his chair as his cock sprang to life.

Now is not the time.

He puffed on his cigar as a kitten leapt to his lap, making itself comfortable as he absently stroked its fur.

This sudden realization posed a great problem. What if his physical difficulty continued? What if he could never father children? Annabel deserved better than that. She deserved better than *him*. He could never court her.

Damn it, he could never be with Anna.

Chapter 3

Annabel covered a yawn with the back of her hand as she entered the morning room. The scents of freshly prepared toasted bread, ham, eggs, and an array of other alluring aromas teased her senses. Her stomach rumbled loudly in response. She covered it and fought a blush. Thank goodness it was just her parents in the room.

"Good morning, Papa." Anna bent to kiss her father on the cheek, then turned to her mother and did the same. "Good morning, Mama."

"Good morning, my dear." Mama spread some marmalade on a piece of toast, and her father grunted his greeting from behind the newspaper.

She went to the sideboard and selected an assortment of fruit and toast.

"You appear tired this morning, Annabel. Did you stay up late reading again?"

Anna covered another yawn as she took her seat at the table. "The book was just too entertaining to put down. I started reading, and the next thing I knew it was nearly dawn."

"Oh, bother." Her mother took a sip of tea. "I do hope that will not affect you at the ball this evening."

Anna hid a frown. "Bother. I had completely forgotten about Almack's." She detested the pretentious display she always saw at Almack's. The young ladies acting like witless, tittering fools in order to attract a husband, and the men who *expected* the women to be witless, tittering fools.

She sighed. She could not avoid it; last week at Miss Rockton's musicale Anna had promised a waltz at Almack's to Lord Anthony Walstone, Viscount Boxton. He was handsome enough, but in desperate need of a dowry to pay off his father's gambling debts.

Anna had a dowry…a handsome one, at that. Could Lord Boxton have a genuine interest in her? *Ask yourself the question that matters, Anna.* If he spoke to her father to request permission to court her, would she be amenable to such a match?

She did not have a long enough acquaintance with him to know whether or not she enjoyed his wit or conversation. It was commonplace for husbands and wives to spend very little time in each other's company, so she supposed that would not be problematic.

It was a simple enough matter. Anna dreaded spinsterhood. She had spent far too long pining over a man who did not share her intimate affections. She may not love Viscount Boxton, or be particularly fond of him, but if he wished to give her his name and was willing to father her children, she would accept his proposal without a moment of doubt.

"Do not fret, Mama. I will take a nap this afternoon in preparation for Almack's."

"Be sure to not nap too long, Annabel. Your mother and I would like to have an early repast before we depart. The fare at Almack's is abysmal." Her father, Joseph Bradley, youngest brother of the Marquis of Greydon, put down his newspaper and stood. "If you will both excuse me, I have a meeting with my solicitor."

"Have a pleasant day, Papa." Anna poured herself a cup of steaming tea.

"Until supper, Joseph."

"Annabel, Margaret." He gave them both a kiss on the forehead before quitting the room.

Anna added cream and sugar into her teacup and took a sip. It did not satisfy her proclivity for sweetness as well as her favourite hot chocolate, but it was pleasing nonetheless.

"Good morning, mother!" A booming male voice echoed in the small space. "Annabel, you look well. Such a pleasure to see the both of you." Her older brother, Major Charles Bradley, strutted into the breakfast room with a self-satisfied smirk on his face, his blonde hair handsomely—and, she thought, *deliberately*—dishevelled.

"Good heavens, Charles, what have you done now?" Mama said in a reproachful voice. "You know how irksome your father and I find it when you cause a scandal." She put the last small piece of her marmalade toast in her mouth and chewed it slowly.

Anna smiled behind her teacup. "Yes, Charles, do tell us what you've been up to. Nothing too mischievous, I hope." She took another sip and returned it to its saucer.

"No, indeed," he said in mock affront, his eyes glittering with humour. "I merely spent the evening at White's and won ten quid off Stanton at the tables." He paused with a teasing glance toward their mother. "Then Harvey and I retired to a very nice house down the street where we met two very fine young ladies—"

"That is quite enough, Charles!" Mama's eyes were wide. "You will hold your tongue. Those tales are not fit for a lady's ears!"

Annabel couldn't suppress the inelegant snort of laughter that escaped her. Mama turned sharp eyes on her, while Charles' crinkled in the corners.

"You know he says such things only to shock you, Mama." She sent an impish grin to Charles. "He could not possibly have won ten quid; he is not nearly that skilled a card player."

Charles let out a bark of laughter while their mother gasped, a hand fluttering to her chest.

"*Annabel*," she scolded.

Charles leaned forward to place his palms flat on the table. "I could win against you easily, little sister. Name the time, game, and wager."

"I shall! I have no prior engagements tomorrow afternoon—"

"Indeed you shall not!" Mama tossed her napkin to the table. "There will be no wagering in this household." With an exasperated sigh, she stood and stalked from the room, sending them one last warning glance over her shoulder before disappearing through the doorway. "You two will be the death of me, yet."

As soon as their mother was out of earshot, Charles heaped his plate with pork and eggs and sat at the table across from Anna.

"I do love teasing her so." He grinned at her.

Anna swallowed a mouthful of fruit and smiled back at him. "I don't think I could ever tire of it. Now," she paused, "what did you *really* do last night?"

Charles did not look up from his plate. "Precisely what I said."

"Come off it, Charles. I know you better than that. You are an abysmal liar."

His midnight-blue eyes grew shuttered, but the look vanished so quickly that she wasn't sure she had actually seen it. That concerned her more than anything.

Since her brother had returned injured from war four months ago, he had been different. He had erected a wall around himself, exuding only the happy version of Charles. But Anna knew he was hiding something behind his jokes. He was quick to temper and grew defensive very easily. Even his closest friend, Bridget, Lane's younger sister, had stopped coming around except to visit with Anna. Those two had been nearly as inseparable as Lane and Anna, but something had obviously occurred to change that. Annabel was burning to know what it was.

"Very well, my sister, the sleuth," he grumbled. "I saw a play at Drury Lane."

Anna's eyebrows rose. "You? A play? I am all astonishment!"

Charles chewed on a mouthful of egg. "I did, in fact, go to White's after the play and won ten quid from Stanton. But that is where my evening ended."

Something told her that there was more, but she did not press him. He was entitled to his secrets.

"Sounds dull," she ventured.

"Not so dull as yours, I imagine. What did you do? Read?"

"As a matter of fact, yes," she said defensively. "I would not consider that *dull*. And do not look so smug. I thoroughly enjoyed my evening."

"I am pleased to hear it."

Anna dabbed at her lips with her napkin. "I am afraid, brother of mine, that I will leave you to continue breaking your fast alone. I must do some reading before I nap this afternoon."

"You *must* read?"

"Hush," she admonished. "Will you be attending the ball at Almack's this evening?"

"I will. Save me a quadrille?"

"For you, brother, of course."

Chapter 4

"Goodness, what a crush!" Mrs. Margaret Bradley exclaimed as they neared the assembly rooms at Almack's.

Anna's shoulders brushed against those around her, lending truth to her mother's words. They walked en masse into the spectacular room. Chandeliers glittered above them, their bright light reflecting off of the gold accents throughout the opulent space. The walls were adorned with fine draperies and painted in pale tones. On the floor was a sea of colourful gowns and evening finery, swaying and swirling like the ocean's tide.

The sea parted briefly, allowing Lord Boxton to find his way through.

Anna smiled politely at him as he approached. He was dressed impeccably; black trousers and coat, an emerald-green waistcoat that made his forest-green eyes sparkle, topped with a snowy-white shirt and cravat. Not a dandy was Lord Boxton.

He sketched a shallow bow, and she responded with an appropriate curtsey.

"Good evening, Miss Bradley," he drawled.

"Good evening to you, Lord Boxton." Anna turned, gesturing toward her brother and making the introductions.

"Miss Bradley, would you do me the honour of partnering me for the next quadrille?"

Anna smiled at him and held out her dance card. "I would be delighted. Thank you."

Lord Boxton bent to jot his name on her card, a lock of his wavy auburn hair falling over his brow. When he straightened, his expression was a combination of satisfaction and challenge.

Anna glanced at her card and suppressed a cluck of her tongue. Lord Boxton had put his name beside the first quadrille and two waltzes.

"My lord, you know I cannot—"

"Please, call me Anthony."

Anna's eyes widened briefly at his presumption. Surely her family would interfere. But a cursory glance told her that sometime during the past few minutes they had made themselves scarce.

Hadn't she just been considering saying *yes* to this man, should he propose marriage? Why, then, should she feel resistant to being on familiar terms with him? *Silly, Anna.*

She gave him a toothy smile. "Why thank you, Anthony. You may call me Annabel." She hesitated, but broached the subject of his improperly claiming three dances. "I fear I must—"

He stepped nearer, clasping her wrist before wrapping her hand around his elbow. "I believe this is our dance."

Indeed, the strains of a quadrille were echoing through the ballroom from the orchestra on the balcony.

Lord Boxton—Anthony—*must feel quite pleased with himself,* Anna supposed. She could hardly mention his misstep now that the moment had passed. She would merely have to claim a headache or express a desire for some punch to avoid appearing discourteous.

He led her toward the assembling group of dancers. Men and women lined up across from their partners, the women on one side and men on the other. Anna joined the ladies, facing Anthony. His gaze held pride and glinted with what she could only interpret as humour.

She should feel honoured to have the attention of not only a titled gentleman, but a handsome one as well, but the emotions in her heart fell short of joy. She could not possibly expect him to be a replica of the men she often read about in her novels, nor could she expect him to be a friend to her, such as Lane was. With him, she did not feel desire or passion. There was nothing more than the indifference she would feel toward an acquaintance.

Was that enough to hope for in a marriage…or in the marriage bed?

Do not do this, Anna, she chided herself as they began the dance. *He is a perfectly amiable gentleman. He will, with good fortune, give you the children you so desire.*

They came together, his gloved palm hot against hers, and turned in a circle in time to the music.

Most marriages were ones of convenience rather than love. Many entered into the marriage state out of a necessity for a dowry, a desire for a title, or the need to produce an heir, *not* for desire.

Lord Boxton—Anthony—was a handsome man in his thirtieth year. She would not be opposed to sharing the intimacies of marriage with him, passionless though they might be.

Anna struggled to find words to cut through the silence between them. They had already complimented each other on their skill at dancing at the previous

16

ball. Should she speak on the weather? Comment on his attire? Make a note of those in attendance?

Before she was able to think of something to say, the quadrille came to an end and Anthony led her off the dance floor. Anna's gaze scanned the crowd milling around the edges of the ballroom and spotted her parents speaking with Lane. But he was watching *her*.

Anna's stomach twisted as he stared. His expression was serene, but his eyes were troubled…and furious. Something distressed him.

Anthony began to steer her toward the refreshment table. "Would you care for a glass of Madeira or champagne, Annabel?"

She broke eye contact with Lane to smile gratefully at Lord Boxton. "Champagne, please. Thank you, Anthony." He responded with a pleased grin that she could not help but return.

He left her side to retrieve their refreshments, and Anna stood in wait.

"You look ravishing this evening." A deep, familiar voice came from behind her, sending a shiver of inappropriate delight down her spine.

She turned to face him, the knot in her stomach tightening. He looked absurdly handsome in his black trousers and cutaway tailcoat, deep-red waistcoat, and white shirt and cravat. He had dressed similarly to Lord Boxton, though Lane was the one to set her heart to galloping.

"Good evening, Lane. Thank you," she said. "You look very fine yourself."

He sent a cursory glance over her pale-rose evening gown with capped sleeves and scooping neckline before his gaze returned to bore into hers.

"I noticed you dancing with Lord Boxton."

A quick frown marred her brow before she cleared it. "Yes, he requested a dance and I accepted. He has also requested a waltz later this evening, which I have also accepted." She failed to mention the *second* waltz that Anthony had claimed.

His jaw tightened before he glanced away.

"Why do you appear as though you disapprove?" she asked. "You have never before given much notice to my dance partners."

His brow lowered briefly. "I do not disapprove, precisely…"

"Do tell me what is the matter, Lane. I do not wish to see you upset."

"I—"

"Lord Devon, good evening."

Annabel tamped down on her irritation at the interruption and turned to smile as Lord Boxton appeared at her side with two glasses of champagne.

"Boxton." Lane nodded in greeting.

"Thank you, Anthony." She pressed her lips together in an artificial smile, accepted her glass, and took a small sip.

Lane cast her a sharp glance of irritated accusation before smoothing his expression. "Tell me, Boxton," Lane drawled, "Have you by chance read any interesting novels lately?"

Anna's gaze riveted on Anthony, genuinely curious to hear his answer.

"Lord no, Devon." Anthony chuckled derisively. "I haven't the time at my disposal to spend on such frivolous pursuits. My reading material consists of estate and account management ledgers." He flicked the wrist of his free hand through the air. "And the newspaper, of course."

Anna's heart sank at his admission, though she understood that not everyone enjoyed reading for pleasure as much as she did.

She glanced at Lane and stilled at the haughty expression on his face. He had known precisely what Anthony's reply would be, deliberately encouraging Anna's displeasure.

Anger abruptly surged through her. Lane had no right to attempt to manipulate her opinion of Lord Box—Anthony in such a way. She turned to the Viscount. "No one can fault you for your diligence in your duties, Anthony. I find that admirable."

A barely audible snort escaped Lane, and she knew her comment had hit its mark.

"Thank you, Annabel." Lord Boxton smiled at her. "I happen to know a splendid part of Holland Park that is breathtaking this time of year. Would you, by chance, care to ride with me on the morrow to view it?"

She sent him a blazing smile. "I would be delighted, Anthony. Thank you."

"Splendid. I shall pick up you up at eleven of the clock."

"Annabel, may I have a word with you, please?" Lane grabbed her elbow and half dragged, half led her through the crowded ballroom and into the vacant corridor.

"Lane, what in heaven's name is the matter?" She staggered, pulling her arm from his grip before setting her now-empty champagne flute on a nearby side table.

Lane raked his fingers through his hair. "He is not the right man for you."

"Not the right man," she said incredulously. "And who would you suggest I let court me, Lane? I am no beauty. My chances of finding love are slim to none." *Since you will not marry me.* "At least with him, I can achieve my dream of having children before I am too old to bear them."

"You *are* beautiful, Anna. And you deserve better."

Despite the leap to her pulse, she clucked her tongue. "You know that I meant my external beauty, not that of my personality."

His jaw worked. "He is a fortune hunter, Annabel. Surely you can see that."

"I *know* he is." She swung her arms exasperatedly in the air before they dropped to her sides once more, her beaded reticule and dance card bumping against her leg.

Lane's eyebrows rose in shock while his eyes were alight with anger. "And yet you continue to let him court you?"

"Which one of my *many* suitors would you have me choose in his stead, Lane? Are *you* prepared to begin a courtship with me? Would *you* marry me?"

Anna's heart beat a tattoo in her chest. *Have I just proposed marriage to Lane? Oh Lord, I think I may have…*

He blanched, his spine ramrod straight. "I cannot, I *will* not," his voice rumbled in a low timbre. "I value our friendship too highly to—"

"Rest assured, Lane I do not need to hear an excuse." Anna hid her hands in her skirts to cover their trembling, her imprudent, hopeful heart aching. But she dared him to look in her eyes. "I believe my point has been made. If no other man will have me, why would I, in good conscience, refuse the suit of a young, titled, handsome, and charming gentleman of the *ton*?"

Before she lost what little nerve she possessed, Anna curtseyed, spun on her heel, and strode purposefully toward the ballroom, her heart breaking a bit more with each step.

Chapter 5

Lane struggled to focus through the pulse drumming in his ears and the pain clouding his mind as he made his way back into the ballroom. Had that quarrel truly occurred? Had he allowed his unjustified jealousy control over his mouth? Had he slighted the woman he loved?

Thunderation! He was not in top form this evening.

He nodded at a matron whose name escaped him, then at a lordling he knew from Parliament. Then his gaze found Lord Boxton looking fondly at Anna as she spoke, and that unfamiliar, heated jealousy burned through him once more.

He hadn't the faintest idea what he intended, but he started for them. Then a hand caught his arm.

"Don't do it," Charles Bradley muttered.

Lane narrowed his eyes at Anna's brother. "Do what?"

Charles shook his head, his grip tightening. "Look around you, Lane. Tell me, what do you see?"

Frowning, Lane turned his gaze on the members of the *haute ton*, the gentlemen, the ladies, the patronesses of Almack's, all grouped together in one grand space. His gaze reached Lady Juliana Herring, the haughty curiosity evident in her shrewd gaze as she watched Boxton's exchange with Anna then turned it on Lane.

The woman was not merely a gossip; she took delight in making others suffer from the tales she told. Lane suspected that she was horrid not only because she was in possession of a vile personality, but also to divert attention away from her own proclivities.

Charles was correct. Now was most certainly not the time to confront Boxton, with whatever it was his jealousy-controlled tongue would have spouted.

"I see," Lane murmured, "enough wagging tongues to embarrass Anna should I do something foolish."

What has gotten into me?

The strains of a waltz echoed from the balcony, and Boxton led a smiling Anna among the other couples. Lane's stomach tightened as though he'd been winded in a round at Gentleman Jackson's.

"Have a cup of punch," Charles suggested. "It is dreadfully watered down, but you need something to do other than stare at my sister."

Lane turned his sharp, searching gaze on the Major. "She is my friend," Lane asserted. "I merely wish for what is in her best interests."

"Of course you do."

The centre of the ballroom was a mass of swirling silk and coat tails. Lane's chest ached each time Anna and Boxton passed. He was holding her indecently close. Lane tried to make out their conversation, but before he could, they were swallowed into the crush of waltzing couples.

Finally, the music came to its crescendo and the dancers strode to the outskirts of the room. Lane scanned the crowd for Anna's high, blonde chignon with cherry blossom sprigs, then spotted her striding, her arm linked through Boxton's, toward the French doors to the balcony.

His jaw tightened. "Nothing good can come of this."

"Lane," Charles softened his tone. "Lord Boxton has begun a courtship of my sister. They should have some allowance for a private walk in the garden."

"Are you not concerned that he is a fortune hunter, Charles? Surely you want better for her?"

"Of course! I want what is best for my sister, and that is for her to be *happy* with her position in life. Despite the common way of thinking, she is a grown woman and is capable of making these choices on her own. If she chooses Boxton as her husband, I shall not stand in her way." He put his hand on Lane's arm once more. "And neither shall you."

Lane stared hard at the man standing beside him, their eyes locked. Charles' gaze was full of meaning, but that meaning was lost on Lane. *Is it a warning?*

"You have had years in which to put your claim on my sister, Lane, if that was your wish. Do not interfere with Anna's contentment merely because you fear the loss of a friend."

Lane was lost for words. The truth pained him far more than he thought it could. "I will not impede Anna's happiness," he swore. *But I will not allow her to live a life devoid of the adventure she so craves.*

"Where are your sisters this evening?" Charles' enigmatic gaze turned with deceptive disinterest to the milling dancers.

Struggling to adjust to the abrupt change in subject, Lane cleared his throat. "Emaline and Katherine are here this evening and currently standing with my mother. Bridget is at home with the headache."

Charles' gaze became alert, but Lane did not take the time to think on it. He watched the French doors through which Anna and Boxton had disappeared and left Charles without another word.

He could not leave Annabel alone with the man any longer. He had to know that she was safe, that he was not attempting anything nefarious. It was *not* because of the pure, aching jealousy that roiled in his gut. Most assuredly not.

He wove his way through the crowed ballroom and out the French doors, halting as the doors closed behind him. It was dark, chill, and silent. He blinked to acclimate his eyes to the shadows. Anna and Boxton were not within sight.

Lane's heels clipped on the stone beneath him as he strode to the edge of the balcony. He peered over its edge but did not see any shadowy figures in the gardens. He walked toward the side of the building where the balcony rounded the corner to a small alcove.

There he saw them.

His heart lurched as rage flowed hot through his veins to pound at his temples. Lord *sodding* Boxton's arms were wrapped around Annabel's waist, his lips on hers.

Lane didn't take the time for rational thought as he let out a roar and pulled Boxton bodily from Anna's embrace. He heard her cry of protest but paid it no heed. He grabbed Boxton's cravat and lifted the man to his toes. He pulled his right fist back, ready to deliver pain to the man who would dare to kiss his Anna.

"No, Lane!" Anna's cry of alarm pierced through his fury. She put a hand to his raised arm, a frown on her pale face. "No. Release Anthony. *Now.*"

"He was taking liberties with you," Lane said lamely.

"I was *letting* him! For heaven's sake, Lane, I *have* been kissed before."

"*What?*" Renewed jealousy fired his blood as he turned wide eyes on Anna. "Who was he?"

"Lane, I am not going to have this discussion with you right now. Release Anthony this instant."

Lane reluctantly unclenched his fist, slowly freeing Boxton's cravat one creaking knuckle at a time.

Once Boxton was free, Anna went to him, spreading her hands over his chest as if to look for injuries.

"I am so sorry, Anthony. Are you well?"

"I am fine, thank you." He sent a venomous glare at Lane. "Though I think your friend should learn to control his temper."

"Indeed he should." She turned her own glare on Lane. "What have you to say for yourself?"

Bloody hell. "My apologies, Boxton. I thought—wrongly—that your attentions were unwanted."

"Accepted." Lord Boxton held out his hand, and Lane reluctantly shook it. "It is admirable that you would wish to protect your friend. Especially one as lovely as Annabel."

Lane swallowed past the bile that threatened to rise up his throat. How could Boxton so readily forgive him? His financial woes must be great, indeed.

"Anthony, would you be so kind as to give me a moment alone with Lane?" Anna asked sweetly. "I must discuss something with him."

Lane caught the stiffness to her spine and the stubborn set to her jaw. *Blazes.* She was furious with him—and rightly so, damn it. He hadn't thought before he'd acted.

"Yes, of course, Annabel." The man sent Anna a toothy grin. "I will see you in the ballroom." He sketched a bow at her then nodded at Lane. "Lord Devon."

As soon as he was out of earshot, Anna rounded on Lane. "How *could* you? You humiliated me, Lane! What in heaven's name were you thinking, attacking Anthony like that?"

He ignored her question. "How long have you been calling him '*Anthony*'?" He sneered the name.

Anna's frown deepened. "Stop avoiding my question. That has nothing to do with why you attacked him just now. You storm in here huffing and stomping like a rampaging bull, with not so much as an explanation as to why!"

Her lip quivered and Lane's heart sank. "I did not intend to hurt you, Anna."

* * *

Anna fought to keep her chin from trembling.

"But you did," she confessed. "You *did* hurt me, Lane. But more than that, I am so…" she took a shuddered breath, "*cross* with you! You are my closest friend; I thought you would understand my desire, nay, my *need* to have children." Anna's eyes began to fog over with unshed tears, and she cursed herself for her weakness. "I am not prepared to become a lonely spinster. I am not prepared to watch life pass me by as acquaintances and friends parent children of their own and live rich, fulfilling lives while I moulder away as someone's companion or unfortunate relation. I cannot. I *will* not." She swiped angrily at her eyes and stiffened her spine. "I have made a decision about my life, and I shall not waver from my path. If Anthony should deign to propose marriage, I will accept him."

"Anna, I…" Lane put a hand to her elbow, his eyes troubled. "I wish you the greatest happiness in life, you know that, don't you?"

24

She nodded, unable to speak through the lump in her throat.

"I did not mean to cause you distress." His hand caressed her upper arm, spreading gooseflesh over her skin. "For that, I am truly sorry."

She let out a long breath. "Thank you, Lane."

His jaw tightened for a moment, his gaze calculating. "What of your desire for adventure, Anna?"

She let out an undignified scoff. "What woman—outside the realm of fiction—ever *truly* has an adventure?" Her lips curved in a mirthless smile. "I fear my childhood fancies of being whisked away in some melodrama or another have long since passed."

He nodded his understanding, releasing her arm. She suddenly felt cold without his touch, and the sadness that had settled in her heart gave a decidedly sharp pang.

"I had best return to the ballroom. Anthony and my family will most assuredly be wondering where I am."

"Of course," he murmured.

Anna hesitated for a moment longer, part of her hoping that he would claim a dance with her. When no request was forthcoming, Anna sent him another small smile and returned to the ballroom, leaving him standing alone on the balcony.

How had she allowed herself to be so open to heartbreak when it came to Lane Mason, Earl of Devon? And why had she not moved past these feelings long ago? Whatever the reason was, she would be free of them from that moment on. Lane was, and would remain, her friend and nothing more.

* * *

Hell and blazes. Lane raked his fingers through his hair as he pondered the insanity of his newly forming plan.

Anna's intention for her future was a noble one, and his heart ached to see her in pain. But he could not allow her to live her expected, mundane life without first having a taste of the sort of excitement she found in her novels.

He would give her what she had always wanted.

He would give her an adventure.

Chapter 6

Five days had passed since Anna last spoke to Lane. Five abysmally long days. She missed him dreadfully. What was he doing? Had he received the book she'd had delivered to his family's town house? Did he think of her? What was it that kept him away?

She shifted her position on the heavily stuffed chaise near the low-burning fire in the library. Her bottom was sore from the many drives she had been on with Anthony over the past several days. He was inordinately proud of his phaeton, though he drove rather poorly.

Anna sighed. She may have missed Lane's company, but she had certainly been kept occupied since their last meeting. Anthony had called on her every day. On the days that they did not go for a drive, he had stayed for tea or luncheon, and several times for supper. Their courtship was progressing, and it was only a matter of time before he proposed. She should feel ecstatic, but instead she was filled with a sort of neutral acceptance for his proposal's inevitability.

Every spare moment she'd had over the past five days had been spent reading. It was her only comfort. Her only escape.

A knock sounded at the library door, and she called out, "Come."

The door opened, and a footman, Bernard, entered, a large silver tray balanced on one hand. "A missive for you, Miss Bradley."

She accepted the letter with a "thank you" for the footman. He bowed and retreated out the door.

One glance at the handwriting, and her heart skipped a beat. *Lane.*

She hurriedly broke the seal.

My dear Annabel,

Please do me the honour of going for a ride with me this afternoon in Hyde Park. The day is lovely; it would be a shame to waste it. Also, I have a matter that I wish to discuss with you.

I will be in your front drive at one of the clock precisely, should you wish to join me. There is no need to reply to this letter.

Lane

It was a strangely unemotional and undetailed missive, which was entirely at odds with his customary letters.

She glanced at the mantle clock and gasped. It was nearly noon! She leapt from her seat and fled the room, pausing in the foyer. Bernard stood at attention against the far wall.

"Bernard, would you have Lady Maximus saddled and brought round front for one of the clock, please?"

He bowed. "Certainly, Miss Bradley."

"And if you could send Marie to my bedchamber, I would be much obliged."

"Of course." The young footman hurried to do as he was bid, and Anna continued up the stairs.

Within moments she sped through her bedchamber door, closing it behind her. She pulled her deep-blue riding habit from the wardrobe and draped it over the foot of her bed.

There was a tap at her door, and she called entrance.

"You rang for me, Miss Anna?"

Anna smiled at her maid. "Yes, I'd like to wash and change into my riding habit, if you please."

"Of course, Miss."

Together they worked at giving Anna a standing bath and getting her riding habit on in time to meet Lane. By the time Marie was fixing her hair, it was nearly time.

Anna's stomach jumped with nervousness. She had hoped to be mounted on Lady Maximus before Lane arrived.

"This will do, Marie. My bonnet will cover my hair anyway."

The maid was hesitant but acquiesced. "Very good, Miss."

Annabel left her bedchamber with a *thank you* to Marie and hurried down the stairs.

Tim looked on as she descended. "Miss Bradley, your mount is on the front drive, and Hawkins is ready to accompany you," he said from his position at the front door.

"Thank you, Tim!" she said breathlessly.

She accepted her bonnet and gloves from a footman with a smile and began to put them on.

"Anna." Charles stepped into the foyer from the parlour's opened door, his expression uneasy and a mite pale.

"Oh, hello, Charles." She stepped forward in concern. "Are you well? You look positively ashen."

He grinned at her. "Quite well, I assure you. Must have been something I ate." He cleared his throat. "Where are you off to?"

Reassured, she tied her bonnet ribbons beneath her chin. "I am to go riding with Lane."

He nodded. "I will see you at supper, I trust?"

"You will. Have a pleasant day, Charles. Do feel better."

"Thank you, dear sister."

She sent a smile to everyone in the foyer then strode quickly through the front door. The day was indeed lovely. The sun shone brightly, the sky was nearly cloudless, and the birds were happily chirping in the nearby trees. It was a splendid day for a ride.

She slipped her hands into her white kid gloves and fastened the button at each wrist. Had Lane met a woman that he wished to court? Her stomach knotted at the thought. Perhaps he had finished reading the novel she had lent him and wished to discuss it.

"Good afternoon, Hawkins." She smiled at the head groom as he made a step with his hands to assist her onto her horse.

"Good afternoon, Miss Bradley," he grunted, as she placed her weight into his awaiting palms.

Comfortably situated on Lady Maximus, Anna gave the grey mare a pat and a rub to her neck. "We will have a good ride today, my Lady."

The *clip-clop* of a horse's hooves came from behind her, and she turned Lady Maximus to face the rider.

Her heart began to drum wildly against her ribs as Lane walked his big, black gelding toward her. He made a striking figure on that horse. His tan riding breeches fit snugly on his muscular thighs, paired with a brown riding coat that reminded her of her evening hot chocolate and matched his warm eyes.

Hawkins mounted his horse just as Lane reached them.

"Good afternoon, Annabel," Lane rumbled as he pulled Pegasus to a halt.

"Hello, Lane." She studied his face but couldn't discern what it was he wanted to discuss with her. Blast the man for keeping her in suspense.

"Shall we?" He gestured for her to lead the way.

Nervousness clutched Lane. He had spent the past four sleepless nights and five restless days planning an adventure for Anna. Once he had decided what his plan of action would be, he'd needed to find actors willing to play the parts he required, and retrieve the agreed-upon pound notes for their willingness. Today he would set the foundation for their adventure, and tomorrow it would begin.

He had his moments of doubt, wondering if this was an entirely foolhardy plan or if Anna would enjoy it as much as he anticipated. He hoped for the latter.

They rode in silence to Hyde Park. He knew Anna was brimming with curiosity as to why he had asked her here today, and likely more than a little perturbed with him for being absent for so many days.

She was stunning in her deep blue riding habit. He bit back a smile. Her impatience showed; long curls had begun to come loose from beneath her bonnet. She must have rushed her maid.

He pulled Pegasus to a halt and cleared his throat. "I had thought that we might leave our horses with your groom and stroll around this shaded pond. What say you?"

"I am amenable to that." She held her reins out to her groom. "Hawkins, please watch Lord Devon's gelding and Lady Maximus while we stroll about the pond."

"As you wish, Miss."

Lane leapt to the ground in one fluid motion then went to aid Anna's descent. He placed his hands on her waist and felt her quick intake of breath as his own caught in his throat. Did he affect her? *Damn it, Lane, it wouldn't matter if you did. You are broken, and Anna deserves better than that.*

He would give Anna the adventure she desired, then she could return to her life and he would—

"What is it that you wished to discuss with me, Lane?"

Lane stepped back and held his arm out to her. "I shall tell you in but a moment."

She wrapped her hand around his elbow, and they strolled into the thicket.

A duck *quacked* and splashed in the pond while the leaves rustled in the trees around them. Twigs cracked under their weight as they walked, the sun's rays shone through the spaces in the trees, and a dog barked somewhere off in the distance of the park.

What he had to tell Anna would be difficult—most particularly because it was an untruth. He had never lied directly to her before. He not only needed to lie to Anna, but he also needed to act while doing so. If she knew he was telling a falsehood, the adventure would end before it had even begun.

Once they were out of view—and of earshot—of the groom, Lane stopped and turned to her, putting on a fretful mien. The shadows from the leaves overhead flickered over Anna's matching concerned countenance.

"Anna," he hedged a nervous glance around them as he spoke, "there is something about which I need to speak with you."

"You said as much in your letter. Please do go on."

"I'm in some trouble."

The skin between her brows crinkled. "What sort of trouble? Please do not tell me that you have to face someone at dawn. I could not bear the thought of—"

"No," he interjected, "this is not about a duel. This is much more serious, Anna." He spoke as earnestly as he could manage without appearing melodramatic. "I borrowed some funds…"

"Funds?" Her frown deepened. "I did not think that you were on want of funds, Lane."

"Not many people do." Which was true, because he was, in fact, quite wealthy.

"Did you bring me here to request a loan? Because I do not have any to hand, but I do not mind requesting it of my father if that is what you—"

"No, Anna." He shook his head. "Please listen to me." He gripped her shoulders.

"I'm listening." Fear threaded the concern on her features.

Lane looked up and down the path for effect. "A few weeks ago, I borrowed funds to pay off some gambling debts…but instead of paying them off, I thought I could…increase the amount."

Awareness dawned. "Oh, Lane, you didn't." She put a hand to her mouth.

"I did. I lost the money. Now I not only owe the bank, but several other money lenders."

"How much do you owe?"

He dipped his head in shame. "Thirty-two thousand pounds."

She gasped, her eyes growing wide. "*Thirty-two thousand*? Lane, how could you accumulate such a tremendous debt?"

"Truth be known, that isn't what should concern either of us at the moment. My troubles get worse, Anna."

"*Worse*? How could they possibly get worse, Lane?"

"I promised certain fellows that they would have their money two nights past. I did not have it in time, and they are now searching for me. I think they mean to kill me, Anna."

"*No*! Good heavens, Lane, what are we going to do?"

He was heartened by the fact that she said *we* but kept his pleasure from showing. She believed his tale. Now he simply had to set the scene for tomorrow when his actors came into play.

He opened his mouth to speak but closed it again when he saw the blood leech from Anna's face. She stared somewhere over his left shoulder and gasped as a twig snapped behind him.

"*Lane!*" She leapt toward him just as something hit him from behind and the world went black.

Chapter 7

Lane awoke to the sound of muffled rumbling. He grimaced at the heavy scent of body odour so foul he had the urge to gag. He was swayed, bumped, and jostled, which could only mean that he was in a poorly sprung hack.

His head ached fiercely. What in blazes had happened? The last he remembered he had been speaking with Anna—

He sat upright, swaying for a moment with the pain in his head, and opened his eyes. But everything was in darkness. He had been blindfolded.

"Anna?" he called, almost desperate.

"Oi!" a distinctly male voice barked from beside him. "The gent's awake."

Someone across from him grunted. "I fought 'e was one a' them gents wot'd be out fer days wi' a blow like tha'."

The actors he had hired must have misunderstood their instructions; they were supposed to kidnap him and Anna on the morrow. Their accents and scent were genuine, for which he must applaud them. Their master had assured Lane that their parts would be played convincingly. Lane was convinced. The mistaken day was of no consequence, he supposed. He had already informed his household staff that he would be away for a few days, and Anna's groom could take care of his horse.

He cleared his throat. "Excuse me, but where might Anna be?"

One of the men chuckled "The li'le miss is ri' ere in the 'ack wi' us. She's a feisty one, she is. A real…wha' they call 'em, Frenchie?" The man remained silent. "It's tiger some-ot anyway."

Lane felt ill. "Tigress?" he offered.

"Aye, tha' be the one. *Tigress*. Nearly scratched Billy's eyes out. 'E 'ad te knock 'er out. 'E's ridin on th' perch, lickin' 'is wounds like."

Outrage burned in his chest. "Now wait just one minute! You lot weren't supposed to harm her at all. That is not what I'm paying you for!"

The men laughed.

"This is not a laughing matter," Lane insisted, taken aback. "I am paying you very handsomely, and I expect a certain amount of respect for my wishes in this charade. Miss Annabel Bradley will *not* be harmed in any way. Do I make myself clear?"

"Got no idea wha' yer goin' on about, mister, but yer mighty annoyin'."

Unable to see their faces, Lane hadn't a clue if they were in earnest.

"Just butt 'im, Toby."

"Butt him?" Lane asked in confusion.

He felt Toby shift beside him, followed by a blinding burst of pain on the right side of his head. With a grunt, his world went black. Again.

* * *

"They *what?*" Mrs. Margaret Bradley screeched.

The head groom, Hawkins, twisted his hat in his hands and shuffled his feet where he stood near the door in the dining room.

Major Charles Bradley sat at the table in abject horror, the blood drained completely from his cheeks. *No! This isn't happening.*

"Th…they d-disappeared, Madam. They left their horses with me to take a stroll about the pond, and they didn't return. I waited then looked around for them, but they…disappeared!"

"Where could they have gone?" Mama cried. "Why would they leave the park without their horses?"

Charles shot up from his seat at the table, his chair scraping noisily against the floor. "Please excuse me," he mumbled. "I must go." He started for the door, but his father stopped him.

"What could be more important than your sister missing, Charles?"

"I wish to help find them, Father. But I do not wish for this to ruin Annabel, so I will keep my search quiet."

"Oh. Very good, then."

"I will do my best to return swiftly, Father." Charles stormed out of the house and dashed into the stables. He went directly to his stallion, Riot, and saddled him. Most of the stable hands refused to saddle Riot due to his tendency to bite, but Charles liked to think of them as comrades. He respected Riot, and Riot respected him.

With the saddle secured, Charles mounted him and rode away from the house. Things had gotten much worse. He'd had a terrible feeling that this would happen if Anna left the house that afternoon. Despite what he had thought would be adequate protection, he should have prepared. He should have had someone watching her at all times. He should have taken those letters more seriously instead of brushing them off as idle threats. *Bloody hell.*

Riot's hooves pounded the cobblestones beneath him as he pushed his stallion as fast as he could. He needed to find Annabel immediately. There was no telling what they might do to her.

*　*　*

Anna awoke in a room as dark as pitch. She twisted her wrists against the decidedly rough ropes that bound her behind her back. She hadn't any idea where she was, or whether those awful ruffians were in this room with her.

What had happened to Lane? The last she had seen of him, some giant lout named Toby had attacked him from behind then dragged him away through the park. She fought as best as she could, but another behemoth of a man knocked her unconscious. She rubbed at her sore bottom.

Wherever she was, it smelled horrible. If only she had a kerchief to cover her nose. If only she could *reach* her nose. *Good gracious.*

"Anna?" Lane's sweet whisper to her left sounded loud in the silence of the room. "Annabel, are you in here?"

"Lane, oh Lane, thank goodness you're here!" Relief flooded her. "Where are we? Who were those men?"

"I don't know, Anna, but I'm going to figure a way out of this."

"Lane, can you help me out of these ropes?"

"I will do my best. I have been tied, as well." He shuffled across the floor toward her. "Perhaps we can sit back-to-back; it might be easier to untie each other."

She turned her back to his voice and waited while he continued to shift. His hands gripped her sore bottom, and she gasped, gritting her teeth together.

"Apologies," he mumbled.

"It's all right," she assured him. "I am merely sore."

He was silent for a moment. "Did the ruffians *do* anything to you?"

"Besides kidnapping? Nothing that I did not provoke them into doing, I assure you." He reached her wrists and began to untie them. "Were those the men to whom you owe funds, Lane?"

"No. I have never seen those men before." She kept pulling at the ropes that tied his wrists. "I have a confession, Anna," he continued. "I didn't really—"

"Oi! Tha's 'nuff ye two!" Anna jumped as two of their burly kidnappers burst into the room.

She squinted in shock from the dim light in the hall beyond their abductors. The four silhouettes made her frown. She'd thought there were only three captors. Though, she supposed someone must *drive* the hack.

The fourth man had red hair and ghastly red scars puckering up the side of his neck, over his jaw, and onto the lower portion of his left cheek.

"Get up off yer arses. It's time te move."

Anna hesitated, her internal voice screaming at her to attend to her own needs. She licked at her suddenly dry lips. "May I please have a few moments to take care of some…personal needs?"

The taller of the giants, Toby, gestured to a tattered privacy screen positioned in one dark corner of the room. "Ye got one minit."

Anna was aghast. Surely he did not mean that. "There is no conceivable way that I am going to use a chamber pot with all of you in the room! The screen is very nearly transparent!"

"Couldn't we step out of the room and give Anna some privacy?" Lane asked.

"No." Toby scowled at Anna. "Ye either do 't wi' us in 'ere or ye piss yer prissy dress." He spit on the floor not two feet from her. She recoiled in disgust. "We ain't gonna leave ye, so get on wi' it."

Her stomach in knots, Anna reluctantly made her way to the privacy screen. She used her fingertips to lift the back of her skirt, but could only manage to raise one side. She spread her legs and tried to rest some of the riding habit's long skirt on the top of one thigh, but it kept slipping off. Uninhibited, a growl of frustration escaped her.

"'Avin' a problem, missy?" The ruffians chuckled.

"As a matter of fact, yes." She knew she had no other recourse but to plead for help. She sighed. "Is there any way that I can request Lane's help?" She felt her blush rise from her breasts to her hairline. One more humiliation and she would dissolve into tears.

The sound of shuffling came from the other side of the screen, then heavy, approaching footsteps. *Please let that be Lane and not one of the blackguards!*

The relief she felt when Lane rounded the side of the screen was fleeting once she remembered that he had to help her lift her skirts.

With a meaningful glance that she could not possibly interpret, he turned his back to her and they worked together to lift her skirts. She managed to arrange herself in a way that allowed her to perform her necessary functions, mortifying though it was. Once Lane had helped her rise to her feet once more, she turned to face him while straightening the back of her skirts.

Now that she thought of it, she had read innumerable gothic novels, and not one of them mentioned having to use the chamber pot while one's hands were tied, nor of needing help to do it. It was a terrible oversight.

Her blush flamed hot in her cheeks as embarrassment swamped her. "Thank you."

His eyes softened. "Everything will turn out well, Anna," he whispered, then led the way around the screen.

"Took long 'nuf." Toby watched them suspiciously.

"With our hands tied behind our backs, you left us little choice, sir," Anna snapped.

"Grab 'em, will ya, Billy? The Boss wants 'em there by wensdee night."

Three days? They were to ride for *three* days in close quarters with these barbarians?"

"Sure thing, Toby." The man named Billy grabbed them both by the elbow and dragged them out the door.

Anna narrowed her eyes against the light in the corridor. They appeared to be in a small inn. She assumed it to be far from town on a road not frequently travelled, as was wont to be the way villains travelled in her books.

The scent of burning tallow wax, smoke, and stale urine assailed her nostrils. The acrid odour grew stronger as they strode down the hall, forcing Anna to breathe through her mouth.

Oh Lord, I can taste it.

She distracted herself by asking the question that had been niggling at the back of her mind. "Why?"

Chapter 8

Lane waited with interest for one of their kidnappers to reply.

"Why have you abducted us?" Anna clarified.

Lane wanted to learn the answer to that question, as well, for he had quickly realized that these were *not* the men he had hired.

"We gots orders," Toby grunted.

"From whom?" Lane probed.

"Ain't none o' yer business!"

Billy's grip tightened on Lane's upper arm as they tramped through the inn's taproom. There were two rough-looking patrons huddled together in deep conversation near a low-burning fire. Did they not find their presence alarming? What of the innkeeper? Surely he found two bound persons being led by four villains out of the ordinary?

A blast of cool, humid air hit them as the inn's door opened. They were quickly ushered out into the innyard where their hack awaited them. Thick, heavy droplets of rain pelted them mercilessly from the dark night's sky.

Lane dipped his head instinctively as Billy thrust them toward the hack. "In. Now," the big man grunted.

Another blow to the head was keenly undesired, so Lane did as was demanded of him, though his gentlemanly instincts allowed Anna to precede him. She struggled with the length of her habit's skirts and tumbled forward into the dreadful equipage.

"Anna!" He stepped forward and peered inside. "Are you well?"

She groaned as she fumbled to right herself. "As well as anyone can claim to be in this circumstance," she grumbled sarcastically.

She was well enough, then.

Lane climbed in the hack just as Anna settled herself on the forward-facing seat. Toby pushed him to the seat opposite Anna and entered to sit beside him. Frenchie and Billy clambered in and took their seats as one of them hit the ceiling with their fist.

The hack lurched into motion, the wheels rumbling over dirt, hay, and manure. The damp from the rain was seeping through Lane's riding coat, leaving him chilled.

The rainwater and cold night were not the only things sending shivers down his spine. Whoever had hired these men to kidnap Lane and Anna had a reason behind their actions. The question was, *why*? And what did they intend to do with Lane and Anna when they'd been delivered to *The Boss*?

Those questions, however, paled in comparison to the one glaringly obvious problem they faced. How were they going to escape?

* * *

The past forty-eight hours had been the worst of her life thus far. Anna sat on the edge of a hard mattress, which had been placed on the rough, dirty, wood-planked floor of a miniscule and tattered room. This was the fifth inn, what Anna was sure was a long line of inns, at which they would stop.

Their journey had been long and rough, as was evidenced by her very sore bottom.

A loud snore echoed through the room, and Anna's gaze slid toward one of her captors, Billy, where he sat in an armchair that was dwarfed by his large size. Their kidnappers took turns watching Lane and Anna in their respective rooms. And though she was grateful that *hers* had fallen asleep, his chair was pressed against the door to the hallway, and the other door connected to Lane's bedchamber, where his guard would surely stop them from escaping, should they attempt it.

Faint candlelight flickered over the walls, lending the dilapidated room an air of intimacy, though it was anything but. Something scuttled around in the corner of the small bedchamber, searching for food or the materials for a nest.

She shivered, running her fingertips over the once fine material of her dark blue riding habit. How she wished she had a clean frock…and a bath…and a meal…and hot chocolate.

Anna grimaced at the loud rumble from her stomach. Their captors had only fed them scraps of stale bread and weak, cold tea for sustenance; her body craved so much more.

She removed the hairpins from her flagging, bedraggled coiffure and tied the dark-blonde strands in a knot at the base of her neck. She had lost her bonnet and gloves at some point over the last two days, but she couldn't muster any outrage over the loss.

As much as she wished to have the comforts of home, Anna settled for having her wrists unbound and a night of sleep.

How had Mama, Papa, and Charles taken the news of her abduction? Were they terribly concerned? By now the fact of her kidnapping would be circulating around the *ton* as the latest scandalous gossip. Anna sighed. She was ruined. She had been in a hack with four men, without a chaperone, for two full days and had spent time with them in five separate inns. There was no possibility that the *haute ton* would forgive those iniquities, deliberate or not.

She couldn't hold back the tears that welled in her eyes. Her hopes for a future were gone. Anthony would no longer wish to wed her...*no* gentleman would wish to wed her! Her hopes for children were gone. And she hadn't a clue what was going to happen to her and Lane. Would they expect him to repay the debt he had incurred in his own blood? Would they be tortured? *Killed?*

Her shoulders began to shake as she openly wept, letting out her fears, pain, and sadness in a cathartic release.

The adjoining door suddenly opened, and Anna swiped at her eyes and cheeks with the backs of her hands.

"*Lane*," she whispered wetly as she stood, her arms outstretched.

He hedged a glance at her guard before he glided forward to pull her into his embrace.

"I was worried about you," she murmured into his travel-worn riding coat.

"*Me?*" He pulled back to search her face. "I was worried for *you*, Anna." His astute gaze locked on hers. "You have been crying." Anger burned in his gaze. "What have they done to you?"

She rolled her stinging eyes at him. "What an absurd question, Lane. We have been *kidnapped*." She sniffled. "What *haven't* I to cry about? Anthony will no longer wish to seek my hand—"

"If Boxton cannot see past something that is not your fault, then he is not worth fretting over."

"This is not merely about Anthony, Lane," she said, her voice a heated whisper. "This is about *all* gentlemen. Don't you see? I am ruined! Not only will I not marry, but I will also be shunned. Women will shield their daughters from the sight of me. I have no care for the state of my pride, but my heart desires a child to love. And Charles! Poor Charles will be in want of a wife in a matter of years, and having a pariah for a sister will render his efforts futile.

"Our current circumstance has me frightful that..." Her chin trembled and her eyes clouded over once more. "I would," she squeaked, "I would hate for anything ill to happen to you, Lane."

His arms came around her once more, and she sank into his warmth.

"Shh, shh. It will be all right, Anna. We will find a way to escape."

She nodded against his shoulder.

"I..." His grave voice rumbled against her ear. "I have a confession."

He pulled away from her once more and gestured for her to resume her seat on the mattress. She sat, watching him pace the floor for several moments before he sat beside her.

He was agitated and tense, his hair dishevelled from raking his fingers through it.

Anna dried her eyes and waited nervously for him to speak.

"I am not in debt," he blurted.

Her brows drew together. "I beg your pardon?"

"I am not in debt," he repeated. "I am, in fact, very wealthy."

"You *lied* to me, Lane?" Hurt cut through her.

Lane ran his hands through his blonde hair. "Yes, I lied to you. But I had what I thought was a good reason. Though, in retrospect, it was a ridiculous plan." He faced her, his expression pleading. "I arranged to have us kidnapped."

Anger charged through her, quickly replacing all feelings of sadness and self-pity. She surged to her feet in indignation. "You did *what?*" she hissed.

He rose to his feet as well, his hands open in a pleading gesture. "Please allow me to explain, Anna."

She crossed her arms beneath her breasts, her jaw clenched tight as she awaited his excuse. As little as she wished to hear him speak through the growing fury in her chest, he *was* her closest friend—or so she had thought—and deserved to be heard.

He sighed, as though in relief. "These are not the men that I hired."

"Who are they?"

Lane shrugged helplessly. "I do not know, Anna. I truly do not know. But this is most certainly *not* what I had orchestrated."

Anna chewed on her bottom lip as her anger began to ebb. She did not know what to think, what to feel. If these were not the men that he had hired, if this was not his scheme, then they were precisely where they were before his confession; kidnapped by blackguards with no knowledge of where they were headed and what was to happen to them.

Lane watched her uneasily for a reaction, his posture stiff.

She took a deep breath and released it slowly. She had no reason to be cross with Lane for their current circumstance. *Thank goodness.*

"What was your plan?" she couldn't help but ask.

His gaze was wary, as though fearing a trap.

She clucked her tongue. "I believe you, Lane. I believe that you would never hire men to abuse us in such a way."

He sighed gustily, relief written on his features.

"If you will not tell me what your plan was," she murmured, "at least do me the courtesy of telling me why you arranged the deception."

He held her gaze, though she could sense his great desire to look away.

"I wanted to give you an adventure, Anna."

His admission took her aback.

"I knew you intended to accept a proposal of marriage from Lord Boxton, should he ask. I merely wished for you to first experience something grand. Something about which you might read in your books."

Anna gazed at him in silence, her heart thundering in her chest.

He stepped toward her. "Annabel, there is something else I need to discuss with you."

His neck and cheeks turned a ruddy rouge. Anna kept her jaw from dropping. *Is he blushing?*

Suddenly, Billy snorted, falling in a heap to the floor with a winded *oof*. *Heavens*, he'd made the ground shake!

"Wha'? Whazzit?" He rose clumsily, blinking his eyes in the dimness of the room. "Oi!" he shouted at Lane, pulling a pistol from his pocket to aim it at them. "Back te yer own room! Y' ain't gonna plan no escape on my watch. Off! Go!"

With one last, enigmatic glance at Anna, Lane quit the room, closing the door behind him.

What was it that he had wished to discuss?

"Git some sleep, girl. The Boss 'spects us te be there on time. Ain't no one crossed The Boss an lived te tell the tale." He resumed his position in the chair blocking the door and closed his eyes.

Anna curled on her side, resting her head on her arm, unwilling to put her head directly on the mattress. Her thoughts were consumed with their circumstance. How were they to escape? Would they find an opportunity? What was it that Lane had originally planned for her *adventure*? Why had none of these men attempted to harm her? She was eternally grateful for their restraint, but what did that mean for their intent?

Was it wrong for her to feel flattered that Lane had thought to orchestrate an adventure for her? Did it mean anything more than a gesture of friendship?

Her thoughts wandered from one question to another until she finally drifted into a fitful sleep.

Chapter 9

Anthony Walstone, Viscount Boxton, leapt fluidly from his chestnut gelding and stalked up the front steps of the Bradley family town house. He had not received a single letter or note from Annabel over the past two days, and he was getting fed up with this entire charade. He would rather tup the plump wench, force her to wed him, and get his hands on her satisfyingly large dowry.

If it were not for the stipulation in his grandfather's will that he marry a well-bred, untarnished female in order to receive the vast estate outside Bath, Anthony would continue to fuck his way through the ladies of London until his cock shrivelled to nothing. Unfortunately, there *was* a stipulation in his godforsaken grandfather's will. And he needed Annabel's dowry. It was the largest of all the unmarried ladies in London, and his father's debts were great, indeed. Annabel was the female he required as his wife.

Anthony raised the door's knocker and let it fall with a *clunk*.

He had come by the Bradleys' home yesterday, but Major Bradley had said that Annabel had the headache and refused him entrance. He did not for a moment believe the bastard's tale.

The front door opened, and the Bradleys' butler, Tim, stood in the opened doorway.

"Good evening, my lord."

"Good evening, Tim. I am come to inquire after Miss Bradley's health." He didn't give a rot about the chit's health.

"Miss Bradley is not at home, I'm afraid, your lordship."

Anthony heaved a sigh as sharp annoyance jolted through him. "Might I inquire as to her whereabouts?"

"Miss Annabel has responded to an urgent letter from her grandmother in the country and left directly to her aid. The remainder of the family have gone to the Massingale ball this evening and are not expected to return for several hours."

Rage began to burn its trail through him. "Thank you, Tim. Good evening." He turned and mounted his gelding, Nightmare, and brought him into a gallop down the drive.

That fat *bitch*! How dare she leave town without so much as a word to him? He would not stand for this unruliness, just as he would not accept any disobedience or rebelliousness during their marriage. He would find out exactly where she went, and he would ensure that this did not happen again.

* * *

The hack jolted along the rutted dirt road, Lane, Anna, and their captors jostling with each roll of the wheels. The curtains had been pulled closed, creating muted light in the interior of the equipage.

Lane clasped his hands in his lap, fearing that if he moved them separately, their abductors would realize that they had forgotten to tie them again.

They swerved in a turn, and fear spiked in his gut. He'd thought on several occasions over the past few hours that they should reduce their speed, but despite his advice, Frenchie continued to hit the ceiling with his fist, demanding the red-haired, scarred driver increase his speed.

He had scarcely slept the night before, his thoughts warring with his need to sleep. It had pained him to see Anna so distraught, so fearful for her future. He had not realized how very much it meant to her, being regarded well in society. He should have, of course; it was a terrible oversight on his part. Naturally, being kidnapped, such as they were, would ruin her in the eyes of the *ton*.

It was a quick decision he'd made last evening that he'd meant to discuss with her, but for Billy threatening him with a pistol. He could not see Anna hurt, could not witness her destruction by society's hands. So while he may not be able to bed her, or father her children, he would most certainly give her the protection of his name.

Abruptly, the hack lurched as it sped in a turn, interrupting his thoughts. Lane pressed his feet to the seat opposite, pressing his shoulders deep into the squabs and wedging himself as securely as possible.

There was a strangled yell, several crude exclamations, and the frightened whinny of horses before the hack lurched again. He reached for Anna, wrapping his arms tightly around her, and prayed that she wouldn't get hurt.

The horrifying *crack* of wood and glass rent the air as the hack flipped.

Their three kidnappers were thrown across their seats in a mass of tangled limbs, but Lane pressed his shoulders deeper into the cushions and held Annabel tighter to resist the force of the roll, one arm across her shoulders and one around her hips.

Garbled shouts and dreadful curses were lanced through the air as the men tumbled about.

They rolled twice, the roof crunching and cracking before the hack made its last roll and settled on its side. Lane caught Anna's gaze as they lay horizontally. She returned his stare with wide, crystal-blue eyes.

"Are you well?" He ran a hand down her sweetly curved cheek and delicately angled jaw.

"Yes, I believe so," she murmured. "I will certainly have some bruises and perhaps a scrape or two, but I am relatively unscathed. How are you?"

Lane shifted and flexed his muscles. "I am experiencing some pain, but I do not believe I have any broken bones."

He turned his gaze to their surroundings to assess the damage. Billy sat wailing miserably over the broken arm he cradled in his hand, but the other two, while abraded and bruised, appeared to be fine. Just their damned luck.

"Dammit, Billy, shut yer trap!" Toby barked. "Wha' the bloody 'ell 'appened?"

"We've had an accident," Anna said softly.

Toby's lip curled back in a snarl.

Lane unlatched the door above them and swung it flat against the side of the hack—which currently served as its roof—with a loud *thud*. "Ladies first." He grabbed Anna's waist and lifted her through the doorway, ignoring the sharp pain in his shoulders and back.

He moved to lift himself from the hack, but Frenchie pushed him aside, glaring darkly at Lane. "You are not going to escape zat easily," he uttered in a French accent, then pulled himself out.

Blazes. Lane exited next, followed by Toby, who helped Billy climb out.

Clouds hung low in the sky, blocking the sun and threatening rain. They had rolled into a ravine next to a field of tall grass and a small copse of nearby trees. He wondered how far they could run without being caught.

Lane steadfastly ignored the trickle of sweat running down his spine and sidled closer to Anna. Perhaps this was the moment?

He scanned the area; the horses were nowhere nearby. *Oh hell.* There went the chance to ride away from these villains.

There was a shout in the shrubbery, before the red haired man struggled to his feet.

"We need to reach an inn and have a doctor summoned." Anna wiped absently at her hands.

Abruptly concerned, Lane placed a hand on her arm. "What has happened?"

Her look was full of meaning. "I am fine, Lane, but Billy obviously requires tending from a doctor, while you, Toby, and Frenchie will likely wish to be examined, as well." Her eyes widened before she winked. "Additionally, I presume we are unable to walk to our destination; therefore, another hack must be procured."

"No," Frenchie said in a fine, French accent.

"Surely you do not mean to—"

"*No!*" Frenchie cut his hand through the air. "We will not stop for doctors. We will reach ze next inn and find anozer carriage and will continue." He started walking back the way they had come, but Anna reached a hand out to stop him.

"You cannot simply expect your men to—"

"Zat is exactly what I expect. We must reach our destination tonight," he spat.

"At the very least, allow me to fashion a sling with some—"

Frenchie spun, his arm raised.

Lane acted on instinct and stepped between Anna and Frenchie, blocking the slap with his arm. "True men do not hit ladies," he growled.

"True women know zeir place." Frenchie's voice veritably dripped with distain. "Step aside so I may teach zis *lady* a lesson she obviously needs."

"I am afraid I cannot do that."

Without warning, Frenchie's fist connected with Lane's jaw.

Anna gasped. "No! Lane!"

He motioned her back with a wave of his hand. "Leave this to me, Annabel." Recovering from the blow, Lane faced Frenchie squarely. "I will never stand aside and watch a man—*any* man, let alone loathsome degenerates like you—abuse a woman. If you wish to hit anyone, it will have to be me."

* * *

Anna watched in horror as Lane and Frenchie faced off. She wanted to thank Lane for defending her, but she wished there had been a way for him to do it without the threat of danger to his person.

Toby and Billy cheered their comrade on, while the red-haired man watched in silence.

Frenchie shrugged. "Very well." He raised his fist and Anna cringed.

Lane dodged the hit and instead planted a fist into Frenchie's ribs. The man hunched over on a wheeze, and Lane struck him hard in the back of the head, knocking him to the grassy ground.

He spun to face Anna with determination. "Run!"

They started at a sprint toward the road. Anna could hear Lane's heavy footfalls behind her, rapidly catching up to her own. She pushed herself farther.

The loud *crack* of a pistol firing echoed off the trees and roamed over the distant hills.

"*Ah!*" Lane hissed a breath between his teeth.

"I have another," an unfamiliar voice rumbled.

Anna spun to see the scarred man aiming a pistol at them and Lane holding a hand over his right arm.

"Lane! Lane, are you hurt?" It was a foolish question, but it was the first thing that slipped from her lips.

He lifted his hand to reveal his bloodied coat sleeve.

"You've been shot!" she exclaimed, as though it wasn't already obvious.

"I've been grazed," he corrected. "I am fine." He turned to face their kidnappers, leading the way back toward them.

The man tossed the spent pistol to Billy, who caught it mid-air. "Reload it," the scarred man grunted. "Wouldn't want these two attempting another escape." He grinned with malicious delight. "Or I might well have to kill 'em."

* * *

Major Charles Bradley threaded both hands through his hair in aggravation then slammed his palms against the desk in his study. Three days. *Three damned days!* He was responsible for his sister's abduction, but he wished to take responsibility for her recovery as well.

Charles and his family had managed to keep Lane and Anna's disappearance quiet among the *ton* by saying that she had journeyed to the North to visit their grandmother in Leicester. He sincerely hoped that they continued to believe the tale.

Bonaparte may have been sent to Elba, but Charles knew that the short, bastard Frenchman had spies planted all across England, doing their best to discover a way to free him. He needed to find those spies and silence any information they may have uncovered. He needed to find his sister.

Charles turned his attention back to the letter spread upon his desk. He had contacted his superiors at the Home Office and made every argument possible to have more men brought on to this case, but he had only been granted the aid of five. Only five bloody men. Each of those men had already been assigned watch of different roads out of town, but none had reported back to him. *Damnation!* His only other method to resolve this was to track Anna and Lane down himself.

He put the letter in the top drawer of his desk and locked it. It was time he packed his saddlebags and did what he should have done the moment his sister was kidnapped.

It was time to go hunting.

* * *

One hour of walking down the dirt road in the warm, humid spring day brought them to the nearest inn. Lane suppressed a sigh of relief. He very much needed to sit; his injuries were beginning to ache something fierce. He could feel his face swelling where Frenchie had punched him, his skin pulling across his cheek. His shoulders and neck were stiff and aching from their carriage accident, and he was tense from half expecting Frenchie to turn to violence or molestation with Anna, merely to teach Lane a lesson.

This situation was getting worse; he still had not found an opportunity for escape, and now their captors were more alert than ever. He needed to rethink his stratagem.

They walked through the innyard, passing chickens, bales of hay, and several stray dogs. The inn's door opened directly into the taproom, a bell jingling as they entered. Toby spoke with the innkeeper, presumably to request a carriage and four to take them to meet with "The Boss" at their ultimate destination, wherever that might be. The innkeeper eyed them suspiciously before returning his attention to Toby.

Lane glanced around the nearly empty taproom, an idea forming in his mind. He needed to get Anna alone in one of the rooms above stairs.

Blazes. He would have to act, and he wasn't terribly confident that he could fool these men. It would have to be the performance of his life.

Lane took two steps then stumbled, grabbing on to a nearby table. Anna rushed to his side. Despite looking drawn herself, she was willing to help him, bless her. He gave her a meaningful glance before holding his stomach.

"Oh dear, Lane, you do look dreadful." She winked at him. Thank the Lord she understood his silent message.

"I *feel* dreadful. In fact, I'm afraid if I don't get upstairs, I may disgrace myself by casting up my accounts here on the floor." He put a fist to his mouth for effect.

"Oi! Toby, we need t' get 'im te a room!" Billy bellowed, still clutching his broken arm. "If 'e gets sick, I will, too."

Lane was rushed to a second-floor room and closed inside. He stumbled to the chamber pot to one side of the room and fell to his knees, hoping that they would hear him from beyond the door. He added sickening gurgles and horks as he took in the room and thought through his plan.

The bedchamber was lacking in furniture, but it would suit his purpose. There was a small, low bed, a sturdy writing table, and a window in the wall behind the table's matching chair.

"I need assistance," he called toward the door over his shoulder.

A short argument echoed in the corridor before the door swung inward and Anna was pushed gracelessly inside.

"No," she pleaded. "Please do not make me go in or I shall be sick, as well!"

They pulled the door closed behind her, just as he'd hoped. He smiled at her reassuringly and motioned her toward him.

She crouched beside him. "What is the plan?" she whispered. *Ever the intelligent and practical woman.*

He made a nauseating sound then whispered back at her, "We need to get out the window, but there has to be a distraction to keep them from hearing us leave. Then we run. Make an excuse to open the window then request fresh water and rags to be put outside the door."

She nodded and sprang into action. "This room smells something awful," she said in a carrying voice as she moved to the window. "Let us get some fresh air in here."

Lane was filled with pride as he watched her put her head out the door to speak to their abductors. He greatly admired her cleverness and keen sense of intuition. Of course, her mind was not the only thing that he admired about her…

Anna appeared before him, taking him out of his reverie. "Let's go," she whispered.

Lane made another awful sound and followed her to the opened window. It did not seem a very far drop to the ground; he was sure they would make it down with minimal difficulty.

Anna sat on the window's sill and swung her legs over the side. Lane grabbed her hands, hooked his ankles around the writing table, and lowered her out the window. They both stretched as far as they could, yet Anna still hung several feet above the ground. He locked gazes with her, questioning with his eyes. She nodded her understanding and acquiescence. Lane sent her a wink…and let go.

Chapter 10

Anna hit the ground with a ragged gasp, as a prickly, tingling sensation crept up her legs. She blinked rapidly against the pain as it slowly faded. She turned as Lane leapt from the window and landed with a grunt.

"Are you well, Anna?" He went to her side.

"I am." She tested her feet. "Are you?"

He nodded, clasping her right hand in his. "Run."

Anna lifted the front of her long skirts, and they ran.

She could not recall ever running as fast or as hard as they were then. She had run excitedly and with exuberance as a child, before her father put a stop to her "hoydenish" behaviour, but never had she run in fear. Certainly, she had read of characters running in such a manner in several novels, but reading it vastly differed from experiencing it.

They reached a copse of trees but didn't slow their speed. Branches tugged at her fallen hair, ripped at her sleeves, and pulled the long skirt of her riding habit, but Anna paid them little heed. She focused fully on getting as far from the four burly men at the inn as they possibly could.

Their breath huffed around them, her blood pounded in her ears, and their feet crunched twigs and brush as they rushed between the trees. She heard nothing but their immediate surroundings; no shouts of anger behind them, no shots from pistols, no pounding hoof beats. It was just Anna and Lane, hand-in-hand, dashing through the forest.

Their escape was both exhausting and exhilarating. Anna laboured for breath, her muscles aching, her throat going raw, and her lungs tiring. She hadn't any notion of how much time had lapsed, or how many miles they had covered, but Anna was certain about one thing; she was about to collapse. Her feet throbbed, and she felt the desire to itch at the sweat running between and under her breasts.

She slowed to a stop, pulling Lane with her.

"I…cannot run…any…further," she huffed, bending over to place her hands on her knees. "I…need…to rest…"

A horse whinnied nearby, and they both froze. Anna struggled to keep her breathing silent as her chest heaved. Lane crept toward the noise, slowly and steadily, until the brush swallowed him whole.

Anna wrung her hands as she fretted over his safety.

Scant moments later the leaves rustled and she jumped back, her arms raised in preparation of self-defence. What she would do against a man with a pistol, she knew not.

Relief flooded her as Lane appeared.

"We have reached another inn!" he announced triumphantly, a grin on his sweat-streaked face. "We haven't much time. Our captors will be searching for us. I will procure a room under false names and request a meal. Is that acceptable to you?"

She laughed airily. "Truthfully, I am so overjoyed at the prospect of a meal that I haven't a care for how we get it."

Lane's grin spread to a smile, but Anna saw the fear behind his eyes. He was worried.

Having stopped running, Anna began to feel the enervation of her limbs, but she held firm. They must, still, continue their escape; they were not entirely free of their abductors, yet.

Lane gripped her hand in his, wrapping it around his elbow, as he led her through the shrubbery. They stepped into the clearing around the inn. It was bustling with activity; stable boys leading horses through the yard, carriages awaiting their passengers, chickens clucking, dogs barking or sleeping in some discovered shaded spots.

They strode across the cobblestoned walk toward the door to the "Lazy Inn." They must look affright. Their clothes were torn and muddy, and Lane's were stained with his blood. Her hair was down about her shoulders, and Lane had not shaved in days.

Anna raised her chin as they entered the establishment, hoping that a show of pride would prevent anyone from commenting. Lane immediately sought the innkeeper to request a room for "Mr. and Mrs. Roberts." They spoke for several minutes while Anna stood, looking about in the taproom.

The room held warmth and appeared to be moderately clean—a vast improvement from the inns of the past several days.

Lane gestured toward Anna as he conversed quietly with a young woman. She nodded vigorously before hurrying away.

Anna's brows drew together as a new thought came to her.

Lane returned to her side with a self-satisfied expression. "Come, our room is prepared."

She stood still then spoke in an undertone, "Please excuse me for being gauche, but how is it that we are able to *pay* for this room and our meal?"

Lane matched her frown with one of his own. "I must admit to my own bewilderment on the matter," he said quietly. "Our captors failed to remove any effects from my person, including my purse."

Anna shook her head but allowed Lane to lead her toward the stairs, a maid in their wake. What could their abductors have wanted, if not to abuse Anna or steal from Lane? She was frustratingly perplexed.

Her legs felt heavy as she trudged up the steps, her muscles aching with each movement.

Soon, they were in their temporary bedchamber. The space was of average size and contained all of the necessary pieces of furniture with pleasing accents of pale green.

"Shall I have a hot luncheon sent up to ye, then?" The maid took in their attire with open curiosity.

"Oh yes, please do." Anna felt ready to weep at the possibility of having a full stomach. "Oh, and if you wouldn't mind having some liniment, a poultice, and some hot water brought up as well, that would be lovely."

"Right away, madam." Anna was taken aback at being addressed as "madam," but then, she and Lane were considered married by the servants here.

The moment the door closed behind the maid, Anna dashed to the washbasin and poured water from the pitcher into the ceramic bowl. Grateful for the soap on the stand, Anna washed her hands and face, then poured water over her hair. It wasn't a bath, but it would suffice while they were under time constraints. She wrung out her long locks and tied them in a knot at the base of her neck, then dried her face and hands with a nearby towel.

She turned to look at Lane over her shoulder. "Would you care to wash, as well? There is plenty of water remaining."

He visibly shook himself before nodding.

Anna tossed the bowl's contents out the window then set it down for Lane's use. The water sloshed behind her as she stared longingly at the large bed monopolizing the majority of the room. What she would not give for a full night of sleep in a clean, comfortable bed such as that.

A knock sounded at the door, and she called out entrance. A maid entered, a tray with hot water, liniment, and poultice atop of it.

"Your meal will be brought up soon, Mr. and Mrs. Roberts," the maid said, placing the tray upon the chest of drawers. She curtseyed and retreated.

"What do you mean to do with that?" Lane inclined his head toward the tray. He set the towel aside and crossed his arms over his chest.

Anna clucked her tongue. "Pray do not be thick, Lane. I mean to clean your wound." She gazed meaningfully at the dried blood on his arm.

He shook his head. "We haven't time, Anna. The bullet scarcely grazed me. Our food will arrive directly, and I fear we have hardly enough time to *eat*, let alone—"

Anna pulled a chair out from beside the table, its legs scraping noisily across the floor before she settled it in front of her. "I do not intend for you to die of infection, Lane. You *will* have your wound cleaned. If you would stop grumbling about time and merely sit down, I could have you bandaged by now."

His jaw tightened. "Demanding woman."

She sent him a thin smile. "Remove your clothing."

His eyes widened, and the lobes of his ears reddened. Anna realized what she had said and fought down her own blush.

"I—I mean," she stammered, "your coat, waistcoat, shirt, and cravat, if you please."

Lane hesitated for another moment before acquiescing and carefully removed the clothing from his upper body. He hissed a breath as he reopened the wound on his arm, and Anna grimaced in empathy. It must be dreadfully painful.

He pulled the material of his shirt from the waist of his tan riding breeches, and Anna could not help but be riveted. A line of coarse, dark hair ran down the centre of his abdomen and peppered his chest. He was lean and muscular, but not overly so. Anna longed to trail her fingers over the dips and curves of his muscles.

Heat pooled in her belly at the sight of him. *So this is what a man's upper body looks like without the veil of clothes... No. This is what* Lane *looks like.* Her gaze travelled over his finely toned arms, broad shoulders, and—

Lane's throat cleared, and Anna jumped guiltily. "H—have a seat, if you would." She indicated the chair in front of her before turning her back on him to pick the items off the tray.

Foolish, Anna. Foolish! Their lives were in danger; the very last thing they needed was to waste time and be caught. Most particularly when Anna's distraction was lust...*for Lane.* Yes, foolish, indeed.

Chapter 11

Lane sat in the proffered chair, his body's shameless response to Anna's brazen gaze hidden by the stained shirt balled in his lap. Had he truly seen what he thought he saw in Anna's eyes? Did she *desire* him?

He gazed ruefully at the overeager appendage straining the front of his breeches. He certainly felt desire for *her*. But while his body easily *prepared* for the act of lovemaking, following through with the deed proved—as of yet—to be impossible.

In the back of his mind, he heard the sloshing of water. Anna reappeared at his side, her demeanour aloof as she pressed a wet cloth to the wound on his arm.

Lane ground his teeth and hissed his breath through the intense pain as she administered to him.

"Anna…"

"Mmm?"

"Last evening when I…" How did one propose marriage to their closest friend, but warn her that they may never have intimate relations? How did he express his regret for her state of ruination and offer her the protection of his name without having her feel as though she had inconvenienced him?

"Yes?"

There may be no other recourse but to announce his intention and hope for the best. "I intend to marry you." *Perhaps that was a touch too blunt*, his conscience admonished.

Her hands stilled in the process of wrapping the poultice over his wound. "I…pardon?"

Out with it, Lane. "Last evening," he began, astonished at the nervousness besetting him, "you lamented the potential collapse of your engagement to Lord Boxton and your state of ruination. I am offering you my protection."

Anna moved behind him, handling the items on the tray. Her silence only intensified his anxiousness. *Blazes.* He had not realized how important her answer was to him. Should he tell her that he loved her? Should he confess his inability to—

A knock at the door interrupted his thoughts.

"Come," Anna called shakily.

He fought a grimace. Had he made her so discomfited?

Two maids entered, one holding a tray of covered dishes and the other burdened with the clothing he had requested.

The time for lingering had passed. Lane stood and one of the maids squeaked. *Oh hell.* He'd forgotten that he was not properly dressed. He pressed his stained shirt to his chest and smiled weakly at the maids before retrieving his purse.

"What ye requested, sir," the blushing maid said quietly.

"What is that?" Anna stepped toward them as the other maid put the food on the table.

Lane placed several coins in the maid's hand. "Thank you very much." He glanced over his shoulder at Anna. "This is a suit of clothes for me and a dress for you. I did not suppose you wished to continue on in your torn riding habit."

Anna bit her lips together. "Thank you, Lane." She paused. "But…where in heaven's name did you manage to purchase a new dress?"

He smiled at her. "I asked the maid in the taproom if there were any dresses in your size available for purchase in the inn. She informed me that they had cleaned one such dress that had been left her by another patron several days ago. She believed it would fit you well enough."

"That is wonderful!" She clapped her hands delightedly, the sight warming him far more than it should have, though part of him was also saddened that she was reduced to wearing another's used frock.

Both maids bobbed curtseys, received Lane and Anna's thanks, and quit the room.

"Mmm," Anna moaned as she lifted the cover off of one of the dishes. "Beef, vegetables, buns… *Oh!*"

"What is it?" Lane stepped forward.

"Chocolate cake!" Her eyes lit with joy, and Lane swallowed convulsively as his body responded inappropriately.

What is the matter with me? Now is not *the time to become aroused.*

He spun the table's chair around and held it for her to sit. She did so eagerly, and he followed suit, both of them removing the dishes' covers to see what was beneath.

Anna moaned, her eyes closed, as she chewed. Lane bit the inside of his cheek to slow the flow of blood to his already throbbing erection. He took a breath and released it slowly.

"I am not certain if it is because I have not had proper fare in the past three days, but this is positively the most *marvellous* beef I have ever tasted." Anna took another bite.

Lane sent her an absent smile then focused on his plate. He ate quickly, steadfastly ignoring Anna's moans and sighs of pleasure. He wiped his lips with his napkin and stood to dress. "Please excuse me."

* * *

"What do you mean to do?" Anna asked Lane. He had behaved so strangely through their luncheon, perhaps he felt unwell. She rose and placed the back of her hand to his forehead.

His eyes closed on a groan, but he was not hot. "You do not have a fever. Is it your stomach?" she asked in concern as she continued to test his skin for heat.

She wished she could put her hands elsewhere on his body. Was he hot there? Was he aware that he still wore no shirt? She'd been hard pressed not to stare while she ate.

His voice was gruff. "No." He pulled her hands from his cheeks, his intense brown gaze searching hers. "I do not feel ill."

Anna's stomach fluttered as he stepped back, releasing her.

"I will leave you to your meal." He sketched a halting bow. "We must both dress and catch the mail coach before it leaves without us."

Her heart thudded in her chest. It had felt, for the briefest of moments, that he might kiss her. What was she to make of that? Lane's behaviour was so erratic, so withdrawn. Was he displeased with her?

He retreated with his suit of clothes behind the privacy screen.

Anna resumed her seat at the table and put several desserts on her plate; a slice of chocolate cake, two raspberry-lemon tarts, and an orange.

Throughout luncheon, she had tried to distract herself from the riot of emotions hurdling through her. The euphoria at Lane's proposal had quickly faded once he had given his reasoning. *A marriage of obligation.* She was conflicted. For countless years she had waited—*longed*—for a proposal from Lane. But was a marriage such as this what she truly wanted?

The rustling of his movements echoed through the bedchamber. Had he taken off his breeches? Did he wear smallclothes beneath, or did he go without? What would his *man part* look like? Was it like Greek statues? Or was it larger? Smaller? Anna blushed at the indecent thoughts.

She bit her tongue and grimaced at the metallic flavour of blood.

Could her lack of a response to Lane's proposal be the cause of his unease? It was possible, she supposed. But she could not give him an answer! Would their marriage be a *true* marriage, or did he imagine that they would continue on as they were—as very good friends—in addition to her change in name? Did he feel forced to offer a proposal, or did he do so out of a genuine desire to be her husband?

Anna tore into the orange then licked its juices from her thumb.

Could she wed Lane with the knowledge that he proposed merely to preserve her honour? Likely not. Anna had no desire for a marriage with one-sided passionate love. She would forever be wishing he would ravish her, and he would merely expect their friendship of old.

The object of her thoughts came out from behind the privacy screen, the previously used suit of clothes hanging loosely across his shoulders. He wore slightly long, brown, woollen trousers, a black waistcoat, and a light-brown coat, with a white shirt and cravat. The material was not as fine as he would ordinarily commission, and his hessians appeared particularly odd peeking from beneath his trousers, but he was as handsome as ever.

He cared for her, of that she was certain. But could he view her as more than a very good friend? Could she inspire lust in him? Could his fondness then turn to love?

Lane placed his pocket watch in his waistcoat's pocket, glancing at the time as he did. "We have tarried far too long, I'm afraid."

Anna stood, wiping her hands on a napkin. "Of course."

She gathered her new—used—dress in her arms and brought it behind the privacy screen. She stifled a laugh at the sight of Lane's riding breeches folded neatly on a chair, in vain though the effort was. Would he fold his other clothing while she changed?

Anna draped the dress over the chair and withdrew from behind the screen. "Lane?" She caught his attention as he had bitten into a tart.

He looked up, startled at her reappearance.

"Would you be so kind as to help me out of my dress?" She turned her back to him, partly hoping that such an intimate service would help induce a passion in him. "I cannot reach the buttons."

* * *

60

Bloody Hell. Did she know what she asked? She very obviously had no notion of how miniscule his self-restraint was. He'd been hard pressed not to pull her into his arms and—

He shook his head to clear his thoughts, then swallowed his bite of tart. "Certainly."

Anna turned her back to him, and he strode forward, his gaze never leaving the gentle curve of her neck. He began unbuttoning her once-deep-blue riding habit. The alluring scent of lemons wafted to him. How could she still carry that fragrance after being among those blackguards for three days? He was tempted to press his lips to her skin…to trail them over the slope of her neck and into the curling tendrils of hair that managed to escape their knot.

Lust roared through him as he exposed the skin of her shoulders.

"Would you…" He hesitated. "Do you wish for me to unlace your corset, as well?"

Anna was quiet for a moment, then nodded. "If I am to flee for my life, I would prefer to do it without the restraint of a corset. Please do."

Lane continued down until the gown had been unlaced, then he worked on her corset. He swallowed back the saliva that had gathered in his mouth and tugged at the knot of her corset strings. *Now is not the time for yearning, Lane. We must continue our escape!*

His fingers brushed her back with every movement of his hands, and the heat from her skin sent hunger straight to the maypole in his trousers. His breathing became harsh, ragged.

He concluded his task, then abruptly turned and made his way back to the table.

"Thank you," she called after him.

He cleared his throat. "You are welcome."

Lane busied himself about the bedchamber while stalwartly ignoring the sound of Anna dressing…and attempting to garner control over his body.

If *The Boss'* henchmen did, in fact, find them, he imagined that they would not be lenient with their punishment. He required a weapon of some kind. His gaze searched the room, then settled on the serrated knife brought with the beef. It would have to do. He slipped it into his breast pocket, bulky though it was.

A throat cleared behind him.

Lane turned and nearly swallowed his tongue. The woman who had owned that frock before Lane purchased it for Anna had been in possession of a smaller…bust. The pale-yellow material stretched tightly across Anna's bosom, creating pert, smooth mounds above the bodice.

He took an involuntary step forward. What if he kissed her? Would she be repulsed by the action, or would she embrace it?

The room faded. He found himself leaning toward her, the diminishing space between them charged with energy.

Did she want it, too? He looked into her heavy-lidded blue eyes. *She wants it, too.*

Suddenly, his conscience gripped him. *What will happen when she believes that you can give her a proper married life? She would accept your proposal under the false assumption that you will take her to the marriage bed. It would be a lie…*

He took a quivering breath. "I will request a basket of sustenance for our journey," he said lamely.

A chill washed over him as he turned toward the door. *You are a fool, Lane Mason. A bloody damned fool.*

Chapter 12

Major Charles Bradley pulled his stallion to a stop and leapt to the ground. He handed the reins to the waiting groom outside the Hog's Inn.

"He bites," Charles warned him.

The sun shone brightly in the partly cloudy sky, its rays heating him through his dark riding coat.

He strode with purpose toward the inn's door. He needed to find Anna, Lord Devon, and their captors, but first he must learn their direction. The first three innkeepers he had questioned had denied ever having seen Annabel or Lord Devon. Charles hoped that this one would be different. He was running out of options.

The men Gilley had allowed him to aid with this rescue mission had, as of yet, not reported back. He was at his wit's end, and damn it, he was worried.

He entered the cigar-scented taproom and located the innkeeper.

"Pardon me, my good man. Might I trouble you for a few moments of your time? I would like to ask you some questions." He slipped two pound notes into the man's greasy palm.

Greedy anticipation widened the innkeeper's bloodshot eyes at the outrageous sum, and he furtively slipped the pound notes into his pocket. "Yes, yes, come into the back if you will, sir."

Charles inclined his head. "I am much obliged."

He followed the rotund innkeeper to the untidy back office and sat in the proffered threadbare armchair.

"What can I 'elp you with, sir?" The innkeeper looked quizzically at him.

"I need to know if you have seen any bizarre behaviour here over the last three days."

The man rubbed his chin in thought. "Aye, we 'ad a group o' ruffians come through 'ere a few days back. They was big 'uns, they was. Giants!" He spread his arms high, as though to indicate the "ruffians'" heights.

Charles watched the man's eyes. "Had they anyone else with them?"

The innkeeper hesitated for a moment, fumbling with the ink blotter and some papers on his desk. "Those men paid the staff 'ere to keep quiet that they 'ad a man and a woman tied up in one of our rooms. I knew we shouldn't a' let it 'appen, but they were big men with pistols, and they said that—"

"Your reasons for keeping quiet are not relevant to my search. I do, however, appreciate your telling me the truth." Charles' heart hiccoughed as dread filled him. "Now, could you describe the man and the woman?"

"I only got a quick look at 'em, but they were both wearing them riding clothes wot the fancy folk wear. The gent was tall and 'ad light hair. The woman had medium coloured hair—not brown, but not light—and was a mite plump…" The innkeeper gestured obscenely with his hands.

Charles felt ill. "Thank you," he said. "Do you happen to know in which direction they were headed?"

"Southeast, I'd say. It's wot I figured from the way they was talking."

The blood drained from Charles' face as he stood to shake the man's hand. He gave him another pound note for his time. "Thank you, again."

Bloody, bloody hell.

The groom was still waiting with Riot, though he'd been watered and fed. Charles tipped the groom, leapt on Riot, and started him at a gallop. They must be headed to Dover. It was the only conceivable location that had a harbour on the southeastern part of England.

This situation was terrible, and getting worse by the moment. Goons hired by French operatives had kidnapped Anna and the Earl of Devon. Charles needed to get to them before they reached their destination and were interrogated on subjects of which they had no knowledge.

His greatest fear for his family had been realized. His sister and her closest friend could potentially be the victims of torture. Of murder. His heart gave a sickening lurch and he pushed Riot harder. *He would not let that happen.*

* * *

Anna resisted the pull of sleep as the mail coach trundled down the road toward the next inn. Rain had started some time over the past four hours. The soft *patter* of the droplets trickled along the coach's roof.

Her mind drifted as she dazedly closed her eyes. Lane had been about to kiss her at the inn, she was certain. What had stopped him? Would he rebuff her if she made an overture?

She'd had plenty of time over the past hours to contemplate their circumstance. She was unquestionably ruined, despite nothing untoward having truly occurred between her and Lane, or their abductors. Lane had proposed marriage to protect her name. And something had changed between the both of them that she absolutely wished to explore.

She shamefully desired his kiss, his intimate touch. Would it be frightfully terrible for her to act on these physical urges? She thought of all the delightfully naughty things she wished she could do to Lane, and molten heat pooled low in her belly. She squeezed her legs together in response, the pressure on her *mons* a fleeting relief.

The mail coach jolted to one side, pushing Anna into the large woman sitting next to her. "Beg pardon," Anna mumbled as she righted herself, blinking her eyes into wakefulness.

"What's that, dearie?" the woman yelled, her jowls rippling at the movement.

Anna caught Lane's glittering gaze from where he sat across the coach, then returned her attention to the woman beside her.

Anna raised her voice so she could be heard. "I bumped into you, Madam, so I said, 'Beg pardon.'"

"Oh, it's no trouble at all, dearie." The woman waved a plump hand through the air, wafting the scent of stewed beef toward her. "What's your name, pet?"

"My name is Anna B—Roberts. Mrs. Anna Roberts." Anna quickly recalled that she and Lane had agreed to continue the pretence until they were safely returned to London. Anna gestured to Lane. "And this is my husband, Mr. Roberts."

The woman nodded, her jowls jiggling. "Pleased to meet you, Mr. and Mrs. Roberts. I am Miss Bligh, and the milk-and-water miss beside you, Mr. Roberts, is my niece, Miss Regina Bligh." The little mouse of a girl sitting next to Lane blushed profusely then turned her gaze to her clasped hands in her lap.

"A pleasure, Miss Bligh, Miss Regina Bligh," they uttered in turn, nodding at them both.

"So where are you two off to at this time of the day? Why, it is well past the time for a country supper." Miss Bligh's loud voice echoed in the small space.

With a quick glance at Lane, Anna turned back to Miss Bligh. "There were no available accommodations at the last inn. We intend to retire at the *next* inn."

"Oh yes," Miss Bligh shouted. "'Tis a shame when one cannot find appropriate lodgings."

"Where are you headed this evening, Miss Bligh?" Lane raised his voice for the hard-of-hearing woman.

Miss Bligh fanned her round face and sent Lane a flirtatious wink. "You impertinent rascal." She giggled.

Lane and Anna exchanged a perplexed glance.

Miss Regina shifted in her seat. "We are returning to my father's home in London," she said quietly. Anna had to strain to hear her words. "My aunt and I ventured on an excursion through the South of England to take in the sights."

Anna smiled. "That sounds lovely. How long was your trip?"

"Speak up, dears," Miss Bligh bellowed.

Lane snorted with repressed laughter, and Anna grinned.

The mail coach began to slow.

"Are we at the next stop?" Anna turned to look out the window. "I do not see an inn or stable."

Lane looked through the opposite window then muttered a curse under his breath. He caught Anna's eye, worry written on his features, then reached below his seat and retrieved their packaged supper.

"It's them," Lane rumbled meaningfully. "We have to leave before they come any nearer."

The rumble of male voices echoed outside the equipage.

"*Now.*" Lane pressed the door's latch and opened the door silently.

They nodded in unison and leapt from the coach. *Thank goodness Miss Bligh had the good sense to remain silent, or we would surely have been discovered!*

Lane put his mouth to her ear, sending a shiver down her spine. "*Run.*" He gripped her hand and made a run for the copse of trees at the side of the road.

* * *

Lane's chest heaved with his laboured breaths as he and Anna ran through the forest. He hadn't the faintest idea in which direction they sprinted, but they could not turn back. They had alternated between running and brisk walking since they had left the coach. He had hoped that they would come across another inn or a suitable place to rest in the past hours, but they'd had no such luck.

Anna tugged on his hand as she started to slow.

"We cannot stop, Anna," he huffed over his shoulder. "I will not risk your getting hurt."

"What if...we...walk quickly?" She gasped each breath, clearly struggling.

You should not push her so. He slowed his feet to a brisk walk. "Is this pace to your liking, Anna?"

"Much," she breathed. "Thank...you."

Sweat beaded down his forehead and over his temples. Another trickle wove its way between his shoulder blades. The rain had stopped some time ago, to be replaced by the brightly shining spring sun. Their only protection from its rays was the fluttering leaves of the trees. They needed to keep out of sight until nightfall; they were far too visible in this forest.

He stopped, his back and legs aching from constant strain. He put down the package of food and checked his pocket watch.

"It is very nearly seven of the clock." He blinked sweat from his eye. "Sunset is in just over an hour. We need to find a place to settle for the night; we should search for shelter."

To her credit, Anna did not appear as appalled as she must have felt. Anna might love nature, but sleeping out of doors was not equal to admiring it.

Lane picked up their packaged meal and, hand in hand with Anna, continued their way through the forest. He kept his attention on navigating the path and searching for a place to spend the night, not the soft, warm hand gripping his…or the lovely woman attached to it.

A loud grumble sounded, and he let out a small chuckle.

"Feeling hungry, Annabel?"

She looked sheepish. "Yes, I am. Do you think we will find a safe place to stop? I have been fantasizing about the contents of that package for well over an hour."

A smile tugged at Lane's lips. "I believe we can arrange something."

He scanned their surroundings as they walked. The air smelled of damp soil and distant flowers. A shrill *squawk* rent the air, and small forest animals scuttled along the ground. The sound of running water and frogs croaking caught his ear and he steered them towards it.

"Oh!" Anna exclaimed. "This is lovely!" She stared at their surroundings.

Lane watched the play of emotions on her face as she entered one of her dreamy moments. Anna had a refreshing amount of wonder and appreciation for their daily surroundings that Lane found addictive to watch.

What had she thought of his marriage proposal? Had she not answered because she intended to refuse him? Or did she merely require an inducement to accept?

"This glade is delightful." Anna's voice shook Lane out of his musings.

He cleared his throat. "Indeed."

"You sound so cynical, Lane. Can you not appreciate the beauty of this place?"

Lane couldn't break her gaze. "I can."

The blush brought to Anna's finely curved cheeks from their sprint through the forest slowly deepened. The sight roused his blood.

They entered a small clearing where blue flowers dotted the grassy ground and trees drooped overhead. A narrow stream trickled nearby.

"Well, my dear, I would certainly describe this as an ideal place to sit."
She huffed a panted laugh. "Ideal, indeed. It is positively enchanting."

Chapter 13

Major Charles Bradley had been running his horse from posting inn to posting inn all day, with no luck of finding Anna or Lord Devon. He and Riot were exhausted and in need of rest, so it was with relief that he had come upon an inn hidden off the main road to Dover.

He must find them before they reached their destination. If they had not stopped along the main roads, they could have been there several times over, but Charles would wager that they had made frequent stops. He was three days behind, but with them travelling together in a hack, they would be significantly decelerated, most particularly with time spent at inns, changing horses, sleep, and meals. With his stallion, Charles was able to maintain a more expedient pace.

He sat back in his chair in the private dining room in the Wild Rose Inn, his glass of brandy resting on the table in front of him, and sighed. Finding his sister had been more of a challenge than he had anticipated. If he had been in possession of a position higher up in command, he would have put more men on the case, but his was a limited reach.

The five allotted men to whom he'd assigned tasks had still not reached him. Henderson and Jones remained at his town house, awaiting news. Stevens had travelled in a southwestern direction, Davis had journeyed north to Scotland, and Thomson had gone toward Dover. He'd hoped that Thomson had been able to trace Anna and Lord Devon's trail, but he'd not heard from the man.

Charles took a sip of his brandy. He would retire before supper, sleep for an hour or two, then be on his way at dusk. He was so damned tired.

The door to his private dining room burst open to reveal Thomson framing the doorway. Charles stood quickly, his chair falling backward to the wood floor. His heart plummeted at the expression on his comrade's face.

"Thank the lord you're here, Hyd—er, Major Bradley." He glanced over his shoulder as he spoke. "I have been searching for you for the past several hours, stopping at every inn along the road. But once this innkeeper said you were—"

"Get on with it, Thomson." Anxiousness clutched at his chest. "What news have you?"

"I found them."

Charles' stomach leapt.

"But I've lost them."

"*Damnation*!" Charles' dread returned. "Where did you last see them?"

"Y'see I'd been following the hack for a mile or so after happening upon them at an inn, when…" He swallowed convulsively, and Charles had to refrain from barking at him. "There was an accident."

"*Accident?*" His heart constricted. "Is Annabel well?"

Thomson nodded once. "Everyone survived, but the horses ran off, and the hack was a right mess. One of the abductors broke his arm, and the others looked right mussed. But, Major, it is what happened *after* the accident…"

"*Quickly, man!*" Charles' heart thudded mercilessly in his chest.

"The group walked for an hour and reached another inn, while I remained unseen in among the trees. They all entered, so I went after them for an early luncheon…"

Charles suspected that he knew what Thomson was going to say, and it was decidedly *not* good news.

"I waited for nearly an hour before I heard a commotion from above stairs."

"Good God!" Charles exclaimed.

"It is likely not what you are thinking, sir, bit it is not good. Your sister and Lord Devon escaped. According to what I overheard, Lord Devon feigned some sort of illness, and they leapt through a second-floor window.

Charles paled. "But if they've escaped, surely they must be on the road returning to London. Neither Anna nor Lane have any experience covering their tracks. They'll be found and interrogated for certain."

Thomson cleared his throat. "I overheard the men expressing anger with regards to Miss Bradley and Lord Devon's actions. They no longer wish to interrogate them. They mean to hunt, torture, and kill your sister and her friend…for sport, sir."

* * *

Anna looked on eagerly as Lane opened the bundle of food and removed its contents. Her senses were teased by the scent of beef, vegetables with white cream sauce, buns, and… *Oh my*! Tarts and chocolate cake! Her stomach rumbled, and her mouth watered.

The stream had satiated her thirst, the water cool and refreshing; however, her stomach begged for sustenance.

Anna enthusiastically accepted a napkin, which she placed on the grass in front of her. They divided the food and ate with fervour. Once her initial hunger had been satisfied, Anna turned her gaze on Lane.

"Does your arm pain you terribly?" she inquired.

The bruise on his cheek had not darkened but appeared to be a dull brown that could easily be mistaken for a smudge of dirt.

Lane shook his head and swallowed his bite of beef. "There is an ache, and I'm certain it will require a doctor's expert touch, but it does not pain me greatly."

"I am pleased to hear it."

The sun began to hide itself behind the trees, lending a faint blue hue to the clearing.

"Dusk will be upon us presently," she noted.

Lane grunted his agreement. "It is a pity that we do not have time to enjoy this spot."

"Do you suppose our abductors will pursue us through this forest?"

He swallowed a bite of cake. "It is impossible to know what the Misses Bligh confessed under duress, but it would be safest to assume that our abductors know we absconded into the forest, yes." He glanced around the clearing. "We must find shelter so we may sleep."

"I daresay I could sleep where I sit."

Lane grinned at her, and her heart flipped over. She sighed at its overzealousness.

Anna very much wished that she could soak in a hot bath and enjoy a night spent in her own bed. She knew not how long it would take to heat the ache from her muscles and soothe the blisters on her feet.

It would be decidedly lovely to sit in her favourite chair by her window and read a book…drink her chocolate. It would be blessedly peaceful.

Annabel noted, reluctantly, that it was rather contradictory to her character to spend the majority of her life fantasizing about experiencing the adventures in her beloved novels, yet now that she was living one, she only wished to return home.

She could certainly focus on the positive aspects of her misadventure; she had faced danger and prevailed, had been kidnapped and escaped, and had…well *no*, she had not kissed the hero.

Lane bit into a piece of chocolate cake, the muscles in his jaw jumping as he chewed. *I couldn't.* Her stomach began to quiver with nervous fluttering. They were sitting close enough together that if she leaned forward, she could touch his lips with hers. *How could I think of doing such a bold thing?*

71

They must continue on soon; if she were to do it, the moment would be nigh.

The fluttering in her stomach intensified, her heart pumping a staccato beat in her chest.

Lane bunched the remaining food into the package and wrapped it closed. "Anna, do you suppose—"

His words were cut short as she thrust herself forward and covered his lips with hers.

* * *

Lane stilled, his body reacting immediately to Anna's kiss. He did not wish to frighten her with his eagerness, so he forced himself to be outwardly calm. Inside, however, he was bursting. His heart thundered, yet sang, his stomach knotted, yet felt ready to float, his ballocks... *Well*, he thought ruefully, *they were tight and near-frantic to release their burden.*

He leaned into the kiss, nudging himself closer. Lane raised his hand to cup her jaw, thumbing the smooth skin under her chin. He traced the line of her lips with the tip of his tongue, gently urging her to open for him.

Her jaw dropped open on a sigh, and he delved inside, elation washing over him. She tasted of lemon raspberry tart; the hint of sweet was enough to drive him to desperation. He tangled his tongue with hers, urging her further, deeper with his actions.

This is Anna! The jubilant realization hit him hard. *Finally*, he was kissing her, tasting her. *Blazes*. He wanted more!

She tangled her fingers in his hair, the gentle, almost painful tugging sending tingles of delight down his spine.

She was intoxicating. He wanted to touch her, to feel her. He didn't care if he couldn't complete the act of lovemaking, he just wanted to give her pleasure. Endless, erotic pleasure.

He wanted to trace his hands—nay, his tongue—along the ridge of her collar, circling her breasts to tease the sweet buds of her nipples. *Blazes*, he wanted to taste her womanly centre, to have her body sing with sensual desire and reach her peak over and over at his hands.

His thoughts hardened him unbearably. He throbbed...he *ached* for her.

Lane let his hand wander to her waist, his fingers fisting in the sunny material. His entire will went into not laying her down in the damp grass and—

"Lane," she moaned, breaking their torrid kisses. "Do you hear that?"

The distant rumble of a horse's hooves and wheels on a dirt road invaded his senses.

"No," he groaned, pressing his forehead to hers. *Please do not let this end!*

* * *

Anna quite felt like groaning, herself. She'd never known kisses like Lane's—so passionate, so... *addictive.*

Her heart fluttered and her *mons* throbbed. She most certainly wanted more.

The distant rumbling drew nearer, pulling her once more from her thoughts.

"You don't suppose it's…" she trailed off.

"No," Lane assured her as he stood, aiding Anna to her feet along with him. "That is a single horse with a light," he scrunched his face in thought as he listened, "two-wheeled equipage." He tightened his grip on her hand as he retrieved the bundled the remains of their supper. "Come."

Anna went along with him, his hand hot on hers. The faint flutter continued low in her belly as they moved quickly through the forest toward the noise. The light was rapidly fading, casting a grey-blue glow on the trees around them.

Branches tugged at the skirts of her butter-coloured frock and the petticoat beneath. A chill ran through her, and she realized just how cool the air had become since the sun retreated.

Abruptly, the forest opened onto a dirt road, where they halted. Not thirty paces to their right was a figure sitting on a horse-drawn wagon, a lantern held aloft, swinging with the wagon's motion. Anna squinted against the light, holding one hand to block it out.

"Ho there!" called the hesitant voice of an elderly man. "What seems to be the trouble?"

Keen relief rushed through Anna. This could be their saving grace!

They strode forward, meeting the man and his horse as they stopped in the road.

"Hello, sir! My name is Mr. Roberts," Lane prevaricated. "My wife and I have been unlucky in our choice of equipage, I'm afraid. Had an accident some miles back and have been wandering through the forest ever since."

"Bad luck, wot?" The elderly man's eyes crinkled warmly in the corners as he leaned forward in his seat.

"I do hope it is not too bold to ask, sir," Lane continued, "but my wife is exhausted from our walk. Would you be so good as to bring us to the next inn? We would be ever so grateful, and I could pay you handsomely for your trouble."

The man waved a hand through the air. "No need to pay me, Mr. Roberts. I am headed that way meself." He smiled, revealing one missing bottom tooth. "My name is Peter Collins."

Anna curtseyed. "It is a pleasure to meet you, Mr. Collins. We are forever in your debt."

"Nonsense, Mrs. Roberts. I'd be happy te take ye te the inn. It's not far from here, but a few miles more."

The kind Mr. Collins gestured to the back of his wagon and waited for them to get themselves situated before he started his horse with a *click* of his tongue.

Anna held on to the side of the wagon, uncaring that she sat upon bales of hay. Her feet stung, her body ached, she was in dire need of a proper bath. Her mind caught on that thought, and she nearly sighed aloud. Would she get the opportunity to bathe at the inn?

The wagon bumped along the dirt road. The greenery in this part of England was exceptionally picturesque. It was a shame that she could not see it through the growing darkness.

"Dover," Lane grunted beside her.

"I beg your pardon?" she asked in an undertone, unsure if Lane had intended for Mr. Collins to overhear.

"We were headed toward Dover."

Anna frowned. "But isn't that just a—"

"Yes," Lane interjected. "We could have reached Dover several times over by now."

With a sidelong glance at Mr. Collins' back, Anna whispered, "I do not mean to bemoan our success in escaping, but why would they delay their meeting with The Boss? Why not journey directly there?"

Lane shook his head, a lock of his uncombed blonde hair falling over his forehead. "I haven't the faintest. But I am relieved that they didn't. Lord knows what would have happened to us if they had."

"Perish the thought."

Lane poked at the faint bruising on his left cheek as a young boy would pick at a scrape. Anna hid a grin.

She swivelled to watch as they crested a hill. The wagon continued bumpily along as the sun all but disappeared beyond the horizon. The sky was streaked with bright pink and deep purple. Anna sighed, rubbing her arms with her hands to ward off the chill.

She covered a yawn with the back of her hand and groggily leaned her head on Lane's shoulder. Her eyes drooped as Lane's arm came across her back, pulling her tighter against him. Anna soaked up his warmth, her eyes refusing to open from a blink.

The rumble and sway of the wagon slowly lulled her into a deep sleep

.

Chapter 14

Lane adjusted Anna's weight in his arms as he strode up The Swan Inn's stairs. The innkeeper had given them the last available room. Evidently, there was a large party of travellers there this evening.

The inn was warm and inviting; they had small fires lit in the main rooms, and those enjoying a late-night repast sat at tables in the taproom. A low hum of conversation drifted up the stairs after them.

The innkeeper's wife walked ahead of him with the keys in her hand. She stopped before a door and swung it wide for Lane to pass.

"This here is one of our finest," she said, her low voice soft and smooth like honey. She smiled, spreading the wrinkles around her mouth until they were flat. "Your bath shall be brought up directly."

"Thank you, madam." Lane could not help but smile in return.

He placed Anna gently on the bed that dominated the small room. A fire had already been lit in the hearth, and candelabra graced each of the bedside tables, lending an orange, flickering warmth to the room.

Within a matter of moments, a group of burly footmen entered with a large brass bathing tub. The Swan Inn must do very fine indeed to be able to bear the expense of such a fine tub.

"At the foot of the bed," the innkeeper's wife directed the footmen. "That's it. No, Harrison, just a mite to the left. Yes, there." She smiled with satisfaction.

The footmen bowed before retreating, the innkeeper's wife following in their wake.

Lane sat on one of the overstuffed cerulean armchairs, stretching out his legs and crossing his ankles one over the other. His body ached…in more than one sense.

Damnation. Had that kiss truly happened? He had never felt so deeply involved in a kiss. Never felt such a burning need to continue. Could Anna be the cure to his *problem*?

The footmen returned with buckets of steaming water, the innkeeper's wife following with towels and soap. The *splosh* of water in the tub was enough to make Lane's eyes roll backward. The air filled with humidity, steam curling alluringly above the bathwater's surface.

"Here y'are, Mr. Roberts. Nice and hot, fresh from the fire." The innkeeper's wife smiled kindly at him. "Ring the bell if you feel hungry. If not, the morning meal is prepared at seven of the clock."

Lane stood and took two steps toward the woman. "Thank you very much, madam. This is lovely."

She beamed at him, her round, wrinkled face positively bursting with pride.

Soon she made her exit, closing the door after her. Lane slid the bolt into place, the *snick* echoing through the room over the crackles from the fire and Anna's soft, even breathing.

His eagerness to be in the heat of the tub overruled any notion of behaving with the proper decorum. He flung his clothes off, tossing them negligently to the chair. Hopping on one foot, he removed his boot and stocking, then did the same for the other.

Finally nude, Lane stepped into the tub. He hissed his breath out as his skin tingled from the heat of the water. He inhaled deeply, sinking fully into the tub, careful to keep his bandage above the water as he allowed his body to adjust to the temperature.

He rested his head against the rim of the tub, closing his eyes and silently encouraging his muscles to relax.

Anna shifted on the bed, drawing his thoughts toward her. Could she be the woman that would change everything? That kiss had certainly *felt* different.

Lane cast a regretful glance downward, where his overly fervent cock stood proudly in the hot water. It was clear that he wanted Anna. But would she accept his proposal of marriage?

Seemingly without conscious thought, his hand crept downward, gripping his stiffness beneath the water. Slowly his hand began to move. But he let it happen. He was exhausted, his body worn from the past days of misadventure. He needed a release from his built-up restless energy.

Lane tilted his head back, resting it once more on the rim of the tub, his eyes closed.

* * *

Anna awoke to a gentle, rhythmic sloshing. Her body begged her to return to sleep, but her mind focused on the fact that she was lying on the comforting softness of a bed, her body engulfed in the warmth of thick bedclothes.

She opened her eyes. Warm, flickering firelight wavered about the room. The air was humid from steam and smelled of soap and burning coals. She inhaled longingly. She would very much enjoy a bath.

The sloshing continued, and Anna's gaze was drawn to the foot of the bed. Her eyes widened, immediately riveted by a very obviously *nude* Lane reclined in a tub at the foot of the bed.

But what…what is he doing? Her mouth dropped open on a silent gasp as awareness dawned. His eyes were closed, his head back, and his arm was moving beneath the water's surface. He appeared to be enjoying himself immensely.

Goodness! She had never thought… But then, if she had explored what was beneath her restrictive clothing, she could only assume that others had done so, as well. *But this is Lane. Lane* was touching himself intimately!

An answering throb began in her *mons*, spreading liquid heat to her womanly core. *What would he do if I joined him?* Oh goodness, what a thought! Could she? Should she? *Dare* she?

Lane moaned softly, and her decision was made for her. She wanted him. He'd already proposed marriage, for heaven's sake. She could easily accept his proposal and marry him upon returning to London. Surely making love to your intended before marriage was not so terrible a thing.

A quick, naughty grin quirked her lips. She pushed aside the bedclothes and rose to a seated position.

Abruptly, Lane sputtered. He sat up, his arms flailing to grab for purchase. "*Blazes*, Anna! What do you mean to startle a man like that?"

Anna felt rooted in place. What could she say? Her bravery of a moment before threatened to dissipate, but she couldn't allow it. She wanted Lane. She wanted this.

Without replying, Anna reached for the ties of her front-fastening gown. Lane blinked, seemingly at a loss for words. Feeling emboldened, she allowed the frock to slide down her arms and pool at her feet.

"Anna—" Lane croaked.

Her stomach knotted, her heart sped. She was anxious to touch him…to *bathe* with him. Her fingers fumbled with the ties and fastenings of her undergarments, but she made quick work of them nonetheless.

Within moments she was standing nude before him, her skin heated with the flush of anticipation.

Lane's heavy-lidded gaze travelled down her person, pausing over her breasts, her waist, and the thatch of curls at the apex of her thighs.

"Sweet Jesus," he breathed.

A tingle travelled down her spine, his aroused gaze sending a thrill through her.

"May I join you?" she inquired.

His jaw dropped before he caught it. "Of," he croaked, then cleared his throat. "Of course."

She lifted her foot over the tub's edge, earning another groan from Lane, then brought her other foot in and sat in the hot bath water.

What do I do now?

Anna extended her hand for the soap. "May I?"

His throat bobbed, but he handed her the soap.

Anna resisted the urge to stare at him through the water. She knew his upper body was sculpted from boxing at Gentleman Jackson's and riding his horse, but, she wondered, was his bottom half just as muscular? What did his *man part* look like? She urged her impatience to ease. She would see him when they left the bath.

Despite her boldness, her stomach fluttered with nervousness. What she was about to do would change her life forevermore. She would be irrevocably and truly ruined.

She shook herself internally. She was likely ruined in the eyes of society anyway, and if her abduction concluded with an engagement to Lane, society would forgive her.

Anna rubbed the soap between her palms and washed herself. She spread the suds over the column of her neck, her collar, and around each breast. Her nipples puckered and her stomach quivered under Lane's penetrating scrutiny.

He put his hands on her waist, the tips of his fingers digging lightly into her flesh. The intensity in his gaze both intrigued and mystified her. She knew that his seeing her naked body would be arousing, but could washing herself be exciting him, as well?

His groan emboldened her further as she slid her soapy hand downward below the water's surface. Lane shifted agitatedly, his eyes following each of her movements. *Fascinating!* She washed swiftly between her feminine folds, her gaze on Lane's tense features.

"Anna…"

A flush flamed her cheeks at her own, decidedly lascivious behaviour. She was shocked at her own daring.

Her gaze roamed over his body; she could no longer hold herself back. She watched his eyes carefully. "May I?" She gestured toward his chest.

Lane's throat bobbed captivatingly, but he nodded. "Please."

Finally able to give in to her keen desires, Anna lathered the soap in her hands once more, pressing her frothy palms to Lane's chest. She worked her fingers into his muscles, using suds and water to get him clean, careful to avoid the bandage on his arm. Lane's eyelids grew heavy and a low groan escaped him, his chest rising and falling with his rapid breaths.

Her stomach gave another nervous kick as her hands delved below the water's surface. While she might not know what he liked, his response to her touch was certainly encouraging, and there was no better way to learn than to try.

The muscles over Lane's abdomen quivered as she felt along the hard, muscular ridges. She ought to go slowly to prolong their enjoyment, but if she did not continue quickly, she might very well lose her courage.

Her hands reached his hips, and Lane's jaw clenched tightly, his fingertips digging subtly deeper into the skin of her hips. She pushed herself through the water, aligning herself between his spread knees, until her stomach lay flush against his. The ridge of his arousal pressed insistently against her, stirring her own desire to greater heights.

His brown gaze caught hers; deep, though hesitant…and, she thought, somehow anxious.

Anna leaned in closer, their lips a breath apart.

"Anna…" he ground out, his fingertips digging yet deeper.

She pressed her lips firmly to his. The kiss started slow but built in intensity. Soon their tongues tangled, their breath coming rapidly.

"Oh." Anna broke their kiss. "Your bandage will become wet."

"I don't care," he growled, catching her lips once more with his.

Then his hands roamed. He felt along her ribcage, the sides of her breasts, and then moved downward. His hands slowed as they reached her hips, as though he were unsure of her reaction.

Anna pressed her hips against his erection, and his breath hitched. He cupped her bottom with his large hands, pressing her further against him. Unbidden, a soft moan escaped her. He squeezed, his fingertips digging into her *derriere*.

Then his hands were gone. Anna whimpered in protest, but then his firm grip was on her waist once more. She gasped and water sloshed to the floor as he flipped her. Her bottom pressed against his erection, and her back lay against his chest, her head comfortably on one of his muscular shoulders.

His arms extended above them, lathering up the soap.

"I want a turn," his voice rumbled beneath her, sending a shiver of delight down her spine.

He set the soap aside and lowered one hand to her breasts.

Her gasp filled the room, and she instinctively arched her spine. He palmed first one breast and then the other, the soap creating a slippery barrier between her skin and his.

Anna's eyes slid closed. His ministrations were exciting...*arousing*. His fingers circled one nipple before he pinched it between forefinger and thumb. The pleasure-pain sizzled through her body, her nerve endings taught with want.

Anna's body twitched at the sudden contact to her *mons*. While he'd distracted her with the playful flick of his fingers on her breasts, he slid his other hand beneath the water's surface to tangle with the hair at the apex of her thighs. Slowly he edged closer, and yet closer, until the tips of his fingers reached her folds.

Oh heavenly day! Could she be dreaming? She'd most certainly never imagined anything like *this*, even when exploring her own body in the dark of night.

Then his soap-covered fingers delved inside.

Anna's body was alight with sensation as Lane explored. To have *Lane* touch her so intimately... It was a fantasy come true.

His hands worked in tandem; one swirling around the soft flesh of her *mons*, and the other plucking nimbly at her breasts.

She began to pant, entirely out of her control. Her pelvis lifted of its own accord, urging him on.

"Anna..." Lane groaned.

Her eyes still closed, she turned her head to meet his kiss. His movements became more insistent, more urgent, their kiss more passionate.

Something was building within her. Something that started in her toes and worked its way up her legs while simultaneously fluttering in her stomach. Something...

"Lane, I..." she gasped.

"Shh-shh," he rumbled. "Let it come, Annabel." He moved his fingers faster. "You cannot know what you do to me. I feel positively mad with desire..."

His words faded from her consciousness as an explosion began.

It started slow, but built quickly. Light burst behind her eyelids, her body shaking with wave after wave of pure pleasure. A cry was pulled from her lips as she arched away from Lane's chest.

Distantly, she heard Lane curse before she was lifted bodily from the bath. She was dimly aware of their movement as Lane placed her, sopping wet, upon the bed's coverlet.

Her body still throbbed with the delightful aftereffects of...whatever it was the *explosion* was truly called.

She watched in anticipation as Lane joined her on the bed, his muscles flexing as he braced himself over her.

Then she caught sight of *it*. His magnificent appendage jutted impressively erect from a thatch of dark-blonde curls that beaded with bathwater. It visibly throbbed with the beat of his heart. It was covered with blue veins that disappeared beneath its head. It looked strong…and *enormous*. *Would it even fit?* As quickly as the doubt appeared, she brushed it away. Men and women were meant to fit together, no matter how impossible it might seem.

Her hand moved before she'd consciously thought of the action. Her first finger extended as she touched the ruddy tip of his erection. It bobbed away from her finger, and she turned her questioning gaze upward to meet his.

The stark desire burning in the dark depths of his eyes was mesmerizing. Anna knew what was coming next. As painful as she had been warned that it would be, Anna was immeasurably pleased that it was Lane who would take her maidenhead.

Chapter 15

Lane's body shook with his desire to be inside Anna. He needed her. But at the back of his mind, doubt nagged at him. Could he do it? Would he make an ass of himself? Would he be able to complete the act?

He wanted to. *Bloody hell*, he wanted to bury himself deep inside her and remain there indefinitely. Uncertainty warred with need in his mind.

He'd nearly come off when Anna came apart in his arms. Could he make her come again?

The thought sent a jolt of want to his cods and flushed the uncertainty from his mind. If anyone were to understand his *problem*, it would be Anna. He hoped to God that it wouldn't happen, but if it did, he knew he would only receive compassion from his kind-hearted friend. Besides, he wanted nothing more than to see Anna come for him again.

"Anna," he said gruffly. "I want you. I want to be inside you. If…" His jaw tightened. "If you have any reservations, please tell me so now."

Anna lifted her head up to connect their lips in a slow, ardent kiss. Her hand, still poised below, boldly gripped him. He broke their kiss to hiss a breath between his teeth.

She quickly released him. "Oh! I'm sorry. Did I hurt you?"

He groaned. "No. That was the farthest thing from pain, my dear. In fact, it felt far *too* good."

Before she could digest his words, Lane positioned himself atop of Anna, spreading her legs wide with his knees. He pressed the tip of his impatient *pego* at her sweet, damp entrance, then paused.

His voice was low and rough. "Are you certain you wish to do this?" He needed to hear her say it.

Anna lifted her hips against him, driving him mad. "Yes, Lane. I'm ready."

He needn't have any further encouragement. With one hand to guide him, he coated himself with her wetness then slowly slid inside. It took every ounce of self-restraint for him to go slowly. But his desire to keep from hurting her prevailed over his wild desire to pump frantically within her.

Blazes, she felt amazing. Her body was perfectly shaped to fit him.

Her cheeks flushed a deeper rose, and she spread her legs wider to accommodate him.

His body trembled as he slowly pushed further, a knot of nervousness settling in the pit of his stomach.

Lane gazed down into Anna's half-lidded blue eyes and pushed past his doubt.

The tip of his member reached her maidenhead barrier, and he paused. He saw no apprehension, no uncertainty in her gaze. Only lust, openness, and warmth shone in those sky-blue depths.

With a deep breath, Lane pressed his lips to hers and thrust his hips, sheathing himself fully in her heat. Anna's gasp of pain was absorbed by his mouth but clearly heard.

He broke their kiss to press his forehead to hers. "I'm so sorry, Anna. I did not wish to hurt you." His voice quavered.

She took a shuttering breath, and Lane's gut clenched.

"I am well, Lane," she assured him. "Mostly startled."

Beads of sweat formed on his forehead, and his body began to act of its own accord, slowly moving within her. He pulled his steely flesh from within her and entered her a fraction at a time.

"Oh…" she moaned. "Oh, Lane. That is…mu…much better…now."

"Anna," he grunted, unable to form any other intelligible thought.

He sped his movements, pumping faster and faster. Anna's face flushed deeper, her body moving against his. Her arms wrapped around his shoulders and her legs rose to encircle his waist.

His cods tightened, his stomach jumped; Lane had never experienced anything like this. Never had this rush of blood surging through his body, this anticipation, this longing, this thorough desire taking over his entire being. Certainly, he'd climaxed by his own hand, but reaching this point with a woman—with *Anna*—was so different. He was in heaven. He was *beyond* heaven, with this writhing, moaning, gorgeous woman beneath and around him.

Blazes. He couldn't hold off his orgasm much longer. He pulled back to watch Anna's face just as she came apart for him once more, her cry of pleasure echoing off the walls of the small bedchamber.

"*Lane!*"

It was too much. With one final, fervent thrust, Lane buried his face in the crook of her neck and poured his seed inside her.

His heart galloped in his chest. *He'd done it!*

Anna was much more than he had anticipated. She was sensational, a marvel. No, a *miracle*. For Lane to experience the entire act of lovemaking so wholly and emotionally in Anna's arms had to have been a sign. He and Anna were meant to be together.

* * *

Annabel blinked languidly as the sun began its ascent the next morning, awakening her slowly. She was slightly sore, particularly after that second bout of lovemaking, but supremely exultant. Lane had awoken her at some point in the middle of the night and made love to her leisurely…sweetly. He had been heartwarmingly gentle, taking the time to kiss every inch of her before he entered her once more.

She stretched, raising her arms above her head dreamily. Her nipples puckered. There was a slight chill to the morning air as the fire had died out long ago.

Anna eyed Lane from her position beside him. The coverlet had been pushed down to his feet, and the sheet lay draped casually across his tight abdomen. He had a spectacularly defined body.

Curiosity grabbed hold of her. She had not gotten a very good look at him last evening. With a furtive glance at Lane's face to ensure that he was still sleeping, Anna stealthily lifted the edge of the sheet and bent to examine his body more closely.

Goodness. Even when not erect, his member was quite large. She tilted her head to see the soft sacs between his thighs. They certainly had an odd look to them, being wrinkled and hairy. She steadfastly resisted the urge to poke one.

Slowly, his manhood began to swell. Her eyes widened, and she looked on in amazement as it grew. How fascinating!

"Do you like what you see?" Lane's deep voice rumbled.

Anna jumped, a hand fluttering to her chest and a blush flaming her cheeks. "Oh! You knew I was observing you! How long have you been awake?"

"Since you reached for the sheet." He winked at her.

"You sneak!" She cuffed him playfully on his uninjured arm, hiding her embarrassment.

"Yes, but you like me this way." Lane reached for her, pulling her down to lie atop of him.

A quiver went through her as Lane kissed her neck, his several days' growth of beard gently abrading her soft skin. He skimmed his hands down her sides to cup her buttocks.

He moaned. "You smell good."

She pressed her lips to his in a quick kiss. "Thank you, but I am *quite* sore this morning," she said with a regretful grimace. "And we do not have much time. I would like to return to London by nightfall."

"Yes, of course." He kissed the tip of her nose before releasing her.

Anna rolled to the edge of the bed and stood in one fluid motion. Before last evening, she would have felt insecure with his seeing her flop about in the nude, but after witnessing the lust glitter in his eyes, she could not conceivably question his desire for her, extra padding and all.

But would he mention marriage again?

Something cold slithered down her upper thigh, and she quickly made her way to the washbasin. She would never have imagined that intimate relations between men and women would be so very *messy*. She resisted the urge to stare at the white substance, knowing he observed her from his position on the bed, but instead rinsed and wrung the cloth to continue cleaning herself.

Would Lane consider proposing once more? It was in his nature to be the honourable gentleman, but what if he was offended at her previous lack of a response? Would he wish to preserve his pride and not ask again? *No.* Surely not. Perhaps he wished to wait until he spoke with her father once they returned to London. Yes, that was most definitely plausible.

Anna's lips curved into a grin. She would wait, then, until they returned to London and Lane had enough time to arrange an appointment with Papa.

She heard Lane shuffle from the bed behind her, and she moved to conclude her morning ablutions behind the small privacy screen at the opposite corner of the room.

They smiled at each other as they passed, a companionable silence settling over them. Is that what it would be like once they married? Them reading quietly or playing chess in the evenings, strolling through the gardens, enjoying alfresco luncheons, a friendly rivalry coupled with contented tranquility. It sounded heavenly.

Anna gathered her clothing from the previous day and began to dress.

Lane strode about the room behind her, his heavy footfalls causing the floor to creak with each step. Anna turned to smile at him as she drew her arms through the sleeves of the sunny-yellow frock.

He stood, gloriously nude, smiling back at her. She fought a blush at the sight of him. He was tall, broad… Heavens, but he was positively perfect. He combed his fingers through his dishevelled blonde hair, his muscles bunching and his brown eyes crinkling.

He watched her expectantly, and Anna stifled a frown. What did he want from her?

She licked her suddenly dry lips. "We had best request the morning meal and obtain tickets on the day's first mail coach."

He turned his gaze quickly to the floor, hiding what Anna thought to be an expression of hurt. But he returned his gaze to hers once more, his jovial mien in place. "Indeed, Anna dear. I will dress and inquire." He hesitated. "But first, would you be so good as to re-bandage my arm?"

Anna blinked. "Oh! Of course."

Lane stepped into his trousers and pulled them up, covering his impressive male appendage. Did he always forego small clothes beneath his trousers?

* * *

Lane's breath caught at the sight of Anna's heated gaze. His eager cock sprang to life, making it nigh impossible to button his trousers' falls. One night of not being a sodding virgin and his body did not want to stop making love. He wanted more, and more, and yet *more* of Anna.

She was the first—the *only*—woman to inspire such feelings in him. She attracted his body, his heart, and his mind in a perfect symphony of need.

"If you keep staring, love, I might have to request a second night at this inn." His voice was pitched low and rough with desire.

Anna's gaze flicked to his, a blush staining her soft cheeks. Her shock, however, quickly turned to reproach. "You teasing man." She frowned, but Lane saw the humour lurking in her gaze.

He thought to correct her, to tell her that he was entirely serious, but prudence won the battle, and he kept silent. He winked at her as he buttoned his falls. They had spent long enough away from their homes and their families; it was time to return to London.

He sat, shirtless, upon a chair and waited while Anna redressed his wounds. The bullet's graze scarcely pained him any more, though he couldn't quell the hiss of his breath as she dabbed at the injury with a cloth. Within moments, she had his arm cleaned and bound.

With a smile, she stood and left him.

Anna went about the room doing Lord knew what while Lane dressed, his mind buzzing. He could not deny that her lack of eagerness hurt. It did. Hell, it nigh tore him apart inside. But she'd given him her maidenhead; surely she felt more for him than a means to gain some pleasure. Indeed, it was not in Anna's nature to behave thusly. She must expect something more from him. Perhaps she waited for their return to London where he could properly court her.

The thought hovered around in his mind, teasing him with the possibilities. Courting Anna would be wonderful. They could do all of the things that they ordinarily did, no longer as close friends but as intended husband and wife. He could hold her closer as they danced, clasp her hand for longer than a polite friendship would allow. They could attend the theatre together, Covent Garden, they could go riding… The options were endless.

Anticipation pumped through his veins, banishing any disheartened feelings from his heart.

Lane moved to stand in front of the room's tall mirror. He slid his cravat around his neck and tied it in a tasteful knot, wrinkled though the blasted thing was, then put on his overlarge brown tailcoat. He adjusted the sleeves and tugged on the waist until it fell comfortably.

"I will go below stairs and arrange for our morning meal and transportation," he said to the room.

"Mmm," Anna replied absently.

His gaze found her as she attempted to make sense of a knot in her hair. His chest swelled. A courtship would be pleasing, indeed.

Chapter 16

Anna blinked rapidly at the startling sunlight as she stepped out the front door of The Swan Inn. At that moment, she wished she hadn't lost her bonnet on their journey. Instead she shaded her eyes with her hand and scanned the innyard for Lane, who had preceded her out the door.

Then there he stood, attractive as ever, with the reins of one mount in each hand and a boyish grin on his face.

"What," she asked, "in heaven's name are you doing with those?"

His grin deepened. "These," he mocked, "are horses. They are for riding." He gestured with his hands and galloped his feet. One of the horses sidestepped away from him in agitation.

"I have a mind to hit you, Lane."

He barked a laugh, his head thrown back.

Anna clucked her tongue. "I had thought we would take the mail coach. Or at the very least, hire a hack for the journey." Her body still ached from running yesterday and their vigorous activity of last evening. Her muscles trembled already; how was she to make it through a day of riding?

Lane's grin slipped, and his eyebrows curved upward in apology. "There are no equipages to be had, Anna, and the taproom is full of patrons awaiting a ride on the day's coaches." He shrugged his shoulders. "My apologies, but riding is our only option if we wish to reach London today."

Shame washed over her. Lane should not feel the need to apologize; he had done his best. If she had not been so very concerned with her own welfare, she would have realized that he must be sore, as well. For goodness' sake, he had carried her to their bedchamber last night!

Anna strode forward and placed her hand on Lane's chest. His heart beat rapidly beneath her palm as he watched her questioningly. "Thank you, Lane," she whispered.

She was aware of the servants and patrons going about their business in the innyard, the dogs roaming, the chickens clucking… But she didn't care. Here, they were husband and wife, Mr. and Mrs. Roberts.

Anna pressed her lips to his in a short kiss. The contact sent a tingle of awareness through her that she determinedly ignored. "I appreciate what you have done for me," she murmured, her gaze catching his.

He cleared his throat. "I must remember to do more for you if that is how I am thanked." He winked, and Anna laughed.

She turned to the chestnut gelding with the sidesaddle upon his back. "Hello, handsome boy," Anna cooed. She gave him a pat before allowing Lane to assist her in mounting him.

"His name is Rainbow," Lane said.

Anna blinked.

Lane continued, "Apparently, his master's daughter named him."

"Ah." Anna nodded her understanding as she attempted to tug her skirts over her woefully exposed ankles.

There was nothing for it. She could not very well bemoan the loss of her riding habit; the thing had become a veritable pile of rags. She turned to smile down at Lane who was frowning at her stockings.

"Come, Lane. Let us return home." She sat with her spine stiff as her bare hands controlled Rainbow's reins. "I would hate to miss the steaming cup of chocolate and good book that await my arrival."

His frown disappeared, replaced by a challenging grin. He mounted his grey gelding in a smooth, practiced motion. "The first one there wins a kiss."

* * *

The sun hit Lane's brown coat, which seemed to soak it up and multiply the heat before it reached his skin beneath. He wiped at his forehead and around his neck with a kerchief before he returned it to his pocket.

They had been riding for hours. His body ached, but he relished the movement of the beast beneath him. He had missed riding. The sense of freedom was exhilarating.

The horses' hooves pounded the dirt-and-gravel road, the hammering of his heart echoed in his ears, and the mingling of his and the horses' breath resounded in the air around them.

Their morning meal had been large and satisfying, but he could feel hunger beginning to gnaw at his stomach. They had stopped to water and rest their mounts at the inns that they passed, but they would want a more extended rest soon.

He led his mount to ride beside Anna's. Once he'd gotten her attention, he slowed Pigeon to a trot, and Anna followed suit with Rainbow.

"Would you care to stop at the next inn for a meal?" he called over the din.

Anna beamed at him. "You have read my thoughts precisely."

He nodded with a smile of his own then nudged his mount faster.

The inn was not terribly far down the road. They rode into the small innyard, and a groom ran out from the stables and held their horses while Lane dismounted. He resisted the urge to shake out the stiffness in his legs, but cringed as one hip popped in its socket.

He rounded the horses and lowered Anna to her feet, a bolt of pleasure shooting through his hands and down his arms at the contact.

Lane willed his heartbeat to decelerate as he tossed the groom a coin. The young lad caught it midair with a nod. "I'll 'ave 'em brushed, fed, watered, 'n' rested fer ye, sirrah."

"I am much obliged," Lane returned.

The inn was not particularly large, but the building appeared to be well maintained. A maid reached out of an upper floor window and flicked a cloth in the air, dust falling from it.

Anna accepted Lane's arm, her small hand wrapped tightly around his elbow, and he led her toward the inn's front door.

A large dog lifted his head as they entered, but he soon resumed his nap near the door. Lane scanned the room for the innkeeper, and spotted him in deep discussion with two men near the door to a back room.

"Charles?" Anna's voice was soft, but one of the men in conversation spun around.

Hell, what is he doing here?

Anna's gasp rent the air. "*Charles!*" She released Lane's arm and ran to her brother.

"*Annabel?*" Charles' eyes were wide. "Thank God!" He opened his arms and caught her in a hug.

Lane watched the reunion with a mixture of relief and annoyance. He was most certainly relieved that they had another man there to aid in preventing another kidnapping or attack should their abductors catch up to them, but he was damned annoyed that now he could not request a private dining room…or a bedchamber to *freshen up*.

His heart sped at the thought. Blazes, but he was far gone in his lust for Anna.

Tears streamed down Annabel's cheeks, and an uncomfortable knot wedged itself in Lane's chest. Was she so distraught with their misadventure, then? Guilt assailed him. He'd thought she was well. Had he not been attentive enough to her needs?

"Oh Charles, I am so pleased to see you!" Anna's grip tightened around her brother as Lane strode toward them.

"Where have you been, Annabel? How are you? Are you hurt? How did you get away? Where ar—" Charles paused, his jaw taut. "Why do we not have this conversation where we might have a modicum of privacy?"

Lane stepped forward, putting a hand on Anna's shoulder. "I would suggest a private dining room, as Anna has not yet eaten a midday meal."

The Major sent him a terse nod then turned to the innkeeper. "Would you be so kind as to show us to a private dining room, if you have one available, Mr. Barlow?"

The man nodded his balding head. "Right this way, Major Bradley, Mr. Thomson." He nodded again at Lane and Anna, as though to include them.

Anna dabbed at her eyes with the back of her hand as they followed the innkeeper. The third man in the group marched silently beside them, his expression impassive. Who was he? What was he doing here? How did he know Charles?

Lane's internal questions floated about unanswered as Mr. Barlow led them into a large, modestly furnished dining room.

"I will have a meal prepared for the four of you. My wife will bring it in directly."

"You are very kind, sir. Thank you." Charles inclined his head.

The innkeeper smiled at them as he backed from the room, closing the door quietly behind him.

Lane pulled a well-padded chair out for Anna, waited for her to be seated, then took the chair beside her. His heart ached for her distress. Her cheeks and eyes were red and slightly swollen. If only he could take her into his arms and comfort her with his kisses and his avowal of love…

The chair scraped along the floor as Charles took the seat across from them. His expression was entirely indecipherable. It boded ill. What was Charles doing this far from London? Was he searching for Anna? Did he fear that *Lane* had taken her?

Lane's gaze flicked toward the enigmatic Mr. Thomson, who hovered just inside the closed door.

"From the beginning, if you will." Charles cleared his throat. "I would like to hear first Anna's detailed account of the events, and then I would like to hear it from

Lane's perspective. Do not leave anything out, no matter how minute or unimportant you feel that the detail might be." He paused to watch them both. "Anna?"

Suddenly she looked drawn and pale, her lips quivering ever so slightly. Lane interjected on her behalf. "Charles, why do you not allow me to speak first? Anna requires sustenance; she can eat while I recount events."

Charles shifted in his seat, his jaw clenched. "Very well. Please begin, Lane."

Lane gently cleared his throat and began his relation of the events leading up to the kidnapping. He noted the disapproval in Charles' expression as he explained his plan for hiring actors to abduct Anna and himself, but that swiftly changed as he continued his account.

Lane went into as much detail as possible; he made sure to mention descriptions of all four captors, their names—but for the unnamed, red-haired man—and the fact that Billy had broken his arm in the carriage accident. He described their method of escape, their change of attire and identity, their near re-capture on the mail coach, and their stay at the inn last evening, naturally withholding any information on his and Anna's newfound intimate relationship. That was something he most certainly did not wish to discuss with Anna's older, and very protective, brother.

"We rode for several hours on horseback and decided to stop at this inn for our midday meal. Upon entering, we encountered you and your...mysterious friend." Lane glanced at Mr. Thomson, who continued to hover enigmatically at the door. "That would bring us to date on the events of the past four days, and my small fiction in the days before."

While he spoke, their meal had come; a feast of pheasant, lamb, and vegetables with an added tray of tea and cakes. Thankfully, Anna had helped herself to the food and regained some of her colour.

Charles leaned back in his chair, having not touched the meal himself, and eyed Lane thoughtfully. "Interesting. Very interesting. You say that the men were working for a man they called 'The Boss'?"

"Yes," Lane confirmed. "They referred to him several times, as a matter of fact. I assume that we were to rendezvous with him somewhere in Dover. What I failed to understand, however, is to what purpose we had been kidnapped. They did not attempt to steal my purse or discuss ransom. And neither of us have been made privy to any kind of political or prudent information that would have been useful to them."

Guilt and defensive anger mingled and passed over Charles' expression, but it disappeared so quickly that Lane questioned having seen it at all.

"No one can know for certain what possesses villains to behave as they do. But we can be sure that it will *not* happen again," Charles stated vehemently. He watched Anna as she took a sip of tea. "Anna, have your nerves calmed enough for you to recount your perspective on the happenings of the past four days?"

Anna shrugged one shoulder. "I do not see the point, as I would relay precisely the same information that Lane has just divulged." She put her hands up in surrender as she caught Charles' irritated mien. "I can see, however, that you are quite adamant." She glanced at Lane and licked at her lips. "I had not heard from Lane for five days after the ball at Almack's, and I had grown concerned, and, to be truthful, slightly bored. On the fifth day, I received a note stating that he had something about which he wished to discuss with me…"

For the next hour, Lane listened to Anna's perception of their abduction, travels, their stops, their escape, and journey here. She, too, omitted their sexual encounter, but it was not relief that Lane felt. He had not expected to be so moved by her account. Annabel's unique way of experiencing the world gave the past four days a dream-like quality. He'd had no notion that Anna had been so affected by the abduction, by the men, the smells, and the way their journey had made her feel.

Anna's tears were evidence of her inner struggles. She had expressed such anxiety, such worry and horror, that Lane felt as though he were in her mind, living the past four days over again.

He was a cad for having not realized her struggle sooner. She had been so brave, so fearless…

He slid his chair closer to Anna's and put his arm around her shaking shoulders, pulling her against his chest in a hug. "Shh, shh. Don't cry, sweetheart. It is quite over now." His heart leapt as Anna settled into his embrace.

Mr. Thomson stepped forward to whisper something in Charles' ear. They engaged in a brief, whispered conversation before Thomson straightened and left the room. *Curious.*

"You did not withhold anything, did you, Anna?" Charles combed his fingers through his hair in a gesture of nonchalance, but his eyes were wrought with concern. "I am aware that there was a period of time in which you were unconscious and there were moments in which you and Lane were separated…" He hesitated, seemingly unwilling to continue. "What I am trying to ask is…are you *positive*, Anna, that nothing untoward occurred with these kidnappers?" Charles' serious demeanour of the past hours melted beneath his brotherly concern.

Anna nodded against Lane's shoulder. "Yes. I am positive."

"You mean that you are still...you are still...*chaste*?" Charles choked the last words out.

Anna hesitated at the direct question about her virginity. *Hell and blazes! Please do not answer that question with the truth!*

She pulled away, slightly, from Lane's embrace and opened her mouth to answer. Lane could not allow that to happen. Anna had never been untruthful to her brother, and he would not allow her to begin now. Nor, God forefend, could he allow her to tell the truth!

"Anna has already confirmed that nothing untoward occurred between her and our captors. It is quite evident that re-living the past four days has upset her greatly, and I, for one, am ready to move on. If we wish to be home by nightfall, we should make haste."

Charles clearly wished to continue with his line of questioning and was displeased with Lane's interruption, but Lane could not bring himself to care. He turned his gaze down to meet Anna's stunning blue eyes, still swimming with tears.

"Would you like to continue on with our journey right now, or would you prefer to have some more tea before we depart?"

Anna smiled damply. "I would prefer to leave now, if you please. It would be heavenly to bathe and have a cup of hot chocolate before bed."

Charles stood. "Very well, but I would like to ask more questions of both of you when you have recovered. I will have a hack brought around." He sent them both an inscrutable glance before he quit the room.

The moment the door closed, Anna turned to Lane. "Oh! Thank goodness you spoke just then!"

Lane inclined his head. "Indeed. I have no wish to meet your brother at dawn, for I fear I would lose. Charles can be rather...severe."

Anna nodded her agreement. "More so since his return from war."

They were silent for a moment, then Lane cleared his throat, trying to dislodge the lump that had formed there. Something about the moment compelled him to speak from his heart. "Anna, last night meant a great deal more to me than I can ever express. Our friendship has stood through the trials of time and of life, unwavering in its strength and endurance." He took a deep, quavering breath as nerves clutched his stomach. He found purchase in Anna's sky blue eyes. "Anna... I l—"

The door swung open and Charles entered. "The hack is awaiting us. I have had your horses sent back to the inn at which you acquired them, and my horse has been tethered to the rear of the hack."

Lane surged to his feet. *Thunderation!* He had been about to confess his love for Anna, most ham-fistedly, in the dining room of an arbitrary inn. How foolish could a man be?

"Of course, Charles." Lane turned his gaze on Anna, his trembling hand held out for her. "Shall we?"

Chapter 17

Anna's heart thumped erratically in her chest. She placed her cold hand into Lane's shaking palm, and he curved her fingers around his elbow. *What had just happened?* It had almost sounded as though he was about to tell her that he loved her! It couldn't be… Could it?

But what if he did love her? Nervous excitement rippled through her abdomen. Would he profess his love when he next proposed marriage? Would he lower himself on bended knee among the cherry blossom trees and beg her to become his wife?

Oh heavens, she should not fantasize about such things! It might only serve to disappoint her.

She looked up at him as they followed Charles to their hack. Lane walked proudly, his spine erect and his square jaw set at the perfect angle. He was striking, beautiful both inside and out.

Anna wanted to make love to him again. She loved him, and she had every intention to accept his next proposal of marriage. Why not surprise him in his bedchamber one evening, or invite him for a tryst in her bedchamber? A blush stole its way up her neck to flame her cheeks. Goodness, she was being far too naughty.

The afternoon sun bathed them in a welcoming heat. Hopefully her brother took her blush as warmth from the weather.

"After you, Anna." Lane helped her into the hack then followed, sitting beside her in the forward-facing seat. Charles entered behind them and sat facing them.

"Where is your friend, Charles?" Anna inquired.

"He has business to attend to. I will rendezvous with him in London." He rapped on the ceiling with his fist, and they rolled into motion.

"How do you know him?" Anna persisted. "I do not recall seeing him before."

"Nor I," Lane added.

"I met him through an army friend." Charles looked directly into her eyes and raised an eyebrow as if in challenge.

Charles was hiding something; Anna could sense it. "Very well. I will pretend that I believe you. For now. But do not think you are fooling me, Charles Ellesmere Bradley."

Lane brayed, and Charles sent her a warning look. Anna raised one eyebrow in response, a laugh escaping her.

"Your middle name is Ellesmere?" Lane wiped a tear from the corner of his eye. "I have known you from infancy. Tell me, how is it that I never knew your middle name?"

"Do shut up," Charles grumbled, his face scrunched in a sour expression.

Anna had missed their familial camaraderie. "How have Mama and Papa been in my absence, Charles?"

"Frantic with worry. They will be vastly relieved to have you home."

Anna gazed out the window at the hedgerows that passed by. "I will be pleased to see them, as well." She sighed. "I do hope I have not shamed them too greatly."

Charles frowned. "How the devil would you have shamed them?"

"With my ruination, of course!"

Fury blazed in Charles' gaze. "I thought you had said that nothing untoward had occurred with those kidnappers!"

"That is not w—"

"At the risk of being pulled into a sibling spat," Lane interjected, "I believe that what Anna is trying to say is that her absence and travel in the company of four men with no chaperone for four days would be cause for her ruination, and she did not wish to shame your parents."

The anger visibly faded from Charles' expression. "Oh. I see." He nodded at Anna. "My apologies, Annabel."

"Accepted, Charles."

"As to the question of your ruination, you have nothing to fear in that regard."

Anna's brow furrowed. "I beg your pardon?"

Charles waved a hand through the air. "We informed your beau that you had come down with the headache on the first morning of your absence. After the first day, we informed those who would spread it around that you had received an urgent letter from our Grandmamma requesting your presence at her home in the North."

"That's positively brilliant!" Anna exclaimed in unison with Lane's panicked "*What?*"

Profound relief swept through Anna. "Thank you, Charles." She reached across the confined space to place a hand on her brother's knee. "You have saved the family a great deal of grief."

Charles shrugged. "It was what had to be done, Anna. I am simply grateful that we managed to find you. I confess, I was quite fearful for your safety."

Anna smiled reassuringly. She had not realized quite how deeply their abduction had affected her until she had recounted the tale. Her emotions had entirely gotten away from her. She feared that her reaction might have given her brother further cause for concern. "I am perfectly fine, Charles. We are returning to London and shall resume our routine come the morrow."

But it would not be the same. Not to Anna. Because she had given her maidenhead to Lane, she could not, in good conscience, allow Anthony to continue to court her. In fact, her hopes were quite altered in that respect.

She discretely slid her gaze toward Lane. He sat rigidly in his seat, staring out the window, his hands fisted in his lap. Perhaps his muscles ached; hers certainly did. She resisted the urge to reach over and hold his hand.

Anna turned to gaze out her own window, her eyes blind to the passing scenery.

She must arrange a meeting with Anthony—Lord Boxton—on the morrow. Would he be cross with her for not writing to him? Would he be terribly disappointed with her for ending their courtship?

Anna sighed, the heat from her breath fogging the window's glass. She reached a hand up to draw a squiggle in the fog, holding back another sigh. It would not be a pleasant task, letting the Viscount down, but the outcome would be beneficial to all involved, she was certain.

* * *

Lane gazed sightlessly out the window as anxiety clutched his chest. *Annabel was not ruined in society. Hell and blazes!*

Would Anna return to Boxton and continue their courtship? Or would she throw him over for Lane? Surely she would break the courtship; Anna would not allow one man to bed her if she intended to wed another.

No matter what he assured himself of, part of him still feared the worst. He did not know what he would do without Anna in his life.

She shifted beside him, and a ripple of desire went through him. *Blazes,* that was decidedly not how he should react at the moment. Her brother was sitting across from them, for God's sake.

Lane cleared his throat. "Charles, have you by chance heard any news from my staff or family?"

"Nothing particularly interesting. They merely mentioned that you were expected to be 'out of town' for an undisclosed amount of time. Your family has carried on in your absence. I have not seen any of them, though before I departed in my search, I heard that your mother and sisters had been keeping themselves busy with shopping excursions and teas with friends and acquaintances." An odd expression that Lane could not recognize crossed Charles' features, then was instantly gone. *Charles has become distinctly odd since his return from war.*

"Good." Lane nodded in satisfaction. "I had not wished for them to worry. Especially Bridget; she has not been feeling well of late."

Charles' eyes sharpened. "Not well? Whyever not?"

"We are not positive as to the reasons behind her decline, but should it continue or affect her overall health, we will consult a physician."

Charles' frowned fiercely. "Why wait? Why not have a doctor come to see her right away? It seems careless, does it not?"

Lane matched the man's frown with one of his own. "I do not think so. I believe what she is experiencing is more emotional than physical. She has become short-tempered and weeps very easily. The additional crying and melancholy gives her the headache; consequently, my staff, family, and I have been doing what we can to avoid a fit of tears."

Charles sat back against the poorly padded seat cushion and gazed out the window, his jaw tight and his hands fisted. Charles and Bridget had been friends for nearly as long as Lane and Annabel, but since his return from war, he had distanced himself.

Every friendship had its periods of distance and connection, of course, just as his and Annabel's had. It appeared, however, that something had occurred between Charles and Bridget that had caused their discord. It must have been sizeable for it to create such a large rift in what had previously been a very close bond.

Anna shifted beside him once more, stirring the heat in his blood. *Damn*, but he wished he could have this time to speak with Annabel privately. Should he beg her once more for her hand? Profess his love? Hell, he didn't know. At the very least, he should arrange to speak with her father on the morrow to seek permission to court her.

Fields, trees, and shrubbery passed by the window in a blurry haze of green. The sun shone brightly in the sky as the carriage wheels trundled down the road, and the *clip clop* of horses' hooves floated on the air. It would be a few short hours before they returned to London. He had best utilize that time preparing his speech for Mr. Bradley.

Chapter 18

Annabel was ready to weep with relief when the hack pulled up to the front of the Bradley town house. Night had long since fallen, and the windows glowed with warm, welcoming light.

Home! She gazed longingly at the tall building, anticipating a long soak in a steaming bath filled with lemon zest, a hot cup of chocolate while her hair dried by the fire, and her favourite book. She nearly sighed.

A footman opened the door, a gust of cool night air rushing in and ruffling her yellow skirts. Charles leapt out then reached a hand in to assist Anna. Lane followed, and paid and thanked their driver. A groom untethered Charles' horse from the rear of the hack and walked him toward the stables, but Lane called to him before he had gotten too far.

"Hold, if you please." He looked questioningly at Charles. "I assume my gelding is being held in your stables?"

Charles nodded tersely, the sound of rattling wheels and clopping horses' hooves cutting through the silence.

Lane turned back to the waiting groom. "Have my gelding saddled, if you would. I intend to ride him home."

The groom bowed and did as he was bade.

"Thank you for protecting my sister, Lane." Charles extended his hand, and Lane shook it.

"I was doing as any man would do for his friend."

"It was more, and you know it." Charles eyed him.

"This manly discussion is lovely," Anna interjected, "but I would dearly love to get inside and begin soaking in a hot bath."

An odd, arrested expression passed over Lane's face as he stared back at Anna. Charles stood mutely.

"What has gotten into the both of you?" Anna put her hands. "No. Do not answer that question. I have had enough excitement. I am going inside." She met Lane's brown, piercing gaze. "Thank you for…everything. You saved my life on more than one occasion. You are wonderful."

She rose up on her toes and kissed him on the cheek, his four days' growth of beard tickling her lips. With one last smile, she turned on her heel and strode up the front steps and into her London home.

A rush of warmth greeted her as she entered. She was absurdly grateful for the silence. As much as she longed to see Mama and Papa, she could not abide another moment of answering questions.

"Welcome home, Miss Bradley." Tim's comforting voice echoed in the foyer.

She sent him a toothy grin. The poor man had been readying himself for bed; his livery was crooked, and he wore his nightcap over his grey hair. "Thank you, Tim. It is very good to see you again."

"Shall I arrange for a meal and hot chocolate to be brought up to your bedchamber, miss?" The light from the foyer glinted off of his spectacles.

"You know precisely what to say to a woman, Tim." Her smile grew. "Yes, please. And a hot bath, if you would."

He bowed. "As you wish, Miss Bradley."

Anna made her way up the stairs. She took a deep breath, inhaling the familiar scents of her home. It was nearly enough to bring a tear to her eye. *My, but it feels good to be back!*

* * *

Despite the dreadful ache in his body, Lane relished the feel of his horse beneath him as he rode toward his Mayfair home. He had missed riding Pegasus.

The warmth that the springtime sun had lent the air had all but gone, leaving a chill to the night. Lane needed the cool air, particularly after the way Anna had left him. It was commonplace for him and Anna to be familiar with one another, but part of him feared that Charles suspected something. Not only had her mention of bathing sent wild images of her naked, wet body through his mind, but her kiss had also heated his blood nearly to boiling.

Charles did not seem to take note of the maypole in Lane's trousers, but he unquestionably perceived his internal reaction to Annabel, if his threat was any indication.

"I know you protected my sister during this ordeal, Lane," Charles had said, "and I thank you for it. But Annabel is very dear to me, and I will *not* have you engaging in any tomfoolery in my home. So wipe that lustful gaze off your face when you look at her, and we will get on just fine." His jaw had twitched. "You are

Annabel's closest friend, and I would hate to have to kill you if you hurt her. It would make her cross with me, and I am not fond of the thought of that."

Lane had looked Charles directly in his deep, blue eyes. He did not owe the man a damned explanation. He was not Anna's father, curse it. The only man he would speak to on the subject of his courtship of Anna would be Mr. Joseph Bradley, not her overbearing, overprotective bear of an older brother.

He had put as much meaning in his glance as he could. "Likewise," he'd spat, furious at the man for implying that Lane would hurt Anna when Charles had done the same damned thing to Bridget.

Charles' Adam's apple had bobbed as he swallowed. *Good.* Lane's response had hit its mark. The man had turned and followed Anna up the steps, disappearing into the warm glow of the town house and leaving Lane alone with his thoughts until the groom returned with his horse.

Lane's jaw clenched as his home came into view. Most of the windows held only a dim, flickering light, but they were a beacon through the darkness of night. He pushed his gelding harder until he reached the front steps. His head groom came out to hold the reins as he leapt smoothly to the ground.

He fleetingly wondered what new animals Emaline had brought into the house during his absence. She had a penchant for helping sick animals, just as Bridget had a habit of beginning friendship with horrid people in the hopes that she could change their ways. Both sisters would have him go mad if he were not careful.

"Thank you, Jenkins," Lane murmured to the groom before he bounded up the front steps to his town house.

Geoffrey held the door open for him as he reached the top. "Welcome home, m'lord."

"Thank you, Geoffrey. It is good to be back." Lane continued across the foyer toward the wide, curved staircase. "Would you be so kind as to have a bath and a meal brought up to my chambers?"

"Right away, your lordship."

"Oh, and Geoffrey, do have a physician summoned at first light, will you?"

"Of course, m'lord. Shall I inform the ladies of the household that you have returned?"

Lane halted half way up the staircase and turned to face the butler. "They are not yet to bed?"

"Ladies Katherine and Emaline have retired for the evening. The Dowager Countess and Lady Bridget are in the drawing room."

He had told his staff and family that he would be away meeting with farmers and business owners, doing research for the best farming equipment for the familial estate. If his mother and sister saw him dressed as he was, there would be far too many questions for him to answer without revealing the truth.

"I will refresh myself before I greet them. If you could keep my return home quiet until then, I would be much obliged."

"Not at all, your lordship. I will have the footmen prepare a bath directly."

"Oh, Geoffrey?"

"Yes, my lord?"

"Are there any new members of the household of which I should be made aware?" Lane preferred to not be surprised by an unexpected houseguest.

"Lady Emaline has acquired one new puppy she has aptly named Soot, and an injured bird she is calling Tweeters."

"I see. She has certainly been busy in my absence."

"Indeed, my lord."

Lane nodded and continued up the stairs, through the maze of corridors, and into the master chambers. His bath would be brought to his personal sitting room that adjoined his bedchamber, as was usual. The room was decorated minimally; several sitting chairs and a chaise lounge were positioned in the center of the room, around a low, rectangular table, a brocade rug beneath them. To his right was the double-door entry to his bedchamber, and to the left was a massive fireplace. He had several bookshelves filled with books, most of which were on loan from Annabel. On the far side of the room were a writing desk and his Tantalus, filled with liquor decanters. He had chosen dark colours while decorating; deep reds, greens, and blues, coupled with dark, rose-hued wood.

Lane poured himself two fingers of brandy while he waited. It was several minutes before the footmen entered with the tub and hot water, and by then he had finished his drink, its heat settling nicely in his stomach. His valet, Peters, arrived carrying a fresh towel while the brass tub was being filled.

Lane quickly requested his solitude, smiling at his servants as they quit the room. He wasted little time divesting himself of his clothes and entering the steaming water. He sank deeply, resting his head on the back of the tub as he allowed his aching muscles to relax.

Closing his eyes, he recalled the last time he had been sitting thusly in a bath, Anna had joined him—nude, wet, and sultry. She was reminiscent of Venus de Milo rising from the water, though with larger breasts and buttocks made for squeezing.

A lustful shiver ran through him. Making love to Anna had certainly not been a part of his original plan, but he was elated that he had.

His body reacted predictably to the course of his thoughts, and he grimaced.

He now knew the reason for his inability to complete the act of sex with another woman. It was his heart. Unbeknownst to him, he had been hopelessly in love with Anna for years, and deep down, he had not wished to be with anyone else.

He was a fool for not seeing it sooner. He could have courted her long ago, been married…had children. *Bloody hell*, he was a fool!

The wait for Anna had been worth it, however. She was remarkable. He had never thought making love could be so powerful, so beguiling. He would speak with her father on the morrow, begin a proper courtship, and have her pregnant with his babe before the year was out.

The thought of making love to Anna over and over had him hard once more. He would take her slowly, then quickly; he would guide her in riding him; he would bend her over his bed and take her as a stallion does a mare. *Blazes*. He wanted to do so much to her, *for* her. He would teach her the delights of lovemaking while experiencing them fully for the first time himself.

Lane's hand crept toward his throbbing cock, gripping it firmly to ease the ache that had begun there.

"Lane?" A soft voice and a knock sounded at the door.

"*Damn it!*" Lane shot up from the bath, sending water sloshing over the rim, his heart hammering in his chest.

"I am sorry for disturbing you, Lane. I will see you in the morning." The quiet voice called, muffled by the door.

"No, no, Bridget. Just a moment."

He hurriedly dried himself, his once proudly erect cock sadly flagging at the disturbance. As much as he wished to continue what he had scarcely started, he did wish to speak with Bridget.

He dressed quickly, foregoing his coat, cravat, and stockings, and opened the door to admit his younger sister.

"Bridget." Lane smiled and pulled her in for a hug.

Bridget was his closest sister, both in age and in camaraderie. After their father had passed away, she and Lane had become much closer.

"Please come in." He stepped aside for her to pass. A small tabby followed her in, making itself comfortable on a chair by the fireplace.

"I apologize for disturbing your bath, Lane. I had no intention of bothering you."

Lane shook his head. "Do not concern yourself, Bridget. I am pleased that you came to see me.

"I am as well, big brother." Her lips pulled back in a smile, but her green eyes lacked their sparkle of old.

"Please, do be seated." Lane gestured toward the tray of food sitting on the low table. "I hope you do not mind that I eat; I have not yet had supper."

Her white-blonde eyebrows rose. "Not at all! Please, eat."

Bridget sat on the chaise, straightening the skirt of her lavender dinner dress. She looked impeccable tonight, with her white hair done up in the latest fashion, ringlets framing her thin, heart-shaped face.

Lane sat opposite her and began to eat with gusto.

Bridget waited patiently as Lane consumed his meal. He ate quickly, then wiped his lips with a napkin and sat back in his chair.

"Apologies," he susurrated. "I was very hungry."

Bridget chuckled. "You needn't explain yourself or apologize, Lane. I quite understand."

"Did Mama retire for the evening?" Lane asked.

"Yes. She does not know yet that you have returned."

"Good. I will speak with her come the morn." Lane eyed his sister. "How did you know that I had returned?"

Bridget cast him a coquettish grin. "I have my ways of knowing." At Lane's raised eyebrows, she let out another laugh. "I have excellent hearing, or had you forgotten? I should think you would remember; you've exploited my talents once or twice."

Lane barked out a loud laugh. "Indeed I have. I should have known I could not sneak past you, Bridget."

"Of course." She paused, eyeing him carefully. "Tell me, Lane, where you really were for the past four days."

Lane froze, unsure what to say.

"I do not," Bridget continued, "for one moment believe that you were doing research for the country estate. So, out with the truth."

"Good God, but you are a termagant."

"And you are a lying—"

"That is quite enough, *dear* sister." He raised an eyebrow at her. "I will tell you where I have been, but you must promise to keep this information to yourself. It is of a very…sensitive nature."

Bridget leaned forward in her seat. "I will keep your secrets, Lane. I always do." She winked at him, and Lane wondered of which secrets she was speaking.

"Very well, I will trust you with my secret. This one, however, is not solely my own." He took a deep breath and let it out in a resigned sigh. "I was with Annabel."

"*Annabel?*" Bridget's eyebrows shot up in surprise.

"I can see that you are shocked. Allow me to explain…" Lane told Bridget about discovering his love for Anna, his plan to have them kidnapped, and the subsequent events of the past four days, once more omitting his and Anna's sexual encounters, leading up to the moment he returned home.

"Goodness," Bridget breathed. "How does Annabel fare?"

"I am uncertain." He shook his head regretfully. "I had thought her well enough, but I was proven wrong while she wept at the inn. It affected her far more deeply than I had thought. Though more the fool am I. Of course she was frightened…" He trailed off with a self-loathing sigh. "I need to make my feelings known to her. I intend to speak with Mr. Bradley tomorrow and request permission to court Anna."

"I would dearly love to have her as a sister, Lane. She nearly is, already. But you obviously botched your first proposal; this one must be done properly."

Lane nodded in agreement. He must do something spectacular.

He blinked. *Of course!* He still owed Anna her winnings from their last chess game! He could find her something particularly wonderful…

"What of the kidnappers?" Bridget's voice cut through his thoughts.

"I intend to find them!" Lane blustered.

"That could be dangerous."

His jaw clenched involuntarily. "Yes it could. But is it any more dangerous than those blackguards loose in England, terrorizing hapless victims?"

"I suppose not," Bridget said grudgingly. "How do you intend to find them?"

Lane shook his head. "I do not know. Alerting the magistrate would only serve to ruin Anna after her family had taken such pains to preserve her reputation. Perhaps Charles knows of a way." He nodded to himself as he decided on a course of action. "I will speak with him, as well, on the morrow. I am certain that he would like to see those villains in Newgate just as much as I."

"How is Charles?" Bridget's voice was deceptively nonchalant. She cared far more about the answer than she wanted him to see.

"Odd," he admitted.

Her brows pulled together in a delicate frown. "How do you mean? Is he well?"

Lane looked into Bridget's concerned, emerald-green eyes. Yes, something had definitely occurred to separate them. And neither was pleased with the situation.

"Charles is fine," he assured her. "He is merely behaving very oddly. I am not certain what caused it, but I have noticed it since his return from war. He is increasingly distant, more proper, reserved, quick to anger, and he is unmistakably hiding something. God help me, I cannot figure out what that something is."

"I understand precisely what you mean. Before he left for war, he and I were the best of friends. I received letters weekly from him during his years on the continent. Then one day, nearly two years ago, he stopped. I worried myself sick, as you recall, for months. It was only once I heard of his impending return to London through Annabel, that I—" She took a deep breath. "When his ship docked, I went to greet him...but he behaved as though he did not know me." Tears began to form in her eyes. "I am sorry." She stood and walked toward the door. "I should leave you to your rest," she said over her shoulder. "Good night, Lane."

Lane stood and followed her. "Wait, Bridget. Are you well?" He put a hand to the door, halting her retreat.

"I am fine, merely tired."

"Your behaviour would suggest otherwise, dear sister. This is hurting you. Did anything..." He'd wanted to ask this question for nearly two years. He braced himself for Bridget's evasion. "Did anything happen between the two of you that you have been heretofore unwilling to share?" The tears that had threatened to fall began to stream down Bridget's pale cheeks. He suppressed a sigh. She would not answer. "I should like you to know, my dear, that if you feel the need, or the desire, to unburden yourself to anyone, you are welcome to confide in me."

Bridget threw her arms around Lane's shoulders and buried her face in his chest. Lane returned her hug, wrapping his arms around her small form.

"Thank you. You are a wonderful big brother, Lane." Her voice was muffled by his shirtfront and waistcoat. "I am not prepared to discuss it quite yet." She pulled back from his embrace and wiped her tear-streaked cheeks with both hands. "You will be the first to know when I am ready, however."

"You are more than welcome, Bridget. Good night." He stood aside and held the door open for her.

"Good night." She tilted up to kiss him on the cheek, then paused. "A word of advice, Lane. When you see Annabel tomorrow, be sure to shave. You look like a bushman." Bridget turned and walked silently down the hallway.

Lane tugged the bell pull while he thought. He had grand plans for the morrow, but he was also concerned for Bridget. He retrieved a cigar, lit it on a candle, and sat languidly on his chaise. He needed to deliberate.

110

Chapter 19

Major Charles Bradley lay in his bed, staring at the canopy as the rest of the household slept. He had not yet heard from Thomson, nor had he read any reports from the others.

He had found Annabel and Lane, which had been a great relief. But now he must focus his energy on finding the wretches who had abducted them. He snarled, his lip pulling back to reveal his teeth. *The Boss*, he spat in his mind. The devil of a Frenchman remained elusive. He and his men had somehow discovered who Charles was and aimed an attack at his family. And they weren't done.

The Boss and his men would continue to come for him until the job had been done. Unless Charles found him first.

Damn but he wished he knew for certain what had transpired with those ruffians. He had a distinctly uneasy feeling that something nefarious had happened to Annabel that she was unwilling to admit. The thought made him feel ill.

A memory of his discussion with Lane on the journey home danced tauntingly—and entirely unwanted—through his mind. The thought that Bridget was ill made his heart sink further. She could not be despondent because of *him*.

Could she?

His heart thumped against his ribs. Lord, but he missed her. Bridget was his everything.

Which was precisely why he could not be with her.

* * *

Anna awoke early the next morning, after a night of restlessness. She had thought the past several nights of fitful sleep would ensure a night of rest upon her return home, but she had lain awake late into the night thinking about Lane. Would he speak with her father? Did he wish to court her? Or seek her hand in marriage? Once she had finally fallen asleep, Lane had followed her into her dreams, leaving her hot and frustrated upon awakening.

Annabel sighed and swung her feet over the side of her bed. She was not one to be patient. She was becoming far too old to spend her nights dreaming of love and lust. And Lane. She was no longer a child, in *any* fashion. She was a woman, and it was about time that she started behaving like one. Today she would arrange a meeting with Lane. She would be bold, like one of the heroines in her favourite novels, and she would declare herself confidently, directly, and honestly.

Anna tugged the bell pull to summon her maid, Marie, then sat at her writing desk to pen a note to Lane. She smiled to herself as she blotted then reread the missive. It was bold, indeed! Anna folded the letter and sealed it with her personal wax and stamp, just as Marie scratched at the door.

"Come," Anna called.

"Good morning, Miss Bradley. What shall we dress you for this morning?"

"A good morning to you, Marie." Anna thought for a moment. "The azure-blue walking dress with the sky-blue ribbon and lace trim. Oh, and would you please have this letter sent immediately to Lord Devon?" She extended her arm out toward the maid.

Marie took the missive from her with a shallow curtsey. "I would be happy to, miss. Then I shall fetch your ensemble, with the walking shoes, gloves, and bonnet to match."

For the next three quarters of an hour, Annabel and her maid worked at perfecting her attire and hair. Anna had stressed upon the fact that today's outfit was a very important one, without revealing *why*. Her eyes must sparkle; her skin must glow. For today she would tell Lane that she loved him.

A knock sounded at her door just as Marie finished Anna's hair. "Come."

The door opened to reveal Charles' wearied form.

"Charles!" Anna sped forward to place a concerned hand upon his shoulder. "Are you well? You look affright."

"That is neither here nor there."

Hurt, she withdrew her hand from his shoulder. "There is no need to be snappish. I was merely concerned."

Charles' shoulders slumped briefly, then returned to their customary rigidity. "My apologies, Annabel. I had a sleepless night, I'm afraid. Thank you for your concern." He glanced about the room, his gaze fleetingly resting on Marie, then back to Anna. "I came to fetch you. I had wondered what had kept you from breaking your fast. You are not ordinarily late."

Anna pasted on a placating smile for her out of sorts brother. "You are forgiven, Charles." She wrapped a hand around his elbow and allowed him to lead her down the hallway. "I was just about to come down to join you. I am famished."

"Mama and Papa are also awaiting your arrival. They will be pleased to hear from your own lips that you are safely returned and doing well."

He pulled her to a stop before the staircase then glanced around, as if to ensure their privacy. "Anna, did you sleep well?"

She watched her brother with curiosity. "I had some difficulty, but I eventually fell asleep. Why? Whatever is the matter, Charles?"

His face cleared. "Nothing. I just wished to be certain that you are telling me everything you should about the kidnapping. That nothing…inappropriate occurred while you were gone."

His blue eyes searched hers as she steeled herself for the lie she was about to tell. She had never lied to him about something so serious. Although, this was more of a lie of omission.

"No, Charles. The kidnappers did not do anything 'inappropriate.' Besides abducting us, that is."

Charles' expression was of stormy disbelief, but he nodded nonetheless. They continued their walk to the morning room in silence.

Anna halted just inside the morning room door. "Good morning, Mama and Papa."

"Annabel!" her parents exclaimed in unison. They both rose from their seats to envelop her in a tight embrace. She may have only been away for four days, but they were trying days, indeed, and she had missed her parents very much.

Mama released her, holding her at arm's length. "Charles informed us of your…" She trailed off, clearly unable to finish the thought as she bit her bottom lip. "Are you well? Are you not hurt?"

"I am fine," Anna assured her. "Lane was there to ensure that I was as safe as possible, given the circumstances."

Mama eyed her critically while Papa *harrumphed*. "You look thinner." Mama shook her head. "That is not good. Come, eat." She gestured toward the sideboard piled high with all of Anna's favourite morning meal foods.

Anna's mouth began to water as she filled a plate with eggs, ham, and fresh fruit.

"I am pleased to see that you have an appetite." Charles served himself, his previous tense demeanour gone. How strange that he could change his manner so swiftly.

With a shrug, Anna took her seat at the table. Her first bite of eggs was heavenly. Somehow, she had forgotten just how wonderful her parents' cook was. She continued to eat with delight until all the food on her plate had been consumed. She dabbed at her lips with a napkin and sipped from her second cup of tea.

"I beg your pardon, Miss Bradley, but you have a caller." Tim stood in the doorway, holding a silver salver.

Before Anna could respond, Mama interjected, "So soon? But Annabel only returned last evening; who could know she is at home?"

Tim stepped forward and held the salver out to Anna. She picked up the calling card and leapt up when she saw Lady Bridget Mason's name on the card.

"It's Bridget!"

"Bridget?" The colour leeched from Charles' cheeks.

Anna turned to Tim. "Is she in the front parlour?"

"The family parlour, miss."

"Even better. Would you be so kind as to have tea brought in?"

He bowed. "I shall inform cook, Miss Bradley."

"Thank you, Tim." She smiled at her family still sitting around the table, then fled the room.

How lovely for Bridget to call on her! Anna made her way to the family parlour, toward the back of the house, which had a wonderful view of the garden.

She entered, closing the door behind her, and saw Bridget gazing out the wide French doors toward the garden. The light from the window created a halo of light around Bridget's nearly white hair, done up in a neat chignon.

"Good morning." Bridget turned at the sound of Anna's voice, a patently false smile upon her lips. The poor dear had been struggling with her emotions of late. "It is wonderful to see you, Bridget."

Anna strode forward to clasp her friend's hands in her own, kissing her on her pale cheek.

Bridget's voice was soft and breathy. "Good morning, Anna."

They both sat on the settee. Bridget stared mutely at her hands.

"Is everything well, Bridget? Is there something that you wish to discuss with me?"

Bridget straightened her already impossibly stiff spine and notched her chin outward. "I spoke with Lane last evening. He told me what really happened while you were away."

Anna's stomach sank. Had Lane told her *everything*? Oh no.

"He told you that...that he and I..."

Bridget nodded. "Yes, he told me."

Annabel was aghast. "He told you that we *made love*? How could he—"

* * *

Bridget's shocked countenance told Anna that she had assumed incorrectly.

114

Oh no, oh no, oh no! A blush flamed from her toes to the roots of her hair. Anna held her hands to her burning cheeks, stood, and began to pace the room. "Oh! You didn't know. How could I have been so senseless?"

Bridget stood and held a hand out to halt Anna's pacing. "Annabel, everything is all right."

"No." Anna covered her face with her hands. "No it is not. I should not have said anything, and now I have gone and—"

A scratch sounded at the door just before it opened. "Your tea, Miss Bradley." One of their downstairs maids entered with tea and teacakes on a large tray.

"Thank you, Tessa," Anna said absently.

The maid placed her burden on the low table, curtseyed, and left, closing the door behind her.

Anna slumped on the settee once more and poured a cup of tea with trembling hands. Lord, how could she have admitted to such wanton behaviour? And to Lane's sister no less! She couldn't suppress the humiliation blazing through her belly and firing her cheeks. She kept herself busy adding milk and sugar to the teacups and putting biscuits and cakes on small plates.

"Annabel," Bridget's barely audible voice said beside her. "Anna, it's all right. I do not judge you."

Anna frowned. "But why not? You *should* judge me. I've been a hoyden, a— a lightskirt." Her hands covered her flaming cheeks once more. "And heaven help me, I would do it again in a heartbeat." *Oh, why did I confess that?*

Bridget unexpectedly encircled Anna in a hug. "All will be fine soon enough, Annabel. Trust me." She pulled away and gave Anna a warm smile.

Anna blinked, entirely perplexed by Bridget's astonishing understanding.

Charles' barked laugh echoed through the hall from his study, and Bridget paled.

"I do apologize for being abrupt, but I must be on my way." She stood and glided gracefully toward the door. Anna took a small moment for envy as she watched the petite woman effortlessly exude such femininity.

"Just a moment, Bridget." Anna followed her across the room. "Will you please keep this discussion… That is to say, would you mind terribly…"

Bridget clasped one of Anna's hands in hers. "Rest assured, Anna, that this conversation will remain between the two of us." She gave a half-hearted smile, her complexion pallid.

Anna's muscles relaxed as she sighed. "Thank you, Bridget. You do not know how much your friendship means to me."

"And yours to me." She gave Anna another hug before she turned and walked down the hallway.

Anna resumed her position on the settee and picked up her plate. *It would be a shame to waste these teacakes.* She smiled to herself as she took a bite of lemon cake. *Delicious!*

"Lord Anthony Walstone, Viscount Boxton," Tim intoned from the hall.

Anna jumped, the cake crumbling to her plate. She carefully placed the plate on the table, and brushed her hands clean of crumbs as she stood.

"I see you have returned home," a deep, ominous voice boomed from the doorway. Tim was nowhere to be seen.

Lord Boxton's dark form was framed in the doorway, a foul look of satisfaction on his once handsome features.

Anna took an instinctual step back. His auburn hair was windblown and his green eyes glinted with perniciousness. A frown touched her brow. She had never seen him like this. She did not like it.

He wore all black, from his riding boots to his cravat. Never before had she seen a man wear so much black at once.

He stepped into the room and closed the door behind him. The *click* that echoed through the room feeling like a death knell.

Chapter 20

"Lord Boxton!" Anna forced a smile. "What a pleasant surprise."

"You called me 'Anthony' the last time I saw you…when you had your tongue down my throat." Anna refrained from wincing at his coarseness. "Of course, you could always call me *darling, my love*, or…*master*. We could reserve that one for the bedchamber. We are to be married, after all." He strode forward ever so slowly, but Anna retreated to match him.

"I have not agreed to marry you, Lord…Anthony."

His voice dripped with malice. "Oh, but you will, sweetheart." Anna flinched at his endearment.

Fear prickled up her spine. Anthony's character had distinctly altered from last she had seen him. "Given your present behaviour, I am not certain that I would wish to marry you, even had you asked." Her bottom bumped against the back of a chair, stopping her retreat.

Lord Boxton seized his opportunity and pounced, trapping her against the chair's back. "I have ways to change your mind." His whisky-soaked breath heated her ear, and a shiver of disgust rippled through her.

"As I said previously, I am afraid that it would prove very difficult to change my mind. Your current comportment is abhorrent." She pushed against his chest. "Please release me."

He whispered nastily in her ear. "Tell me where you were over the past several days. And please, be *honest*." Anna flinched as he hissed the last word.

She could tell the truth, but Anthony could ruin her in the *ton*, and she had no wish to disgrace her family. "I had an urgent letter from my Grandmamma, and I left to assist her," she repeated her brother's convenient falsehood.

Her teeth pulled back in a grimace as he ground his pelvis against her and trailed his slimy tongue up the rim of her ear. "With what did she require help?"

"She was ill," Anna improvised. "Her housekeeper suggested that she summon me for assistance after her illness had lasted for more than a fortnight. By the time I arrived, however, she had already recovered." There. That was a sufficient excuse. "She did not wish me to miss more of the season in London, so she insisted I return directly."

Lord Boxton stepped back, his face a mask of rage. "You lying bitch!" The crack of his hand against her cheek echoed through the room.

Her vision blurred, and her balance faltered. She landed on the floor with a *thud*, knocking the breath from her lungs. She blinked, holding a hand to her cheek as she watched the viscount in disbelief.

Anger suddenly replaced her fear. "You, my lord, have gone too far." She held the side of the settee and pulled herself to her feet. "I must demand that you leave at once, or I shall have my footmen throw you out! I no longer wished to be courted by you, nor will I *ever* marry you."

The door's latch rattled. Lord Boxton must have locked the door upon entering. Anna fought the fear gnawing at her.

A loud knocking followed the rattle. "Annabel?" Charles' concerned voice came from the other side of the door. "Anna, is everything all right? I heard some loud noises."

Anna opened her mouth to request assistance, but before she could utter a sound, Lord Boxton's hand clamped around her neck. His body pressed hotly against her back, and his mouth pressed to her ear.

"If you so much as utter one word against me, I will shoot him through the heart." He pulled the cock back on the pistol as he aimed it unwaveringly at the door. "I am an excellent shot." He pressed his nose to her hair and inhaled deeply, sending another shudder of revulsion through her.

The door's latch rattled again. "Annabel?"

She swallowed past the sudden lump in her throat as nervousness and fear took hold of her. "Everything is fine, Charles. You may be at ease."

Lord Boxton shifted his hold on her neck, tightening his grip ever so slightly. "Very good, my dear," he whispered into her ear. "You had better be certain that he departs quickly, or I might get bored with waiting and kill him just for sport."

Anna's stomach knotted to the point that she feared she might become ill.

"Are you positive, Anna?" Charles called through the door.

"You may go now, Charles." Her voice quavered, and she hoped that Charles could not hear it.

"Very well. But please call if you have need of me." The dear man!

"Thank you," she called out.

Charles' footsteps faded down the corridor, and with each step Anna felt her hope diminish drastically.

Lord Boxton lowered his pistol and released her neck. "Now we have the opportunity to discuss the terms of our marriage in private."

Anna touched her fingers defensively to her neck. "You might be capable of bullying me into an engagement with you, your lordship, but the moment you leave I will contact the proper authorities and have you put in gaol."

His lips pulled back in a nasty snarl, a mirthless laugh barking from deep in his throat. "Why do we not sit?" He gestured toward the sitting area.

With a wary glance in his direction, Anna sat carefully on the edge of the settee, poised to run should the opportunity present itself. His lordship sat on a chair to her right, appearing for all the world to be at his ease. His smile was congenial, but his eyes glinted dangerously.

"I made some inquiries," he said in an eerily soft voice. "I had some…acquaintances look into your tale. Your grandmamma did not send you an urgent letter, nor did you travel to the North to visit her."

He casually waved the pistol in his hand, and Anna shifted backward in her seat.

"You were, in fact," Boxton paused to pin her with his irate gaze, "with Lord Devon, travelling toward Dover."

Anna spared a moment for surprise. The viscount certainly had well-informed connections. Who could know of her true location?

His green eyes watched her with malice. She sat perfectly still, entirely unwilling to show him that he frightened her. How had she not noticed his true character prior to this moment? He had been all charm and congeniality, amiable and attentive during the beginning of their courtship. Could she have been so consumed with the desire to have children that she had been blinded to his true nature? She certainly saw him now, and he was ugly indeed.

"If this is a desire for my dowry, Lord Boxton, I would be pleased to acquire funds for you. There is no need to go to such trouble as to—"

He lifted his hand to deliver a backhanded slap, and Anna flinched, pressing her back hard against the settee. She waited, but no stinging impact was forthcoming. She released a silent sigh of relief, but the threat remained.

He lowered his arm. "It is not only your dowry that I wish to possess, dearest. It is also your womb." His sickening gaze swept her body. "You are built for making children, and I require an heir and a spare."

Revulsion swept through her. The thought of making love to *this* Lord Boxton was a nauseating one.

"I will *never*—"

His low voice rumbled. "If you do not agree to marry me, Annabel, I fear you will force my hand."

She watched his smug smile grow as he thought he'd trapped her.

Anna notched her chin mutinously despite the fluttering in her stomach. "I shall state my point again, your lordship, that you may bully me into accepting your hand this morning, but there is nothing you can do that would stop me from reporting you to the magistrate upon your departure."

His expression became increasingly malign, as impossible as it seemed. "Not if I tell all of England what a *whore* you have become? You would have no one to blame for your family's disgrace but yourself."

She hid her flinch at his coarse language. "Even then. I shall not marry you."

As upsetting as her true ruination would be, Anna would gladly sacrifice her good name to avoid a future as a wife of this…*monster*.

His eyes narrowed portentously. "You will marry me, Annabel." He trailed a finger along the barrel of his pistol. "You will also not tell a soul about my gentle…*coercion* in this matter."

Anna opened her mouth to disabuse him of this fantasy, though her gaze followed Boxton's stroking of his pistol. He spoke first. "If you do…" he had the smile of a man who knew he possessed insurmountable power, "I will kill the ones you love."

Anna's eyes widened as her heart stalled.

"Your mother," he goaded, "your father. Your brother…your *lover*." He chuckled evilly. "I will have them all murdered in their beds. And do not think for one moment that you can escape my watchful eyes. I have them everywhere."

He crossed one leg over the other, seemingly contented with his threat. Despite herself, Anna trembled. She did not fear the threat of her own mortality, but that of her family? Of *Lane*? She was petrified.

"Why are you doing this?" Her voice quavered.

He gestured wildly with his hands, the pistol dangling frighteningly from his careless fingers. "Why does a man do anything?" His countenance darkened menacingly. "Because I can."

Anna gathered her courage and licked her dry lips. "Why me? There are other women with wide, childbearing hips from good families. Why do you care enough to threaten me?"

He shrugged his shoulders. "Because I chose you." He said it as though his simple explanation answered her question.

She daren't ask again, however.

"What say you, Annabel?" His vile, knowing green gaze bore into her. "Shall we announce our engagement to your family?"

Anna bit the inside of her cheek as she thought. She could not marry this man. But neither could she allow harm to come to those she loved. She had no choice.

Her heart ached as she thought of Lane, her hopes for a life with him now dashed. There must be a way to both protect her family and avoid a life with this dreadful man. She would, unavoidably, have to accept his proposal this morning, but surely she could find a way out of the arrangement.

Oh, how she wished she could confide in Lane or her family! She would not risk their lives, however. She must do this on her own, while ensuring that those closest to her believed her happy with the impending union.

Her stomach knotted. Could she do it? Could she find a way to end their engagement in such a way that he would not harm anyone?

Anna cleared her throat against the tightness that had formed there. "I—I…" Anna hesitated. "I will marry you."

Chapter 21

Lane dipped his pen into the inkpot and touched it to the side, catching the hanging drop on the rim. He had neglected his property management and accounts for far too long. He was obliged to review tenant letters and several agricultural forms from his solicitor and was nearly finished for this morning.

He covered a yawn with the side of his fist. He'd had very little sleep. He'd spent the night imagining the ways that he wished to make love to Anna. His feverish mind had created some very intriguing positions.

He shifted uncomfortably in his seat and retrieved his cigar from an ashtray. He puffed as a knock sounded at his study's door.

"Come." A smoky haze rose up around him, and he waved a hand to clear it.

Geoffrey entered with a silver salver. "A messenger came, my lord." The butler extended the tray and Lane accepted the letter.

His heart leapt as he saw Anna's familiar, curving handwriting. "Thank you, Geoffrey. Is the messenger awaiting a response?" He returned his still-lit cigar to its place with its ashes.

"No, your lordship, though I should inform you that the missive arrived an hour past. The new footman apologizes sincerely for the delay."

Lane nodded in dismissal, then turned his attention to the breaking the seal for the note in his hand.

Dearest Lane,

I have thought only of you since our parting last evening. I would like nothing more than to see you.

Please do me the honour of meeting me for a tryst at our favourite spot at half past one this afternoon. Do be sure to bring something sweet, for I have a mind to share the flavour with you...

Yours affectionately,

Annabel

Lane read, then reread the missive several times.

Annabel was propositioning him! The eager appendage in his trousers sprang instantly to life.

He glanced at the clock on his mantle. It was nearly a quarter to one. He surged to his feet, pulling his charcoal coat off the back of the chair in one fluid motion.

"Geoffrey!" He slid the coat over his white shirtsleeves and deep blue waistcoat.

He reflexively adjusted his cravat and ran his fingers through his hair as he strode determinedly toward his study's door.

"Geoffrey!" he hollered through the doorway.

The butler appeared before him, unruffled as ever. "My lord? You bellowed?"

"I am in too cheerful a mood to chastise you for your sarcasm, Geoffrey." Lane smiled. "Please have an alfresco luncheon prepared immediately, with added desserts, if you would. I require it within the quarter of the hour."

"Right away, your lordship." Geoffrey bowed and hurried away.

Lane felt light and elated. Had Annabel decided upon her answer to his proposal? Had she lain awake, as he had, wishing that he were next to her? Anticipation charged through him as he made his way toward the doors to the garden.

The sky was dark with the threat of rain, casting a shadow upon the earth. But Lane cared not. He would enjoy this rendezvous with or without rain.

He checked his pocket watch. *Blazes!* Only ten minutes had passed.

"Geoffrey!" He sped to the parlour's open doorway and nearly bumped into Bridget.

"Good heavens, Lane, what is the fuss about?"

"Apologies, Bridget," Lane murmured. "I am in a dreadful rush to depart."

She entered and closed the door behind her, ignoring what he'd said entirely. "I thought I should inform you that I had a brief visit with Annabel this morning. We had a very enlightening conversation."

That made him pause. "When did this discussion occur?" he asked carefully.

"An hour ago, approximately."

Lane met her hard gaze, suspicion crawling up his spine. "What happened? What did I do?"

She tilted her head. "I believe you know what you did, big brother. And I believe you know how to fix it. So get to it." She swung the door open and left the room.

Lane stood mutely for several long moments, his mind whirling. What in blazes did Annabel say to Bridget?

"Your alfresco luncheon, my lord." Geoffrey entered, the laden basket in his arms, his expression harried.

"Wonderful!" Lane accepted the burden with a "thank you" and strode quickly through the French doors.

* * *

Annabel swiped furiously at the tears coursing down her cheeks. *That evil, manipulative…rat bastard!*

She paced back and forth beneath the cherry blossom trees, awaiting Lane's arrival. It felt wrong, somehow, to soil her favourite spot with the discussion she knew must take place. But Lane must believe it; he must accept it, walk away, and not look into the veracity of her feelings on the matter.

Anna wiped at her cheeks once more, holding back a fresh wave of tears. Her heart pounded with dread, and her stomach was in knots.

She would find a way out of this, and then she could confess her love for Lane. But for now, she would save his life, even if it tore her apart inside to do so.

"I thought I might find you here." Anna's heart skipped a beat as Lane's deep timbre rumbled behind her.

She spun to face him just as Lane's mouth closed in on hers. *No, Anna! You must stick…to the…plan…*

He smelled of soap and sweet cigars. Anna melted.

Lane's lips were hot and delicious. For a moment Anna let herself be immersed in his embrace, the way his tongue played with hers, the way his arms held her tight… But it needed to stop.

She pulled back. "No. Stop, Lane."

His heavy-lidded gaze met hers, but slowly his countenance changed. He unwound his arms from around her, holding her shoulders with his hot palms as he watched her carefully.

"What has happened, Anna?"

"Nothing at all. Everything is perfectly well." Remembering her falsehood, Anna smiled. "Better than well, as a matter of fact."

He brushed her claims aside with a tilt of his head. "Your eyes are red, Anna. You have been crying."

She waved a hand through the air between them. "It is merely the wind; my eyes have become dry."

Ordinarily, she would turn her face away to avoid further scrutiny, but he mustn't see through her lie. She would face him directly, meet his gaze, and dare him to refute her.

He withdrew further, seemingly nonplussed by their encounter. "I understood from your missive that you wished to, er, enjoy some moments alone. I had not anticipated a sombre discussion."

"Our conversation will be quite the contrary, I assure you," she lied. "The letter was meant to tease; I wrote it on a whim, though I did wish to see you."

She didn't miss his flinch. Her chest tightened as she smiled brightly at him.

"Truthfully, my reason for requesting this rendezvous was to impart some rather exciting news!"

A frown touched his brow as he waited for her to speak. She was about to destroy something beautiful, turn it foul and unrecognizable. She only hoped that she could turn it back once this was all done.

"Anthony came to call on me this morning." She did her best to sound cheerful as she bounced on her toes. "I wanted you to be the first to know… He proposed marriage—"

"*No!*"

"—and I have accepted."

Anna fought back the desire to weep at the sight of Lane's blanched countenance, to tell him that it was all a lie, that she loved him…

"*Have you lost your bloody mind?*" he growled. "How could you consent to a marriage to that—that damned whoreson?"

* * *

Lane's chest ached with a pain akin to the fiery depths of Lucifer's lair. He had not known this level of pain was possible.

"Anthony is a gentleman." She notched her chin defiantly high as she toyed with the ribbon that circled her waist.

Anthony was a blackguard for taking his Annabel away from him. He couldn't let that happen.

"Marry me instead, Anna." He gripped her hands in desperation. "We have been friends since we were on leading strings. We are so good for each other. Break off your engagement. Marry me."

Her lips thinned into a hard line as she watched him pityingly. Damn it, he did not want her pity.

"I cannot." She pulled her hands from his and stepped back. "I am engaged to Anthony. I will not break my promise to him."

This must be what a breaking heart feels like. The ache spread to his limbs, his heart thundered while simultaneously being shattered into pieces. He gasped for breath, his soul struggling for purchase as he watched Anna's stoic countenance.

How could she be so calm when he felt as though his world just crashed around him?

Anger slowly crept inside him, protecting his heart from further pain while lashing out at the one who had hurt him. Anna's lemon scent wafted toward him on the chilled breeze, and he grit his teeth against its lure.

He growled. "Does your *fiancé* know that you well-nigh begged me to take your maidenhead? Does he know how you screamed my name when you found your pleasure in my arms?" Lane tried to stop the flow of hurtful words from leaving his lips, but his pain and anger controlled his mouth. "Does he know that you—"

"Yes." Her softly uttered interruption halted his hateful speech.

To Lane's mortification, his eyes began to sting with the threat of tears. *Hell and blazes.* He hadn't cried since his father died eleven years ago.

She softly cleared her throat, her pitying gaze meeting his through a haze of his unshed tears.

"Anthony knows of my lack of virtue, Lane."

He couldn't catch his breath. He couldn't slow the painful hammering of his heart. He couldn't have the woman he loved.

"Very well," he croaked. "I will not importune you further."

"Lane." She reached for him, but he pulled away. He couldn't have her touch him. He would either grovel at her feet or shout tearful profanities at her. He didn't relish the thought of doing either.

He turned, ignoring the basket he'd set upon the grass, and tramped back toward his town house. He could not stand there any longer. He could not turn back. He needed to be alone, to escape the crushing pain assailing him.

With a low rumble, the skies opened, raining droplets over the grand expanse of London. It suited his mood impeccably.

Tears flowed freely down his cheeks, mingling with the warm spring rain, while his feet drove him home.

Chapter 22

Reading books allowed Anna to escape into a life not her own. She'd wanted to escape the past eight weeks in their entirety.

The moment Lane had turned his back to her and the skies had wept, despondency had swept her. She'd lost her very closest friend; the man she'd grown up with. The man she loved.

Anna shifted uncomfortably in her seat. Any spare moment in which her time was not consumed with Anthony, she spent in this chair in her bedchamber, reading.

She was terribly lonely without Lane. They used to share their feelings with each other, go for walks, play chess, read aloud to one another… When she'd found her newest favourite novel, *Pride and Prejudice* by Miss Jane Austen, Anna had had no one with which to share it. With whom would she discuss Elizabeth Bennet and Mr. Darcy's obstacles, Lydia's foolish decisions, and the dastardly Mr. Wickham? With whom would she joke? With whom would she share her deepest desires and fears?

She sighed. Her heart hurt when she thought of Lane. She was haunted by the image of his pale, distraught features from when last she saw him. She despised herself for what she'd done that day. And she was beginning to fear that it was all for naught, for she had yet to concoct a plan to free her from Anthony's clutches.

She had thought of—and quickly dismissed—several plans, from abandoning him at the altar, running away from home, or pretending a dire illness, to feigning death or poisoning Anthony. None seemed possible.

With a sigh, Anna put a ribbon between the open pages of her book to mark her place, then pressed it closed. This was the first day since they had announced their engagement in which Anna had not seen Lord Boxton, and she could not enjoy it. She was exhausted from the countless carriage rides through Hyde Park, the evenings at the theatre or balls, the musicales… And at every opportunity, Anthony made certain to remind her of what would happen if she spoke a word or broke their engagement.

He would murder her family.

She could scarcely imagine that someone could do such an odious thing. She had often wondered how a man could be so despicable and volatile in character as Lord Boxton, but she had yet to find an answer other than madness.

A yawn caught her by surprise, and she quickly covered it with the back of her hand. She had been dreadfully tired of late, for she slept very poorly, scarcely for more than two or three hours at a time. Being exhausted, and her predicament with Lord Boxton, had diminished her appetite significantly. She feared she was beginning to waste away.

How did Lane fare? She had learned from Bridget that he had travelled to their country estate in Hertfordshire and had not been seen or heard from since. Did he think of her as often as she thought of him? The letters she had sent him had all been returned unopened, each one deepening the ache in her heart.

She sighed once more. The season was in full swing, and tonight would be another performance. She was due to attend the second Merrington ball of the season on Anthony's arm. How she loathed the façade of happiness that she displayed to the world. She smiled prettily, laughed at humourless jests, danced all the dances… Acted the dutiful fiancée.

A knock sounded at her bedchamber door, and she called out a welcome.

Charles' head appeared from around the door. "Anna? Would you care to come down to luncheon?"

She glanced at her mantle clock as he stepped into the room. "Is it that time, already?"

"It is." He nodded, holding his elbow out to her. "Shall we?"

Anna placed her book on the window's sill and stood, but stumbled. Her vision went blurry, and her head swam dizzily before the room went black.

Charles was suddenly at her side. *How had he gotten here so quickly?* What was she doing on the ground?

She put a hand to her head. "Goodness! What happened?"

"You fainted. You are fortunate I was here, Anna, or you would have hit your head." He tilted his head toward the tea table several feet away.

These dizzy spells were terribly bothersome. "I am grateful for your aid, Charles. I believe I am much improved now." She moved to sit up, but Charles put a hand to her shoulder.

"I disagree. You have been experiencing moments of faintness far too frequently of late. I will have a physician called."

Anna waved a hand. "Oh pish. There is no need to go to the trouble. It is merely a lack of sleep, and I am rather hungry, as well."

She rose to her feet with Charles' grudging assistance.

130

He eyed her disapprovingly, his blue eyes glinting. "I warn you, dear sister," he pointed a finger at her, "if I see you take so much as one more faltering step, I will summon a doctor to examine you."

Charles' eyes were lined with worry, and as much as Anna found his overprotective nature irksome, she did not wish to be a burden on his nerves. "Very well," she agreed. "I will submit to a doctor's examination if, after I get some rest and have eaten, I still have dizzy spells."

Her brother nodded his head in satisfaction, holding his elbow out to her once more. Anna accepted with a smile, and they both strolled from the room.

The dining room was bright with midday sunlight, where it cast its glow on Mama through the grand windows.

Their mother looked up from her seat to the right of the table's head. "I see you have been torn from your books, Annabel, dear."

"Yes, Mama."

Charles walked her to her seat across from their mother before he rounded the table and took his own seat. The footmen arrived with their meal and plates and placed them upon the table. Anna's stomach roiled as the scent of herring wafting from beneath one of the silver domes. Her appetite fled.

"Lady Kipling informed me that her nephew is returned from war," Mama said conversationally. "The poor man lost most of one arm and is dreadfully scarred." She sat forward eagerly. "He was a dear, sweet boy the last I saw him. Do you recall, Annabel?" She continued without waiting for a response, "At the ball Lord Kipling had held in her ladyship's honour? He was but a boy, then, but as Lady Kipling informs me, he is eight-and-twenty and quite grown now." She looked at Charles. "Did you happen to see him while you were in battle, dear?"

Charles' jaw tightened. "I did. But I do not believe that it is fit conversation for a lady's ears, Mama."

"Ah yes, you once more refuse to reveal any information about your time overseas." She sniffed delicately. "Very well." She took a small bite of herring and chewed daintily.

Anna watched her plate, a perpetual grimace of distaste on her lips. Charles cleared his throat, and Anna knew he was watching her. She skewered a small potato with her fork and brought it to her mouth.

She fought a gag. It had been soaking in fish-flavoured sauce. Her stomach roiled, but she managed to swallow.

"My dear Charles," Mama cooed, "how fares your search for Annabel's abductors?"

Anna's fork clattered to her plate, catching the attention of the room's occupants. "Please excuse me," she murmured as she stood.

"You have scarcely touched your meal, Anna." Charles stood as she did.

"I have lost my appetite," she uttered lamely before fleeing the dining room.

A walk out of doors would benefit her—truly, *anywhere* away from that dreadful fish smell would do—but the beautiful June day warranted a stroll in the gardens.

* * *

Lane grunted as he stared sightlessly out his estate's study window. The sun heated him through the glass, but pain clutched his heart. *Anna would have loved this day.*

He puffed on the last bit of his cigar and ground it out on a dish, blowing the smoke against his reflection in the window.

The past seven and a half weeks had been among the worst of his life. He had little appetite and few hours of sleep. He'd made the excuse to himself that he was required to be at the estate to oversee several agricultural projects, but in truth, he simply could not see Anna go about town with Lord *sodding* Boxton.

She'd refused him. His chest tightened, and he took a sip of his brandy. He still could not quite accept that she was gone, out of his life, as quickly as all that. One moment he had been ready to make love to her—marry her—and then, as quick as a flash of lightning…

With a groan, he slumped in the chair behind his desk. He had not shaved or bathed in nearly a sennight. He'd missed several appointments with fencing partners, nor had he been riding. He felt distinctly sloth-like.

The only true thing that Lane had done was aid his solicitor in overseeing the agricultural projects and have runners investigate his and Anna's kidnapping. All of the men had come back with nothing to report. It was as though Billy, Frenchie, Toby, and the scarred, red-haired man had all but evaporated into nothingness.

He tapped the paper on his desk as frustration rode him.

According to the gossip rags, Anna and her fiancé had been quite busy about town. No date had been set for their wedding, but Lane would wager that an announcement was forthcoming.

He shook his head against the backrest of his chair, regret burning inside him. He had not even expressed his love for her! She would marry Boxton, have a passel of children with the bastard, and forget about Lane entirely.

His heart stalled in his chest, his breath freezing. He could not allow that to happen. Anna was his confidante, his love, his…his friend. He could not lose her.

He cursed foully, the awful words echoing off his expansive study walls. What the devil was wrong with him? He was hiding away like a coward! He needed to tell Anna his feelings. He needed to hand her his heart and give her the power to make an informed decision.

Bloody hell. He could not live without her; sexless friendship with Anna was better than living as he was now. If she refused him, he would gratefully accept a position as a confidant in her life.

He stood and tugged on the gilt rope that hung near his study's door.

Moments later, his housekeeper, Mrs. Buttersworth—whom they affectionately call Mrs. Butter—entered.

"You rang, my lord?" She wrung her hands, distinctly uneasy.

He smiled reassuringly. He'd been a bear of late. "Yes. I am feeling more the thing, Mrs. Butter. I require a bath sent up to my room, as well as my valet and two footmen. I intend to return to my house in town posthaste."

Her expression instantly brightened. "Right away, your lordship." She hesitated then placed a thick hand on his arm. "I am right glad that you are feeling more yourself, my lord. We were all worried about you."

"Thank you, Mrs. Butter. It feels good to be back." It certainly did.

Lane strode from his study and wound his way through the long, wide corridors, and entered his chambers. A rare anticipation tingled up his spine as he thought of confessing his love to Anna. Would she break her engagement to be with him? She hadn't when he'd begged her to marry him, but what of love? Would she choose love over a marriage of convenience?

He tossed his rumpled waistcoat over a chair and unknotted his loosened cravat. The anticipation rushing through him intensified. He had an outstanding debt to settle with Anna for winning their last game of chess.

Chapter 23

Annabel gazed at her pallid reflection in the mirror of her dressing table while Marie styled her long, dark-blonde hair. She would prefer to remain in this evening, but then, she did every evening. Anthony would be very cross if she chose to snub him, however. She must attend.

Her gaze lowered to her attire. She wore a new, daringly cut, scarlet evening dress, as dictated by Viscount Boxton. It was a pleasing enough frock, but rather bold for her taste, as it exposed nearly all of her large bosom. Of course, it wasn't her taste; Anthony had taken control of the appointment—from corsets and lace to slippers and nightdresses. He had chosen it all.

She must find a way out of this engagement or this could very possibly be what the remainder of her life would be like. Anthony would tell her what to eat, wear, and do. She would no longer be Annabel, but Lady Boxton; perfect, docile, and submissive in every way.

Anna refused to become one of the ladies of the *ton* whose husbands dictated their lives. They were soulless, walking, talking versions of their husbands, spouting opinions that were not their own. They may be living, but they were not alive.

She dearly wished that she could confide in her brother. But God help her, she couldn't. Lord Boxton was a frightening, mad man, most particularly when holding a weapon. She daren't put her loved ones in the path of such dangerous insanity.

Marie tugged on a lock of her hair, and Anna grimaced as her gaze dropped to her décolletage. *Goodness!* If her bosom giggled at such a small movement, Lord knew what society's matrons would make of her attire this evening. She would be on all the wagging tongues on the morrow. Most particularly since Lady Juliana had peculiarly observed her at every function she had attended since her impending nuptials to Anthony had been announced. Anna had spotted her not merely attending said engagements but watching Anna. It was baffling and, quite frankly, disturbing.

Lady Juliana was a shrill woman of low morals, if the gossip was to be believed. She had been engaged to the elderly—and obscenely wealthy—Lord Whitmore, but had purportedly been caught nude in his bed on the night that he had died. Rumour stated that he had died atop her while engaged in the marital act. Since that scandal, no man had deigned to court her, and her parents held her bedchamber under tight guard.

"There you are, Miss Bradley. Pretty as an angel." The sweet maid clasped her hands to her chest.

"Thank you, Marie." Anna gave an indulgent smile as she stood and made her way to the door. Anthony would be cross with her if she were late to arrive below stairs, and heaven forbid she face his wrath.

"I shall await your return, Miss."

Anna waved a hand through the air. "Please do not trouble yourself, Marie. I will manage on my own. You may have the evening to yourself."

The maid thanked her profusely and made her exit.

Anna held the side of her scarlet skirts as she strode down to the main floor. Charles and their Mama stood at the base of the stairs, talking to Lord Boxton; Papa was likely at White's, engaged in a game of cards. The three of them looked up at her entrance, then froze.

"There you are, Annabel. I am pleased that you are ready." Anthony sketched a shallow bow over her gloved hand, then wrapped her palm around his elbow.

Mama and Charles still stared with wide eyes at her audacious gown, and Anna resisted the urge to cover her bosom.

"Shall we depart?" she asked. "The Merringtons await."

She knew she did not appear as herself, nor would she, now that her new wardrobe had arrived from Madame Adriane's and replaced her wardrobe of old. She felt exposed and ridiculous.

Anthony's voice whispered, hot and revolting, in her ear. "Wipe that discomfited expression from your face or I shall remove it for you."

Anna smiled brightly as he led her out the door. The evening was dark, but the air held warmth from the day; but Anna was ice inside—a living statue of marble continuing the façade while her heart and mind were elsewhere.

The carriage emblazoned with Boxton's family crest rolled into motion. Anna blinked heavily over her tired eyes. She scarcely recalled entering.

"How kind of you to allow us the use of your fine equipage this evening, Lord Boxton," Mama said into the silence.

"It is my great pleasure, Mrs. Bradley. Your daughter is a delight; I am truly a fortunate man." He smiled down at Anna and gave her hand a heavy pat.

He seemed so sincere, but Annabel knew what lay beneath his gentlemanly veneer.

If only she had accepted Lane's proposal when he had asked. They could have travelled to Gretna Green rather than return to London. What would her life be like if they had? Anthony would not have been able to force her into an engagement.

Would she be within Lane's warm embrace or curled by the fireside reading to one another? Or perhaps they would be engaged in a rousing game of chess.

She suppressed a sigh. Any of those scenarios was vastly more appealing than where she currently sat.

The carriage rocked gently as it righted itself from a corner, and Anna felt her stomach churn uneasily. She should have requested a tray of tea before readying herself for the ball, for her empty stomach felt distinctly unsettled.

"Are you well, Annabel? You look rather pale." Charles' concerned voice echoed from across the carriage.

"Yes, you look quite ill." Mama leaned forward to put a hand to Anna's knee.

Anna quickly nodded and turned her attention out the window. Lord, but she hoped she did not disgrace herself in this carriage. As they neared the Merringtons' large home, the streets grew increasingly crowded. Anna discreetly held her stomach as the carriage jolted forward, slowed, and then jolted again as they awaited their turn to disembark.

Finally they pulled to a stop. The door swung open, and Anna breathed a deep sigh of relief. The air was perfumed with the pungent scent of manure, but it was preferable to being confined in the rocking carriage.

Anthony exited first then helped her down the step, his hand needlessly tight on her own. The Merrington ball appeared to be the event of the season. There were carriages and people in abundance.

They made their way up the steps and into the grand foyer, following the other finely dressed ladies and gentlemen as they joined the receiving line to greet their hosts.

Lord and Lady Merrington were pleasant people, with greying hair and stout figures. Their son, Simon Claridge, heir apparent to the Earldom, was a very gentlemanly man. He had briefly courted Annabel, but they had agreed that they suited much more comfortably as friends than husband and wife. He was a handsome man with black hair and crystal-blue eyes. Many women swooned in his presence, but Anna felt nothing but warm friendship for the man, infrequently though they saw each other.

Lord Simon Claridge kept himself very busy with his "diversion" of doctoring. Annabel knew, however, that he took his position far more seriously than his parents. They did their utmost to dissuade him from continuing, but he was very persistent.

As Anna had predicted, they were greeted with warmth and congeniality by their hosts. Anna, Anthony, Mama, and Charles expressed their appreciation for the invitation, smiled, and continued to the ballroom.

Anna stared with wide-eyed wonder as they strode into the ornately decorated room. The chandeliers hung high and blazed with light. The walls were draped with gilt and violet hangings. She lowered her gaze to the mass of colour and flourishing silks, satins, and lace. It was quite the sight to behold, disappointing as it was that she had to attend on the arm of the evil man beside her.

"What a crush!"

"It is, indeed, Mama." Charles bowed to them. "If you will excuse me, I see a friend with whom I wish to speak." He turned to Annabel. "Save a dance for me?"

She felt Anthony's arm tense beneath her hand, but she could not very well refuse a dance with her brother. She smiled. "I would be honoured, Charles. Thank you."

He nodded and left to seek out his friend.

"Oh! There is Mrs. Humphery." Mama waved a delighted hand. "I must speak with her about her new gardener. I must know where she found him! Will you be all right, dears?"

A knot of apprehension formed in her stomach. She did *not* wish to be alone with Anthony.

"I would prefer—"

"We shall be fine, Mrs. Bradley." Anthony smiled amiably at her mother. "Thank you for your concern. Seek out your friend, and enjoy your evening."

Mama smiled and disappeared into the crowd.

Dread crept up her spine as Anthony turned to whisper in her ear. "If you think for one moment that being in the company of your ridiculous relations will release you from our bargain, you are sadly mistaken." He bit her ear, causing an intense, sharp pain. It took all of her will to avoid a flinch. *Good Lord, had he drawn blood?* "You will *not* give a dance away to anyone but myself. The dance you foolishly promised to your brother cannot be avoided, however."

"Yes, Anthony." She smiled at a passing couple.

"Splendid." He straightened. "Shall we get a refreshment?"

"That would be lovely, Anthony," was her automatic reply.

They wove through the milling members of the *ton* and found the refreshment table. Annabel eyed the pastries and decidedly alluring lemon tarts but selected only a glass of champagne, as dictated by Anthony. She comforted herself with the knowledge that she only had to follow Anthony's rubrics until she found a way out of the engagement. But for now, she did this for her family. For Lane.

"Very good," Anthony said under his breath. "Before long you will not require my guidance to make the correct choices."

"Yes, Anthony," she said meekly. She very dearly wished she could say more. *Much* more.

"Good evening, Lord Boxton, Miss Bradley," a familiar, trilling voice said from behind them. Anna grimaced. *Lady Juliana.*

Anna turned, smiling convincingly. "Lady Juliana, what a pleasant surprise." She dipped in a curtsey, as was due the lady's station.

Anthony followed suit, his greeting far more effusive.

"You would not believe what I learned from my dear friend, Lady Darling, this morning." She smiled smugly, evidently overjoyed to be spreading rumours and gossip. "It is to her understanding that Miss Clarke is the bastard daughter of a certain Lord of the realm. A *duke* to be precise."

Anna resisted the urge to roll her eyes as Lady Juliana continued her tale. She could not abide the mindlessness of such things. It was no wonder that Bridget had attempted to mentor Lady Juliana. Sadly, the lessons never took.

Anthony's booming laugh shook Anna back into the present. She forced a smile.

"Oh, there is Lady Ellis. I must share my delicious news with her. Please excuse me."

Anthony bowed, and Anna curtsied as the lady dipped quickly and left them.

Anna sipped at her champagne and gazed about the room. She spotted Ladies Bridget, Emaline, and Katherine, and the Dowager Countess of Devon speaking with a group of young gentlemen. No matter how embarrassed Anna still felt in Bridget's company, she wished she could speak with them. She had briefly exchanged missives with Bridget, but they had not discussed anything of consequence. She too had not spoken with Lane since his departure.

Bridget seemed to excuse herself from the group and slipped into the corridor toward the ladies' retiring room. Now might be her only opportunity to speak with her!

She turned to smile at Anthony. "Would you mind terribly if I excused myself to use the retiring room?"

He heaved a sigh and nodded with obvious reluctance. "Very well, but do not be long. The first waltz of the evening will begin shortly, and I require you here to partner me."

"I will not be long," she promised. "Thank you."

A strangely exhilarating anticipation ran through her as she strode toward the corridor. Anthony had kept her so long from conversing with her friends and acquaintances without his presence that she scarcely knew how to contain her joy at the prospect of being alone with someone else.

An odd sensation prickled at the back of her neck, and she slowed her steps down the hall. Her gaze darted from side to side as the feeling of being observed intensified. *Who could it—*

Before she could complete the thought a heavy hand clamped over her mouth and another wrapped around her elbow. It dragged her into an empty room, closing her into the pitch dark.

The hands released her, and Anna prepared to scream, her lungs taking a long, deep breath.

"Anna." Lane's voice echoed in the small space.

Her breath left her in a *whoosh*, and tears sprang foolishly to her eyes. "Lane!" She felt for his shoulders and pulled him into her embrace. "I have missed you, my dear friend."

He was silent for a moment before he cleared his throat, pulling away. "And I you, Anna."

"Do you intend to remain for supper?"

"I'm afraid not."

Anna squinted through the darkness, cursing her eyes for not adjusting quickly enough. She wished she could see his face.

"Are you well?" she asked.

"Quite well, thank you. I had urgent business to attend to at the estate. We are testing a new till and different seeds this year. I hope for a plentiful crop."

"Oh, good!" She smiled into the darkness, wishing she could speak to him form her heart. As trivial as the conversation was, however, she was simply pleased to speak with him again.

"How have you fared, Anna?" His voice lowered a fraction.

"Well, indeed. I have been quite busy planning the wedding," Anna lied. Her heart ached.

She heard him swallow. "Have you set a date, then?"

Chapter 24

Lane held his breath as he awaited Anna's response. His heart thundered in his ears. Her greeting had thrown his intentions off course. He had planned to confess his love, but Anna's greeting of *friend* had cut him short.

"We have not, but once my gown has been fitted, we shall."

His breath hitched, but he managed to exhale.

"Anna." He hesitated. Perhaps this was not the time or place in which to profess his love. "Would you care to join me for a stroll on the morrow?"

It was her turn to be silent. He could hear her toying with the fabric of her skirts. "I would love to," she said haltingly.

Relief swept him. "Shall I come for you at ten of the clock?"

"I—I would prefer to meet at the cherry blossoms, if that is sufficient."

Lane's gut clenched. The last time they had met at those trees, his life had been torn apart. "They are no longer in bloom," he stated baldly.

Anna's lemon scent swept over him. He had to bite his inner cheek to keep his body under his control. Anna would not appreciate being rumpled in front of her affianced…the blackguard.

Anna shifted. "I quite enjoy their purple leaves."

"Very well." Lane's lips formed a thin smile. "We will begin our promenade at the cherry blossom trees."

His nerves jumbled and his heart flipped over as Anna pulled him into her embrace once more.

He'd missed her dreadfully—her charm, her wit, her humour, her unique perspective on life. Which books had she been reading lately? She was so clever; she always found the best novels.

"I must go," she whispered.

Lane nodded, foolish though the action was in the darkness.

"Until tomorrow," he replied.

She opened the door and slipped into the hall, leaving Lane distinctly bereft without her company. They had discussed nothing of consequence, and yet he felt lighter merely having been in the same space as her.

He was a fool for leaving London. He should not have marred their friendship with his hurt heart. He should have… *No.* There was no sense in wasting time on regrets. He must focus on the present and the future. He would walk with Anna on the morrow and give her both his heart and the truth. Pride and fear be damned.

* * *

Anna's steps faltered as she neared the ballroom and heard the familiar chords of the waltz. The sickening knot in her stomach that had formed while she spoke to Lane tightened. She breathed a deep lungful of air, the scent of melting beeswax and the nauseating mixture of perfumes and colognes assailing her senses.

She smoothed her skirts with trembling fingers and rounded the corner into the grand ballroom. She saw Anthony immediately. He was hovering nearby, his expression vacant and his complexion a mottled red. *Oh, no.* He was furious. Anna could not miss the glinting rage in his eyes as he noticed her entrance.

Anna braced herself for a verbal thrashing and walked toward the devil. Before she reached his side, he came forward with a congenial smile. He put a hand on her arm and gave it a painful squeeze, though to anyone observing it appeared to be a solicitous gesture.

"Where have you been, my dear?" The steel behind his kind demeanour could not be mistaken.

Anna's smile turned brittle as she looked up at him. "In the retiring room, darling."

Anthony eyed the doorway to the corridor and stiffened. His hand tightened its grip, his fingers digging deeply like talons into her soft flesh. His head lowered, and his mouth touched her ear. Anna disguised her flinch by turning her head.

Oh, Lord. Lane had entered the ballroom, his gaze finding hers.

"You lying whore," Anthony hissed in her ear. "How *dare* you tell me falsehoods? Do you have any idea what I could do to you?"

Anna tore her gaze from Lane's and faced the furious Anthony. "I apologize. He surprised me in the hallway," she confessed.

The muscles in his jaw tightened, and a thick vein bulged on his forehead, running through its center as a bolt of lightning would the sky.

"A word in the gardens, if you please."

Anna fought to keep the quaver from her voice. "Of course."

He roughly wrapped her hand around his elbow and strode purposefully between mingling members of the *haute ton* and out the French doors to the terrace. She struggled to keep up with him as he moved swiftly past the terrace and into the darkness of the garden. They traversed the winding paths of fragrant rosebushes, orchids, and foxgloves to a secluded part of the garden hidden by shrubberies and trees.

Anthony released her arm from his grip, spun around, and slapped her hard across the face. Anna's vision spotted as she fell to the ground.

"You *dare* to lie to me, not once, but twice?" he snarled. "You will learn your lesson, wench, and it will be my pleasure do be the one to teach it to you!"

Anna held a hand to her smarting cheek as she blinked back the dots. She moved to stand but Anthony pushed her back to the ground. She stared, aghast, as he removed his coat and draped it over a bush before lowering himself atop of her.

The realization of what he intended dawned on her as his hips pressed hard into hers.

"No!" She bucked her hips and pushed at his chest, but she was powerless against the strength of his heavy body.

"You will learn to adore this, I promise you. Not as much as I, but that is not my concern."

Anna squirmed, kicked, and bucked, but Anthony's weight would not yield.

"It is more pleasurable for me if you resist, my dear." He licked her ear, the loud lapping sound making her stomach flip over in disgust. "Your movements excite me."

Anna stopped, the champagne churning in her stomach. "Please," she pleaded, helpless to do anything but. "Please wait until our wedding night. I will be more prepared for you then."

He sneered at her as he ground the ridge of his erection into her pelvis. "I don't give a bloody damn if you are prepared or not. I am having you tonight."

Anna held back a gag.

He trailed his tongue down her neck and along the décolletage of her gown and a shiver of revulsion travelled through her. She let out a squeak of protest and swallowed another gag as one of his hands slid up her waist and cupped the underside of her breast. He laughed cruelly at her as he lifted her skirts with his other hand and ground his member into the soft juncture between her thighs.

Oh Lord, I'm going to be sick! Anna turned her head in time to cast up her accounts on the grass beside her.

"Ugh!" Anthony leapt off her in abhorrence. "You disgust me." He checked himself to ensure he was clean of vomit and, upon clear inspection, pulled on his coat.

Despite her illness, Anna was relieved to have him off of her. She rolled to her side and shivered in the cool air of the late June evening.

"Get yourself together," he derided. "I am returning you to your brother directly. I do not want to contract whatever ailment has befallen you." He straightened his sleeves and ran a hand through his wavy auburn hair. "And be quick about it."

He stood impatiently several feet away, muttering to himself about repulsive sick women.

Anna brought herself to a seated position and breathed deeply of the fresh air. Despite a slight tremble, she felt better. She retrieved her embroidered handkerchief from between her breasts and dabbed at her mouth. Thankfully, her hair had only been mussed from the grass and not from her illness. The rest of her appeared to be clean but for grass and dirt stains.

She extended her hand toward Anthony, but he stared back at her with indifference in his malevolent green eyes. How had she ever thought him handsome?

Sighing, she struggled to her feet on her own. She straightened her gown and fixed the few fallen strands of her hair from her coiffure.

"There we have it," Anthony murmured, as though he had aided her in righting herself. "Let us return you to Major Bradley."

"Might I freshen myself in the retiring room first?"

Astonishingly, he nodded. "I will fetch your brother."

He sped ahead of her, leaving Anna to walk alone to another side door into a long, dark corridor. It took her only minutes, but she found the ladies' retiring room.

She stared in disbelief at herself in the mirror. Her face had narrowed; her skin was ashen and her eyes despondent.

How had her life turned so askew in so short a time? It felt a mere few days past that she and Lane had been kidnapped and dragged hither and yon at the whim of some scoundrel named "The Boss." It felt months, however, since she and Lane had lain together.

With a tired sigh, Anna poured fresh water from a nearby pitcher into the large washbasin on the table in front of her. She dipped her handkerchief in to clean it, then dabbed her forehead with the wonderfully cool water. This evening had gotten out of hand rapidly. She had not thought that she would have been caught lying to Anthony, let alone attacked by him.

Another wave of nausea came over her so quickly, she had just enough time to reach the chamber pot before she once more cast up her accounts.

"Good heavens," she muttered to herself.

"Annabel?" Charles' dear voice came from just outside the door. "Annabel, are you well? Do you require assistance? I have sent Mama to summon a hack, but I could fetch her if you wish it."

"No, thank you, Charles," she called from behind the division screen. "I will be out directly."

Anna replaced the chamber pot lid, then returned to retrieve her handkerchief. She wrung it out and placed it between her breasts. She scooped some water from the washbasin and rinsed her mouth out as best she could without tooth powder and a brush. She dumped the bowl out the window into the garden below then replaced it on its stand.

With one last look in the mirror at her pallid complexion, Anna quit the room. The moment she was through the door, Charles pulled her into his embrace. The comfort he offered was too much for her tried and tired emotions to bear, and tears sprang to her eyes.

"There, there, Anna." Charles crooned. "We will have you home soon."

Anna sniffled, pressing herself against his chest. "You are a wonderful elder brother, Charles. I do not know what I would do without you."

"Nor I you." He kissed her damp forehead and dabbed her eyes with his own kerchief.

He slowly led her down the hall and through the side door. Anna was grateful that he did not take her through the ballroom in this state. She could not abide the curious stares and probing glances.

"Where did Anthony go?" She looked up at Charles as he helped her into the hack—where she sat down comfortably beside her Mama.

Charles' expression was carefully blank as he entered after Anna and knocked once on the ceiling. "Lord Boxton expressed his confidence in Mama's and my own abilities to escort you safely home. He sends his well wishes for your health."

Anna nodded, hiding her relief with great effort. She had certainly dealt with enough of his company for one evening.

"You poor dear." Mama turned in her seat and laid the back of her hand on Anna's forehead. "You do not feel feverish, thank the good Lord."

"I feel fine, Mama. There is no need to be concerned. I think it may have been something I ate, or perhaps the champagne, that is all." *Or it was the thought of being intimate with a monster like Boxton.* She smiled for their benefit.

"Regardless of how you claim to feel, Anna, you will be examined by a doctor when we return home."

Anna thought instantly of the bruises that were sure to be fully formed on her upper arms, her cheek, and her bottom, and shook her head. "Oh, no. That is not necessary," she assured them. "All I require is a hot bath, some tea, and a good night of sleep."

"You will not avoid this, Annabel," Charles warned. "You swore to me that you would submit to a doctor's examination if you had another spell. I will not allow you to go untended any longer. This ends tonight."

Her heart flip-flopped. Charles was concerned for her welfare, it was evident by his angry and overbearing demeanour, but if he learned of her bruises, he would suspect Anthony of abuse. And if he tried to end their engagement, then all of this would be for naught, and Anthony would strike.

"I understand your concern, Charles, but I really do feel fine."

"Fine or not, you are seeing a physician. It is futile to argue, Anna. My decision will not be altered."

Oh, dear. She would have to fabricate an excuse for the colourful marks on her body. "Very well."

The ride home was silent and uncomfortable, but blessedly short. Upon arriving at their town house, Annabel went straight to her room with Marie—who thankfully did not complain about having to work after Anna had given her the evening off—washed, and dressed in her nightclothes.

"Would you like me to fetch you some tea, Miss Bradley?"

"Yes, please, Marie. Thank you."

Her maid left silently as Anna gazed out her window into the night. The doctor should arrive shortly, and Anna believed that she had formulated a plausible explanation for her bruises. *Please let it work.*

Good heavens, but she was exhausted.

Chapter 25

Major Charles Bradley paced the foyer, waiting for the doctor's forthcoming arrival. He'd suspected that Annabel was hiding something from him since she had been abducted, but she had been frustratingly tight-lipped. But she could not hide it from the good doctor.

The clipped sound of his tread echoed through the room with every step. He had sent the servants to bed an hour past, after he had sent for the physician.

His heart leapt as a knock on the door reverberated through the house. Charles quickly opened it and stood aside.

"My Lord, thank you very much for coming. I apologize for taking you away from your parents' ball."

Lord Simon Claridge, heir apparent to the Earldom of Merrington, stepped over the threshold. He had obviously changed out of his evening attire before he'd departed his home, for he was wearing a brown coat and trousers, a plain black waistcoat, and a simple knot in his white cravat. A very practical ensemble for a doctor.

"It is my duty and my pleasure, Major. But please, call me Dr. Claridge or Simon." He smiled amiably.

"Very well." Charles gave a half smile in return. "Please accompany me to my study." He motioned for Dr. Claridge to follow him as he started across the foyer to the hall.

"Is Miss Bradley in your study?" He sounded surprised.

"No," Charles grinned mirthlessly. "She is in her bedchamber. I, however, have several matters which I wish to discuss with you prior to your examination of Annabel."

"I see." Though by the tone of his voice, Charles could tell that he didn't.

He preceded the doctor into his study and closed the door behind him.

"Please, have a seat. Would you care for a drink, Dr. Claridge?" Charles went to his Tantalus and poured himself a glass of fine brandy.

"No, thank you," the doctor replied. He placed his large, black physician's bag on the floor and sat in the chair that Charles had indicated. "What did you wish to discuss?"

Charles brought his glass with him as he sat in the grand, leather wingback chair behind his desk and gazed solemnly at the man across from him. "I would first like your vow of discretion when it comes to your examination of my sister."

The doctor shook his head. "I never discuss my patients with anyone but the patient or guardian, unless previously authorized to do so. You have my promise to be discreet."

Charles inclined his head, wishing that it did not have to come to this. "My thanks. I am going to tell you something, regarding my sister, that also requires your secrecy."

Dr. Claridge watched him curiously. "As you wish."

Charles uttered a humourless laugh, shaking his head self-deprecatingly. "Truthfully, I have difficulty believing that I am about to confide in you in such a manner, Dr. Claridge. I believe, however, that this is necessary if you are to examine Anna properly." He drank deeply of his brandy, then took a deep breath. "Approximately nine weeks ago, my sister and Lord Devon were abducted from Hyde Park—"

"You're bamming me!"

Charles raised one eyebrow. "I assure you, I am not." The shock on Dr. Claridge's face did not abate as Charles recounted the basics of the tale.

"Bloody hell." Dr. Claridge rubbed his face with one hand. "I mean… Pardon me, but…*bloody hell.*"

"My thoughts, precisely. My concern at this moment, however, is that I suspect Anna is hiding something. Something that occurred during her experience with the blackguards hired to abduct her. Her appetite has diminished, she is not sleeping, and she has been feeling rather ill. I fear that her harrowing experience has affected her emotions so greatly that she is sinking into a decline." He finished the last of his brandy with one swallow, scarcely taking notice of the liquid heat burning its way to his knotted stomach.

"I will only know more once I have examined your sister."

"I have a request to make of you, then." Charles sat forward in his chair, resting his forearms on his desk. He looked Dr. Claridge directly in the eye. "I need you to inform me *exactly* what it is that my sister has been hiding from me, and what it is that ails her." He paused. "Cost is no object. Annabel's health is of the utmost importance to me."

* * *

Anna reclined in her bed as Dr. Simon Claridge continued his examination. She felt distinctly exposed, sprawled before him in only her night rail. The room was bright, with the fire in the hearth and several candelabras lit nearby, putting her scantily clad form in stark relief.

"How did you come by these bruises, Miss Bradley?" His searching blue gaze traveled over her face.

"I fell." It was plausible. She could have very easily fallen and gotten marks from it.

He nodded his head, a lock of his ebony hair falling over his brow. "I see." He put his fingers to her wrist and stared at his pocket watch. "Very good," he murmured. "Please sit up."

He assisted her into a seated position and put an odd contraption to her back. "Breathe in." His voice was low and calm. "Very good, now breathe out. Good. Now lie back down, please."

Anna did as she was told while marvelling at his soothing voice.

"For how long have you felt ill?" He returned the contraption to his black bag.

"It has only been a few days."

"What are your symptoms? Could you describe them to me?"

"I have been dizzy, which is most certainly due to a lack of sleep. My appetite has fled, but, I rather put that to emotional stress. And most recently, I became ill after...after I ate some rather foul-smelling fish sauce." She carefully avoided mentioning Anthony's attack.

"I see." He smiled warmly at her then hovered his hands above her torso, his gaze questioning. "I am afraid that I must be slightly forward with you for a moment."

Anna nodded.

"Do you mind if I ask you some rather personal questions?"

Something about him made her feel quite comfortable with anything he wished to do. "I give you permission to continue your examination, your lordship."

His smile grew. "Thank you. But please, call me Simon. We have enough history, I believe, between you and I, for you to call me by my Christian name."

She grinned at him in return. "Indeed. Then you must call me Anna."

He pressed his fingers into her stomach, causing her to flinch.

"My apologies. Did that pain you?"

Anna nodded. "Yes. A sharp pain through to my hip."

"Have you experienced any other pains like this before?"

"A few, yes."

"I see. And what of your breasts? Have you experienced any tenderness or pain?"

149

Anna blushed, but nodded. Personal questions, indeed!

His smile was warm. "You have no need to feel bashful with me, Anna. I have been trained by the very best and have helped many patients."

She felt foolish. "I know."

He stepped back and leaned a hip against a nearby table. "What of your menses? When was your last cycle?"

Her blush deepened. "I…" When had her last menses come? Her brow furrowed as she thought. "Goodness, I do not recall. I apologize. Will that affect your diagnosis?"

"Greatly, actually. But it is quite all right." Simon put his tools back in his black bag, then assisted her to a sitting position.

"Do you know what is wrong with me?"

He gazed steadily at her, his mien solemn. "Nothing is *wrong* with you, Anna."

"Then why—"

"You are with child. Nearly eight weeks along, I should say."

Her jaw dropped, and her eyes widened as shock tore through her. She was *enceinte*? How could she not have known? She had not paid close attention to her menses, though stress could have easily caused it. The thought of pregnancy had not crossed her mind over the past weeks, nor had it been a concern when she had decided to make love to Lane.

A baby! I am going to be a mother! Tears sprang to her eyes, then quickly spilled over her lashes. Oh heavens, a baby!

Simon approached her bedside and held a handkerchief out to her.

Anna gratefully accepted his offering, then dabbed at her eyes. He placed a warm, comforting hand on her back.

"In my experience as a physician, I have treated several women through the duration of their pregnancies, and delivered countless healthy babes. You will be well, Anna. And if you should wish for me to be your doctor throughout your pregnancy, I would be honoured to do so."

Anna nodded. "Yes, thank you, Simon."

"Many women have similar symptoms in their *enceinte* state." She heard the smile in his voice. "One being a propensity for weeping."

Anna let out a small, damp chuckle as she looked up at him through tear-filled eyes. "What are some others?"

"Some women have intense cravings for bizarre foods."

Anna crinkled her nose.

"Others," he continued, "are repulsed by food they previously adored."

150

"Well that is silly." She smiled. "I shall never be rid of my proclivity for chocolate."

Simon barked a laugh then patted her shoulder. "I will allow you to rest. Be sure to get some sleep, eat, and drink plenty of water. Baby needs you to stay healthy." He winked. "I will come to see you again in a fortnight." He sketched a quick bow and gathered his doctoring bag in one hand. "Take care of yourself, Anna."

She returned his smile. "I will. Thank you, Simon."

He made his way to the door, opened it, and paused to look back at her. "I want you to know, Anna, that you will always have a friend in me."

More foolish tears seeped from her eyes at his kindness. "Likewise."

Chapter 26

Major Charles Bradley paced his office as he awaited Dr. Claridge's return. Was Anna well? Was it exhaustion, as she claimed? Or was it as he suspected? The anxiety clutching his chest was too much to be borne.

"Major Bradley?" Charles spun at the sound of Dr. Claridge's voice.

"Please, come in, sit down." Charles took his own seat, his gut roiling. "Would you care for a drink?" It was a question out of habit.

"No, thank you." The doctor shifted in his chair. "You, however, may wish to partake."

That made him pause. His heart faltered. *Damnation.* What news could the doctor bring that required Charles to imbibe before he heard it?

"What news have you? What is wrong with Anna?"

The doctor winced. "There are two things which we must discuss. The first…" He heaved a gusty sigh. "It appears as though someone has attacked your sister."

"Attacked?" Dread gripped him in its painful vice.

"Yes," Dr. Claridge confirmed. "She is very nearly covered with bruising, both old and new. Some are scarcely discernable any longer, while others are dark and fresh."

"Bruises?" Charles' fists clenched upon his desk's surface as anger began to bubble within him.

The doctor nodded. "She claims that she fell, but it is clear to me that they were made by a man's hands."

"Someone used force with Anna?"

"According to the formation of her bruises, yes." He scratched at his chin. "There are several bruises along her upper arms that suggest rough handling. There is also a large bruise beginning to form on her left cheek, which tells me that she had been hit with someone's right hand. She allowed me to give her a thorough inspection, and I discovered two more new bruises, one on her right hip and one on her thigh. Those would suggest that she had, indeed, fallen, most likely due to the blow to her cheek."

"*Bloody hell!*" Charles exploded. "Who would dare to lay their hands on Annabel?" His heart pounded against his ribs as his growing anger pumped through his veins. He needed to find this villain and give him a taste of what he had delivered to his little sister.

Dr. Claridge grimaced once more. "I am afraid that there is more, Major Bradley."

"More? What could be worse than the abuse of my most beloved sister?"

"Anna is with child."

"*She is what?*" He roared with rage as he surged to his feet. Sweet, innocent Anna was pregnant? It couldn't be. "No. Not Anna."

The doctor inclined his head. "I fear so. She is approximately eight weeks along and will be due some time in late December or early January of next year."

Eight weeks… The kidnappers! Anna had evaded his question about her virginity… *Good God.* He had been searching for the blackguards since Anna and Lane had returned home. Now, he would not rest until he had each of their necks in a noose.

* * *

Anna lay curled on her side, the bedclothes pulled up to her chin. She stared past the reflections in the window to the dark sky beyond.

She had heard Charles shouting below stairs minutes before. *He knows.* Simon must have informed him of her increasing condition. He would have learned of it eventually, she supposed.

She still had difficulty believing it, herself. She was *enceinte*! With *Lane's* child! The thought nearly made her excited to be a mother. There was one large matter that stood in the way of her happiness, however. Lord Boxton. She must find a way to break the engagement! What if his abuse damaged the baby? What if he found out about the baby? Would he take his anger and disappointment out on her family?

A tremor of fear rippled through her. She *would* find a way out of this.

A tap sounded at her door before it slowly swung open. Anna watched Charles in the window's reflection as he strode toward her bed.

"You spoke with Dr. Claridge, I presume?" She hardly need ask; his fury was written on his face.

Her question was greeted by silence. With a sigh, she sat up, propping pillows behind her back as she met Charles' fuming stare.

"Did you tell Mama and Papa?" she asked.

"Who was he?" Charles demanded. His voice was terse and cold.

She could not tell him the truth. Charles had always been overly protective of her. If he knew Lane was the father, he would not force them into a marriage; he would call Lane out. It was irrational, but she knew her brother. Besides, Lane should learn of it before anyone else. And only after she had found a way to break her engagement to Anthony.

"*Who was he*, Annabel? Who was the rogue that got you with child and then left you to face the consequences on your own?"

"I—I would rather not say."

Charles stepped closer, looming over the side of her bed. "You would rather not say?" She shook her head. "I do not care if you would *rather not say*, Annabel, you will tell me who did this to you, and I will ensure that he never treats another female the way he has treated you!"

"What will you do?"

A vicious glint entered his blue eyes. "I would rather not say," he said through gritted teeth.

"Now, that is not fair, Charles—"

"Not fair? What is not fair is that my little sister will have to endure ridicule and shame for some villain's wrongdoing. What isn't fair is that my niece or nephew will be born a bastard!" Anna flinched. "Now, I will ask you again. *Who was he?*"

Charles was furious, which was a clear validation of her decision to not enlighten him as to the identity of her unborn child's father. Heaven forbid she let it slip!

"Was it one of your abductors?"

"I will not tell you, Charles." She could not let him guess the truth.

His jaw clenched, and he ran his fingers agitatedly through his blonde locks. "Then tell me this." His voice faltered. "Is it the same scoundrel that has been abusing you?"

His question came as such a shock that Anna's jaw dropped open before she could catch it. How had he known?

"I fell," she said lamely.

He reached out to touch the marks on her arm, and she reflexively flinched. *Blast.* He paused to watch her with shock and concern, then sat on the edge of her bed.

"Anna," he said, his voice softened. "Whoever taught you to flinch when a man moves toward you is a bastard, a coward...and should be punished." He grabbed her hand and held it between his own. "A man who abuses women is someone who is too spineless to take out his anger in constructive ways; he is someone who wishes to wield power over someone for his own nefarious purposes, and he is a putrid piece of a man who is going to end up burning in the pits of despair with Lucifer for all eternity." He lightly touched the bruises along her arm, then the bruise on her cheek, where a tear had left a hot trail. "The man who did this needs to be taught a lesson for his misdeeds. Please, Anna. Tell me, who did this to you?"

Anna squeezed her eyes tightly shut as more tears fell. If only she could confide in her brother. Confess to him all that had happened since her abduction. But she could not. She feared for his and for Lane's lives, both from Lord Boxton and from each other. This matter would have to be resolved, her engagement dissolved, and a new life begun, before she could tell him the truth.

Tears dripped to her hands, where they sat clasped on her lap. "I cannot tell you that, either, Charles. I am so very sorry."

He stood in indignation. "And why the devil not?"

Because I love you and Lane far too much to allow anything bad to happen to you.

A squeak escaped her as she realized she was going to be sick again. She leapt gracelessly from the bed and ran to the chamber pot that her maid had mercifully left by her bedchamber door. She fell to her knees and wrapped her hands around the pot as she cast up her accounts.

Charles moved behind her.

"Here you are, Anna." He held a damp handkerchief out to her, and she accepted it gratefully.

She dabbed at her face, wiping away sweat and tears, then rubbed the back of her neck. "My thanks, Charles." Her hands shook as she picked up the pot and quietly placed it outside the door.

As she stood, she squared her shoulders, then turned to meet Charles' gaze. "I am sorry to have disappointed you, brother. I have my own reasons for keeping this information secret, and I would appreciate it if you did not pry."

Anger once more flashed in his eyes, but he said nothing as he kissed her forehead and left the room.

Anna blew out the candles placed around her bedchamber. The firelight flickered from the hearth, lending a warm, golden glow to the walls of the room.

She was far beyond exhausted, but as she lay in bed, tears streaming unbidden from her eyes, Anna placed her hands upon her womb and prayed that all would turn out well.

Chapter 27

Lane Mason, Earl of Devon, sat at his morning room table, sipping his steaming cup of coffee. But his mind was not on his coffee, nor the partially consumed plate of eggs and ham. It was on Anna. Why had she departed so hastily last evening? And what of their impending stroll? What should he say to her? Should he blurt his feelings out or prepare an eloquent speech?

"Why are you frowning, Lane?" His youngest sister, Katherine, furrowed her brow from her seat beside him. "Is there a hair in your cup?"

He smiled reassuringly. "Thank you for your concern, sweet one, but I am fine. Merely tired. I am rather surprised at how early everyone has risen after the Merringtons' ball last evening."

The other women at the table watched him searchingly. Bridget, unlike Kat, Emaline, and Mama, gazed knowingly at him. She was far too intuitive for her own good.

Lane made eye contact with each of them, then returned to breaking his fast. They will think what they will.

"I, for one, feel rather refreshed." Kat quietly stirred her tea. "We *did* leave the ball earlier than many of the other guests. I slept for a full seven hours, I am absolutely certain. Of course," she sent a pointed glance at Emaline, "if it weren't for the dogs, we would all have slept much later. But," she brightened, "if we look at the positive in this, we will realize that we all have many more hours with which to enjoy the day." She smiled at everyone.

"Quite right, Kat." Emaline nodded, then turned to address the table at large. "I have put Tweeters in a larger cage, as Whiskers and Willie have become obsessed with the poor fellow." She took a bite of her eggs.

Bridget and Katherine smiled fondly at Emaline.

"That is lovely, dear." Mama dabbed daintily at her lips with a napkin before placing it on the table beside her empty plate. "How fares the new—"

A loud, booming knock sounded at the front door, sending the morning room into mayhem. Emaline's prized Great Dane, Artemis, leapt to his feet and let out a string of frenzied barks, which frightened the new kitten, Whiskers, into bounding off its perch on the sideboard and scampering across the table. Its little paws clumsily knocked over several cups of tea and plates of eggs, and sent the ladies into shrieks. Footmen rushed about, searching for rags and napkins to soak up the mess.

Lane stood, knocking his chair to the floor behind him as his hot coffee spilled, narrowly missing the very sensitive area of his lap.

"*Hell and blazes!*" He turned his furious gaze on Emaline, who appeared contrite, holding a napkin and attempting to clean up the table. "I would speak with you later, Emaline, about your habit of inviting pets into our eating rooms."

Her gaze lowered. "Yes, Lane. I am truly sorry, everyone."

The morning room door opened and Geoffrey entered. "My lord, a Major Bradley is here and requests an urgent audience with you."

Bridget straightened and gaped at the opened doorway, as though waiting to get a glimpse.

Lane's stomach dropped. Had something happened to Annabel? Did it have something to do with her hasty departure last evening? Or could he have learned something about their kidnappers? "Yes, I will see him."

"I have put him in the drawing room, my lord."

"Thank you, Geoffrey." He sketched a short bow to his mother and sisters. "Please excuse me."

Lane ignored the servants rushing to clean up the mess and instead focused on the thunderous beating of his heart and the rapid *clip* of his boot heels on the wooden floors. He breathed steadily through the riot of anxiety creeping its way into his chest in an attempt to calm himself.

He entered the drawing room and closed the door behind him. Charles was pacing in front of the settee but halted when Lane entered.

Lane strode purposefully forward. "What can I do for you, Charles?" He couldn't help but ask, "Does it concern Anna?"

Charles was harried, his eyes sagged with lack of sleep, and his hair was mussed, as though he had run his hands through it too many times. But what frightened Lane most was Charles' lack of control over the emotions on his face. He was worried…and he was furious.

"Yes," Charles ground out. "This happens to be a very sensitive topic and requires the utmost discretion." With a groan, he rubbed his hands over his face and dropped into a nearby mauve, floral upholstered chair. "Bloody hell. This is a seriously horrendous issue, and I have no one with which to discuss it. I do not know what to do, or how to solve it." He looked Lane in the eye. "I need your help, Lane."

158

Lane sat upon the edge of the settee beside him, fear winding its gnarled claws into his chest. "I will be happy to help in any way that I can, Charles. What has happened to Annabel?"

Charles pinched the bridge of his nose and groaned.

"Damnation, man! Tell me what has happened to Anna!"

"Two things." Charles held up his fingers. "I just do not know which to discuss with you first." He paused. "Before I impart the recent issues, I would like to pose a question to you." Lane waited for him to speak. "I know that you have already given me your account of what occurred during your abduction, but I wanted to be certain… Are you aware of any amount of time in which Anna may have spent alone with one—or, God forbid, all—of your kidnappers during your journey?"

"Yes," Lane answered without hesitation. "There was an unknown span of time in which we were both unconscious, and we were separated into different rooms in the majority of inns that we stayed at, guarded by our kidnappers." Lane's jaw ticked, and his heart flipped over. "What has changed?"

Charles slammed his fist on the side table at his elbow, which crashed to the floor with a vase.

Lane watched it dispassionately. "Not to worry, that was not of value." He leaned forward in his seat. "What, Charles, does this have to do with Annabel now?"

"Everything," he growled. "I scarcely know where to begin." He clenched his fists and trained his tortured gaze on Lane's. "Anna has bruises on her body."

Lane shook his head in disbelief. "I beg your pardon?"

Charles nodded. "Someone has been abusing Anna. She has bruises up and down her arms, her thigh, hip, and one on her cheek. She claims that she had fallen, but we know that is untrue."

Lane's chest felt tight, his breathing constricted. He did not want to believe that Anna had been the recipient of any form of violence. "How can you be certain?" he asked hopefully. "Perhaps she did fall."

Charles shook his head regretfully. "The bruises are in the shape of a man's hands." He rubbed his eyes with the insides of his wrists before he dragged his fingers through his dishevelled hair. "From what the doctor and I can deduce, those on her hip and thigh were caused by a fall, most likely due to the slap to her face."

Rage exploded in Lane. "Who the bloody blazes would *dare* to hit Annabel?"

"My sentiments, exactly," Charles growled. "I need to know who it was that did this to her."

Lane's mind raced through the possibilities. "Lord Boxton. It could be Lord Boxton. He has the opportunity due to their engagement, and they have enough privacy for others not to notice when it occurs."

"It is possible, but why would he wish to abuse his future wife? And why the devil would Anna accept a proposal of marriage from an abusive man?" Charles shook his head. "If she did not know he was abusive before she accepted his proposal, but learned of it afterward, why would she not then inform me or break off the engagement? It does not make sense."

Lane surged to his feet and ran a hand through his own hair, his mind whirling. "What if Lord Boxton has threatened her?"

"You think he is forcing her to marry him?"

"Blackmail? Perhaps he learned about our being kidnapped and is threatening ruination if she does not marry him?" He began to pace.

Charles brusquely shook his head. "That does not sound like something Anna would submit to. If that were the case, she would accept ruination and move to the country with our grandmamma."

"At the cost of ruining your chances to find a wife?" Lane pointed out. "You know that Anna would put your priorities ahead of her own."

Charles pinched the bridge of his nose, his eyes squeezed tightly shut. "I do not believe that she would submit to being abused if he were only threatening ruination, Lane." He sighed. "None of this makes sense." He paused. "This may sound terrible, but I hope it *is* Lord Boxton."

Lane frowned at him. "Why the blazes would you hope for something like that?"

"Because I hate the man. Something about him gets under my skin and festers there. He is not right. He puts on an amiable front, and Anna seems to like him, so I've gone along with it. But damn it, if he's abusing her…"

"On that, you and I are in accord," Lane jerked his head in a nod.

"I shall have an inquiry made with regards to Lord Boxton's behaviour toward women, and Annabel specifically." He clenched a fist. "I will find the man who has abused her."

"I am glad to hear it." Lane hesitated, his curiosity getting the better of him. "How is she? What happened last night at the Merringtons'?"

Charles put his elbows on his knees and rested his face in his hands. "That question," he said, his voice muffled, "brings me to the second, much worse, issue that we are currently facing."

Lane's stomach wound tighter as he waited for Charles to speak. "What could be worse than someone harming Anna?" Surely there was nothing.

Charles lifted his head and straightened, fisting his hands upon his knees. "The second issue has to do with the question that I posed at the beginning of this discussion."

"About Annabel being alone with our kidnappers." *Hell and blazes, would the man speak faster?* Lane could not stomach the suspense.

"You have confirmed that she had, in fact, been alone with your abductors..."

"That is correct," Lane snapped. "Please get to the point, Charles."

The muscles in his jaw jumped as he ground his teeth. "She is with child, Lane."

Chapter 28

Lane felt paralyzed; every part of his being stopped.

Anna is with child... My child! Suddenly his breath came fast and hard, his heart following as fast as thunder would lightning. *Sweet blazes, I'm going to be a father!*

His knees gave out, and he slumped on the settee, unable to regain control of his stunned senses.

"I can see from your expression that this has come as a shock." Charles sat forward. "You are looking rather pale, in fact, perhaps you should have something to drink."

Lane was unsure if he'd blinked in the past several moments. Perhaps he should. Yes, a blink was in order.

"No, no," Lane said absently as he internally shook himself. "I am fine," he lied.

He gulped air, and sweat began to bead on his forehead. Possessiveness swept him as he thought of what Anna carried in her womb. Regardless of whether or not Lord Boxton was guilty of abusing Anna, she would be *his* wife, not Boxton's.

"When did she find out?" he found himself asking.

"Just last evening. Evidently she had gotten ill while in Lord Boxton's company. He had retrieved Mama and I from the ballroom. We escorted her home. Lord—that is, Dr. Claridge, as he has requested we call him—was summoned immediately."

"Claridge? You mean Lord Simon Claridge, heir to the Earldom of Merrington?"

Charles nodded. "The very one. He is a trustworthy and highly praised doctor."

Unwarranted jealousy rushed through Lane, quick and searing. "Was he not a suitor of Anna's at one time?"

Charles shrugged one shoulder. "Yes."

"But does that not make things uncomfortable for Anna?"

"Not in the least, I should imagine. In fact, she has requested that he continue to be her physician throughout the pregnancy and during labour."

Lane tamped down on the inappropriate jealousy. He was to be a father, for God's sake! But how much did Charles know?

"What of the father?" Nervousness clutched him as he awaited Charles' answer. What would he do if he knew? Lane had best speak to Anna before he revealed anything, if the man didn't know already.

Charles' face grew mottled with anger. "She has refused to tell me who he is. Dr. Claridge has stated that she is approximately eight weeks into her pregnancy, which is quite early, but determines a timeline. I suspect it was one of your abductors." He ran a hand through his tousled hair. "The bastard that took her virginity will be on the receiving end of my blade when I find him."

Lane carefully avoided continuing the discussion on the babe's father. "Is Anna about, or is she to bed for rest? We had an engagement for a midday stroll in the gardens."

"When I left this morn, Anna was reading in the family parlour. She had eaten very little at the morning meal before secreting herself away. I've the feeling that she does not wish to see our parents, nor answer any questions. Mama and Papa are visiting those of their acquaintance; Anna should be pleased that she successfully evaded them." He reclined against the back of the chair.

"I would like to speak with her." Lane straightened his coat, anticipation ripening in him.

"Splendid notion." Charles stood. "You are friends with her; you should be able to glean more information from her than I ever could." He clapped Lane on the back, and they both quit the room.

They passed his butler in the hall, and Lane motioned him to follow. "I am glad you are here, Geoffrey. Please arrange to have Pegasus saddled; I aim to leave directly."

"Of course, my lord." Geoffrey bowed and sped off ahead of them.

They reached the foyer, and Lane began to pace. Charles leaned casually against the far wall, his stance one of ease, but his expression thunderous.

It was fortunate that Lane had dressed in preparation for a ride this morn. He patted his waistcoat pocket and felt the comforting bulge there. Since he had returned from his estate, he had carried it with him everywhere. One never knew when the moment would arise.

"Lane?" Bridget appeared at the top of the stairs.

He stopped his pacing as he turned to gaze up at her. "I apologize, Bridget, but I do not have time at this moment for a discussion. I am awaiting my horse and shall be on my way."

She started down the stairs, watching him uneasily. "I heard shouting a few moments ago and thought I would see if everything was well." His eyes widened, and he held up a placating hand. "I did not hear specifics, mind, but one could not help but hear you when you raise your voice." She paused. "You have me quite concerned. Has something happened?"

His jaw tightened. "Yes, but I am not at liberty to discuss the details at the moment."

She reached the bottom of the stairs.

"Nor should he." Charles' deep voice echoed off the walls of the foyer as he pushed off against the wall and strode forward into view.

Bridget visibly stiffened and turned her burning gaze on Charles. "Why are you here, Charles?" Her cheeks lost what little colour they'd had.

"I had business to discuss with Lane."

Bridget looked between the two of them. "Is there something the matter with Anna?"

Lane winced. "It is complicated."

She frowned, her delicate brow crinkling. "How is it complicated? She is either well or she is unwell."

Charles stepped forward, his heavy footfall echoing off the walls, and grabbed her arm. "For God's sake, keep out of it, Bridget!" he said gruffly.

Tears formed in Bridget's eyes, and she roughly pulled her arm from Charles' grip. Without a word, she retreated up the stairs.

"Oh, hell." Lane bound up the stairs after, catching her arm to halt her.

She brought her tearful, questioning gaze to meet his, and he smiled tenderly at her. "I will speak with you once I have returned. Not to worry, things are not as dire as they may seem." He tapped her under the chin with his crooked index finger.

Bridget pulled him into an abrupt hug.

"It will be all right, Bridget." He tightened his hold on her shaking form.

"Thank you, Lane. I wish you luck today."

He released her to press his lips lightly to her forehead. "Thank you, Bridget." He turned and trotted down the stairs, eager to be on his way to Anna.

Charles' watched his descent, his mien indecipherable.

"Bloody hell, Charles. You do have a way with women," Lane murmured as he reached the other man.

"Do shut up." Grimacing, Charles tugged on his riding gloves and preceded Lane out the front doors.

* * *

Annabel lowered her novel to her lap and looked out the window at her elbow. The leaves of the trees and garden plants flickered with the wind, birds hopped from one branch to another, and busy honey bees hovered over the flowers.

She tucked her feet further beneath her as her mind wandered. She could scarcely keep her attention on the pages of her book, her thoughts were so scattered. She should focus on devising a plan to release her from her promise to Lord Boxton, but she feared that she had run out of ideas.

Her stomach rumbled sickeningly, and she instantly regretted not having eaten more at the morning meal. Her head began to swim, and she dropped her book on the table beside her. She surged to her feet and rushed to the chamber pot that had kindly been left to one side of the room. She lowered to her knees just as her stomach lurched.

She heaved once more, but nothing came forth. Tears sprang to her eyes, and her face reddened as her stomach rebelled against her. Slowly, the wave of nausea passed, and Anna attempted to regain her breath.

She reached between her breasts in search of her handkerchief. "Oh, bother," she grumbled. She felt the short sleeves of her day dress, but failed to find one there.

Abruptly, a clean, white kerchief appeared before her blurry eyes. "Oh! Thank you, Charles." She accepted the offering and dabbed at the corners of her eyes. "I had not realized that you were home." She wiped at her lips. "How was your morning?"

"I had an unexpected visitor disrupt my morning meal with some very interesting news." Lane's deep, rumbling voice sounded behind her.

Anna gasped, spinning quickly to face him. The quick motion made her head whirl and the parlour go blurry. Then the room went black.

Chapter 29

Lane's heart plummeted as Anna fell. He swiftly moved forward, catching her in his arms before she hit the ground. He shifted his hold on her and brought her to the settee. He laid her down comfortably before rushing to the opened doorway.

"Tim!" he called, his head in the hallway. "Tim! We have need of your services!"

The butler of middling age shuffled down the corridor toward Lane. "You called, my lord?"

"Yes," Lane said hurriedly. "Miss Bradley has fainted. We require a cool, damp cloth, and full tea service, if you would."

"Right away, Lord Devon." The butler bowed and strode quickly down the hall.

Lane returned directly to Anna's motionless form on the settee, kneeling beside her. He leaned in close, pressing his lips to her ear. "Wake up, sweetheart. Wake up, my darling, and return to me."

Several moments passed before a brusque set of footsteps approached from the hallway. Lane sat back on his heels just as a small maid, carrying a large tray laden with cakes, sandwiches, tea, and other covered dishes, entered the parlour. He stood to assist her in placing it on the low table.

'Thank you." He nodded at her. "That will be all."

The maid left as Lane turned to his task. He withdrew a cool, moist cloth from a dish and placed it, folded, on Anna's forehead.

"Anna? Anna, sweetheart, please wake up." He ran his hand absently through her long locks.

Concern gripped his heart as he watched her. She breathed deeply and slowly, and her cheeks were naturally rouged, her skin taking on a lustrous quality, though one cheek sported a dark bruise.

Anger rushed through him at the sight of it, but he quickly pushed it back. Anna needed him.

Lord how he'd missed her! Her clever mind, her unabashed sense of humour…and one could not deny, her stunning beauty.

He'd thought of her beauty every night they had been apart; he'd thought of the sway of her hips when she walked, her generous bosom, her flowing locks.

Now is not the time, Lane. For God's sake, hold yourself together!

Anna's eyelids fluttered and slowly opened. She looked dazedly at the ceiling, a hand rising to the cloth on her forehead.

"I would leave it there." Lane put a hand to the cloth.

"Lane!" she breathed.

She moved to sit up, but Lane held her shoulders to the cushion. "For heaven's sake, Anna. Do not make yourself faint again. Lie still for a few moments."

She nodded, her half-fallen coiffure rubbing against the decorative material. "Why are you here, Lane? I appreciate the visit, but we were scheduled to meet at the blossom trees in," she glanced at the mantle clock, "over two hours from now."

"Your brother interrupted my morning meal with a matter of urgent business."

Anna's hands rose to cover her mouth.

"I heard some news," Lane continued, "that quite took me by surprise."

As Anna began to sit up, Lane stood and aided her into a seated position. She removed the cloth from her forehead, and he returned it to the bowl.

"I see," she said carefully. "And what news would this be?"

Lane took the seat beside her on the settee, his stare locked with hers. "I heard two things this morning." His gaze dropped briefly to her unchanged stomach, then returned to hers. "First, is it true that you are increasing?"

Her eyes watered, and she nodded, using the handkerchief that she still clutched in her fingers to dab at her eyes. "Yes," she whispered.

Pride and excitement swelled in his chest, and he could not help but smile. "That is wonderful news, Anna!" He leaned forward and kissed her soundly on the lips. Despite the desire to deepen the kiss, Lane pulled away. "When is the baby due?"

Anna's lips curved in a small, hesitant smile. "Simon has said that it will be late December or early January of next year."

"*Simon?*" Lane's eyebrow quirked upward.

He cursed the jealousy that burned in his gut and tried to ignore it. Anna's calling another man by his Christian name should not bother him this much.

She waved away his question. "I do not see how it is such wonderful news, Lane."

"How could you not?" Lane clasped her hand in his. "This is our baby, Anna! Our baby that is growing inside you at this very moment." He placed his other hand on her abdomen then kissed her again.

"While that is true, I am still promised to Anthony."

Lane straightened, determinedly suppressing the cutting insult to *Anthony's* name. "Break the engagement. Marry me."

Her eyes welled with sadness, and, he thought, fear. "I cannot."

Something was not right. Her despondent gaze revealed her true feelings; she could not hide them from him any longer. "Why?" he pressed. "What is he holding over you?"

Her face crumpled, her tears spilling over her lashes as she shook her head. Her intoxicating blue eyes were so pained, Lane's chest ached with sorrow for her. But he had to know the truth. "Was it he who abused you, Anna? Was it Lord Boxton?"

* * *

Anna's tears fell without abatement, leaving hot paths burning down her cheeks. *You cannot tell him, Anna! Think of what Anthony will do to your family if you reveal it!*

She sobbed helplessly as Lane pulled her into his arms. She wanted desperately to tell him. She wanted help to find a way out of her predicament.

"Please, Anna. It is clear to me that you are unhappy with your engagement to Lord Boxton. Is he holding something against you?" She hiccoughed, and he squeezed her tighter. "I only wish to help you."

Her resolve dwindled almost instantly. She would prove completely useless as a spy, like the one in the novel she had most recently been reading.

His concerned, chocolate-brown gaze and dishevelled countenance were too much. She moaned as more tears streamed from her eyes. "I do not wish for you to be hurt!"

Lane's mien sharpened, and he straightened; he had the look of a hound scenting a fox. He pulled back to grip her shoulders in his gentle hold. "Has he made threats? Is that what he holds against you?"

Anna could not hold it in any longer. The burden was too great to bear. She nodded, then wiped at her cheeks and eyes with Lane's kerchief. "Yes," she confessed. "It was Anthony, and yes, he is blackmailing me." She sighed. "I have thought for so long on the matter, and I have yet to find a solution that does not end in my marrying Anthony, my loved ones' deaths, or my neck in a noose."

Lane heaved a sigh of obvious relief and stiff fury. "How did he make the threats, Anna? What were they, specifically?"

She toyed with the handkerchief in her hands. In for a penny, in for a pound, as they say. "The morning that I had requested a rendezvous in the cherry blossom orchard, Anthony came to see me. He stated that he had made inquiries as to my whereabouts in my absence from London. He…called me some decidedly distasteful names, then threatened my reputation."

169

"Which you did not fall prey to," Lane stated confidently. "You would never allow the threat of ruination stop you from doing as you pleased, particularly when you knew that I had already proposed marriage."

She nodded slowly, careful not to make herself dizzy once more. "You are correct. I informed him that nothing he said or did would induce me to marry him." Lane's form wavered before her as her eyes once more blurred with the threat of tears. "Which is when he struck at my heart."

He noticeably swallowed. "Your heart?"

She nodded again. "He withdrew a pistol, waved it about, and informed me that if I did not agree to marry him, he would kill my family…and you." One tear slid down her cheek, and she brushed it away. "Since then, he has taken great pleasure in proving the power he could have over me."

Lane's jaw tightened, and his gaze hardened.

"I asked him why," she continued, "but he would not give me a reason other than the fact that he *could*."

Lane shook his head. "Monstrous men such as Lord Boxton often have no reason other than desire. A desire to possess, conquer, or control."

Anna felt the weight that had settled upon her chest lighten with the relief of confessing her troubles to Lane. She had missed him more than words could express.

"Anna." He held her hands in his. "I promise you that I will do everything in my power to help you, while simultaneously ensuring the safety of your family."

Anna could not find the words to properly express her gratitude. Instead, she flung her arms around his shoulders and squeezed him tightly. "Thank you."

Goodness, but he smelled delightful. Like warm spring air, soap mixed with horseflesh, and the lingering scent of his favourite cigars. She buried her face in the crook of his neck, her tears drying as fresh arousal took its place.

It had been so long since she had experienced his fevered touch, so long since she had received anything but pain from a man not in her family. She wanted Lane to touch her. She wanted him to be inside her, to make her feel something other than dread, sadness, and agony.

She trailed her lips up his neck to the sensitive area behind his ear. The deep rumble of Lane's groan vibrated against her chest.

Lane withdrew and stood, putting his noticeable erection at her eye level. Anna smiled and rose to meet him.

"Anna," he choked out. "I am not certain… I am… I do not know if this… Oh, *hell*." He crushed his lips to hers, wrapping his arms tightly around her.

In the interest of haste, Anna reached between them and set to unbuttoning Lane's bulging trousers. Her late-night imaginings of this moment paled in comparison to the sheer *need* pumping molten heat through her.

Lane walked her backward until she had her back pressed against the wall. As Lane's falls opened and his throbbing manhood lay in her palm, Anna realized that he had been working on the ties of her gown, which now hung off her shoulders and below her thinly clad breasts. Lane reached for the ties of her chemise, his mouth hot on hers as she smoothed her hand around his shaft.

He pulled the neckline of her chemise below her breasts and bent to cover one with his mouth.

A moan slipped from between her lips before she could hold it back. He suckled and licked, then tugged her nipple in a bite, sending a bolt of need through her.

Frustrated with Lane's breeches hampering her access to him, Anna shoved them down his legs. With one hand wrapped around his rigid length, she explored his sac with the other.

Lane groaned, the sound coming from deep within his chest. "Hell and blazes, Anna," he choked.

Before she could ask if she'd hurt him, he bent to grasp the hem of her skirts and lifted them, exposing her drawers.

He pressed her harder against the wall. "Wrap your legs around me," he grunted as he lifted her off the ground. He groaned his approval. "Link your ankles about my back." Lane reached between them to open the slit in her drawers. "My God, you're wet for me... You drive me to distraction," he breathed. "I cannot resist you."

He impaled her with his pulsing manhood.

"*Oh!*" she moaned breathily. "Lane... You have...no idea how *good* that feels."

Sweat beaded on his brow. "I do, sweetheart," he ground out. "I do."

Anna wrapped her arms around his neck and pressed her lips to his, slipping her tongue inside to play with his in an arousing, jousting imitation of the intimate act they now performed.

Lane growled deep in his throat as he pumped his hips. One hand drifted up the side of her body to cup her breast, while his other gripped her bottom, moving her in sync with his thrusts.

Her pinnacle approached suddenly, the passion of the moment taking hold of her. "Oh, Lane!" It wound tighter and tighter until it exploded in a swirling dance of colour behind her eyelids. "I love you!" she burst out, unable to halt the impassioned words at the height of orgasm.

Lane's lips curled back in an erotic grimace. He held her tighter as he pumped frantically. "I love you…too!" He abruptly stilled, his face flushed and his member pulsing within her as he spilled his seed.

For a moment, they remained where they were; their damp foreheads pressed together, one of Lane's hands palming Anna's breast, his other grasping her bottom, while Anna clung to him, wishing never to let him go.

Chapter 30

Charles sat in his tall, wingback chair, his hands fisted on the knobbed armrests as he seethed with rage.

Thomson exchanged an apprehensive glance with Brown, both of whom had come bearing unhappy news. Charles did not know which to address first. Either of the evils would do, he supposed.

His gaze flicked up at Thomson. "You say that they were last seen outside of Dover, but their trail has run cold?"

"Yes, sir."

Charles tapped the armrest with his index finger as he thought. "Alert the inns on the roads back. Have them alert us if they catch sight of them. I *will* have those bastards found." He sent Thomson a curt nod. "Thank you, sir."

He hated making the men feel awkward in his presence. He was not their superior, after all, but an equal.

Thomson nodded and sped from the room as Charles turned his gaze on Brown.

His insides twisted. "It isn't true… Tell me, Brown, that it isn't true," he implored.

Brown's young face distorted with regret. "I am afraid so, sir. The madam at Madam Bordeau's flash house confirmed it. He picks th' young women and h—hurts them." He wrung his hat in his hands as anger reddened his face. "Beats them to within an inch of their life, but the magistrate don't care on account o' them being whores."

Charles' blood roared through his veins. "And the *other* information?"

"True, as far as I can tell. They always rendezvous in public places. Don't rightly know why."

"I have my suspicions," Charles rumbled with disgust. "Thank you, Brown."

"Of course, sir." The young man bent in a short bow and fled the room.

He needed to speak with Anna. He'd given Lane enough time to attempt to glean information from her, but now he had information of his own. He supposed he could give them another moment…

Charles tapped the armrest of his chair, his mind whirling with possibilities.

* * *

Regretfully, Lane withdrew from Anna's sweet haven and lowered her feet to the ground. "Blazes, Anna. You are amazing."

He pulled his riding breeches up his legs and tucked his shirt into them, doing up the buttons of his falls.

A beaming smile lit her flushed face as she righted her skirt and covered her glorious breasts. "Thank you," she said breathlessly. "You are rather magnificent, yourself."

Pride rushed through him, and he returned her smile with a toothy one of his own. "Shall I fasten your laces?"

She nodded and turned her back to him. Though his fingers still shook with the aftereffects of their lovemaking, he managed to fasten her sky-blue day dress. Her alluring scent wafted to him, and he gave in to temptation and pressed his nose to the back of her neck.

"Mmm," he moaned, scattering kisses up her spine. "I adore the way you smell." He inhaled deeply. "Lemons."

Gooseflesh bumped her skin and with a light laugh she turned to face him. "I bathe with lemon water. It is my favourite."

"It has driven me mad for years." He gave her a quick kiss.

She tilted her head, her gaze searching. "Has it truly?" she asked uncertainly.

Lane's heart flipped over. "I must ask you something, Anna."

Before she could respond, he led her to the settee and gestured for her to sit. He lowered himself beside her as Anna fruitlessly attempted to repair her fallen coiffure.

Lane felt abruptly nervous. He took a deep, quavering breath and held it. "Did you mean it?"

Without breaking his gaze, she nodded, swallowing. "Yes. I know that you may not—"

Lane let out his breath in a relieved *whoosh*. "I do," he blurted, clasping her hands in his. "I have loved you for many years, Anna."

Her eyes widened. "You have?"

He dipped his head. "I was not aware of it until recently, but yes, I have loved you since we were very young. My marriage proposal to you, those many weeks ago, was out of love, not merely a desire to preserve your reputation." He shook his head in self-derision. "I should have told you. It was my curst fear that you did not return my affections that stopped me."

"Oh, Lane." She smiled warmly at him. "I would never have given myself to you had I not loved you." She lowered her gaze to their clasped hands. "I, however, know how men are with their affections; young men being what they are—"

"Not I." Lane cursed himself for his quick tongue and juvenile blush.

Anna's brows drew together in a frown. "Pardon? Surely you have had relations with women before."

Lane's damnable blush deepened. Blazes, he had not blushed since he was in short pants. He cleared his throat. "I have attempted the act of lovemaking on *many* occasions. But never have I once been able to complete the act." His hands tightened on hers. "Not until you. You changed my life, Anna."

A slow smile grew on her lush lips.

Despite the embarrassment riding him, Lane felt compelled to return her smile. He fingered the lump in his waistcoat pocket. *This is the moment.*

"What do you suppose we should do about Lord Boxton?" Anna chewed on her bottom lip, interrupting Lane's thoughts.

Disappointment wound through him at the loss of the moment, but he pushed past it. He would find another.

"I have a thought," he said, "but I am not yet certain that it would work. I think our best course of action would be to speak with Charles on the matter, that is, if you are willing to reveal the truth about Lord Boxton."

She nodded her head. "I believe that I am."

As though only just now noticing the tea service, Anna reached over and selected a sandwich, taking a bite.

"Anna, I had thought…" Lane hesitated, choosing how to phrase his request. "Perhaps until this unfortunate business with Lord Boxton has concluded, we could keep the particulars of our relationship clandestine—"

Anna swallowed her bite of sandwich. "Goodness, yes! I have no intention of informing Charles that—" Lane and Anna both stilled as the door to the parlour swung open.

* * *

Charles strode in and closed the door behind him, his suspicion heightened. "No intention of informing Charles that what?" Anna's face grew ashen. "*What,* Anna?"

He suspected that he already knew, but Anna and Lane were not privy to that aspect of his life.

Lane stood, exchanging a meaningful glance with Anna. "Why do you not sit, Charles? We have something we wish to discuss."

Charles sat in the deeply cushioned armchair, stiff and deliberately unreadable. "You have five minutes to explain yourself, Anna."

She visibly swallowed. "It is Lord Boxton who has been abusing me," she confessed.

Charles surged to his feet and yelled angrily, "I knew it! The scurrilous bastard is going to get what is coming to him!"

"Please, Charles. There is more that I wish to discuss with you."

I should say so. Fury still rode him from his meeting with Thomson and Brown, but he kept it in check as he faced Anna.

She took a deep breath. "He has also been blackmailing me."

Charles felt no better for having his suspicion confirmed. His little sister did not deserve such abominable treatment. Lord Boxton would get what was coming to him; Charles would make sure of it.

"What could he possibly hold against you, Anna, that you would yield to?"

"You, Mama, Papa...and Lane."

Charles' eyebrows rose. "He threatened to harm us?"

She shook her head. "He threatened to kill you." She went on to explain what had occurred the morning of her engagement, how Boxton had delivered his threats and garnered Anna's acceptance.

Charles wanted to shout. He wanted to grab her shoulders and shake her, ask her why the devil she had kept such important facts from him. He could have helped her, for Christ's sake! But he didn't. She was under enough duress with the turn of events in her life; she did not need added guilt.

She touched a hand to his knee. "I apologize for not telling you sooner, Charles."

He nodded. "I do not put the blame on you, Anna; I thank you for telling me." He turned his gaze on Lane. "What thoughts have you in mind for the villain?"

Who were Boxton's *eyes* and how did he feel they were *everywhere*? It certainly bore looking into—and eliminating.

Lane cracked a lopsided grin. "I have an idea, but I am missing an integral piece of this puzzle. I had hoped that you would be able to aid me in that area."

Charles inclined his head. "I am willing to help in any way that I can, so long as it ends in Lord Boxton ruing the day that he ever laid a hand on my sister."

"Excellent." Lane's smile grew. "This is what I'd had in mind..."

Chapter 31

Anna's heart continued to beat unsteadily as she watched the Scarsdales' guests mill about and dance in the grand ballroom. She had yet to see Lord Boxton among the colourful crowd, though having not arrived with him, she did not know how he was costumed.

She adjusted her plain black domino and hoped that no one would recognize her. She had dressed in an unremarkable, plain, long-sleeved, modest, yet slimming emerald gown. Her hair was tied in a simple knot at the base of her neck with no adornments. Utterly forgettable.

Lane had disappeared among a group of his Cambridge acquaintances, and Charles waited nearby but out of sight.

A nervous flutter quivered in her stomach as she ran their plan through her mind. The last fortnight had gone by in a haze of scheming, meetings, and secret rendezvous. Charles had assured her that Lord Boxton's "eyes" would not give them trouble, though Anna hadn't the faintest idea how he would fulfill such a promise.

She had learned several things throughout the plotting that she wished could be unlearned. They were, however, essential to the plan that would hopefully be successful tonight.

After their last encounter, Anna had no difficulty convincing Lord Boxton that she was ill. Angry though it made him, he hadn't come to call on her once in the last fortnight to express it. It also meant that she was not expected to attend Lady Scarsdale's masked ball.

Nervous anxiety quavered in her stomach and trembled her fingers. She straightened the long sleeves of her gown and toyed with the small reticule that hung from her wrist.

She shook herself. They had all memorized the plan. Behaving nervously could damage their chances for success. She must embody a character, like the enigmatic Lady Roving in Mr. Mystery's latest novel, *The Highwayman*. *Yes*. She was the mysterious Masked Lady. She attended a ball on the arm of her one true love in the hopes of destroying an infamous scoundrel, thus freeing her from his evil and manipulative clutches. She straightened her shoulders. *Indeed. The mysterious Masked Lady.*

Anna wove her way through the crowd toward the refreshment table, eyeing the masked members of the *haute ton* with the hopes of finding her quarry.

"Annabel?" A voice whispered.

Anna jumped.

"Don't turn around."

She filled a glass with punch and took a sip. "What is it, Charles?" she whispered back.

"Lady Juliana has been spreading some rather repugnant rumours about you this evening."

"Lady Juliana?" Anna's heart thumped with nervous anticipation. "What are the rumours?"

He was silent, and she feared for a moment that he might have left. Finally, he hissed, "I would rather not say."

Anna clucked her tongue. "It would not be prudent of me to go into our scheme unaware of—"

"Fine," he growled. "She has stated to many of the rumourmongers in attendance that you had spent several days in the company of rough men...and enjoyed it thoroughly."

"Oh dear," she breathed. It was close enough to the truth that it could be easily believed. "Where is she?"

"Moments ago she was entertaining some handsome gentlemen toward the north side of the dance floor. She is wearing a scarlet evening gown, with matching mask adorned with rubies, and a red-and-green tartan sash. I believe her costume is intended to be a Celtic princess of some kind."

Anna nodded, placing her empty glass upon a nearby tray. "Thank you."

"Good luck." Charles' reply rang in her ears as she spun and made her way around the perimeter of the grandly bedecked ballroom.

Lady Juliana came into her view. She was, as Charles had warned, surrounded by men and wearing an unfortunate Celtic princess costume. The evening gown clashed hideously with her orange hair. Why had she chosen that particular shade of red?

Anna pressed her back to the wall in an attempt to fade into the background unnoticed.

"Have you heard the most recent tidbit about Miss Bradley?" Lady Juliana's strident voice cut through the low hum of conversation and the orchestra's enthusiastic rendition of the quadrille. "I have been informed, by a very reliable source, that the prim and proper Miss Annabel Bradley is no longer *prim and proper.*" She tapped the side of her long nose and let out a tittering laugh that was echoed by several lower chuckles.

Anna felt an absurd, burning desire to walk over to the gossip-mongering woman and pull her hair. *Settle down, Anna,* she told herself with a secretive smile, *you will soon have your chance to end Lady Juliana's vicious tongue-wagging for good.* And my, but that would feel good. *I am the mysterious Masked Lady,* she reminded herself.

"Yes," Lady Juliana continued, "it is said that she spent several days in the company of *six* men, days *and* nights, without a chaperone." Several gasps rippled through the crowd.

A loud, male voice rose above the snickering and general surprise of the small group. "That cannot be true. I have known Miss Bradley for many years, and she simply does not seem the type of young lady to behave in such a manner."

Anna dearly wished she that she could see the face of the gentleman that had so gallantly come to her defense. Nevertheless, she was warmed by the gesture.

"I assure you, sir," Lady Juliana's brittle, shrill voice rose, "that it is true. I have heard the account personally from a very close acquaintance of Miss Bradley's."

The crowd muttered and whispered, the low hush slowly spreading through the room. Soon Lady Juliana's credibility would cease to exist, but doubt would likely linger in many a mind…and it smarted. Most particularly when Anna's *enceinte* state began to show and the truth would be exposed for all to see.

She placed a hand over her stomach in a protective gesture.

A large, shadowy man passed her, bringing her thoughts back to the present. The man smelled strongly of Irish whisky and walked with a self-confident swagger. Anna eyed him carefully. He wore black from head to toe with a black half-mask. His auburn hair and glinting green eyes could only mean one man. *Lord Boxton.*

He entered the throng around Lady Juliana, the buzz of conversation slowly dissipating. The discussion turned to the fine weather and other light banter, until the group began to disperse.

Anna continued to observe inconspicuously from her position against the wall as Lord Boxton and Lady Juliana exchanged pleasantries. Lord Boxton left to retrieve some punch, and then they danced a waltz.

The business of spying certainly had its dull moments, but the excitement flowing just under her skin was like molten lava ready to erupt in an explosion of exhilaration at any moment.

She kept her gaze on the couple as they slowly walked away from the other dancers together. Lord Boxton whispered something in her ear, and they went their separate ways. As casually as she could, Anna followed Lord Boxton as he slunk into the hallway, then up the staircase to the upstairs retiring rooms.

Anna kept her distance, ensuring that Lord Boxton would not see her. She stopped at the second-floor landing and crept her head around the corner.

The contemptible man disappeared through the doorway to one of the guest bedchambers, and the door closed quietly behind him. She waited for a moment before sneaking down the hall after him.

Her heart beat hard and steady in her chest, while tense discomfort swelled within her. She approached the door and heard voices within. Tentatively, she put her ear to the door.

"I understand that you have been spreading gossip about my future wife, Juliana."

"Oh come, darling. You know she is a lightskirt in commoners' clothing. You have said as much, yourself."

Anna clenched her jaw.

"She is soon to be *Lady* Boxton," Anthony reminded her. "She should not have so many rumours floating about; it may have an adverse affect on my own reputation."

Lady Juliana sniffed indelicately. "Be that as it may, she deserves a little humiliation before you take her for your own. She will have you, after all, and I must stand to the side."

"Come now, Juliana," Lord Boxton's voice held censure. "You know that I cannot marry you. I do not want your scandalous reputation to mar my good name and ruin my chances at inheriting my grandfather's estate in Bath." There was silence for a moment. "I will continue to see you after I am married; you know how marriages of convenience work. You are open to some very pleasurable acts that not many women will submit to, and are therefore worthy of my attention. You may not be wifely material for a man as distinguished as I, but you will do nicely as a mistress."

There was another pause. "Speaking of entertainment," Juliana purred. "Why do we not think of something more pleasant than your promiscuous wife-to-be, and amuse ourselves with something much more fulfilling?"

"I do wish that your father hadn't such strict guard on you at your home," Lord Boxton murmured. "Trysts in such daring locals could one day find us caught."

Lady Juliana moaned. "Oh, darling, but the danger makes it so much more exciting!"

The unmistakable sound of slurping lips came from the other side of the door, and Anna cringed. *It is time.*

She quickly retreated down the corridor, noting the room's precise location before descending the first staircase. Out of the corner of her eye, she spotted a reflection glass hanging in the hall, and she stopped to gaze at her reflection. *Too pink*. She reached into her reticule and withdrew some white powder and smeared it over her cheeks and under the edges of her mask, giving her a sickly appearance. *Perfect*.

She then withdrew a leaflet of parchment and a small piece of drawing charcoal and quickly jotted the directions to the occupied room. She folded the paper and tucked it in her sleeve. She returned the items to her reticule, clapped her hands together, and adjusted her gown before entering the resplendent ballroom.

Conflicting emotions ran rampant through her as she strolled among the crush. She had always been poor at playing charades, but tonight she would have to surpass every performance she had ever made. It was the performance of her life, for her life.

Charles still stood next to the refreshment table. She caught his gaze and winked one eye at him. He responded with a barely perceptible nod, then stalked through the crowd toward Lady Freeman, the greatest rumourmonger that ever was.

Anna continued to run her gaze through the crowd searching for a glimpse of Lane. Finally, she spotted him across the room watching her through the slits in his domino. Anna withdrew a fan from her reticule and fanned herself with a wink and a smile. Lane nodded.

Apprehension wove its way through her, her stomach lurching. *Calm down, baby*. She could do this.

Anna navigated the milling crush of guests, through puce, emerald, pink, peach, and the occasional virginal white, until she had maneuvered herself into the group of eager listeners standing around Lady Freeman. She felt a tap on her right hip, and then on her left, confirming that Lane and Charles were behind her. She slipped the parchment from her sleeve and held it behind her back. It was instantly taken.

"Do you think that she confirmed it? No! She vehemently denied ever having gone near it, even though I saw it with my own eyes." Chuckles, chortles, and titters moved through the moderately sized group around Lady Freeman; confirming that she was a woman with many years of practice in storytelling.

She always kept her listeners enthralled. She was a tetchy woman, when things did not go as she wished them to, and an easily excitable woman when she came across a new bit of diverting gossip. As Lady Freeman was a spinster in her late fifties, Anna could not wholly blame her for finding her entertainment in the misfortune of others. It was cruel, but Anna empathized with her probable loneliness.

The woman wore only the latest styles; this evening she wore an abundance of gilt and plum, including a purple turban with gilt rope wound around it with hanging tassels that jiggled with each movement. Her mask was an ostentatiously large and over-adorned piece that sat upon a long, painted stick, which she used to hold the mask to her face.

Anna waited until Lady Freeman's tale had come to a sensational highpoint, then readied herself for her performance.

The rumble of laughter and several gasps rose above the din, and Anna let out a cry of distress. She placed the back of her hand to her forehead and collapsed in a feigned faint. Anna put her trust in Charles and Lane, and was relieved when they caught her. A ripple of distress went through the crowd as they saw what happened.

Lane's voice above her was loud and carrying. "This woman has fainted! We need to get her to a private room!"

"My! How pale she looks!" Lady Freeman's voice grew closer.

Anna resisted the urge to open her eyes.

"Lady Freeman, would you do us the great honour of accompanying us as a chaperone as we bring this lady to a guest chamber upstairs?" Anna heard Charles say.

"I would be pleased to help." Lady Freeman sounded so elated to be included in their drama that Anna fought not to smile.

"Please excuse us, we must bring this woman upstairs." Charles' voice cut through the din of voices around them.

They began to move, her brother and love jarring her with their effort. The din of music and conversation faded, and Anna surmised that they were close to the staircase.

"Oh, dear! Is there any way that I might be of assistance?" Anna recognized the voice as Lady Scarsdale.

Lane and Charles shifted their hold on Anna, one on either side of her. Lady Scarsdale was the perfect addition to their plan!

"Yes, please," Lane replied. "I believe that a cool, damp cloth will do this woman a great deal of good."

"I will have it brought up directly." Lady Scarsdale retreated, calling orders to her footmen.

They continued up the staircase. Anna swallowed past the saliva gathering in her throat. She had not considered the possibility that the motion might make her ill. It was not the most challenging part of their plan, however. Keeping her expression blank and her eyes closed had turned out to be exceptionally difficult.

Lane shifted his arms under Anna as they topped the second flight of stairs. Lady Freeman followed, gleefully fussing about Anna's state.

Lane must be nearly ready to burst with some cutting remark or another, and Anna dearly wished she could laugh. But she kept her expression carefully blank, steadfastly dedicated in her role.

Chapter 32

They needed Lady Freeman's expertise in order to carry out this plan, so Lane bit his tongue to hold back the rude remark that threatened to escape. He could not abide gossip-mongering ladies.

Gratefully, Charles spoke before Lane could. "I believe that a cool cloth, a glass of punch, and a quiet place to sit will be just the thing, Lady Freeman. Ah," he notched his chin toward the door to which Anna had directed them, "here is a guest bedchamber. Would you be so kind, my lady, as to open the door for us?"

"Of course, young man." She moved quickly, pressing down the latch and letting the door swing wide…to reveal the most lewd scene that Lane had ever witnessed.

Lady Freeman let out a startled gasp but seemed distinctly pleased to have come across some choice fodder for fresh gossip.

Lady Juliana, who was presently tied to the four-posted bed—her legs tied high so they were lifted in the air—and gagged with what appeared to be Lord Boxton's black cravat, let out a muffled scream. The viscount, however, did not seem startled, but livid. He stood entirely nude on the bed, looming over Lady Juliana, a shining black hessian in his raised hand, and his surprisingly small cock aimed and at the ready.

Lady Juliana had welts and cuts all over her person; as though Lord Boxton had been whipping her with articles of his clothing and items about the room, in what Lane could only assume was some sort of erotic pleasure game. The sight was disgusting. If inflicting pain was what Lord Boxton enjoyed in, and out, of the bedchamber, Lane was exceedingly glad that Anna would not be marrying the devil.

They were all silent as they absorbed the scene, Lane and Charles still holding the "unconscious" Annabel in their arms.

"I have a cool compress for the young miss—*Oh*!" Lady Scarsdale, accompanied by her husband and several servants, stopped to gawk through the open doorway.

"Good Lord in heaven!" Lord Scarsdale's outraged cry sounded beside Lane. "My great aunt Gertrude's lavender counterpane!"

"Oh, my!" gasped Lady Scarsdale. "Is that Lord Boxton and Lady Juliana?"

Lord Boxton dropped his boot, balled his hands into fists, then let out a deep, barbaric growl. "*Get the hell out! Now!*"

"Er…perhaps another room would be better for this lady's recovery." This could get out of hand rather quickly, and it would be best for them to make themselves scarce before it did.

The others agreed and strode quickly to the room across the hall. Lane and Charles placed Anna gently on the bed, then put the cloth on her forehead, leaving her mask firmly in place.

The sight of Anna reclined on the bed stirred Lane's blood. He briefly wished that he and Anna were alone in the room, but he would get that chance later. And hopefully for the rest of their lives. He smiled to himself as he administered the smelling salts that Lady Scarsdale held out to him.

Anna roused convincingly, seemingly dazed and out of sorts. Lane admired her theatrical skills, pride swelling in his chest.

"Goodness," she breathed. "What happened?"

"My dear, *much* has happened!" Lady Freeman put in jubilantly, her hands clasped before her in barely suppressed excitement. "It all began when you fainted. But we have some punch for you, dearie."

"Thank you." Anna sat up, removing the cloth, and accepted the punch gracefully. "It must have been the warmth of the room."

"Yes, dearie, it must have been." Lady Freeman looked impatiently about the room. "It seems that you all have this in hand, so if you would not mind, I will return to the ballroom and leave you to recover."

Lane stifled a laugh as Lady Freeman's lips twitched impatiently. She was obviously doing her utmost to refrain from squealing with delight, positively bursting with the need to tell someone what she had seen moments ago across the hall. *All according to plan.*

"Of course, my lady. We thank you for your kind assistance." Charles and Lane bowed to her as she left the room.

"If there is anything else that you require, please do not hesitate to ask. We will leave you in the care of our staff." Lord Scarsdale motioned for his wife to accompany him. "We have some distasteful business to attend to. We wish you a good evening."

"Good evening," the three of them said in unison.

Anna sat forward in the bed. "Thank you for your aid, Lord and Lady Scarsdale." She took a sip of punch. "The ballroom's décor is beyond breathtaking."

Relief swept Lane as Lord and Lady Scarsdale took their leave, the lady distressing over her aunt's counterpane and waving her hands agitatedly. Their plan had worked thus far; it was simply a matter of time before it played out to its completion.

Anna used the damp cloth to clean the white powder from her face, revealing her beautiful, radiant skin with every wipe.

They let several minutes pass before Charles suggested that they return to the ball, to which Lane and Anna heartily agreed. They thanked the servants and left the room.

Harsh shouts and shrill screeches emanated from within the room across the hall. It would seem that Lord and Lady Scarsdale had informed Lady Juliana's parents of her indiscretion, and they were now having it out with Lord Boxton.

"Goodness." Anna held a hand to her chest as shocking language came from the other side of the door.

"Avert your ears, dear sister," Charles susurrated. "There are some things that no lady should hear."

They descended the stairs and entered the ballroom.

"Lady Freeman has been busy," Lane noted, as an excited hum of gossip resonated through the room, Lord Boxton and Lady Juliana's *affaire* on everyone's tongue.

"Indeed. The orchestra has stopped playing, as no one is dancing." Anna gazed up at Charles and Lane through her domino. "The plan is working."

"Why do we not take our leave?" Charles said in a low voice. "We have completed our task this evening, and I, for one, have seen much more than I cared to." He touched Anna's elbow and led them through the throng toward the exit.

"I concur." Lane kept pace with them. "When we formulated this plan, I had not thought we would see such a bawdy and vulgar display." A shudder wracked him. "Disgusting. You are fortunate, Anna, that you did not witness it."

An incensed shadow crossed Charles' features. Lane suspected that he knew what Charles had been thinking, but thankfully, what Charles believed was not, in fact, true. As Lane had been the one to take Anna's maidenhead, the violence that Charles likely imagined had not taken place. Anna had lost her innocence in a magical moment that continued to take Lane's breath away.

"Good evening, dear brother." Lane started at Bridget's voice as she stepped from down the corridor, blocking their path.

"What in the blazes are you doing here?" Lane growled as they halted.

Bridget strode silently forward. "This evening has proven rather more interesting than I had first anticipated." She ignored his pointed question and gazed critically at him through her shimmering silver mask. "I have a feeling that you are behind it."

Charles interjected before Lane could respond. "Whether this may or may not have been caused by us is none of your concern. Please step aside, we wish to leave."

Anna gasped. "Charles! Why in heaven's name are you being so rude?" She linked her arm through Bridget's. "I apologize for my brother's boorish behaviour." Bridget nodded but appeared markedly hurt. "Why do you not accompany us home?" Anna offered. "We will be happy to discuss it with you there."

"I do not think that is a wise idea." Charles stood stiffly in front of them.

Bridget quietly cleared her throat. "Major Bradley is correct. I do not believe that it would be a judicious decision. Besides, it is clear to me that I am unwelcome."

"Balderdash." Anna frowned at Charles. "Do not listen to what he says."

"Anna..." Charles said through gritted teeth.

She released Bridget and stepped toward Charles, her shoulders squared. "You helped me a great deal this evening, and I thank you for it. But I will not stand by and allow you to verbally abuse a wonderful woman who used to be your closest friend. I do not know what occurred between the two of you, and I shall not pry, but you shan't cut her out of my life as you have yours." She linked her arm through Bridget's. "You are welcome to join us in the family barouche, or you may find your own way home; the choice is yours. Good evening."

She turned with Bridget and returned to Lane's side, before they strode out of the corridor and into the foyer. Lane had to admire her strength. She was a remarkable woman.

"Anna!" Charles marched after them. "Anna, you will not speak to me in such a way."

"I believe that I just did, brother." They continued to walk through the foyer.

"As your older brother, and the acting male authority in this situation, I demand that you treat me with respect."

Anna noticeably seethed. "I will respect you, dear brother, when you have earned my respect. Your treatment of Bridget was unwarranted. I simply stated how it was perceived and indicated that I would not stand for it. You have made the cruel decision to alter your personality for the worse. I will not have it in my presence."

Lane was fascinated by their family dynamic. Anna was a fearsome woman. Judging, however, from Charles' glinting eyes, he was capable of far more than he displayed. Lane would hate to discover what the man would do should he uncover the truth—that Lane had fathered Anna's child.

Chapter 33

The ride to the Bradley household was silent and tense. Charles chose to ride a borrowed horse, much to Anna's consternation. She was dumbfounded by his discourtesy. Before he had gone to war, Charles was a kind, gentle, loving man, but he had returned cold, distant, and quick to anger. There were moments, of course, in which she saw the old Charles shine through, but the majority of the time it was a thin veneer of congeniality over poorly banked fury.

They rounded a corner, and her stomach turned. Anna abruptly wished that she had eaten something from the refreshment table. She quickly removed her domino and took a deep breath.

"Are you feeling well, Anna? You appear pale of a sudden." Lane leaned forward to squint at her pallid complexion.

Anna could not do more than hold up her hand in response and turn to look out the window. It was dark, but it helped slightly.

Slowly, the barouche came to a stop, and Lane leapt out, handing first Bridget down, then Anna. Warmth spread through her as he held her hand longer than propriety dictated. Her stomach lurched.

He leaned down to whisper in her ear. "Are you well?"

She took a deep breath of the blessedly cool night air. "I shall be, once I eat something."

"Noted."

She wrapped her hand around Lane's elbow and allowed him to lead her into her family's town house, where she greeted Tim.

"Finally arrived, have you?" Charles appeared from within the doorway to the front parlour, his frown fierce.

"Shall we gather in the parlour?" Anna's voice quavered when she spoke. She was eager for some of Cook's teacakes; without them she would surely soon embarrass herself.

Charles called to Tim over his shoulder as he led the way to the parlour. "Do have a tea service brought to the parlour, will you, Tim?"

Anna vaguely registered Tim's response as she focused on not casting up her accounts on the way to be seated. She did not look forward to the conversation she was sure would come. Charles would not wish to involve Bridget in their family's secrets, but Anna valued the woman's friendship.

The fire blazed high in the hearth, casting a bright glow on the walls and creating a warmth that comforted Anna's nerves.

She scarcely took notice as Lane closed the door and took the seat beside her.

Charles sat on the chair nearest Anna and leaned forward, appearing suddenly concerned. "Anna, are you quite all right? You look ill."

She gulped at the air, focusing on not becoming ill. "Food," she grunted. "I need food." She took slow, deep breaths while Lane strode to the door to bellow for tea.

Bridget strode forward. "Is there anything I can do for you, Anna?"

Anna hesitated to open her mouth, so she merely shook her head slightly. Hopefully she did not offend Bridget by not speaking to her.

"Just the food; I understand. We will have it for you directly." She gave Anna's hand a light pat before she moved away.

* * *

Lane stood to one side of the room, watching Anna with worry clutching his heart. Increasing women sometimes got ill, but Anna had been doing so with alarming regularity.

"When were you planning on making this right, Lane?" Bridget whispered from beside him.

Lane's brows drew together. "Whatever do you mean?"

Bridget tilted her head in exasperation. "You know precisely what I mean, do not pretend otherwise. I am not as ignorant as you would like to believe, Lane." She glanced meaningfully at Anna, then turned to pin Lane with an intense stare and continued in a harsh whisper. "That poor, ill woman is *enceinte* with *your* child." She ignored his stunned expression. "So I will ask you again, when are you planning on making this right?"

Nervous anxiety sank sickeningly in his stomach. "How in blazes did you know that?" Lane hissed. "And...er...please do not repeat that. Even to Charles."

"Of course I would not betray yours or Anna's confidence. I am not the kind of... Wait a moment. Do you mean to tell me that Charles is not aware of Anna's current state?"

Lane cast a furtive glance at Anna and Charles to ensure their conversation was private. "Yes, he knows. He is simply not aware that…that she and I…" he cleared his throat, "of who fathered the child."

Awareness dawned in Bridget's eyes. "Ah." She inclined her head. "I see. Well then, brother, once again, your secret is safe with me. But you must know that Anna does not deserve the ridicule should you not give her—and that child your name."

"Yes, I intend to make this 'right,' as you say." He eyed her crossly. "I will ask you again, Bridget, how did you know?"

Bridget shrugged one delicate shoulder. "Women tend to see the signs of such things, and as I am familiar with Anna, I saw the changes in her."

A knock sounded at the door, which Lane spun to open.

"Your tea, sir." Two maids entered, arms laden with overflowing silver trays.

Charles directed them to the table beside Anna, then ushered them out and closed the door.

"Your sustenance, Anna." Charles sat across from her and helped himself to a plate of sandwiches.

Anna sat, white as parchment, with a hand to her stomach. Disgusted, Lane marched to the table and filled a plate with teacakes and sandwiches.

He sent a steely glare at Charles with a grunt of derision. "What has happened to you, Charles? Have you no sense of awareness?"

Lane then poured steaming tea into a cup and added several lumps of sugar and a generous helping of cream, just how Anna preferred it.

Charles scowled at him in confused anger. "What?"

"Anna was correct. You have not changed for the better."

Lane turned and knelt before Anna. Her complexion had gained a tinge of green. He held the teacup to her lips and let her drink. Once half the cup had been consumed, Anna slowly brought her hands up to hold the cup on her own, then eagerly finished the tea.

"Would you care for your plate, or would you like more tea?" The vice around Lane's heart eased with relief when she looked at him and smiled.

"The plate, thank you."

Lane placed the plate on her knees. "It is my pleasure."

* * *

Charles sat at his ease, eating a delectable cucumber sandwich. He knew that his behaviour was abominable, but he had no intention of changing. His profession and his family's safety depended on his ability to continue on this mien. He would not fail them.

"Shall we discuss what happened this evening?" Bridget's voice cut through the air of the close room. "Whatever it was that you three did, it caused quite the stir."

Anger and resentment burned through Charles at the sound of Bridget's voice. A part of him wished that he could take back his decisions and actions of the past years, but that was an impossibility. He must continue working to protect those whom he loved.

At any cost.

"I hardly think that it is any of your business, Lady Bridget," Charles derided.

Hurt clouded her eyes even as she kept her expression carefully blank. Lord, but he sickened himself.

"Shame on you, Charles," Anna said weakly. "You know better than to behave in such a manner. There is no harm in telling Bridget what it was that we did this evening.

Charles let his gaze travel over Bridget's entirely too tempting body as she came to sit beside Anna, but he forced himself to close his mind and his heart to her charms.

Despite Charles' protests, Anna enlightened Bridget as to the night's activities.

"You three have gone to great lengths to sentence Lord Boxton and Lady Juliana to a lifetime in an unpleasant marriage. What I fail to understand is why. You appeared taken with him at the beginning of the season, Anna, whatever happened to alter your opinion of him?"

Charles pasted a smug smile on his lips as Anna flicked a glance at him. It would seem that his little sister had not thought that she would be required to explain her reasoning for ending her engagement in such a spectacular way.

"Do enlighten us, sister," Charles watched her with his hard gaze. It had been her choice to bring Bridget into their private affairs, not his.

She toyed with the material of her emerald skirts.

"I believe that this is an adequate moment to end this conversation." Lane put a teacup and saucer back on the tray. "It is plain to see that Anna is exhausted, and we all require rest. Tomorrow should prove to be another busy day, and I for one, would like to be refreshed while I face it."

Compassion lightened Charles' chest at his sister's downcast expression. "Perhaps it is best if you do not share what occurred, Anna. There is no sense in putting undue strain on yourself." *Or the baby. Good God, my sister is pregnant!* He still could not quite grasp the concept. And he still intended to flay the man who…impregnated her.

Bridget leaned forward. "If it distresses you, Anna, I am content with not knowing this aspect of the story."

Anna shook her head. "You are my friend, Bridget. I wish for you to know the truth."

Charles pressed his back against the chair and extended his legs toward the fire as he listened to Anna speak. He'd be damned if he left her to face retelling the story alone.

Chapter 34

The fire burned low in Anna's bedchamber, its light casting an orange glow about the room. She had already snuffed her bedside candle and put away her book, but was unable to fall asleep. She lay reclined on her large bed, staring at the ceiling, her mind replaying the events of the day.

The evening had been a success. Lord Boxton and Lady Juliana had been caught in their tawdry and disgusting act, and Bridget was now a party to the intimate details of Anna's life. She trusted Bridget, and it would be nice to have someone in which to confide should she need the friendly ear.

Profound relief overwhelmed her. She had begun to fear that she might be stuck with Lord Boxton forever. But now that she had enlisted the aid of her brother and Lane, she did not have to hide behind the façade any longer. The threat of tears stung behind her eyes as her chest welled.

The ticking of the mantle clock sounded loud in the quiet room, the echoing *tick-tock* a constant reminder that she was exhausted and should rest. But couldn't. Lord, but she wished she could sleep.

She closed her eyes and thought of pleasant things. Hot chocolate, books, the scent of a flower, a hot bath… *Lane* in a hot bath. Lane's well-formed body, his defined muscles and masculine shape…

Heat began to sizzle through her, and she fought a blush at her indecent thoughts.

A small *thump* echoed in the hallway just outside her bedchamber door, causing her to jump. *Jittery ninny*, she chided herself. She detested sounds that went bump in the night; in the books she read, they often led to someone being kidnapped or attacked in one way or another. Having lived through an abduction did not lessen her fear.

She rolled to her side, tucking herself snugly beneath the covers.

A loud click echoed in her room and Anna sat bolt upright, holding her bedclothes against her chest like a shield. *Foolish Anna!* She stared wide-eyed at her bedchamber door as the latch slowly pressed and the door swung inwards.

Her heart thumped wildly with fear as she grabbed the long candlestick from her bedside table and wielded it like a weapon. The snuffed candle rolled to the floor with a muffled *thud*.

A shadowy figure moved just outside the ring of flickering firelight, and her hands trembled.

"Come any closer and I will scream loud enough to wake the dead." She raised the candlestick above her head in warning.

A light chuckle sounded as the door closed. The dark shadow of a man moved toward Anna and she quickly inhaled, preparing for an ear-splitting scream.

"No, no! Anna, it's me!" Lane's hushed whisper sent relief flooding through her, and she let out her breath in a *whoosh*.

"Oh, thank goodness! You scared me half to death!" She lowered the candlestick-wielding arm. "What in heaven's name are you doing here?"

Lane neared her bed, the light from the fireplace illuminating his handsome features. "Are you displeased that I have come?"

She blinked. "Not at all. I merely find myself curious as to why."

"I did not know if I would be welcome." He twitched his head in a short shake. "I have no pure motive for being here, other than the need to be with you."

Her lips pulled back in a toothless smile, her eyes squinting with both fatigue and pleasure.

He reached across her body and removed the candlestick from her hand, then placed it on her bedside table. "Did I disturb your sleep?"

Anna clasped his hand and pulled him down beside her on the bed. "No. I have not been able to sleep."

"Shall I tell you a story?" His hushed voice was low with a pleasing rumble that vibrated in her chest.

With a dreamy smile, Anna nodded and nestled against her pillow. Lane removed his boots and settled cross-legged on the bed at her hip.

"Once upon a time there was a little boy. He lived on a grand estate with his family in the country. This little boy had a very, *very* good friend who happened to live on the neighbouring estate."

Anna grinned as she caught on.

"The boy and his friend," Lane continued, "spent their days acting silly and gambolling about, terrorizing their siblings and governesses.

"As they grew, they spent fewer days acting silly and more days strolling through the garden, playing cards or chess, reading to one another, and engaging in deep discussions on art and literature. Without this young man's knowledge, he began to fall helplessly in love with his friend." Lane clasped her hand and ran his thumb over her knuckles. "He found himself thinking of her frequently, wondering how she fared or what she thought." His warm brown gaze met hers. "One day the

194

man and his friend were drawn into a wild and perilous adventure. It frightened the man, for he had not realized just how much his friend meant to him until her life was in danger."

Anna watched his unwavering eyes, unmindful of anything but their chocolate-coloured depths.

"That man wants nothing more than to take his friend as his wife…*if* she will have him."

His hand appeared between them, a ring pressed between his forefinger and thumb. Anna's eyes widened as she sat up, a lump lodged in her throat.

"Yes," she croaked, nodding ecstatically and she flung her arms around his neck. "Yes, I will marry you, Lane!"

Her heart thundered in her chest as Lane pulled back to slide the ring on her finger. Goodness, but it was beautiful! The band was gold with a leaf-like design engraved on the sides, while in the center was a cluster of large diamonds in the shape of… Her damp gaze flicked up to his. "Cherry blossoms."

He nodded with a grin. "Do you recall our last game of chess?"

"As I recall, I trounced you." She laughed.

"You did. I also promised you a prize." He looked pointedly at the ring. "I had it especially made with our favourite spot in mind. Now you can enjoy the blossoms even when they are not in bloom."

"Oh, Lane…"

She moved to kiss him once more, but he halted her. "If you wouldn't mind, Anna," he grimaced, "I would prefer to keep our engagement clandestine until I have the opportunity to speak with your father."

Her chest swelled with joy as she smiled into his concerned gaze. "Of course, Lane."

His expression cleared and he swooped in for a kiss. It began slow, but built ever more passionately, until he had lowered her back onto the bed.

* * *

Lane awoke sometime later as the predawn light lent a milky glow to Anna's bedchamber. Memories of the night flashed through his mind's eye.

Anna's pretty blushes, her sighs and moans of delight. The first time had been fast, hard, and powerful. Perfect to slake their lust. But the second…the second time had been slow, leisurely. He'd taken his time tasting every inch of her, bringing her to peak with his lips and tongue. It had been an utterly arousing experience, and one he would never forget.

Anna's mantle clock ticked loudly, forcing Lane to recognize the danger of tarrying any longer. The household staff would rouse soon, and he daren't be caught.

He willed his body to calm as he turned to look at Anna. Her eyes were closed in slumber, her eyelashes dark crescents on her flushed cheeks. He could scarcely believe his good fortune.

I am engaged to be married! To Anna! A smile cracked his lips, and his heart skipped several beats.

He would send Mr. Bradley a missive after the Parliament meetings to request an audience with him. But for now, he must return home.

It took mere minutes for him to gather his clothes, dress, and slink from the room.

Chapter 35

Anna gazed at her reflection in the looking glass above her dressing table as Marie styled her hair. She'd hidden the beautiful ring Lane had given her among her jewellery, to be worn only when out of sight from her family. She could scarcely believe Lane had proposed! What a wondrous feeling!

She had slept remarkably well after the…*activities* of last evening. Lane had done something with his tongue, that… She fought a blush as Marie tugged on a lock of hair. Goodness, she should not think of such things, enjoyable though they were.

She took a deep breath to calm her suddenly racing heart. They should wait until they were wed before they continued to enjoy the delights of the bedchamber, but Anna could not resist the pull of desire to be with the man. What more could possibly occur? She was already *enceinte*, for pity's sake.

The sound of birds chirping happily floated in through the window, and Anna grinned. It was a bright, sun-filled day, and she intended to enjoy it fully.

"There you are, Miss Bradley. Pretty as a picture, as always." Marie smiled at her as Anna stood to examine her reflection in the tall mirror.

She wore her pale-pink morning dress, which brightened the colour in her cheeks, and her hair was fashionably styled with coils and ringlets bouncing about. Her body appeared smaller than her ordinarily plump shape, which was distressing. Her nausea, and constant fear while being engaged to Lord Boxton, had caused her to lose the soft edges to her frame. She rather missed them.

She turned with a smile, while her stomach ached with hunger pangs. "Thank you, Marie."

Anna hurried down to the morning room, but paused before she opened the door. The rumble of her father's and Charles' voices and the higher lilts of her mother's came from the other side. Nervousness gripped her. Since learning of her increasing state, Papa had been both disapproving and frequently absent. Anna knew not which he disliked more, her refusal to reveal the father of her baby or the simple fact that she was no longer a maiden.

Mama had been surprisingly compassionate and understanding, however, about which Anna was supremely relieved.

She rolled her shoulders, took a deep breath, and pushed open the morning room door.

"Anna, dear!" Mama beamed from her seat to the right of the table's head. "Good morning!"

Anna smiled hesitantly. "Good morning, Mama. Papa."

Her father scarcely glanced at her over his morning paper.

A little disheartened, Anna turned to Charles who sat on the other side of Papa. "Good morning, Charles."

He sent her an apologetic smile and a bright "Good morning" as she passed him on her way to the sideboard.

The aroma of the morning meal lightened her disposition. She selected a plate and piled it high with ham, eggs, toast, and fresh fruit. Anna took a deep, appreciative breath as she returned to the table.

"I see that your appetite has returned, Annabel." Tentative relief flowed through her as Papa eyed the food on her plate.

"Yes," she admitted. "This morning, I awoke feeling refreshed and quite ravenous."

"That is wonderful, my dear." Mama smoothed a silver strand of her hair and patted Anna's hand, an enthused smile on her wrinkled lips.

"Whatever has you so animated this morning, Mama? Has a new shipment of fans been delivered to—"

The newssheet appeared before her eyes, and her gaze flicked up to Charles, who wore a scowl fit to rival Mama's exuberance.

Her gaze flicked about the table, worry gnawing at her. "What has happened?"

"Read this column." Charles reached across the table and pointed to the opened newspaper before her.

Her heart pounded as she read the article heading. It was a review of the Scarsdales' ball last evening. She continued reading.

It was an event-filled evening last night at the beautifully bedecked Scarsdale masked ball. The costumes were creative and colourful...

Anna scanned down the column past the dresses and attendance.

By far the most interesting—and scandalous—event of the evening was the hasty announcement, by Lord B and Lady J, of their impending nuptials. This came as quite a shock to the members of society, as most were already anticipating the upcoming wedding of Lord B and Miss A. B.

Lady J already has an infamous past filled with shocking, hoydenish behaviour and illicit liaisons, or so gossip has told us. Could this unfortunate circumstance bring Lord B lower on the proverbial social ladder? This columnist believes so.

But we must think of the woman he left behind. It must have been something of a surprise to Miss A. B. as she reportedly fled the ball on the arm of her brother, the strapping Major B, and Lord D, after coming upon the unsightly scene of her intended and Lady J en flagrante delicto.

* * *

Anna gasped. "How could they have known it was us?"

"I daresay we were difficult to miss upon exiting," Charles growled. "Or it could have been Lady Freeman. She could very easily have guessed our identities and spread the word around the ballroom of not only what she had seen, but our involvement, as well."

Fear swiftly replaced the elation she had felt this morning.

"Could this not mean that Lord Boxton will know that we were behind the ill-timed exposure of his depravities and subsequent engagement? Do you not fear that he will take his anger and disappointment out on—" She broke off, unable to voice her fears.

Mama wrapped an arm around her shoulders. "Do not worry, my dear. We will keep Charles indoors today as the excitement settles."

Charles shook his head. "I am afraid that is impossible. I have a luncheon appointment that I cannot miss." He paused to send a pointed look at Anna. "If your next inquiry is regarding Lane, he will also be unable to remain indoors, as Parliament is in session today."

Charles had assured her that they would have nothing to fear from Lord Boxton, or his "eyes," but without learning the details of his plan, Anna could not be certain of its veracity. She must send a missive to Lane.

"Stay safe, Charles."

He nodded, one cheek puffed with an overlarge mouthful of food.

She cleared her throat, dropping the paper to the table. "I assume that Charles has enlightened you both as to the events of last evening?" She swallowed convulsively. "And the reasoning behind it?"

A shadow of anger covered them.

Papa leaned forward, seemingly incensed. "Yes, Anna. Charles informed us of Lord Boxton's despicable behaviour. I must say that I am both shocked and appalled. I wish that I had known; I would have refused to allow his courtship of you. The man is a disreputable blackguard, and I am glad to be rid of him."

"Thank you, Papa."

"I am greatly displeased that you did not inform me of your attendance at the Scarsdales' ball last eve. I had not even known that we'd received an invitation until Charles mentioned it this morn."

Mama took a sip of her tea while Charles and Anna muttered their apologies.

"Was it as beautiful as the columnist implied?" she asked.

Anna swallowed a mouthful of food before replying. "Yes, Mama, it was quite resplendent."

"Tell me, what did you wear?"

"My emerald evening gown with a black domino."

Her mother scoffed. "Such a simple costume for such a grand event?"

Anna had thought that it accentuated her generous curves rather well, plain though it was.

Charles dabbed at his lips with a napkin and placed it beside his empty plate. "I fear I must leave you." He stood and replaced his chair beneath the table, then sketched a bow. "Good day to you all."

Anna squelched her nervous anxiety and bid Charles a good day as he quit the room. Would Lord Boxton accept his fate with Lady Juliana, or would he attempt to seek retribution by following through with his threats?

She finished her breakfast, not out of a desire for food but for mere distraction, as her mother discussed her latest shopping excursion and teas with her acquaintances. Papa read the paper silently before retreating to the library. Finally, Anna had concluded breaking her fast and excused herself from the table.

In the interest of saving time, Anna sped to her brother's study. She procured a piece of parchment and a quill and sat at his desk to pen a note to Lane.

Dearest Lane,

I assume that you have read the paper this morning, but in the event that you missed the gossip column, I felt the need to warn you. Our names were revealed in connection to the events of the Scarsdales' ball last eve, which concerns me greatly. Please be cautious in your activities today, as I fear that Lord Boxton might seek to make good on his threats.

On a more pleasant note, I am always *pleased to have your company, no matter the hour.*

All yours, with love,
Anna

Anna grinned as she blotted and folded the missive. It was so naughty of her to be so forthright in her desire for Lane. Perhaps she was a hoyden, after all. She sealed it with her brother's wax and seal.

As she was about to stand, a letter on Charles' desk caught her eye. She ran a finger over the intricate seal at the bottom of the page. *Who in heaven's name could this be from?* The letter was not signed, and the words on the page were nonsensical. She squinted at the delicate writing for several long moments before she shrugged. Charles had some very peculiar friends, evidently.

She strode from her brother's study and down the corridor into the foyer. An unfamiliar footman stood by the door, and she smiled at him. "Would you have this delivered to Lord Devon, please?"

"Right away, Miss Bradley." He sketched a bow and left to do her bidding.

In a mere matter of minutes, Anna was settled on the cushioned window seat in the family parlour with a book in her hands. She had come to sit on this very seat as a young girl during the season. She had never truly enjoyed routs, soirées, balls, fêtes, or teas, but had vastly preferred the company of a good book. Or Lane.

Such was fine with her. She rather enjoyed her life, without Lord Boxton in it.

She settled herself comfortably and began to read.

Anna did not know how much time had elapsed since she began, but all too soon a knock sounded at the door. She looked up as the door crept open and one of their downstairs maids entered.

"I apologize for the interruption, Miss Bradley, but this just came for you." Henrietta came forward and handed a sealed missive to Anna.

Her heart leapt as she recognized Lane's handwriting. "Thank you."

"If I may, miss, luncheon has been prepared. Would you care for a tray?"

"I will take my luncheon in the dining room, if it is not too much trouble."

"Oh, it is no trouble at all, miss. I will have it set out directly."

"Thank you, Henrietta."

The maid bobbed a curtsey and left the room. As the door closed, Anna eagerly tore the seal and opened the missive.

My lovely Annabel,

I appreciate your concern with regards to my safety. I assure you, I remain safe.

As I am sure you are aware, Parliament is in session today, which I shall attend. But you have my word that I shall send you a missive when I return home so you are assured that I am well.

I am delighted that you enjoy my company, as I am rather addicted to yours. I must warn you that I intend to visit more frequently.

All my love,
Lane

Anna's heart fluttered as she folded the missive. She hadn't truly thought that he would risk their being caught just to visit her in the night again. A quiver of anticipation rippled through her abdomen at the thought. He must feel for her what she felt for him.

Tonight, she would be ready for him.

Chapter 36

The afternoon moved just as swiftly as the morning. Anna ate a plentiful luncheon, bathed, then sat, inelegantly slumped, in her favoured armchair in her bedchamber.

Sometime in the afternoon, she received a second missive from Lane informing her that he had returned safely to his town house after an uneventful session of Parliament.

Birds chirped outside the window, the bright light of the day slowly fading as evening took its place. She'd heard the faintly muffled comings and goings of her family and the servants shuffling about, completing their duties.

Their housekeeper, Mrs. Johnson, moved about so quietly and discreetly that Anna often forgot that she was there. But this household could not function without the housekeeper's excellent contributions. When Anna was a little girl, she and Lane would jest that Mrs. Johnson was a myth; that the other servants had created the tale of her work and her office sat vacant below stairs. On more than one occasion, she and Lane would sneak into the bottom floor in an attempt to uncover her empty office. But as ever, there Mrs. Johnson sat, diligently working through the menu for the sennight.

Anna was accustomed to the usual comings and goings of her family and the staff; the noise was comforting to her. She had spent many days in that very seat, and even more in the family parlour below stairs, reading her beloved books and sipping at her hot chocolate. Her family understood that she enjoyed her solitude, just as she understood their need to bustle about.

The past fortnight had felt different, however. She had life growing inside of her. She had fallen in love with her closest friend, been kidnapped and nearly forced to wed an abominable man. She no longer read her books as an outsider dreaming of a life of adventure that she could only attain through fantasy. She *was* like the heroines in her books!

Now, reading about kidnappings, sword fights, and all sort of escapades no longer seem so foreign. She knew the fear these fictional women would feel; the excitement of running through the forest and into the hands of safety; of loving and being loved. That knowledge lent that much more delight and depth to her books.

Even now, her heart was still rapidly beating after reading one particularly exhilarating description of a fistfight between the hero and villain of Mr. Mystery's latest novel. It brought to mind the bout between Lane and Frenchie ten weeks ago, which still put fear into her.

A knock pounded her door and Anna jumped in her seat. Charles poked his head through the doorway.

"Oh, hello, Charles." She smiled at him.

"Good evening, Anna." He smirked in return. "Will you be joining us for supper?"

"Is it that time, already?"

"I would think that you would have been aware, due to how famished you have been of late." He winked playfully at her, opening the door fully.

"Of all the nerve!" She stood in mock righteous indignation. "You dare say that to a pregnant woman, you knave."

The humour in Charles' countenance faded at the mention of her current state, but he made a valiant attempt to hide it. "I believe we should put our battle of wits to the test, dear sister, and engage in a game of chess after supper."

"Prepare to be trounced," Anna warned. "What will I receive when I win?" She put her book on her vacated seat and walked to stand before Charles.

"When *you* win? I think not, little sister. When *I* win, you will reward me with the book of my choice from Hatchard's."

"Ooh! Splendid choice! That will be precisely what I will accept from you when *I* win."

Charles chuckled, and Anna blew out a breath of relief—the tension between them had dissipated. She fell into step beside him as they walked through the corridors toward the dining room.

* * *

Charles silently seethed. He would find the blackguard that impregnated his sister and he would see the man hanged for his crimes.

Anna and Lane's abductors had, as of yet, eluded him, but he would be damned if he stopped searching. If only he could ride out himself…but no. Anna needed him here.

With Boxton's men neutralized, he had fewer concerns with his sister, but Boxton himself could still very well be a viable threat. Indeed, he must remain in London.

* * *

Anna ran a brush through her damp hair as she sat before the hearth in her bedchamber. The heat from the fire warmed her through her night rail, and the brocade rug was soft beneath her bottom.

The early evening sun had begun to hide itself behind the plentiful buildings of London town, sending streaks of orange light reaching through her large window.

Her stomach was full of roasted beef and Yorkshire pudding, and her mind was swimming with the night's events. Mama had monopolized the supper conversation, discussing the new clothing that Anna would be required to purchase once her current wardrobe no longer fit her growing belly.

She was grateful that her parents had not demanded answers as to the identity of the baby's father. She was not prepared to tell them, yet. Perhaps once she and Lane were properly engaged, or even married. Heaven knew what Charles would do once he learned the truth.

Despite the anxiousness roiling in her stomach, Anna smiled at the memory of Charles' expression once he'd realized that he would lose their chess game. He had made an admirable attempt at beating her, and he had nearly done so, but the game had concluded with her as the victor. She very much anticipated their excursion to Hatchard's.

A light laugh escaped her as she continued to brush her hair, stroke after stroke.

"You have beautiful hair." The low rumble of Lane's voice sounded behind her.

An unbidden squeak escaped her as she jumped and spun around. "Lane! Good heavens, you frightened me right out of my skin!" She brought a hand up to cover her rapidly beating heart. "How did you enter so silently?"

He lifted the boots he held in his hand. "I have found that when one wishes to be stealthy, lighter feet and soft stockings tend to render one nearly soundless. I waited until I saw the light in Charles' study ignite before I ventured inside. He will likely spend hours pouring over correspondence and other such paperwork, so we must be quiet."

Anna nodded. "My parents have been to bed for an hour, at least, and they are able to sleep through anything."

"So you are aware, I sent your father a letter this afternoon. I am not certain whether or not he has received it, but I hope to seek an audience with him on the morrow."

Anna's lips quirked. "He reads his correspondence in the morning."

His gaze flicked to her brush. "May I?" He notched his chin toward her, and she nodded.

He quickly joined her on the rug, settling himself close behind her. He removed the brush from her loose fingers and stroked it through her locks. She had never had a man brush her hair before. It was a highly intimate and... *erotic* experience. She could feel the heat radiating off his body behind her, and the grazing of his knuckles on her back as he ran his free hand through her hair after each pass of the brush.

They sat like that for quite some time. Anna closed her eyes, enjoying the bristles massaging her scalp and the arousing scent of cigars, brandy, and soap emanating from behind her. She inhaled, letting her head fall back as Lane's actions filled her senses.

He slowly slid her hair aside and placed a soft kiss on the side of her neck, sending a shiver up her spine and gooseflesh dancing over her body.

"Mmm..." she moaned.

He kissed her again, sliding his lips leisurely along her neck. He tossed the brush aside and placed his hands on her hips, gliding them over her waist and fisting them in the material. His lips were hot, his hands even more so.

Anna's breathing became erratic as need wove through her. Abruptly, Lane spun her and dipped to catch her lips on a gasp.

Instinct drove her as she reached for the silver buttons on his grey waistcoat. Lane tugged at the knot of his cravat. Soon, he was on his knees, pulling his white lawn shirt over his head while she reached for the fall of his trousers.

He groaned as she brushed her fingers against the bulging weight of his erect member with every button she unfastened. Finally, his manhood sprang free, and she released a delighted hum. Lane hastily kicked his trousers aside to land in a heap with the rest of his clothes, while Anna enjoyed the sight of him.

Lane was a strikingly gorgeous man. From his tousled blonde hair, knowing smirk, rippling muscles, and shapely, but highly muscular legs, to his amazing and utterly attractive personality. Anna's gaze travelled over his arousal and felt immediately swathed in blazing heat.

In one smooth motion, Anna lifted her night rail off and flung it atop of Lane's clothing pile. An empowered smile touched her lips at his swift intake of breath. She loved that she affected him as he did her.

She placed her hands on his warm chest and pushed him backwards until he lay flat on the rug. She took her time exploring his body, pausing at the scar on his right arm from the bullet that had grazed him. She kissed the reddened tissue before moving on to the rest of him.

He was warm, hard, and soft in all the desired places. She used her mouth, tongue, and teeth to tease, lick, and nip him, similarly to what he had done to her the night before. She delighted in returning the pleasure.

She assumed that one particular act, which he had most wonderfully performed on her, could likewise be done to him.

Slowly, she kissed her way down his body, then the tip of his stiff manhood. Lane gasped, and his member leapt before her. With a smile, she slid her tongue up and down his smooth skin, then around the tip. Heartened by Lane's rapid breathing, she became more daring. She grasped the base of him in one hand and put the tip in her mouth. It was rather interesting. Salty and velvety…and entirely arousing.

* * *

Lane choked out another garbled gasp as Anna created suction with her mouth. *Thunderation!* He had always wondered what this particular pleasure would feel like. Now he knew. He had thought to ask for the experience before, but had never summoned the courage. Hell, he very much wished that he could allow it to continue. Unfortunately, he was perilously close to coming off in her hot little mouth, and he much preferred to climax *with* her.

She bent further over him, her hair teasing his hips as she took more of him into her mouth.

Lane groaned. "Sweet blazes, Annabel. You need to stop."

She lifted, her lips leaving him with a *pop*. Uncertainty and disappointment clouded her features. "I didn't do it correctly. I didn't pleasure you, did I?"

Lane let out a startled laugh. "Anna, if you had gone on for a single moment more, I would have finished our evening before it had even truly began. You are extremely talented in that regard, I assure you."

Her Machiavellian expression returned to her face, accompanied by a self-satisfied grin that made his heart flip over in his chest.

She moved over his body, and he gripped her hips, guiding her where he wanted her. She nipped at his neck, then smoothed the sting with flicks of her tongue.

Lane could not suppress the moan that escaped as Anna grasped his cock and guided it into her slick heat, settling herself atop him. Her hair hung around them as she began to rock back and forth, and her gloriously full breasts bounced and swayed with her every movement. By damn, he could never have his fill of this woman. *You are magnificent.*

"Why, thank you," she breathed.

He hadn't realized that he'd spoken aloud. "It is the truth," he grunted.

Giving in to his desires, Lane cupped her breasts, pinching her nipples and rolling them between his forefinger and thumb.

Anna's eyelids closed on a moan. She was getting closer, he could tell. He hoped he could hold out long enough for her to find her pleasure.

Suddenly, her rocking grew ragged, her breath halting. Her head fell back as she bit her lip to keep from calling out.

The sight pushed Lane over the edge, and he let himself go, growling as he spilled himself inside her.

With contented, panting breaths, Anna rolled to the floor beside him, resting her head on his heaving chest.

"Goodness!" she breathed as she pressed a kiss to his glistening chest.

Lane's lips pulled in a crooked grin. "Come," he murmured, rising from his reclined position and taking Anna with him.

He lifted her in his arms and carried her to the bed, placing her gently on the turned down mattress. The bedclothes were crisp, clean, and cool to the touch. He slid in next to Anna and pulled the counterpane over them.

He wrapped his arm around her shoulders and settled her tightly against him. How could he have been so fortunate as to find a perfect woman? Not only had he discovered a consuming love, but he had also realized the remarkable delights of the bedchamber. This woman. This bloody remarkable woman had brought him into an entirely different life. And he would never let it go.

"I love you, Anna." Lane closed his eyes, enjoying the sound of their combined breathing.

"I love you, too, Lane." Anna's muffled voice was the last thing Lane heard before he fell into a deep, satisfying sleep.

Chapter 37

Anna shifted in her sleep as a soft sound woke her from a dream. She ignored it and turned onto her side, her eyes still closed.

A soft knock echoed against the wood of her door, and Anna's eyes shot open.

The unmistakable sound of her bedchamber door's latch being pressed sounded next, and her heart immediately began a frantic, terrified pounding. Impossibly, time seemed to slow as she reached for the thin cotton of her bed sheet and the door swung open.

"Terribly sorry to wake you, Anna, but I had been meaning to ask you about the—" He froze. "*What the bloody hell is going on?*" Charles roared, waking Lane.

Anna sat bolt upright in bed, holding the sheet up to cover her breasts, while Lane leapt, stark naked, from under the counterpane.

Before she or Lane had any time to react, Charles strode forward and punched Lane in the face, sending him falling back against the mattress.

"Lane!" Anna shuffled forward on the bed, still with one hand on the sheet for modesty's sake. "Lane, are you all right?"

Lane held a palm to his face with a grumbled "hell and blazes."

"*You bloody, ignoble wretch!*" Charles curled his lip in disgust. "All of this time you have been feigning innocence while I labour at discovering the father of my sister's unborn bastard child. And it was *you!*" He bent at the pile of clothes on the floor, picked up Lane's trousers and threw them at Lane as he righted himself. "Cover yourself. I have no desire to see your naked arse."

Anna's heart thundered. "Charles, do not do this!"

Charles pointed a finger at her, his irate blue gaze pinning her on the spot. "You and I shall discuss this later."

Lane stepped into and buttoned his trousers just as Charles stepped forward to punch him again. The *smack* of their skin connecting and the awful *crunch* made Anna cringe.

"Charles, stop!" she cried.

"I expect silence from you, Annabel." He didn't take his furious gaze off of Lane.

"He is correct, Anna." Lane held a placating hand up to her. "I deserve what he is to give me."

Anna bristled. "You do *not* deserve it!" She turned her gaze on her enraged older brother. "Charles, this is not what it seems."

"No?" His frosty regard chilled her to her bones. "He is *not* the father of your unborn child? He did *not* allow me to believe that it was one of the scoundrels that abducted you? It was *not* he who abandoned you when he discovered you were with his child, and leave you to that rogue Lord *bloody* Boxton?"

Oh dear. "He…yes. Yes, it was he. But there—"

"That is precisely what I thought." His eyes flared with hatred and rage as he glowered down at Lane sitting on the edge of the bed.

"We are to be married!" Anna blurted.

"*The hell you are!*" Charles roared.

Gathering her courage, Anna slid from the bed holding the sheet to her front. "Charles, listen to me—"

"I shall not!"

"Damn it, Charles!" Lane said over him. "I *have* proposed to your sister. *Twice*, in fact."

Anna stepped forward, her heart in her throat. "Please understand. I accepted Lane's proposal, Charles. This baby will *not* be a bastard." Her voice strengthened as she defended her unborn child.

Charles' visage was dark and frightening as he stared her down. "*If* Lane lives past dawn."

"*What?*" Her face grew ashen.

"As I am a gentleman and do not kill men in their skivvies—and in the presence of women—I will see you on the field of honour at dawn, Lord Devon. Choose your weapon."

"*No!*" Anna screeched. "I will not allow you to fight!" Anna's heart plummeted, leaving a sickening hollowness in her chest.

"Pistols," Lane grumbled.

Charles sent him a curt nod. "I will see you at dawn. Now get the hell out of my home."

Lane began gathering his remaining clothing and putting it on.

"I repeat," Anna said rigidly, "I will not allow you to fight! There must be some other way to resolve this."

Charles rounded on her. "If you think I will so much as entertain the idea of listening to your lies right now, Annabel, you are sadly mistaken. I have asked you countless times for the identity of the heartless cur that put his bastard inside you, and not once have you said that he was, supposedly, a friend to this family. You allowed me to believe that you had been *raped*, for God's sake, Anna!" He shook his head in disgust. "I have all the information I require at the moment. You are not to see Lord Devon any longer, and you will begin packing your trunks tonight. You leave for Hertfordshire in the morning."

Anna felt certain that her pale cheeks had turned a sickly green. "Pardon?"

"You heard me correctly. You will remain at the familial estate until the end of your confinement, at which time the baby will be given to a distant relative—"

"No!" Anna bared her teeth at him. "You are not my father, Charles. You have *no* right to dictate to me—"

"I will do whatever *I damned well please* when you behave like a *bloody harlot* in my home!" He heaved a heavy breath, his fists clenched.

Hurt lanced through Anna's chest, and tears sprang to her eyes, the curst things.

"That is uncalled for, Charles." Lane stepped between them, his waistcoat unbuttoned and his cravat hanging limp from his hand. A thin line of blood ran from his nose, down around his mouth, and along his jaw, until it dripped down his shirtfront.

Charles' face reddened, and the veins in his neck began to bulge. Anna feared he might have apoplexy.

"It damned well is," Charles protested.

Her brother had been a soldier at war for several years, but never once had Anna seen this side of him. She had witnessed him upset and had seen him hide his pain behind his jokes, she had even observed him angry a time or two recently, but not like this. *Never* like this.

Was this who he was as a soldier? Was this his demeanour when he fought and killed in battle? Lord, but she would hate to face this man again. She wished that the old Charles would return, the one from before the war—the loving and carefree brother who would have seen this situation as grounds for a marriage, not a duel.

"Charles," Anna pleaded, "you are cross now, but what of the morrow? There is no need to go to such extreme measures. Surely you will see things in a different light once you have separated yourself from it for a night."

"The devil I will," he spat. "You've become a whore and our *family friend* has dishonoured his own good name by lowering himself to the despoiler of virgins."

Wholly without her control, tears overflowed her eyelids to leave hot trails down her cheeks. She turned her gaze on Lane, who had pulled his coat on and was attempting to knot his cravat without the aid of a mirror.

She must stop this duel. She went to Lane, desperation driving her. "Lane, you do not have to do this," she whispered in his ear. "Please. Run away with me to Gretna."

She could feel him shake his head. "Your brother deserves to have satisfaction," he whispered back to her. "I will not harm him, Anna, my love. I will not shoot."

Anna tightened her hold on him. "I do not wish for you to be hurt," she said helplessly.

"*Enough!*" Charles barked, pushing them apart and scowling down at Anna. "You two have spent more than adequate time in each other's company. I believe you should be packing, Annabel." He sent her a warning glance then turned to shove Lane toward her door. "Get out."

Lane turned to glance over his shoulder at her before he marched through the doorway.

Desperate, Anna grasped for Charles' arm and spun him around. "Please, Charles! I implore you to see that we love each other!" For the briefest of moments Anna thought she'd seen regret in his gaze, but his countenance hardened to stone so quickly, she was unsure. "I love Lane."

His lips curled back in revulsion. "*Love*," he snarled the word, as though it left an ill taste on his tongue.

He brushed her off, unintentionally knocking her off balance and sending her stumbling back. She quickly righted herself, but when she looked back at the doorway, Lane and Charles were gone.

How could such a peaceful, *wonderful* evening have concluded so horribly? Anna closed the door, tossed down the sheet, and strode angrily to her wardrobe. How could Charles have behaved so abominably? And how could Lane have accepted this fate as thought it were an expected punishment?

She pulled a lilac, front-lacing travelling gown from her wardrobe and laid it on her bed. She might as well keep herself busy, for she would get no rest tonight.

* * *

Lane nudged Pegasus in the ribs as they hit a straight patch of road. His nose and jaw were still throbbing with the pounding of his heart, but the trail of blood on his face had dried and crusted, making his skin pull with every movement of his mouth.

He should not have been so careless this evening. He should have left before submitting to sleep.

Well, if he were to be honest with himself, he would admit that there were many things that he should have done, beginning with not taking Anna's maidenhead at all. He could not regret it, however. Annabel was beyond anything he had ever imagined possible.

Lane rounded the last corner before coming upon his town house. The air was crisp, the night dark, and the roads of Mayfair all but vacant. He pulled up the drive, leapt down, and walked Pegasus to the stables. The household and the stable staff would be asleep in their beds; he would need to care for Pegasus on his own. That suited Lane fine, for it would allow him time to reflect on his idiotic actions.

There would be no hope for sleep as he faced certain injury, and probable death, come dawn.

Lane brought Pegasus to his stall and removed his saddle.

One of Emaline's cats perched curiously on the side of the stall and watched as he brushed Pegasus' coat and prepared him for the evening.

He had not lied to Annabel when he had said that he would not shoot her brother. Charles was justified in his anger, overreact though he did, as Lane had indeed ruined his sister. It was unfortunate that Charles had caught them together this evening, as Lane had intended to speak with Mr. Bradley. The cruel irony did not escape him.

Lane finished with his gelding and left the stall, closing and latching the door behind him. He turned to look back at Pegasus' large, brown eyes over the stall door, then pulled an apple from a bucket and held it out to him. His horse gently accepted the apple and munched while Lane rubbed his nose.

"That is a good fellow."

He inhaled a deep breath, taking in the scent of horses, leather, manure, and fresh hay, letting it out in a gusty sigh. What a fool he was.

He turned and strode out the large stable doors, closing and latching them behind him.

Lane shook his head in self-derision as he rounded the side of the town house toward the front steps. He must focus on what was to come. He had plenty to do before the night was through; the first of which being that he required a second for his duel. He did not have any friends of whom he could request to fill that position. He could convince his valet, Peters, or the head groom, Jenkins, to be his second, but neither would be pleased or very willing to do so.

He suppressed a groan as he opened the front door. He must clean his duelling pistols and settle his affairs, for Lord knew this night might very well be his last.

Chapter 38

Anna lay curled on her bed in the darkness of her bedchamber. The fire had died to only a few embers, and no candles had been left burning. Hours had passed since she had dressed and resolutely *not* packed her belongings.

Charles was being unreasonable. Surely come dawn he would see that she and Lane were meant to be together.

Her head ached from lack of sleep…and the abundance of tears that she had shed. She had listened to Charles pace angrily below stairs in his study, though he had grown silent some time ago. He was likely pouring over the books at his desk or cleaning his pistols.

Tears stung her dry eyes once more at the thought of Lane and Charles duelling on the field of honour. She had read about duels, and not one had ended with both parties uninjured. She feared for Lane in particular, after his statement regarding not shooting. Anna suspected that Charles was entirely earnest in his fury toward Lane and indeed intended to do him harm.

She must devise a plan that will render both Charles and Lane unharmed, and her unmoved from London. Perhaps she could appear at the duel, deliver a clever speech, and prevent them from shooting.

She did not know where the duel was being held. *Drat.*

Oh, but perhaps she could saddle Lady Maximus and follow Charles at a discrete distance when he departed.

She could feign digestive distress and earn Charles' sympathy and forgiveness… *No.* She could not be so deceitful to him. As dangerous as the course of action might be, following him was the only plan that could potentially prevent death or serious injury. Neither man would shoot if she stood between them.

Anna swung her feet over the side of the bed and sat up. She must begin preparations.

A loud thump suddenly echoed behind her. Anna surged to her feet and spun around. She blinked into the darkness but had difficulty seeing anything discernible. It was possible that she had placed her book precariously on the edge of her reading table and it had merely fallen to the floor…

The dark, sinister form of a man appeared before her now-opened window, and fear prickled up her spine, raising the hairs on the back of her neck.

"Lane?" she whispered cautiously into the darkness.

It was a foolish question. She knew it wasn't him; Lane stood tall and proud, his hair and familiar body clearly discernible, even in the darkness. *This* man—whoever he was—was a colossal, looming man; his hair was dishevelled and he hunched to one side.

The dark mass moved closer, and her heart plummeted. Anna instinctively reached to her night table and fumbled for her candlestick, her gaze trained on the man in her room. *Oh, Lord.* The familiar, ghastly scent of acrid body odour wafted toward her, and she abruptly realized who had entered her bedchamber—who had returned for her.

She took a cautious step backward, gripping her paltry choice of weapon tightly in her hand. She *must* reach her bedchamber door. Keeping her rapid breaths as silent as possible, Anna took another step backward.

Her back pressed firmly against a solid, decidedly human form, and her hope fled. Terror clawed its way through her.

Anna took a deep breath and prepared herself to scream, but a firm, filthy hand covered her mouth before a sound could escape. She knew what would come next, and she wanted no part of it. She would have to fight her way out. And if she did not succeed, she intended to do a significant amount of damage while trying.

She pushed past her repugnance at his unclean hand, opened her mouth wide, and bit him as hard as she could. The man howled, yanking his skin from between her teeth.

Anna rounded on him with the candlestick. She hit him everywhere she could, as quickly as she could, before she hurled her weapon at the approaching second man. She picked up her skirts with one hand and ran for her bedchamber door, screeching as loudly as her voice allowed.

Her hand scarcely touched the door's handle, when she was caught from behind and dragged backward. Anna kicked and flailed her arms, inflicting as much damage was possible, her voice growing hoarse from her screams.

Surely, she had made enough noise to alert someone?

She heard movement below stairs, and hope flared in her chest. The man with his arms around her body tightened his grip as the second man quickly bound her wrists and ankles, despite her struggling. She bucked and continued to scream until fabric was wrapped over her mouth and tied at the back of her head. *Double drat.*

Anna stared, wide-eyed with hope, at her bedchamber door, willing Charles to come to her aid. Mama and Papa slept through most anything, but Charles…

One man's breath brushed her ear as he groaned, lifting her in his arms. In a joint effort, the men hefted her bodily and tossed her out the opened window.

Time slowed. Anna's heart all but halted in her chest as she fell through the air. *This is it. This is my last moment alive.*

A muffled scream followed her descent; she was certain that the sound was hers, but she could not know for certain.

She waited for the ground to break her fall, but two large male arms caught her out of the air. The man lifted her over his shoulder with a grunt. Relief briefly rushed through her as she realized that she would not die…but dread quickly followed.

She was being kidnapped…*again.*

* * *

Major Charles Bradley sat behind his desk and attempted to read through a very disconcerting letter. Not only had his men been unsuccessful in searching for Anna and Lane's abductors, but The Boss had also sought him out to issue threats once more. *Damnation*! He would have to increase security.

A *thump* sounded above his head and he glanced toward his study's ceiling. Anna must have dropped a book on the floor. He turned his attention back to the letter in his hand.

He felt guilty about his comportment tonight, but he'd had no other option. If this letter was any indication of the peril that loomed over his family, he should have secreted them away a fortnight ago. As for his behaviour toward Lord Devon… the man deserved far worse than what Charles would give him.

A deep howl and a screech sounded above him, bringing him to his feet. *Was that Anna?* The screeching continued, accompanied by heavy thumping.

Charles dashed to his study's door, tugged it open, and ran down the hallway.

"*Tim*!" he called as he ran.

He sped through the hallways and a flight of stairs, until he came to Anna's bedchamber door. He tried the handle, but it was locked.

"Anna?" He listened at the door, but heard nothing. "Damn."

He took several steps back and ran at the door, hitting it with his shoulder. He heard a small crack, but stepped back and hit the door once more.

"What in heaven's name is going on?" Mama shuffled down the hall wearing a robe and her large lace bedcap. 'Why are you hitting Anna's door, Charles dear?"

"Because my intuition tells me that Anna is in trouble."

He ran at the weakened wood and hit it with his smarting shoulder one final time. With a loud *crack*, it splintered from the doorframe.

"Oh, my!" Mama gasped as Papa appeared behind her, blustering.

Charles' stomach sank as he looked about the room, then at the opened window. He ran to it and saw a hook, often used on naval ships, curved into the window's frame, a rope dangling from it.

The predawn light lit the back garden well enough that Charles could see that Anna and whomever was with her were no longer in sight.

"Bloody rotten hell."

"Language, Charles," Papa chided. "Though I share your sentiments entirely."

Mama pointed to the floor with one slender finger. "What do you suppose this is doing here?"

Charles rushed to her side and stopped her before she picked the item up. "Just a moment, Mama." He knelt down to examine it. "It is the candlestick that Anna keeps on her bedside table. And it has blood on it."

Charles ignored his mother's fearful gasp as she clutched to Papa's side, despite the fresh fear burning through his own heart. This could only mean one thing. The Boss had returned for Annabel.

Chapter 39

Lane Mason, Earl of Devon, stepped down from his phaeton and onto a covered and discrete section of Holland Park. There was a chill to the air, and a low mist had settled overnight, creating a calf-deep blanket of fog.

He had not slept in the hours since he had left the Bradley town house, though it was very likely that he would enter into the eternal sleep very shortly. He'd spent the past hours sending letters to his estate, his family, his solicitor, and preparing his last will and testament, ensuring that he included his and Anna's unborn child in his entails.

Peters descended the phaeton behind Lane, the box containing his duelling pistols under one arm. Lane genuinely wished that he had not put his valet in this position; of course, if he was making wishes…

The rumble of heavy hooves pounding toward them took Lane out of his reverie. He took a deep breath, rolled his shoulders, and turned to face Charles as he rode, hell bent, up the path. Charles, however, was not accompanied by a second, as Lane had expected. In fact, he appeared pale and drawn.

"There will be no duel this morn," Charles stated baldly as he pulled to a stop.

Lane's heart beat frantically in his chest. *No duel?* What could possibly have occurred to change his mind? Anna?

"I accept, but—"

"Anna has been taken," Charles announced.

"Pardon?" His heart stopped. "No. No, this couldn't be. It must be some mistake. She must have found an isolated place to read, or—"

Charles grimaced. "I heard her struggles, Lane."

A nauseating lump formed in Lane's stomach. "We must find her. What clues have you?" He strode back to his phaeton, motioning for Peters to follow.

Charles shadowed them on his horse. "I have already concluded that it is the same group of villains that abducted you both in April. But I must inform you now that I simply came here to call off the duel. I must find her on my own."

Lane froze, then turned to stare incredulously at Charles. "Like hell you do!"

"I understand that you had a…a *physical* relationship with my sister, but it must go no further than that. I would prefer you not accompany me in searching for her, and I would prefer it if you did not come calling on her any longer, either. The 'friendship' between the two of you, and between our families must be dissolved."

Lane's heart tripped over in his chest. "The devil you say!" Anger joined his fear and anxiety, as he glared up at Charles. "There is nothing that *anyone* can do to keep me away from Anna. She is the woman I love." He disregarded Charles' scowl. "She means everything to me. I understand and acknowledge that you disapprove of our union; however, that will not stop me from pursuing her to the ends of the Earth. She has already agreed to become my wife, and I intend to have her, no matter what you have planned to keep us apart."

Charles' horse shifted under the tense pressure of its rider.

"It seems we are at a stalemate." Lane held his hand out to Charles. "Shall we agree to disagree?" He waited. "We are wasting valuable time…"

The man growled before extending his hand and shaking Lane's. "This does not mean that I condone a relationship between you and Anna. This is simply an acceptance of your offer for help in finding her."

Lane nodded his understanding. "I intend to stop at my town house to retrieve my horse, as with him I am able to keep up a more punishing pace. Do you suspect that they will attempt to continue their journey to Dover?"

Charles gave a terse nod. "I expect that is the case."

"I shall need to pack a saddlebag, then. Perhaps it would be wise for you to pack a fresh set of clothes for Anna, as well. She would likely appreciate something clean to wear when we find her."

"I will meet you at the docks in half an hour. If you are late, I shall ride on without you." With a click to his horse, Charles was off down the path.

Lane stepped up to his perch on the phaeton and waited until Peters was settled before he picked up the reins and drove them home.

He *would* find Anna. No matter what it took.

* * *

Anna brought the goblet of water greedily to her chapped lips and savoured every last drop. She hadn't a concept of time since these men had taken her again, but she suspected that several hours had passed since she had been kidnapped from the comfort of her bedchamber. She could guess the time from the hunger gnawing at her stomach, and Lord, but she was hungry! She hoped she vomited on one of them; they certainly deserved it.

Billy reached across the hack and took the goblet from her trembling fingers. She heartily wished that they had given her a piece of bread with the water, but she supposed she must be grateful for the small relief she was provided. Patience was a virtue, after all.

Charles was likely searching for her, and in that she took comfort. He had spent many hours searching for these very men since the moment she had been abducted with Lane eleven weeks ago.

Had Lane and Charles followed through with their duel? Had either of them been injured? She hoped that they were both safe.

She shifted in her seat. It felt as though each hack she entered was increasingly ill sprung.

"Quit yer squirmin' missy." The man she remembered as Toby nudged her in the ribs.

Anna mumbled an apology and gazed out the grease-streaked window. Clouds hung low in the sky, threatening rain.

She had been through this and had found a way to escape before; she could do so again. This time, however, she did not have the protection and companionship that Lane had offered her during her last experience with these barbarians.

She surreptitiously glanced at each of the men. Toby was as large as she recalled, with undistinguishable matted-brown hair and squinty eyes. Billy's broken arm had obviously healed, but he used it hesitantly. Frenchie eyed her with vindictive intent. He was evidently harbouring resentment and anger at her and Lane for having escaped them. The fourth man drove the hack but was one that she recognized. She did not know his name; his face, however, was one that could never be forgotten, with his flaming red hair and horrid scars…

Anna returned her gaze to the scenery that moved swiftly by. The hack jostled them as it hit a rut in the road.

She could not put all of her hopes on being rescued. Did these men intend to interrogate her…or kill her? She had faith in Charles, but Anna suspected that she must rely on her own wits. She needed to find a way to escape. Quickly.

* * *

Lane nudged his knees into Pegasus' ribs, causing the beast to break into a run. Despite the constant ache of worry in his chest, he relished the raw power of his black gelding running beneath him, the wind flying through his hair, sending the tails of his coat flapping behind him, the sound of Pegasus' panting breaths, and the constant ache through his body from hours on travel. He was on the road, on his way to finding Anna, and that thought kept him pushing forward.

What a sight he and Charles must make; both wearing all black, so as not to be noticed come sundown, and both riding large black mounts. Charles' stallion was a larger beast, but Pegasus was just as swift. Charles also wore his sword attached to his belt, as though it were another appendage. Comfortably.

They galloped side by side as if the hounds of hell were after them. They had stopped at several inns, and until they had reached the North Star Inn, Lane had begun to fear that they would not find their trail. Thankfully, the friendly barkeep had seen the unforgettable visage of the fourth kidnapper, whose name Lane had not learned. This confirmed their suspicions that the kidnappers and Anna were once more headed southeast toward Dover.

Lane did not know for how long they had been travelling. At least one night had come and gone, but his lack of sleep had melded days into one. They had eaten and taken short refuge at few inns at Charles' insistence. If it had not been for Charles' argument that their horses required water, feed, and rest, Lane would have foregone respite altogether.

He pushed harder, keeping pace with Charles, until he heard a loud "Ho!" He glanced sideways, slowing his mount to match Charles'.

"What is the problem?" Lane shouted over the rush of blood in his ears.

Charles nodded down the road. "Ahead."

Lane followed his line of sight and saw a rider barrelling toward them. He immediately put a hand to his ribcage, resting over the comforting form of his pistol. In the interest of arriving prepared, Lane had placed one pistol in his coat pocket and one in the back of his breeches. Those, in addition to the dagger he'd hidden in his boot, were the only weapons on his person, but they should be enough.

"At ease, Lane. I know this man."

Lane returned his hand to Pegasus' reins, his kidskin gloves grinding as he squeezed.

"Mr. Thomson," Charles called to the approaching rider.

"Hyd—er...Major Bradley." He saluted Charles then turned and nodded to Lane. "Lord Devon. I come with news."

This was the mysterious young man with whom Charles had been travelling all those weeks ago.

"The young miss and her captors have travelled to Canterbury, where I believe they mean to stay the night. They have acquired a hunting cabin and a small estate. The two sit nearby one another; Miss Bradley resides in the cabin and the four villains in the other. I believe it is possible to retrieve Miss Bradley without alerting the men."

"Good work. Please pass the message on to Brown and Davis. Rendezvous at the hunting cabin once you have completed your duties. You know what to do."

Mr. Thomson saluted. "Yes, sir." He bowed his head at Lane. "My lord."

Lane inclined his head. "Mr. Thomson." The man galloped away, and Lane turned to gaze questioningly at Charles. "Who was that man, and how did he know to look for Anna?"

Charles shrugged as he pushed his horse into a canter. "He is an acquaintance who owes me a debt. I sent a missive to him when I returned home to retrieve a fresh frock for Anna."

Lane followed, disbelieving. "He would ride out in the light of predawn merely at your behest?"

Charles' gaze was shuttered. "He owes me a very *great* debt." He clicked to his mount, pushing him faster. "We know the destination we are to reach before nightfall, Lane. Let us not tarry. On to Canterbury."

* * *

Their journey was long and arduous. Charles was cross with him; that much was evident. The tense silence Lane had endured since they departed, however, was nearly more than he could handle.

His love lay in God knew what sort of peril, at the hands of men who, no doubt, felt bitterness and resentment towards her. Lane hoped that they kept their hands to themselves. As much as he hated to admit it, even to himself, the likelihood of Anna's escape was very slim. Those men had already been outwitted and would presumably fortify their efforts at keeping her in their clutches. Lane still embraced the hope, however, that Anna was well and fully safe.

Charles slowed his horse, and Lane followed suit, pulling up to a canter beside him.

"Knowing what we do about these men," Charles called, "I believe we could safely assume that they are on the outskirts of Canterbury. That they would doubtless take roads not oft travelled to reach their destination." They pulled their mounts to a halt at a crossroads. Charles looked down a dirt road to their right and then back at Lane. "What are your thoughts?"

Lane blinked; taken aback that Charles would think to ask him his opinion. Charles had taken the lead since they had begun their search; it was unlike him to seek advice. What were his motives? "Do you inquire because you genuinely wish to know my thoughts, or simply to be polite? If it is the latter, you are wasting valuable time." He had not intended to sound so noncompliant.

Charles turned to him with a scowl. "I resent your presumption that I would waste time with meaningless inquiries. If you have nothing useful to contribute, Lord Devon, I will thank you to kindly shut up."

"Such inspirational words, Major," Lane snapped.

"If you wish to continue on your own, please do. I believe I will take this path." Charles led his horse toward the side path, when Lane stopped him.

"I must give you credit, Charles; you *do* have nerve. Although, I had hoped you would not show it at this moment. We should remain together, no matter how much you wish to be rid of me."

Charles leapt from his horse and strode angrily toward Lane, who had dismounted as well. Anna's brother clearly had issues with anger, superiority, and resentment. None of those had a place in their current venture, and Lane would make sure that Charles knew it.

Lane prepared himself as Charles pulled his fist back and punched him in his already bruised jaw. Pain speared across his face, and he staggered back.

Charles entered the ready position for a proper match, but Lane merely shook his head to clear it. He experimentally moved his jaw. "Are you quite finished?"

"Fight me, damn it!" Charles put up his fists and circled Lane.

"I have no wish to fight you, Charles. You may hit me if you wish, but as far as I am concerned, we should be en route to rescue Anna." He paused. "Why do you wish me to fight you? Now that I think on it, why did you call me out when you could have merely allowed Anna and I to marry?"

"You have no right to question me, sir, when you should be questioning your own behaviour."

Lane frowned. "What of my behaviour?"

"You took advantage of Anna's innocence and vulnerability, then got her pregnant with your bastard!" Charles exploded venomously.

"I will have you know that I have loved Annabel since I was sixteen. I may have only discovered my feelings for her recently, but that does not change the fact that they are of long duration, deep, and true.

"You, contrarily, informed *my* sister that you loved her, left for battle, then returned only to spurn her!" A blanket of white rage came down over Charles' expression. He opened his mouth to undoubtedly utter a hot retort, but Lane cut him off. "Meanwhile, your beloved sister has been kidnapped by men who unquestionably wish to harm her—or worse—and you are wasting precious time by standing here arguing with me. I may not be the brother by marriage that you desire, but that is not a reason to hate me.

"My unborn child was not created in the despicable manner that you imply." Lane could not help but defend himself on that score. "If we are to continue to search for Anna in an amicable fashion, you must first overcome your resentment toward me and accept that I only wish for what is best for her. I love her, and believe it or not, I do like you." He shrugged one shoulder. "Although God knows what horrible things happened during war to have you turn into such a damnable bugger."

Charles stared at Lane in silence, his jaw working as he absorbed Lane's speech.

"As for your original inquiry, Charles, and in the interest of speeding things along in our search, I rather think that Anna's abductors would continue on the main roads. They know that we would assume otherwise."

Charles' expression was blank for a moment, then he exploded. "By damn, why did I not think of that?" He ran a hand agitatedly through his hair. "You are right, of course. I have been thinking only of myself, and not the tortures that Anna must be enduring at this moment. I am willing to call a truce until we recover Anna. Any outstanding issues we may have can be resolved another time.

Chapter 40

Anna shifted her seat on the hard stone floor. Her bottom had lost its feeling several hours ago, but she knew that if she did not shift, she would only be in more pain. She had several smarting bruises on her person; most were from rough handling from her captors, but the others were from kneeling and shifting on the hard ground of the cabin or from falling sideways and needing to right herself.

While her wrists and ankles were abraded and bleeding from her attempts to pull herself free, she was grateful that they had not gagged her again. The fabric had dried out her mouth, and it tasted horribly.

Her stomach had surpassed hunger long ago, and now bordered on starvation. She had been kept satiated on minimal amounts of water, but had not received any food. She had gotten ill several times, and once, she was slightly pleased to recall, on Toby. He had not looked so smug when she had cast up her accounts directly on his chest.

A cool breeze whistled through a crack in the cabin wall, and Anna shivered. The cabin was chilled and dark, and it smelled of must and dirt. The windows had been boarded over, but Anna was certain that it was nightfall. She was weak and dizzy, but she forced herself to focus on finding a means to escape.

She rolled her hip and pulled her tied ankles beneath her, then pressed her back against the wall and, using all her strength, slid herself awkwardly up until she stood. She waited a moment for her dizziness to pass before she hopped about the cabin. She first tried the door and windows, but with her hands tied behind her back and her ankles tied, her mobility was woefully restricted.

Her gaze darted around the space. There was a tall, narrow table, counters in the kitchen space, two empty bookshelves, a tall mirror, a wardrobe cabinet… *Wait just a moment.* The fog in her mind suddenly cleared. *The mirror!*

Anna cursed loudly as she bumped her hip against a table, but she managed to find the mirror in the darkness. She knocked it hard with her bruised hip, sending it crashing to the floor. She carefully lowered herself to her knees, earning several cuts through her skirts. She disregarded them and leaned to her side, reaching from behind her back with her hands in search of a large piece of broken glass.

A brief wave of satisfaction went through her as she found a piece, before she sliced her finger and cursed again. Her hands trembled as she began scraping the glass against the rope binding her wrists.

Several minutes passed before she felt the ropes loosen. Jubilation rushed through her as the rope snapped and her wrists were freed. She tossed the shard aside and brought her arms around the front of her, grimacing at the ache in her shoulders.

Anna hastily wiped her blood-soaked hands on her skirts before she reached for the binding at her ankles.

* * *

The cabin appeared empty from a distance, but Lane was certain that Anna was within. He worried for her health and safety, and that of their baby.

They had briefly surveyed the home in which the four kidnappers were allegedly housed, but aside from the chimney blowing smoke, they had seen no sign of them. Lane had his reservations as to their whereabouts.

They'd settled their horses in a glade a mile back and walked the remaining distance to the cabin, so as not to alert the villains to their arrival.

Charles nudged Lane in the rib. "It is not wise for them to leave Anna alone in the cabin. They must know that we could easily come to retrieve her. Something is not right." His harsh whisper broke the silence around them.

Lane opened his mouth to reply, his jaw still smarting, but another voice cut in. "You are correct, Major Bradley. Or should I call you *Hydra*," Frenchie's accented voice sneered.

Charles scoffed. "I am aware that you know my identity, fool. The Boss has sent me numerous letters informing me as much."

Lane squinted at Charles in confusion. *Identity?* What in blazes was Charles on about?

"Tell me what you have done with Anna, and I will tell the courts to be lenient with you."

Frenchie's laugh veritably dripped with condescension. "I am not so much a fool as you Englishmen. A Frenchman would never fall for nonsense such as zat." He sighed with apparent impatience. "Now, come out of ze bushes before I lose my patience and shoot you both through your filthy English 'arts."

Charles nodded at Lane, and they stepped into the clearing around the cabin. Frenchie stood with a pistol aimed at both of them, one in each hand.

"You have us at a disadvantage," Charles drawled. "What is it that you would like from us?"

"Zere is only one of you zat I require. I used your troublesome sister to get you 'ere. Now zat I no longer need her…" He let out a sharp whistle, and Toby strode out from behind the cabin with a torch held aloft.

"*No!*" Lane pulled the pistol from the back of his breeches, took aim, and shot Toby through the chest. The large man, and the torch, fell heavily to the dirt-covered ground.

"*Imbecile!*" Frenchie's screech was high and long, but was drowned out as another shot rang through the clearing.

The echo resounded in his ears but didn't detract from the searing heat spreading through his left shoulder. A string of foul curses fell from his lips as he looked down at his shoulder. Dark, shining liquid soaked his black coat, and he cursed again. *I've been shot!*

He was hardly cognizant of the fact that Charles had leapt on Frenchie and the both of them had fallen to the ground and now fought for the upper hand.

Lane shook his head to clear his thoughts as he pulled his second pistol from his coat pocket and hurried toward the cabin. Even if he perished, he would damned well save Anna before he did.

He made it halfway through the clearing when a branch swung before his eyes, narrowly missing him. He stopped as Billy and the red-haired villain flanked him. *Hell and blazes.*

* * *

Rustling and mumbling echoed outside the cabin, and Anna's stomach jumped. Could someone have come to her aid? Or was it her captors come to torment her? She willed the beating of her heart to slow so she could hear past its rushing in her ears.

Finally, she heard Charles' voice and her heart felt buoyant. He had come to rescue her!

She worked faster with the ropes, anxious to be free. Her fingers fumbled with the thick rope as the tips of her nails were shredded. She pushed past the pain. The sooner she freed herself, the sooner she could be at home, in Lane's arms after a long hot bath and a small feast.

She heard a shout that she knew distinctly to be Lane's. Despite herself, her heart flipped over in her chest. *He'd come!*

Shots rang out in the clearing, and Anna went cold.

Oh no, oh no, oh no! Please let Lane and Charles be unharmed!

Finally, her fumbling fingers pulled the knot free and she slid her ankles out.

More shouts echoed outside the cabin and Anna rose shakily to her feet. There must be some way that she could be of help!

She stumbled on her first step, but made her way to the large window at the back of the cabin.

How am I to get the boards off?

* * *

Lane's left arm proved useless. He fought the red haired man while Billy took to a run.

The red-haired man took advantage of Lane's injury and struck from the left. Lane accurately placed each return punch to the man's face. His opponent was wiry and wily, and Lane's only chance was the dagger in his boot.

Charles mumbled curses under his breath as he fought Frenchie several yards behind him.

A burst of light caught his attention, and his startled gaze flew toward the cabin. That damned Billy had retrieved the flaming torch and lit the cabin on fire.

Lane scarcely recognized the hoarse, agonized scream that emanated from him and echoed through the clearing. "No! Anna!"

The red-haired man hit his injured shoulder, knocking Lane to the ground. The man leapt on top of him and laughed in Lane's face, blowing his vile breath at him.

"Yer little miss is gonna meet 'er maker," he sneered in his gravelly voice.

Lane looked again at the cabin, his heart in his throat as the flames licked at the dry wood, spreading rapidly.

Bloody hell! He hadn't much time.

* * *

Anna cried out as the wood covering the window splintered in her already cut fingers. She shook her hands and darted her gaze about the dark cabin for something to use as leverage.

She gasped, then coughed; the cabin was filling with smoke. Someone had lit it on fire!

As quickly as she could, Anna rushed to the small table and knocked it to its side. She felt her way to the legs of the table, then straightened her back. Lifting one foot into the air, Anna stomped her foot against the table's leg with as much strength as she could muster.

Naught happened but a small *crack*. Anna breathed deeply and stomped again, releasing a very unladylike grunt as she did so.

Crack! The leg split from the table's top, and Anna eagerly scooped it up. She spun, wobbling on her unsteady legs as she strode to the window. She wedged the narrow end of the leg between the wooden board and the window's frame and pulled.

Her hands stung, and her body quavered and ached. She gasped for breath, very much afraid that she would not be able to free herself.

A hoarse cry of anguish resounded beyond the door to the cabin, and Anna's heart stalled.

Terror gripped her, and she pulled harder on the table leg. She put the whole weight of her body behind it. She suddenly was possessed of a strength that she did not know she had, and the nail popped easily from the window's frame, the board falling to swing loosely from the other nail.

Without forethought, Anna averted her face and smashed the window with the table's leg, knocking away the shards of glass around its edge.

The opened window seemed to encourage the fire; an inferno of angry flames climbed up the walls and to the roof.

* * *

Lane watched in horror as the fire engulfed the cabin.

In the face of the red-haired man's wicked laughter and punishing blows, Lane miraculously garnered his strength and lowered his hand to his boot. He scarcely took notice of the fists connecting with his flesh and bone, as his fingers reached the hilt of his blade. He slid it up his palm to grasp it firmly.

Lane waited until the wretch's hand was raised, ready to deliver another excruciating punch, when Lane plunged his dagger into the bugger's ribs.

With a cry of agony, the red-haired man fell to the ground, clutching his wound.

Lane's heart fluttered with renewed anxiety as Charles appeared before him, his hand extended. Lane accepted and stood, glancing back at the sputtering form of Frenchie, who lay on the ground with Charles' sword protruding from his stomach.

Despite the considerable amount of pain Lane was in, he forced his legs into a run. "*Anna!*"

Charles kept pace beside him, looking as frantic as Lane felt.

They reached the blazing cabin, and Lane stopped to look at the weakened door. "Help me get my coat off." Lane struggled with his left shoulder and his numerous other injuries, but with Charles' assistance, he removed his coat and draped it over his head. "I'm going in!" he called over the din of lapping flames.

He took two steps forward, when a loud *creak* and *groan* made him hesitate. He pulled his coat from his head in time to see the roof of the cabin collapse.

"*No!*" He leapt forward, but a pair of arms wrapped around him from behind, pulling him back. "Let me go! *Anna! Anna!*" His heart felt torn from his chest.

"I will not allow you to enter," Charles shouted in his ear. "It has to be *me*. You are injured and not fit to retrieve her."

A tear slid down his cheek, and Lane realized that he was crying. He would be embarrassed, but at the moment he did not care. "Nothing will stop me!"

"What about me?"

Lane and Charles both turned to see Anna round the corner of the blazing cabin, the flickering orange light illuminating her dusty cheeks, fallen coiffure, and blood-streaked dress and hands. She looked affright, but his heart leapt to see her standing.

"Anna!" Lane pushed past the pain searing through his body as he ran to her, pulling her into a tight embrace. "I am so glad that you are well." He pulled back slightly to look down at her face through his tear-filled eyes. "You *are* well, aren't you?"

"I am sporting many cuts and bruises, and I am positively parched and famished, but otherwise I am unharmed."

Lane held her lightly, his soul-deep desire to envelop her in a crushing embrace notwithstanding, and leaned down for a short kiss.

"I will never leave your side again," he murmured in her ear. "I love you so very much, Annabel."

She leaned up and kissed him back. "I love you, too, Lane. Now, shall we return home?"

Charles appeared beside them, glowering. "I am pleased that you are well, Annabel." He glanced between the two of them. "But I am still unsure how I feel about the two of you."

Anna withdrew from Lane's embrace and stepped before Charles. "I am pleased that you are well, also, Charles. But I am afraid that there is nothing you could do that would separate Lane and me." She paused while a fit of coughing overtook her, the force of them causing her to stagger. "You will find that I am rather inflexible on the matter."

Charles sighed and pulled Anna into his familial embrace. "Very well, little sister."

"Hyd—Major!"

The three of them spun around as five men entered the clearing. One Lane recognized as Mr. Thomson.

"Pardon me," Charles muttered as he went to greet them.

"Who are those men?" Lane asked as he weakly led Anna further from the flames of the cabin.

"I haven't the faintest notion."

Lane's vision went blurry, and he was abruptly afraid that he would perish before ensuring that Anna knew how he truly felt. "I meant what I said, Anna. I do not wish to be parted from you again. I—I felt as though my heart had been ripped from my chest when I saw that fire begin, then it nearly failed me when the roof fell in. I could not bear to lose you, my love."

"Nor I, you." Her eyes appeared glazed as she cupped his jaw with her hands.

"I truly wish to marry you." His words had slurred slightly, but Anna did not appear to notice.

She coughed again as she threw her arms around him. Lane grunted through ground teeth at the pain. His vision distorted, and he struggled to catch his footing.

Anna quickly pulled back in concern. "Oh, Lane!" Her gaze travelled over his person then stopped at his shoulder, her eyes growing wide. "You have been shot! We must get you home and summon Dr. Claridge directly." She turned from him and shouted at Charles, who was directing the other men in taking the half-conscious Frenchie and the red-haired man away. It appeared that he also sent two men to search for where Billy had hidden.

Lane's eyes rolled in his skull, and he briefly wondered why Anna's voice sounded so far away. He watched the scene through blurred vision that he tried to blink away.

He felt himself waver before everything went black.

Chapter 41

Charles sat at the desk in his study, attempting to concentrate on the letter before him. He had assumed that after the interrogation and trial, his plight would cease to haunt him, but he was sadly mistaken. He had failed to find Billy in the days since the fire at the hunting cabin. He sorely wished that he had shot the man while he'd had the chance. The red-haired man, whose name they had discovered, was Samuel Aspil, and Frenchie had managed to stay alive long enough for questioning. Aspil, however, had died from his dagger wound shortly after the interrogation, and Frenchie, two days following.

He raked his fingers distractedly through his already dishevelled hair. "Damn, but this is tiresome," he grumbled to himself.

Anna had been confined to her bed, as ordered by Dr. Claridge. Apparently, more damage had been done to her than Charles had originally assumed. According to the doctor, in addition to her cuts and bruises, Anna had inhaled enough of the smoke for it to be a potential danger to her and, quite possibly, the baby. She also suffered from dehydration and malnourishment during the time that she had been in their clutches. The combination had created a rather serious affliction.

Lane had been in and out of consciousness for four days. Dr. Claridge had been there to see the three of them every day.

Despite having agreed upon a truce with Lane, Charles had disagreed with the notion of Lane remaining as a guest in one of their spare bedchambers. Upon returning from Canterbury, however, Anna had insisted that they be hospitable, and, *damn it*, in her condition, Charles was not inclined to begin an argument. The man was injured, and as much as Charles wished to deny it, it was simpler for the doctor to pay calls on them when they all resided under one roof.

Lane's words had haunted him since they had recovered Anna. The man was entirely correct in his assertion that Charles had changed into a "damnable bugger" since his return from war roughly seven months ago. He had wished that he would not have to behave in such a way, but… *Damn it*, he would behave in any manner to keep his loved ones safe.

He raked his hand through his hair once more.

To Charles' everlasting annoyance, Bridget had seen fit to visit Lane in his unconscious state, and to sit in with Anna to share news, exchange gossip, and discuss the newest books at Hatchard's. Lane's other sisters, Emaline and Katherine, and his mother, the Dowager Countess of Devon, had also been by to call. Those, however, did not concern him as much as the company of the statuesque, white-blonde-haired, green-eyed beauty, who posed a danger to herself and her family just by visiting.

A soft knock sounded at his door, and Charles looked up, grateful for the distraction from his wayward thoughts.

"Come."

The door opened, and Dr. Claridge entered.

They exchanged greetings as the doctor closed the door behind him.

"Please, have a seat." Charles gestured to the armchair opposite his desk and waited while the man lowered himself into it. "How fares my sister?"

The doctor took a deep breath and placed his large black doctoring bag on the floor beside him. "I believe that she is improving. It will likely be a slow recovery, but she has regained her colour, and her appetite is returning. The baby appears to be fine, but we will only be able to tell as her pregnancy progresses. She continues to cough, but I suspect that it is only temporary and no long-lasting ill effects will come of it. The weight she has lost will likely return with the babe, as well. I strongly suggest that she remain in bed for one more week and maintain a full diet to feed that baby. I shall return and inform you of any changes, should they occur."

Charles nodded. "I see. I am glad." He cleared his throat. "And has she made any comment or given any indication that would lead you to believe that her abductors…abused her at all?" His stomach knotted as he awaited an answer.

"No." He shook his head. "She has not made any allusions to suggest anything of the sort. Nor have I seen any evidence to support your assumption."

Charles let out the breath he'd been holding. "Very good. Now, I wish to inquire after Lord Devon. How is his condition?" He was rather eager to have the man out of his home.

"Lane's fever has broken, but at this point in his recovery, the only thing we can do is wait."

"And what of his regaining consciousness? Now that his fever has broken, should he not—"

Dr. Claridge interrupted him with a shake of his head. "The lack of a fever, while fortunate, does not guarantee that he will awaken."

Charles inclined his head. "Thank you for taking the time to speak with me, Dr. Claridge."

"It is my pleasure to be of assistance." He stood, picking up his doctoring bag and straightening his coat. "Are *you* well, Major Bradley? You appear fatigued and, dare I say, wan."

Charles shook his head. "My health is of no concern. I merely require a good night of sleep."

"It is nearly nine of the clock in the morning, Major; did you not sleep last night?"

He raised a sardonic brow at the doctor, then forced it to clear. "Have no worry for me, doctor. I will sleep."

"As you wish. But as your physician, however, my recommendation is plenty of rest and full repasts. No skipping meals, Major."

Charles waved a hand at the man. "Yes, yes. I understand."

Dr. Claridge gave him a nod and quietly left the room, closing the door behind him.

Charles sat back in his chair as he heard the click of the latch. *What the devil am I to do?*

* * *

Anna sat up in her bed, enjoying her morning hot chocolate. The last four days had been trying ones, but Anna had begun to feel more the thing. Her coughing fits came less frequently, and they no longer made her become ill.

She did, however, feel constantly concerned over Lane's wellbeing. She had not been allowed to see or visit with him since Dr. Claridge had confined her to bed. Unbeknownst to them, however, Anna had waited until everyone was asleep before she snuck out of bed and stole into Lane's bedchamber undetected. She spent several hours with him each night, curled up beside him, shushing him when he became restless.

This morning she had awoken feeling refreshed and pleased. Lane had not felt feverish last night, nor had he shifted agitatedly in the few hours she had spent with him. She had managed to return to her bedchamber before Marie had come to check on her.

Anna took a bite of a lemon teacake, worry still clutching her heart. Would Lane awaken?

A soft knock echoed through her bedchamber, and she looked up. "Come in."

The door opened, and Bridget strode through.

"Bridget! What a pleasure it is to see you this morning." Anna smiled up at her.

"Good morning, Annabel." She placed her gloves and bonnet on a table beside the door, her white-blonde hair catching the sun from Anna's window. She appeared ethereal in this light—delicate and pale.

"How is he faring?" Anna questioned, eyeing Bridget intently.

"According to his nurse, the fever broke early in the afternoon yesterday. He should begin his recovery now…as long as he regains consciousness."

Anna pressed her lips together and twisted her engagement ring around on her finger, nervous anxiety lodging itself within her.

"I must say, Anna, I am very pleased that you are engaged to be married. I confess, I am very much looking forward to having you as a sister."

Anna grinned sadly. "I am, as well." *As long as Lane awakens.* She covered a yawn with the back of her hand. "My apologies."

"Not at all. Would you prefer I leave you to rest?"

"Thank you, but no. I feel I have spent far too much time resting; I would much prefer the company."

Bridget pulled an armchair to Anna's bedside and sat. "I am certain Mama and the girls will be inordinately pleased once you announce your engagement to my family. I must warn you, however, that Kat will likely beg you the opportunity to make your wedding gown."

"My wedding gown?" Anna had known Katherine to enjoy embroidery and materials, but she hadn't the slightest notion that she enjoyed sewing gowns.

Bridget sighed. "Yes, did you not know? Kat has taken it into her head that she would like to become a *modiste*. She has been sewing since Mama first taught her to pick up a needle and thread. She has created all of the frocks that she wears, most of mine, Emaline's, and Mama's, and, truth be told, several of Lane's suits of clothing."

Anna's eyebrows rose in surprise and fascination. "She does tailoring, as well?"

Her friend nodded. "Indeed she does. I am not certain that Mama approves, but she has yet to scold Kat for it. Though we all know that it cannot go on for much longer, as soon Katherine will wish to marry, and no London gentleman will take a wife with such diversions." She glanced at her own clasped hands, and Anna wondered if she was still talking about Kat.

She pushed past the moment and allowed her excitement to bubble through. "I would love for Katherine to create my wedding gown! What fun that would be!" She would not have to explain her expanding waistline to a gossipy *modiste*!

"Truly?"

"Of course. I shall send a letter to her once our engagement is announced, formally requesting it of her."

"Oh, Anna, Katherine will be so pleased."

"As will I." Anna took a sip of her chocolate. "Would you care for some chocolate or tea, Bridget?"

"Oh, no, thank you. I will not stay long. I have a luncheon engagement with a new acquaintance."

"New acquaintance" meant a new project. Anna admired that about Bridget; she did her utmost to improve upon certain members of society, simply by being their friend. "As you wish." Anna took another sip of her chocolate. "Tell me, Bridget, how have you been doing?"

Bridget watched her fingers as they fidgeted with the fabric of her gown. "I am well, Anna. Thank you."

Once again, Bridget hid her true feelings. Anna would have pried, but the moment she did, Bridget would flee. And Anna enjoyed Bridget's company far too much to jeopardize it.

"I am glad to hear it," she said instead. "Now, do tell me about the newest books at Hatchard's. I must begin a list of books to read, as I shall be secreted away to Hertfordshire after the season is through, and I do not wish to be bored."

They spoke for some time, and had tea. While Anna was grateful for the distraction, she could not help but worry over Lane's wellbeing.

Chapter 42

Anna watched from her propped position in bed as Marie ushered their footmen out, carrying the empty bathing tub. She wished her maid a good night before lifting her book from her lap and opening it to her bookmarked page.

"Why was she here again?" Charles' dark form stepped out from the shadow of the hallway.

Anna gasped and suffered a fit of coughing. Her throat honked, and her lungs burned, but finally she regained her wheezy breath. "Good heavens, Charles!"

"Apologies, Anna." He came to her bedside and rubbed her back in circles, waiting until she had finished. "Are you well?"

She inhaled deeply, sending Charles a wry grin. "Well enough for someone whose brother insists on spooking her."

His lips twitched before turning down in a frown. "I will ask you again, Annabel. Why was she here?"

"I assume you mean Bridget. She was here to visit Lane, then she came to my bedchamber to keep me company."

"Lane is not yet conscious; how would he know that she has come if he is not awake to see her? She does not need to come every day, and I would prefer if she didn't." Her heart constricted at the reminder of Lane's condition.

Anna frowned at her elder brother, dear though he might be. "That is uncalled for, Charles. Shame on you."

He stepped closer, his spine impossibly stiff. "This is much more serious than you could know. She *must* not come here."

Charles might not fully approve of her association and pending marriage with Lane, but Anna did not see that as an excuse to be so ill tempered.

"If her presence bothers you, brother, then I would suggest you vacate the house when she arrives. I have invited her to join me here again on the morrow. She is bringing a new book from Hatchard's that we shall begin reading together."

Charles groaned and rubbed a hand over his face. "Listen, Anna, there are only three weeks left in the season, at which time we will return to the estate in Hertfordshire. There, you will be wed. I do not request, I *demand* that you listen to me on this matter."

Anna's good humour dissolved. "You *demand* it of me? Demand, Charles? Not only are you not my father, and therefore not the head of this household, but you have no just cause to demand any such thing! She is a dear friend; you shall not order me to be otherwise." She succumbed to a short fit of coughing. Lord but it was irksome!

Charles leaned into rub her back once more, but she batted his hand away. She waited until she had regained her breath before she spoke. "I would appreciate it if you left." She sent a pointed look at the door. "Good night, brother."

His jaw tight, Charles sketched a short bow and stiffly left the room.

Anna picked up her book only to gaze sightlessly at its pages. Goodness, but Charles was in a foul mood. Anna wondered once more what had caused such a strain on his and Bridget's friendship.

* * *

The first thought that entered Lane's head upon awakening was that he was in overwhelming pain. He carefully brought his right hand up to his forehead, where a damp compress rested. He lifted it off and cracked open his eyelids, but immediately regretted it.

Blazes, the room was bright. Sunlight shone through the opened window. He blinked, staring at the dust motes that danced along the air.

Where the devil am I? The ceiling was most decidedly not his; it was far too elegant and...delicate. He turned his gaze about the room. It was small but well appointed, with bright, cheerful colours and floral patterns.

A soft sigh reached his right ear, and he turned his gaze toward the sound. *Anna.* She lay curled up at his side, sleeping peacefully. She appeared drawn, but was a beautiful and welcome sight. *She had stayed by my side.* The realization warmed him immeasurably.

He moved to reach for her but cursed as searing pain shot through his shoulder. He hissed a breath and flattened himself against the mattress. Holy hell, but he felt awful.

"Lane!" she breathed, awakening. "Oh Lane, you're awake! This is wonderful news." Despite her exhausted countenance, she beamed at him, her eyes misting over. "How do you feel?"

The sun from the window gave Anna's head the illusion of a halo, her sleep-tangled hair appearing nearly translucent. He had the urge to kiss her. If he could have moved, he would have. "I hurt," he croaked. "And I am rather confused. Why am I not in my own bed? What happened?"

Anna straightened herself to a seated position on the bed beside him, her legs tucked to one side. "You are in one of the guest bedchambers in my home. You lost consciousness at the hunting cabin and have been sleeping since then. We brought you here to get the attention you required, and the doctor feared the repercussions should we have moved you."

The hunting cabin… Hell and blazes! "Are you well, Anna?"

She smiled damply. "I am. Just so pleased that *you* are well." Tears abruptly spilled over her lashes. "I had begun to fear that you might not awaken."

Cringing through the pain, Lane reached a hand up to stroke a tear from her cheek and slide a wayward lock of hair behind her ear. "I am well, Anna," he murmured. "A mite sore, but I shall recover."

His wound itched him, but he settled for placing his hand over it. Then a thought arrested him. "Whose night shirt am I wearing?"

Anna grinned, swiping at her reddened eyes. "It is one of Charles'."

"Hell," he grumbled. As grateful as he was for the sleeping attire while he was abed, he was markedly uncomfortable borrowing another man's clothes. He cleared his throat over his discomfiture. "You say that Dr. Claridge has seen to me?"

"Yes." She nodded her adorably rumpled head. "He has been remarkable."

The good doctor, it seems, had been rather busy during Lane's unconsciousness. "How long have I been abed?"

"You have been fading in and out for five days. Your fever broke the day before yesterday."

"Five days! You're bamming me."

She shook her head. "I assure you, I am not." She put a stray hair behind her ear, and Lane followed the movement with his eyes.

A sparkle caught his gaze, and he watched her put her hand back on her lap. She was wearing her engagement ring! Elation and pride pumped through him as he reached his hand out to clasp hers.

Her blue gaze glittered.

"You're wearing it," Lane noted lamely.

She nodded, a small smile on her lips. "Of course."

Lane returned her smile with an absurdly exultant one of his own, just before she leaned down to kiss him.

"What the devil is going on here?" Charles' outraged voice came from the doorway, startling Anna into a fit of coughing.

Lane rubbed a concerned hand on her back until she finished.

"How long has this been going on?" Charles and Lane asked in unison.

Anna looked between the both of them, then laughed breathily. "I do believe you mean different things."

"Of course we do, Anna," Charles muttered, crossing his arms over his chest. "What are you doing in here? How long has this been going on? Do you two meet in the evenings while pretending to be ill during the daytime hours, just so I am forced to keep Lord Devon under my roof?"

Anna let out a bark of a laugh, startling both men. Lane had never heard such derision directed at Charles from her before.

"Not that it truly matters to you, Charles, how I feel or what I do, but I have been sneaking in here at night to keep an eye on Lane. His fever had been quite severe, and I monitored him to ensure that he survived the nights. Last night was his first truly restful night, and I confess, I fell asleep while keeping him company." Her eyes warmed as she turned to look down at Lane. "To answer your question, my love, I have been coughing since the fire. It has improved, however, as I no longer cast up my accounts while doing so."

Concern gripped him. "How is the baby?"

"Well, so Simon informs me." She began to lean down for another kiss, when Charles took a step further into the room.

"This is all so very touching," he sneered, "but if Lord Devon is recovered, then I believe he should return to his own home." He sent an angry glance at Anna. "You should be in your own bed. Off with you."

Despite her brother's disapproval, Anna gave Lane a quick kiss. She then slid off the bed and left the room, sending Charles a frown as she did.

Charles closed the door behind Anna, then turned to face Lane, his arms crossed and his expression irate.

"I thank you for your hospitality, Charles," Lane said, his voice still rough like gravel. "I understand that there is something you wish to discuss with me, however at the moment, I must answer nature's call." Lane struggled to a seated position then gasped, a cold sweat beading on his skin. The blood drained from his face, and black spots danced before his eyes.

"Are you with me?" Charles hovered over him with Lord Simon Claridge, heir to the Earldom of Merrington, standing behind him, an odd air to his startlingly blue eyes.

"With you?" Lane frowned. "When did his lordship arrive?"

"Please, call me Dr. Claridge. And I happened to arrive shortly after you fainted, which I assure you—"

"Fainted? You mean to tell me that I swooned?"

The doctor tilted his head sideways in an odd shrug of his shoulder. "Medically speaking, your loss of blood caused your bout of dizziness, but yes, you fainted. It is nothing to be ashamed of, I assure you."

"Have you ever fainted, Dr. Claridge?"

"No, but—"

"Then I would not speak of embarrassment to me."

The man nodded. "Very well, I concede the point."

Lane swallowed his pride as he asked, "Is it possible for me to use the facilities?"

"Indeed."

The two men assisted Lane to his unsteady feet, then walked with him until he reached the necessary, at which point Lane insisted on continuing on his own. It was humiliating enough having them aid him that far; he needn't have them hovering while he performed his ablutions.

What was it that Charles had wished to discuss with him? He had appeared distinctly put out when Dr. Claridge had insisted that Lane receive a meal, then rest in silence for the remainder of the day. Curious, indeed.

Chapter 43

Anna stood at the altar, waiting for her turn to speak her vows. Mason Hall's chapel was as quaint as it was beautiful. The cream ceiling bordered in gilt arched high above them, while countless tall, narrow stained glass windows divided the cream walls with colourful partitions. The sun shone through from the outside, scattering a rainbow of hues over the floor and their guests.

The wedding dress that Katherine had created was magnificent; it had a soft pink underskirt with a sheer cream overlay and a pale-pink ribbon just under the bust. It had softly rounded capped sleeves, trimmed in pink lace to match the hem. Anna had finished off her ensemble with cream, elbow-length gloves, pale-pink slippers, and artificial cherry blossoms woven into her chignon. Kat had created the gown in such a way that permitted Anna to forego the use of a corset, and allowed for comfort where her stomach had grown over the past several weeks.

Anna glanced sideways at Lane, taking in his impressive physique. Kat was, indeed, a wondrous creator of men's clothing as well. Lane wore a deep-blue cutaway tailcoat, cream waistcoat with silver thread woven through, cream breeches—which, Anna noted, fit his muscular thighs and buttocks in an incredibly desirable manner—and polished shoes.

He was a remarkable specimen of a man. She could scarcely wait until they were alone. She smiled to herself as she returned her gaze forward.

An odd, nervous flutter rippled low in her stomach. Strange, she did not feel nervous at all. In fact, she was rather excited. Anna froze. *Could it be?* Anna's eyes widened as she realized that the flutter she felt was not nerves at all; it was the baby!

She could not enjoy this moment alone, even at the cost of an interruption their wedding service.

As slowly—and inconspicuously—as she could, Anna sidled closer to Lane, until their shoulders were touching and no one in the pews behind them could see their hands. She carefully grabbed Lane's hand and brought it to her abdomen, twisting his wrist so his palm faced down.

The fluttering continued, tiny bubbles of movement proving that life grew inside her.

She looked up into Lane's glistening brown eyes, their depths wreathed with meaning. He wore a breathtaking half smile, though it carried a ripple of emotion. Anna's heart skipped a beat, and the baby's quivering intensified.

The rector stopped talking to watch Anna expectantly. Awareness dawned, and she quickly uttered, "I do."

He nodded and continued, turning to Lane for his response. "I do." His voice was deep and rough with emotion as their baby continued to move.

* * *

Lane's anticipation knew no bounds. His and Anna's wedding ceremony had concluded splendidly. Bridget stood up with Annabel, and Charles had stood with Lane, both startlingly pale for the joyous occasion.

After signing the register, they had walked the short distance to Mason hall, his familial estate, and began their wedding breakfast.

Anna had planned a spectacular meal. There was a variety of hot bread rolls, coddled eggs, roasted pheasant, and an overabundant table of desserts and chocolate.

Lane's gaze sought Anna, where she stood conversing with her parents, his mother, and sisters. *My wife.* He was certain that he had a ridiculous grin on his face, but he did not care. He was a married man and was incredibly pleased with that fact. He had waited far too long to make Anna his bride. His closest friend, his confidante… It was an incredible accomplishment, indeed.

He was startled out of his musings as a loud commotion came from the entrance hall. The buzz of conversation in the room stopped, and several gasps rose above the crowd as one man forced his way into the room.

Lane became instantly alert as he recognized Lord Boxton. The man had changed greatly in the weeks since Lane had last seen him. He appeared drawn, grizzly, and…intoxicated. But that did not make him any less of a threat.

A small, trembling hand entered his and squeezed. He needn't see Anna's face to know she was frightened. This man was a monster who'd mistreated her dreadfully. Lane hated him with a passion.

"I object!" Boxton shouted, stumbling. "Stop the wedding!"

Incensed, Lane released Anna's hand and stepped before the foxed viscount. "I'm afraid you are too late, old man." He slapped him hard on the shoulder. "We are well and truly wed."

The blackguard wavered on his feet and let out a belligerent bellow. "Well, I have some think…somestin…some *things* I wish to say." His breath reeked of whisky and cheap ale.

Charles came to Lane's side. "I believe you have said enough, Boxton. Perhaps you should return home."

"No!" He weakly pushed both Lane and Charles. "I need everyone to be made aware of some inster…interesting news that I learned about dear, shweet Annabel."

Lane growled and stepped forward, but Charles' arm stopped him from pummelling the viscount's jawbone.

"I suggest you leave now, Boxton," Charles said smoothly, his voice low and rippling with a dire threat, "before you get what my new brother by marriage and I have been sorely wishing we could give you for some time."

Lord Boxton's face turned a mottled red and he looked angrily about the room. He'd turned almost purple before he burst out in a verbal explosion.

"Shle… she," he pointed at Anna, "is the reason I was forced to marry *stupid* Juliana! I *hate* that woman! She makes me insane with her inces…insss…incessant pestering! She was just supposed to be a good romp, but this—this *harlot* interfered! I dunno how you did it, but you got me!" He shrugged his shoulders and gestured wildly with his hands. "My network of m-men are all gone!" He burped loudly, then his gaze fixated on Anna. "Little did the g-gossipy wen…wenches of the *ton* know that the perfect Miss…Miss Annabel Bradley had…"

Both Lane and Charles' fists connected with Boxton's jaw simultaneously. The man fell to the floor with a *whomp* like a felled tree.

Gasps and exclamations of shock rippled through the room, while Lord Boxton lay on the ground, groaning in pain.

Anna appeared at their side. "Would you both please do the honours of helping him out? Lane? Charles?"

* * *

"Anything for the bride." Charles smiled wickedly, reminding Anna of the man she sorely missed.

She followed as both men reached a hand under the viscount's arms and dragged him from the room, past the entrance hall and passel of wide-eyed servants and guests, and out the double front doors. Satisfaction surged through her as Lord Boxton struggled to his feet, holding a hand over his jaw. The sun brightened his auburn hair until it nearly flamed a bright red.

"*Bloody hell!* What is the matter with you?" He spat blood on the ground, causing Anna to cringe.

Anna stepped forward, cutting off Charles and Lane. "The matter is, Lord Boxton, that you interrupted a very pleasant wedding breakfast in a drunken stupor. I am rather pleased to hear that your marriage is dreadful. Please give our best to Lady Juliana."

Boxton looked her up and down with an unnerving astuteness. "My God, you've grown f-fat."

Anna reacted before she truly considered her actions. Her fist connected with Lord Boxton's nose with a resounding *crunch*. Blood splattered his face as he fell, his feet lifted over his head as he rolled.

Anan had read of women being aggressive in such a way but had never realized how gratifying it was to be the woman defending herself. It smarted a great deal more than she would have expected, however. She rubbed the back of her hand and shook it out.

Charles likely patted her back. "Good form, Anna. I begin to think I have underestimated you."

She sent a small smile to Charles before leaning over the viscount's groaning form on the ground, his hands folded over his bloodied nose. "I do hope that was a lesson learned, Lord Boxton; never discuss a woman's weight."

Charles pulled the man to his feet and returned him to his carriage, blood dribbling on the ground behind him.

Lane wrapped his uninjured arm around Anna and leaned down for a kiss. "I will brave your wrath to say that I quite adore every inch of you."

Anna smiled up at him. "Thank you." She cupped his jaw. "And I would never punch you, Lane. I am far too fond of your handsome face."

Lane barked a laugh. "You never cease to amaze me, my love."

"Good. Now, shall we return to our guests? I would very much like to have another piece of that specialty confectioner's chocolate."

Lane smiled indulgently. "As you wish, dearest."

* * *

Anna's muscles twitched as Lane kissed a path across her abdomen. She lay in nude repose on the bed in the master bedchamber of Weston Hall. Lane had arranged to use of Lord Simon Claridge's second country home, located just outside of Wheathampstead, which happened to be a short distance from both of their familial estates.

Lane had planned for a skeleton staff to prepare the bedchamber and main rooms of the house. He informed her that he had requested the larder and their wardrobes be stocked for a full month's stay.

One full month! One month of shared baths, private meals, alfresco luncheons, walks in the grand garden, making love by the firelight… Anna could scarcely contain her excitement.

"Right here," Lane murmured, kissing the spot between her belly button and pubic bone, where the small, hard lump of their baby had recently formed. "Right here is where our baby is growing." He looked up at her with adoration in his eyes. "Which do you fancy it is? A boy or a girl?"

"A boy."

He blinked. "You seem very decided on that fact. How are you so certain?"

She shook her head, further mussing her hair against the pillow. "I am not sure I wish to tell you."

"Whyever not? I am your husband now, you know. And still your friend, I hope." He pressed a kiss to her baby bump, sending her skin into gooseflesh. "You may tell me anything."

She easily relented. "I realize that this is silly, but, I had a dream." She reached down and ran her fingers absently through his blonde hair. "It was a lovely dream. The baby was already born; he was a handsome little boy with green-and-brown eyes, and his papa's blonde hair. We were both smiling down at him, admiring what we had made together. The amount of love I felt for you both was nearly overwhelming, but when I awoke the next morning, I felt certain that we would have a baby boy."

Lane's eyes warmed during her tale, and his smile grew. "I would very much like the picture that you have painted." He turned his face into her palm.

"Truly?"

"Truly." He leaned down and kissed the baby lump once more, before rising and slipping his arms into his green silk robe. He handed Anna her scarlet one. "Come. I have something to show you."

"What is it?" Anna's mind ran through the possibilities.

"A surprise. Now, come along."

Anna slid off the bed and hurried into her robe, tying the rope tightly around her waist.

"Follow me, Lady Devon."

A shiver of excitement ran through her as she accepted his hand and allowed him to lead her into the hall. "Lane!" she pulled his hand, forcing him to stop.

"What is it, darling?"

Her gaze darted about. "What of the staff?" She sent a pointed look at their attire, then back into his smiling eyes.

"Fear not, love, they know not to disturb a newly married couple. Besides, one look at your delectable ankles and the aging butler would faint dead away."

"Lane!" Anna gasped in mock outrage.

He laughed. "You know I love to tease you. There is nothing to fear, Anna. I informed the staff that they were free to retire for the evening."

She playfully shook her finger at him. "You rascal!"

He grinned wolfishly at her before leading her further down the corridor. They wound their way through the halls and down a winding staircase until they reached a drawing room.

The room was fashionably appointed, with rich purple and gilt tones.

Lane strode forward and gestured dramatically to the space below the grand window overlooking the gardens. Anna gasped as she spotted the chess board that had formerly stood in the family parlour of Lane's town house.

"You brought this here for me?"

He nodded. "For us. I also requested the newest works of Mr. Mystery and several other novels by your favourite authors. I had thought that we could read them aloud to one another."

Joy burst in her chest and she lifted on her toes to throw her arms around Lane's neck, kissing him with the full force of her love. His arms encircled her waist. It was such a simple gesture, but the small ones were often the biggest ones. "I love you, Lane," she whispered against his lips. "Thank you so much."

His eyes crinkled in the corners. "You are welcome, my darling."

"This is a pleasant moment," she sighed, stating the obvious.

Lane grinned wickedly. "I daresay I am the maker of moments."

Anna's head fell back on a hearty laugh, recalling that long-ago jest.

"Now," Lane pulled back to look down in to her smiling eyes. "Shall we play a game? I am confident that I shall be victorious this time."

Anna left the comfort of his arms to sit at the chess table. "I fear that this will not be your day, but I shan't abuse your pride." She winked at him. "Have a seat, my love, and name your stakes. But please, oh please, let it be naughty."

Epilogue

Major Charles Bradley sat at his desk in his study, opening the day's correspondence. He expected Annabel, Lane, the Mason sisters, and the Dowager Countess to arrive any moment; tonight they were to eat dinner and engage in a bit of frivolity by playing charades.

Charles had come to accept that Anna would settle for no less than a marriage with Lane. However, he did not take kindly to the fact that in his sister's two months of marriage, he was obliged to see Bridget on several very discomfiting occasions.

He hated making her miserable, but it was his duty to keep her from him. She may not see it now—or ever—but Charles was determined to.

He withdrew his pistol from his opened desk drawer, cocked it, and aimed, as his door crashed open to reveal the haggard form of Billy, holding a blunderbuss.

"Came wi' a delivery, Hydra." Billy aimed the blunderbuss at Charles' chest, while Charles had his pistol trained on Billy.

"I am pleased that you could drop by for a visit," Charles drawled. "However, I'm afraid that if you attempt to shoot me, you will not leave alive." Billy snorted. "Where is your delivery?"

The man reached into his pocket and pulled out a wrinkled and dirty missive. "From th' Boss." His lip curled into a taunting sneer.

Charles stood, his pistol still aimed unwaveringly at Billy's chest. He walked cautiously toward the man and accepted the letter.

He placed it in his breast pocket then glared into Billy's gruff visage. "I confess, I am rather shocked that just you and I remain, Billy. I had thought that Frenchie would be the survivor of the four of you. That does not happen easily with traitors like you."

"'Nuff talk." He jabbed Charles in the ribs with the end of his blunderbuss. "The Boss said that if'n I get th' chance, I should kill you in cold blood. But I fancy seein' you read that there letter, and be 'round while you cry like a sissy miss. But ye know, it would be mighty entertainin' to ruff you up a li'le bit first."

Charles had had enough. Quick as a flash, he knocked the blunderbuss out of Billy's hands, slammed the heel of his palm into the man's nose—breaking it instantly—and swiped his leg beneath Billy's, knocking him to the floor in a bloody mess. He untied his cravat, pulled it from around his neck with a *snick*, and tied the intruder's hands behind his back with a neat, tight knot.

He straightened, dusting his hands of the filth that coated Billy's clothing, and reached inside his pocket for the letter. He would bring Billy to the Home Office, but he could not leave until he had satisfied his burning curiosity.

He opened the bit of parchment and scanned the writing.

Charles' thoughts scattered as he read. *No...* His heart skipped several beats, then began to thunder hard and fast against his ribs. *It couldn't be. How could they have known?*

He read through the message once again, then hovered over the lines that filled him with dread.

You may have won against my best men, Hydra, but we have learned several interesting facts since. Now, we will not rest until we have removed your heart.

The Boss

Your heart, the words repeated in his mind.

Charles quickly set down the missive and pulled several fresh pieces of vellum from his drawer. He dipped his pen in the ink and began to write with trembling fingers.

His plans would have to change. It appeared as though he would be required to spend much more time in Bridget's company than he had thought.

The End

About the Author

Cheri Champagne has had a passion for the written word since she was a child; even before she learned to write, she would scribble "stories" into notebooks and read the imaginary words aloud for all to hear. As a child and preteen, Cheri wrote adventurous short stories and heartfelt poetry, filling her notebooks with writing she would enjoy for years to come. Since then, Cheri poured insatiably over the pages of every historical romance she could get her hands on.

In College, Cheri first focused on Creative Writing and English Literature, thus beginning her eternal love of Jane Austen's work. She then graduated with honors with an Applied Business Technology degree in the Administrative Assistant field.

After getting a job straight out of College, Cheri quickly moved up the proverbial ladder to Inside Sales, to Accounts Receivable in a mere four months, where she stayed until she left on maternity leave.

Cheri and her husband married and two years later they had their first son, followed quickly by their second a year and a half later.

When her sons were still very young and Cheri's love of historical romance still very strong, her husband saw one particular receipt for a sizeable bookstore purchase and knew of her partiality to writing, suggested that she try it. Cheri, having been longing for her favourite authors to create very specifically plotted novels, agreed. She began writing her first novel in 2011 and after the first paragraph, was completely addicted.

In Autumn, 2012, Cheri and her husband were overjoyed to discover that they were expecting their third child, but in January 2013 they were shocked to learn that they were having twins in the Spring. With that unexpected but very happy discovery, their lives changed forever.

In addition to reading and writing, Cheri crochets, paints, scrapbooks, gardens, collect antiques (teacups, artwork, books, and skeleton keys, specifically), and above all, plays with her children.

Still passionate about her sizzling historical romances, Cheri writes as often as she can manage and continues to come up with a seemingly never-ending supply of plots, writing them exactly how she likes to read them.

Thank you for purchasing this copy of *Love's Misadventure*, Book One of The Mason Book Series by Cheri Champagne. If you enjoyed this book by Cheri, please let her know by posting a review. If you purchased this book through Amazon, it is eligible for a free Kindle Match.

Read More Books by Pandamoon Publishing!

pandamoon
publishing

Visit www.pandamoonpublishing.com to learn more about our other works by our talented authors and use the author links to their Amazon sales page.

Made in the USA
Charleston, SC
18 March 2016